Freda Lightfoot

Freda Lightfoot was born in Lancashire but lived in the Lake District for many years where she was a teacher, a bookseller and a smallholder. She is married with two grown-up daughters and still visits the Lakes as often as she can. Her first two Lakeland sagas, *Luckpenny Land* and *Wishing Water*, are also available from Coronet.

Larkrigg Fell

Freda Lightfoot

CORONET BOOKS
Hodder and Stoughton

First published in 1996 by Hodder and Stoughton
First published in paperback in 1996 by Hodder and Stoughton
A division of Hodder Headline PLC

A Coronet paperback

4

A CIP catalogue record for this title is available from
the British Library

ISBN 978 0 340 64723 3

Printed and bound in Great Britain by
Mackays of Chatham plc, Chatham, Kent

Hodder and Stoughton
A division of Hodder Headline PLC
338 Euston Road
London NW1 3BH

To the memory of my mother, who first taught me the joy of books

1977

1

'I think this could all be a horrible mistake.'

The two girls stood in the bare cobbled yard, a warm breeze riffling their thin shirts and blue denims, a battery of suitcases at their feet. It would have been plain to an observer, had there been one present, that they were not happy. One, rather small and softly rounded with short brown hair clipped steadfastly behind her ears, was almost weeping. The other, a mass of black curls bristling with temper, violet-blue eyes blazing, could barely stand still. She it was who had spoken her feelings in a sullen and furious pout.

A nine-hour flight, several more hours spent hanging around airports and a long, dusty train journey from Manchester caused the girls, in their different ways, to express their exhaustion and despair.

'There's no one in I tell you.' Sarah hammered for the fourth time on the solid oak door. It was low with an oak lintel above and a threshwood below, leading into the 'hallan' or hall where animal feed might once have been stored but now was no doubt full of old coats and muddy boots. Sarah shuddered. Not her sort of place at all. What on earth was she doing here? 'Didn't you tell them when we'd be arriving?'

'Of course.'

'You can't have done. Incompetent as ever, Beth. Don't deny it.'

The taxi which had deposited the twins with their luggage in the yard of Broombank farm was rapidly disappearing down the long winding lane and while Sarah beat unsuccessfully on the unyielding door then set off round the back of the house to seek another, Beth emitted a sigh of relief and began to gaze about her in awed wonder.

Lakeland was greeting them with one of her rare and perfect days in late May. Painted blue sky, clouds like white socks sauntering over the distant peaks and closer at hand the soft bleating of contented sheep cropping impossibly green grass. Broombank too was at its best, the spiky bushes which gave the farm its name a blaze of gold on the lower slopes of Dundale Knot. Had she been more conversant with Lakeland weather she might have looked more closely at those cumulus clouds banking up on the horizon, but was too absorbed fighting the guilt which Sarah's sulks always brought out in her, to notice.

Beth dug her toes into the cracks of the dry-stone wall and hauled herself up to sit on the flat stones on top. She guessed it was a dreadful breach of country etiquette but couldn't resist, cupping her chin in her hands and gazing about her, drinking it all in.

She'd forgotten it would be like this. So wild, so remote, so utterly beautiful. She could feel its beauty already soothing her and wondered why Sarah could not appreciate its majestic grandeur. But then Sarah was not in the mood to think of anything but her own discomfort. When was she ever?

Yet it was she, Beth, who had the greater reason to be miserable. Less than two months ago she'd been sitting at her dressing table in a white bridal gown, hand stitched by Miss Lester of Boston, when Derry had walked in.

Beth remembered she'd been dabbing at her nose with a powder puff for the umpteenth time, since it always turned rosy when she was excited. She'd felt giddy and carefree, filled with joy, her grey-blue eyes wide and sparkling with the kind of happiness any eighteen-year-old bride would feel when she was about to marry the man she loved.

'You don't look half bad,' Sarah was saying. 'Though that dress would suit me far better. The train is a touch too long for your dumpy figure, darling, and white is not your colour.'

Beth could recall laughing at her sister's outrageous vanity, untroubled by gnawing jealousy for once as she caught her stepfather's gaze through the glass. She had meant to ask his support, which he always readily gave to both girls in their numerous and petty squabbles, when something in his expression stopped the words on her parted lips. She could even now feel the laughter expire to nothing

2

as she'd stared at him transfixed, like a rabbit caught in the glare of a searchlight.

'It's Jeremy, isn't it?' A tiny, breathless whisper, visions of some horrific car crash or similar disaster echoing in it. The room had seemed to turn ice cold.

'I'm afraid so, my precious,' Derry had said, then taking hold of both her hands, saying she needed to be very brave, he'd told her. Yet her mind simply refused to take in the awful words. When he'd finished she'd continued to sit there, a trusting smile of disbelief on her coral pink lips.

For one terrible moment Beth had wished with all her heart that Jeremy had indeed died. Anything rather than this dreadful humiliation.

Downstairs, family and friends waited for the wedding to begin. The hum of their voices, the trill of laughter, the strains of a lilting tune as someone tinkered with the piano keys filtered through into her stunned mind. While out on the lawn, white painted chairs stood neatly in rows.

But there was to be no wedding. Not now. Not ever.

Then Sarah had split the terrible silence by calling him a *Goddamson-of-a-bitch*. Saying how she would screw his balls off, rip his eyes out, *kill* him with her own hands! Beth had sat unmoving, listening to her mother's hurrying footsteps echoing unnaturally loud on the stairs and along the landing, her new high heels clicking on the pine boarding like gun shot.

They'd stripped the wedding gown from her and put her gently to bed. There was to be no glorious, loving wedding night. Jeremy had lied. He didn't love her at all. Probably never had.

Over the next agonising days she had been quite unable to eat, slept only when drugged with dear Doc Barker's little pills and could only lie unmoving, no words, no tears, nothing. Her whole body seemed locked in a cold, despairing emptiness.

Her mind replayed every side-long glance, every hesitant expression of doubt he'd uttered in those busy weeks before the wedding, railing at herself for not taking them seriously. But then everyone had been strung up. It was only natural.

While Sarah had railed at dressmakers and mother had chivvied flower arrangers, he'd kept making cryptic remarks, saying how young he was to be considering the grand state of matrimony, that perhaps he would be no good as a husband, or take her too much for granted.

Now he had gone, with some other woman.

'Never trust a man,' Sarah muttered, 'I certainly won't. I shall never marry.' And defiantly tilted her chin to show off the perfect lines of her cheekbones and nose, as if to prove she was far too lovely ever to suffer Beth's fate, even if she was ever tempted to risk it.

'Of course you'll marry. You mustn't let this put you off,' Beth told her. 'Men queue up for a date, don't they? Haven't you always been the most popular girl in our year?'

'I didn't say I wouldn't find a fella, sister dear. I said I'd never marry one, or risk one jilting me.'

Beth winced, but Sarah didn't even glance her way as she strutted back and forth in the flower-decked bedroom, wrapping wedding gifts which must be returned, sighing from time to time over the beautiful acquamarine dress she would never now wear. 'There's a difference, you know. You can live with a man without a piece of paper to tie you together. Heavens, don't look so shocked. It's perfectly normal these days. What a prude you are.'

'Mom wouldn't like it.'

'Mom would have to get used to it. Men like a sample of what they're getting before they commit themselves. So do women. Why not? Maybe that was your mistake with Jeremy. You're too damned virginal. And he was very weak, you know, darling. If I'd crooked my little finger, he'd have jumped into my bed, quick as a flea.'

Beth didn't attempt to deny it, or show how the imagery behind this thought could still hurt, for it seemed very likely true. Better to keep the conversation general whilst her mind desperately sought a way for her to go on living without him. 'Don't you think commitment is important?'

'Commitment is dangerous,' Sarah said, and stopped her packing for a moment to glare at her sister from beneath silky black lashes. 'It makes you dependent, which must be a bad thing. For goodness' sake, Beth, pull yourself together.'

She gazed critically at her sister, feeling the usual nudge of irritation at the sight of her sweet, forlorn face. 'Don't be so melodramatic and emotional. And for God's sake, scintillate more, and do stop being such a limp lettuce. Put a little make-up on, throw away that childish hair slide for a start. And take my advice, darling, get yourself noticed. Flirt a little. The world is full of men. You'll find another. There's absolutely no reason to pine.'

'I'm not.'

'Good girl.'

Oh, but she had pined. Her heart had felt split into two jagged pieces. But Sarah was right. Perhaps if she were more outgoing she'd be as popular as her twin. Yet how could she trust a man ever again? Not that the question would arise. She was rejected goods now, as well as plain, she told herself, trying to make light of it.

And now, sitting on this wall, already worrying about her future here in Lakeland, Beth pulled the slide from her hair and tucked it into her pocket.

A swathe of chestnut hair fell forward over her cheek and she drew her fingers through it, pushing it back for it only to swing forward again, lifted by the breeze.

But Sarah's words, for all their cruelty, had an edge of truth to them. No young beau had ever come begging her for a date, as they did for her sister. Several had been arranged for her, but she'd always managed to ruin everything by sitting like a tongue-tied fool, not having the first idea what to say to the chosen victim. They'd never asked her out again, of course, and in the end Sarah and Mom had stopped trying. Which was why she'd been so delighted when Jeremy, the boy next door, had taken such an interest in her. Both families had been thrilled with the match. Yet now she came to consider the matter, it wasn't really surprising that he'd grown so quickly bored with her.

Beth drew in the clear, mountain air, banishing the grey thoughts swirling in her head like mist. If she was destined to grow into an old maid, so be it. She'd be old and lonely, crabby and unloved, like the dreadful stories Mom told of her own grandmother. How Rosemary Ellis ever found a husband, Mom often said, must have been a miracle.

This trip back to their childhood roots had been her mother's idea, and on a burst of desperate energy, Beth had agreed. The flights had been booked and she'd written to Meg and Tam, their grandparents at Broombank, to tell them of the intended visit. It would be the fulfilment of a dream. She'd always longed to return to the rural idyll of her childhood, which still lived in her head like a blue and green haze.

Sarah had reluctantly given her blessing to the plan on the grounds that it would restore Beth to full health, though she'd much rather have gone with the Frobishers to Venice and the Italian Lakes. Throughout the long flight, Beth had kept apologising for this fact, saying she could have managed on her own, even though they both knew this wasn't true.

So here she was. Lakeland spread out before her like a magic carpet, scratchy lichen beneath her fidgety fingers, and her heart thudding with new hope. Not quite ready to rebuild her life, since that would mean setting Jeremy aside for ever, but hoping this holiday might at least give her something else to think about for a while, a breathing space in which to heal.

And breathing in the crystal fresh air of Lakeland, her eyes aching from the splendours of its majestic beauty, she decided that she might even come to enjoy it and be happy again, in the end.

Sarah was thinking quite the opposite as she walked round the back of the farmhouse, rattling windows and doors, wondering why she'd ever agreed to come.

Broombank seemed smaller than she remembered. But then they'd been no more than seven or eight when they'd last seen it.

It was a long, low, whitewashed building that had looked out over the fells for three hundred years or more. An awesome thought to a girl brought up largely in America. She remembered a big inglenook fireplace that took up the length of one wall and smelt of smoked hams and pine logs. And two oak staircases and a host of rooms with creaky floors, all different shapes and sizes. But she could see nothing through the narrow windows, blanked out by solid shutters within.

Broombank would have been a 'statesman's' house, so named to indicate the free status of its owner. A house of note in its day. To Sarah, a humble farmhouse nonetheless, which wouldn't excite anyone, she decided. Except Beth, of course. And Mom.

Mom had told them so many stories about the wonders of Broombank that Sarah had been intrigued enough to agree to come and see for herself. Now she wondered what all the fuss was about. But then Beth was the romantic one, always asking questions about how Gran had built up her own sheep farm against the wishes of her family, as if in some way she could emulate this achievement, or discover some sort of rural bliss. What a silly dreamer she was. No wonder Jeremy had run away. Frightened him half to death with her talk of a house and children, and her white-picket-fence mentality. Totally unrealistic expectations of life, in Sarah's opinion.

Now she rattled a window with growing impatience, peering in on the dark interior. 'Damnation.'

Half the building was not house at all. Though the old Cumbrians might still call it the down-house, part of it comprised a long barn, and another lay at right angles to the main house. Wasn't it from here that they operated the knitting machines which supplied the family woollen business?

But that too was locked. Firmly bolted. Not a sign of a living soul anywhere.

There were several other outbuildings. These too yielded not a flicker of life beyond a dozen or so hens and one large, black and white cockerel strutting about the yard. An eerie kind of emptiness emanated about the place, like an echo of loneliness. What was she doing here, pandering to Beth's failures and fancies?

Irritation rose again, hot and furious in her breast. And how dare they be left, simply abandoned without any sort of welcome? It'd been exactly the same at the station.

'I expected a horde of relatives to greet us, with luggage carts, transport, hugs and a warm welcome,' she'd complained, quite justifiably in her opinion.

Since there were no young fit males around for her to inveigle upon to do the service for them, Beth had carried the heaviest bags off the train, without a word of protest. A fact which Sarah accepted as the norm but which irritated her beyond endurance nonetheless.

But then Beth was used to giving in. It had ever been so, even when they were children. As the elder by seven minutes, Sarah had quite early on adopted the right to make all the decisions, have the first choice of plaything and even take Beth's, if her own were broken or lost. So it had been with dolls and bicycles and so it became, in time, with boys. And why not? If it had ever mattered to her twin, she would surely have said so.

7

'Don't you want to see it?' Beth had remarked, not for the first time on that interminable journey. 'Larkrigg Hall? Our inheritance? Left to us by our famous, or rather infamous Great Grandmother Ellis. Aren't you excited?'

'Not particularly.'

Despite every effort on Beth's part, Sarah had managed to hold on to her protesting sulks. 'What do I care about a childhood inheritance extracted as an act of vengeance from a vindictive old woman? You might be suffering as the jilted bride, Beth, but did you have to ruin my own lovely holiday as well? Old houses are quite unimportant. I could be on the Rialto Bridge by now, do you realise? Gazing into some lovely Italian eyes.'

'I know,' Beth had unwillingly agreed, looking so satisfyingly guilty it had quite cheered Sarah up.

'Well then. And it's probably falling down. You do realise that too, don't you?'

'I dare say you're right.'

Sarah had dusted an old seat with her scarf, then smoothed her hands over her jeans, wishing there was a man around to admire the tightness of her bottom which she knew looked good, and perching it precariously on the edge, emitted a deeply weary sigh. 'I do wish you didn't get these crazy ideas.'

'You might like it. It might be beautiful.'

'Maybe I'll change my mind, abandon you and head south, over the blue horizon.'

'Don't say such a terrible thing, not even as a joke. You know how I need you. I couldn't face anything without you here beside me.' The panic in the high pitched voice was almost flattering, and tears welled in the soft eyes.

'Oh, don't be such a baby. Where else would I go? Besides, it's too late. The Frobishers have gone without me.' Sarah had glanced wearily around at the dull station buildings and applied fresh lipstick to her already scarlet mouth. 'Who wants Venice when I can be here in Lakeland?' an unmistakable touch of asperity in her tone. Then she gave a sudden grin, as if by expressing the dark anger she had cleansed herself of ill humour and become agreeable again. 'I'm here though, aren't I?'

'Under protest.'

'Yeah. At each other's throats the whole damned time. Twins, my ass. Non-compatible, let alone non-identical. Now will you move? Stop acting so wet and pick up that flight bag for God's sake. And find us a taxi before I scream.'

'Maybe we should have settled for college in Boston, after all.'

'You'd have hated it. *I'd* have hated it. At least they've put the flags out for us. That's nice.'

'It's for the Silver Jubilee.'

'Why should you know so much all of a sudden?'

'Mom warned me. She said if we were invited to any celebration parties to be sure and stand during the National Anthem.'

'Right now it looks as if we won't even be invited in for coffee.' Both girls had suddenly found this extraordinarily funny and collapsed into a fit of the giggles. Sarah, for one, felt all the better for it. Then, 'Whoops, a porter has arrived. He's giving us the glad eye. Wait here while I go and chat him up.'

Then she'd shaken out her jet black curls and sashayed over to the uniformed attendant, lips curving into her most winsome, poor-little-me smile, violet eyes teasing from beneath long lashes and after several seconds of stunned paralysis, the young man had been galvanised into action. Moments later the twins and their luggage had been stowed aboard a taxi.

As they bowled out of the station, Beth had seen a bright yellow mini drive in, screech to a halt, and a girl with spiky blonde hair leap out and wave frantically at their retreating vehicle. Sarah was too busy lecturing to notice, so she sat back in the leather seat with a sigh and said nothing. It always seemed the easiest course.

After ten minutes of fruitless rattling and knocking, Sarah gave up.

'Come on.'

'What?'

She stood beside Beth, bursting with impatience as usual. 'No point in hanging around here. Doors and windows all locked and bolted. Nobody home. End of story.'

Beth frowned, feeling very slightly let down. 'But Meg . . .'

'Hasn't bothered to welcome us. Probably gone off to market or however sheep farmers spend their time. Not even Tam is here. Come on, will you?' She tugged at her sister's arm. 'We can at least do some exploring.'

'We ought to wait. I expect she'll be back soon.'

'Oh, do come on. Anything's better than hanging about. The thought that the house is so near is beginning to tantalise even me. You wanted to see it, didn't you? Our inheritance? Well, let's get on with it.' Cool, violet blue eyes gazed out over the fells as if they could make it appear out of nowhere.

'Someone might be living there.'

Sarah shook her head. 'Nope. Mom says it's been empty for years. Come *on*.'

Now that she was faced with seeing the house, Beth was suddenly afraid. What if reality were nothing like her imagination? What if it were no more than an illusion, a fairy tale built up over years of childish dreaming? Still she hesitated, then realising Sarah meant to go without her, swiftly changed her mind. 'Oh all right. Wait for me. I hope it isn't too far, that's all.' She scrambled down from the wall and brushed the dust from her denims. 'I'm tired.'

'The exercise will do you good after all that travelling. Best thing for jet-lag. Two miles by road, Mom said, but we can take a short cut over by Brockbarrow Wood and on past the tarn. Maybe it'll all come back to us and we'll remember the way. Experience a *déjà-vu*.'

'I remember so little of our visits here as children.'

Beth set off up the sheep trod in her sister's wake. What would it be like? Damp and filthy as Sarah predicted? Or beautiful and serene as she'd always imagined in her dreams. And how would seeing it in the flesh as it were, affect their lives? Would they find happiness there? Beth shivered but told herself it was only because the sun had slipped behind a cloud and the blueness was now washed with grey, like a water colour. A breeze buffeted them, less kindly.

'It might rain.' she warned.

'Rubbish,' Sarah said, now so far up the track that Beth had to run to catch up.

When the yellow mini careered into the yard there was nothing to show of the twins' presence but two suitcases and several bags crowding the small porch.

'Oh drat. Not again.'

*   *   *

Tessa Forbes glared at the two suitcases and experienced an over-whelming desire to kick one. She'd never seen any quite so big in her entire life. Plus two flight bags, shoulder bags, coats and all the detritus of travel. And then she considered her mini. How many elephants can you get in a mini? Wasn't that the old schoolroom joke? Answer, one grizzling infant, mouth covered in the remains of chocolate buttons, strapped into a car seat. One roll of chicken wire to block up holes in the fence to stop the hens escaping, and possibly, if she ever caught up with them, two travel-weary females. The luggage wouldn't fit. That'd have to be collected later.

Why hadn't she borrowed Meg's van? Even if she'd got to the station on time she couldn't have fitted them all in her ancient tub. What had she been thinking of? Tessa clasped her fingers into the spiky tufts of her hair and gave an anguished scream. The wind brushed it away as if it were of no significance.

'Why do I volunteer to do favours when I am so entirely scatter brained? And why can't people sit still for half an hour?' she groaned.

Tessa went and gazed up towards Larkrigg Fell, certain she could see a blob of colour moving on the hillside.

Mind you, this had been a particularly trying day. Two and a half hour's queuing in the Social Security office, an hour's grilling in a pea-green cell by a fish-faced official. Her bank accounts, or lack of them, tutted over, her sex life investigated in excruciating detail. Guilt and humiliation heaped upon her by the spadeful, as if it had been she who'd walked out, or rather driven off, with the TV, stereo, and most of the furniture and not that useless lump, Paul, her unbeloved husband.

They must have set off up to the house, she decided. Where else could they be? If she hurried, she might catch them before they'd gone too far. Tessa glanced up at the sky. 'Or before that ominous grey cloud empties itself of rain.' You couldn't rely on anything. Not husbands, not visitors, not even the weather.

With a heavy sigh she rammed the two suitcases into the small storm porch and flung everything else beside James in the back seat, the small boot already being full to bursting. He beamed at her and offered a button in a chocolate-smeared fist. Tessa declined and scrambling back into the driving seat, crashed every gear as she tore off up a bumpy track, cursing every time she had to climb out to open or shut a gate. She'd better find them soon or Meg would have her guts for garters.

'I love it here already, don't you?' Beth said, as they strode out across the heaf. 'I feel as if I've come home.'

'It's that *déjà vu* thing.'

'No, it's more than that.' She felt at peace for the first time in weeks. 'It's a spiritual thing. I belong here. Can't you feel it?'

Sarah made a rude sound in her throat.

They came to a pair of standing stones that stood some short distance away from the drive which wound onward up to the house. Beth was instantly intrigued. 'I wonder what those are meant to be? They're huge, yet appear to have been placed here deliberately. Who could have had the strength? Remains of a stone circle, do you think?'

Sarah wasn't listening. She had pushed open the huge wooden gate that hung on a pair of limestone posts. It gave off a loud creak and she couldn't help but giggle. 'It's like something out of a Hammer Horror movie. Hardly your rural idyll. Decaying old mausoleum, more like.'

'Oh, no. It's lovely.' One fat drop of rain fell on to Beth's nose but she didn't notice. She was too enchanted with the bewitching scenery, and with the anticipation of seeing at last the house of her dreams. It formed a dark, intriguing shadow at the end of the long drive. Large, rectangular and grey-stoned, its tall narrow windows blank, just inviting her to peer within. Again she shivered and crossed her fingers behind her back. Let it be lovely, she begged, nudging aside small misgivings of her own, or her precious dreams would be over before they'd hardly begun.

Sarah simply scowled, wishing herself anywhere but here in damp Lakeland.

The sound of a car tearing up the track behind them caught their attention just as they were about to start the trek up the drive.

It lurched to a halt beside them, a window was wound down and a tousled blonde head popped out. 'You won't be able to get in. All doors and windows are locked and shuttered. You couldn't see a thing.'

Both twins turned to stare at this person who had so unexpectedly appeared out of nowhere and seemed to know exactly where they were going. She was now climbing out of a filthy yellow mini, the bonnet of which was decorated with the painting of a huge golden eagle with outspread wings. Beth stared at it, highly impressed.

'Did you do that?'

Tessa nodded, grinning as if they were old friends. 'Hobby of mine. Sorry I missed you at the station. Your taxi was just leaving as I drove in.'

'Par for the course,' Sarah said, rather sourly. 'It's been that sort of day.'

The new arrival pretended not to have heard this cutting remark. Dressed in blue tank top and flared trousers she introduced herself and James.

The two girls smiled uncertainly at the baby, now barely discernible beneath a coating of chocolate, then Sarah asked, 'You wouldn't have a key, I suppose?'

Tessa shook her head. 'Meg probably has.'

'But she isn't in,' Sarah tartly replied. 'That's why we came up here. We were bored stiff with waiting. And cold. Hardly the best welcome, I can tell you.'

Tessa flushed and looked embarrassed. 'Don't blame Meg for that. I offered to fetch you because she'd a meeting she couldn't cancel, only I got held up. Sorry.'

'That's OK,' Beth said, before Sarah had chance to make any more rude remarks. 'We'll see inside Larkrigg Hall some other time. We were simply amusing ourselves,' she finished, trying to soften Sarah's attitude by indicating with her eyes that here was a pleasant enough girl, trying to be friendly. 'It's all so wonderful, isn't it?' The wind tossed a spray of raindrops in her face but she simply wiped them away with the flat of her hand and returned the slide to her wayward hair. 'We've quite fallen in love with the place already.'

Tessa raised arched brows right up into her raggy fringe. 'Bit sudden. You've hardly clapped eyes on it yet. It's a mess inside, or so I'm told.'

'She's a romantic and falls in love very easily,' Sarah explained, casting her sister a scathing glance. 'I, on the other hand, am far more level-headed.'

Tessa gave her an assessing look. 'I can imagine.' Then a roguish smile. 'You both look like something the cat's dragged in, if you don't mind my saying so? Probably because it's raining and you're both getting soaked. Come on. Pile in.'

'Agreed. Curiosity can wait.' Sarah sounded highly relieved. Anywhere which could offer a hot cup of coffee and a spot of dry comfort was fine by her.

'Is Meg OK?' Beth asked, as she lifted bags and boxes so she could squeeze herself into the back seat beside the beaming James. She let him tug at her hair with his sticky fingers and grinned back at him.

'Fine, some problem with the mill I believe.'

'That too was closed.'

'Yes.'

As the mini bounced off down the rutted drive a shutter moved at a window in the house behind them. But they were all so busy chattering, none of them noticed.

2

Meg sat in the private dining room of the Cock and Feathers Public House and gazed blankly out of the window. In her mind she was a young girl again with clear skin, honey-gold hair and smoke-grey eyes. Nineteen years old and caught pulling pints behind the bar here, by her brother Dan. Always jealous of her, he'd been eager enough to hand her over to her father's ministrations.

But they hadn't managed to keep her at home, not either of them. She'd achieved her dream and become a sheep farmer which had totally absorbed her ever since. Apart from Tam of course. There was always space in her life for her dear husband, seated opposite her now, as he always was, keeping tactfully silent.

Meg didn't see the bustle of people in the street going about their business. Nor the traffic searching for parking places, splashing rain over unwary legs, hooting horns at recalcitrant pedestrians. She was glad it was raining. It seemed only fitting. Bad weather suited the hearing of bad news.

'It's all my fault of course,' she said suddenly, the words bursting out at last.

'And why should you be thinking that? Haven't you your hands full already with the farm. How can any woman, even you, Meg O'Cleary, run two businesses.'

'I should have paid more attention.'

'It does no good to brood on the past, Meg. No good at all.'

She plucked at her gloved fingers, barely aware of the hushed voices of the people in the room behind her, mulling over the day's injustices, wondering if they had time for a coffee before they dashed back to work, if it would be fine on Sunday for once, or if the weather would change and the sun come out again. And it had started out such a fine day. As Broombank Woollens had started out as such a fine business. In the beginning.

'I wanted to have something fit to hand on to the twins. Now I feel shame for neglecting it. If Jan hadn't so many children she might've been able to do more. But with those four . . . Or if Lissa hadn't gone off to America. But then Derry's job was there. Oh, dear, we should never have trusted that young manager, never.'

Tam stared gloomily into his pint of best bitter and did not disagree. It certainly had been a blow, a shock even, to learn that the newly appointed manager had absconded with a chunk of their sorely needed profits. Hadn't they trusted him completely? Given him every encouragement to do as he thought fit. *Eejits* that they were. Tam downed half his pint in a single swallow, wiped his mouth with the back of his hand and smiled at Meg, his green eyes troubled. ''Tis a temporary problem we're having. It'll get sorted. Now let me see you smile. Your two darlins won't want to see you in the dumps.' He glanced at his watch. 'Would you have me pick them up?'

Meg shook her head. 'Tess is doing that for me.'

'You'll be glad to see them. Me an' all.'

She met his smile with a weak one of her own and reaching across, squeezed his hand. 'It'll be grand. They must be lovely young women by now.'

'Then let's be away. I'll settle up with the waitress and fetch the car to the door. You get your coat on, I'll not be a jiffy.' He strode out through the door, tall and purposeful and it came to Meg as it did a hundred times a day, how much she still loved him.

The room was emptying. Lunchtime was over and people were going back to their offices and businesses, to their shopping, and their families. She sighed. How she had missed having Lissa living near. America seemed so far away. Not that she had ever said as much to her daughter. Young people had their own lives to lead. Now Meg felt she'd let her down by not taking proper care of the business Lissa had started all those years ago.

The waitress was moving quietly about, collecting spent glasses and dirty plates. The small dining room was almost empty, apart from one other man who was lingering by the door. For a moment there seemed something vaguely familiar about him. Young, twenty-something, lean and dark with the kind of studied scruffiness the young thought appealing these days. With a start she realised he had caught her staring at him, and filled with embarrassment she quickly turned away. But not before she had noted how his eyes were not entirely friendly, which struck her as rather odd. The sound of a car horn in the street outside brought her to her feet, and grabbing her coat Meg headed for the door. By the time she reached it the young man had gone.

The sting of rain on her face somehow brightened her and made her cleanse her lungs on a deep breath. Tam was right, she thought. Brooding did no good at all. The only way to cope with a problem was to meet it head on, and fight. But first she must welcome her lovely twins.

Tessa pushed open the door, baby James propped on one hip, and led the two girls into Broombank's big warm kitchen. A hen followed her in and she tossed it a piece of bread and butter pudding from a dish on the sink. It scurried off as if it had been given a rare treat.

'Bit of a mess I'm afraid.' Tessa sighed, and with one hand filled a kettle at the low stone sink, plugged it in and flicked the switch. 'It's my job to wash up, in return for room and board, but I forgot this morning. One of the peasants, that's me,' she said. 'Tea?'

'Lovely,' Beth said, while Sarah suffered a desperate longing for a decent cup of coffee but was so busy wondering what this odd girl was doing here, that for once she held back.

Tessa lay the patient James flat on his back on the kitchen table, stripped off his dripping pants then rubbed his nose affectionately with her own. 'Potty time, cherub.' She placed the baby on his potty then poured some fruit juice into a feeding cup and gave it to him. James hooked chubby fingers round the two handles and brought the spout straight to his mouth. He started to suck with loud appreciation.

'That'll keep him occupied for a while, with more hope than anticipation of a performance, I have to say. Potty training is the very devil. So, you liked Larkrigg Hall then?'

'Didn't catch more than a glimpse but it looks intriguing,' Beth agreed, fascinated by Tessa who moved about the large untidy kitchen finding mugs, milk, a tin of biscuits, stepping adroitly over her son as he motored about the floor.

She was frowning. 'It's a bit neglected. Nobody's lived in it for years. Sad waste really but your mother apparently didn't like it and refused to have anything to do with it. Wouldn't even bother to let it.'

Tessa abandoned the idea of washing three of the mugs in the already full sink and selected clean china cups and saucers from a pine dresser, every inch of which seemed stuffed with a variety of pretty flowered china that had seen better days. Stacks of papers, leaflets and letters were crammed in the gaps between. 'The tea won't be a tick. Make yourselves at home.'

She placed the cups on a tin tray that said 'Young Farmers Do It Best' and added a sugar bowl and milk jug that did not match the cups or each other. 'Meg and Tam will be back soon. They had some errands in town, including the bank manager, I believe.' She pulled a wry face. 'Meg has her hands full, as usual.'

'Clearly,' Sarah said, not troubling to hide the coolness in her tone.

Embarrassment coloured Tessa's cheeks. 'You can blame bureaucracy for my inadequacy this morning.' She was pouring boiling water into a large brown teapot with a chipped spout. 'Single parent. Unemployed. One of the rural poor seeking a handout from the state. Deserted wife and all that.'

'Oh,' said Beth, her caring nature at once warming to the girl. 'That's even worse than . . .' Then stopped, blushing furiously. 'I-I'm sorry. I'd no right to . . . I mean . . .'

Tessa looked puzzled and Sarah calmly explained. 'My sister means that she's recently suffered a similar fate, only the knot hadn't quite been tied.'

'You had a lucky escape then,' Tessa said and as Sarah calmly agreed, Beth blinked. She'd never thought to look at it in quite that way.

'. . . a handout from Meg.' Sarah was saying.

'True,' Tessa frankly agreed. 'Your long suffering grandmother is forever rushed off her feet yet still finds it in her heart to take me under her wing. And I was grateful since hubby pretty well cleaned me out. I'm one of her lame ducks.'

18

'How very fortunate for you.'

'Yes,' Tessa readily agreed, soberly meeting Sarah's gaze. 'It is.'

James stood up, a red ring round his small plump bottom. 'Wee wee,' he announced, showing two teeth as he grinned with pleasure.

Tessa looked in the plastic potty and squealed with delight. Then there followed such a celebration that soon all three girls and baby joined in with great hilarity and the tension in the room slackened. The tea was quite forgotten while a clean nappy was fitted and the beaming James firmly strapped into his high chair.

'Shall I pour?' Beth offered, when they'd got their giggles under control and the potty had been rinsed in the cloakroom.

'Sorry, yes. If you don't mind.' Tessa started to mix a glutinous mess that might have been porridge had it not been bright orange.

Tessa caught her eye and laughed. 'Orange and apricot pudding. His favourite.'

Beth handed round the cups then set about clearing the stack of dishes in the sink.

'You don't have to do that,' she half-heartedly protested.

'I want to. I like to help. Sarah can dry.' Beth cast her sister a glance which was steadfastly ignored while Tessa spooned food into the baby's mouth.

'Is Meg keen on gardening?' Sarah coolly enquired, staring at a few withered brown leaves from a tradescantia that littered the carpet.

'Hates it. No time, she says. She's usually with her blessed sheep, or at some farming or local event or other, Tam along with her. They're very busy people.'

'And what do you do, besides not wash up?'

Tessa grinned good-naturedly as she scooped more glutinous pudding into the baby's mouth. 'When I'm not with this tyke here, you'll find me in an old shed I dare to call a studio, attempting to paint pictures, or do sculptures, or whatever my latest fad happens to be.'

'How terribly artistic of you. And no other form of employment?' The two girls' eyes met and held.

'Not at the moment,' Tessa agreed. 'No other visible means of support.'

'How fortuitous that Meg is so generous then.'

'You must be awfully clever,' Beth butted in, hastening to soothe the bristling atmosphere, and Tessa laughed.

19

'Don't ever say that. I'm not clever at all. One of life's dabblers, that's me.'

'Oh, I'd love to be able to draw.'

'Drawing is only a part of it. It's paint that's the tricky medium. I love pastels myself.'

As the two chatted on about art and pottery, Sarah set aside the cup with its tea that tasted of perfume and looked about her with open distaste. She'd never seen a room quite as messy as this one. Piles of dirty crocks, a tiled floor smeared with remnants of mud, and walls which probably hadn't seen a lick of paint in a decade. Undoubtedly some might say it exuded comfort with its bunches of drying herbs, pretty dresser, and winking copperware in the wide inglenook. But one chair was covered in an old sheepskin rug and another seemed full of dog hairs. She turned up her nose and took care where she sat.

'Are these your efforts?' A bright abstract on the wall, a pencil drawing of a naked man and a bronze sculpture of an owl propping open a door which presumably led into the living room.

'Do you approve?'

'I know nothing of art.' Sarah turned away, her body language clearly adding that she had no wish to learn, and pointedly studied the most notable feature of the room. One wall crowded with photographs of sheep and dogs, rosettes and certificates that filled every inch of space.

'You seem to have landed well on your feet here.' There was an open challenge in the blunt statement but Tessa only half glanced at her as she dealt with the baby, laughing all the while.

'I don't deny it.'

Since she offered no further defence, there seemed nothing more to say on the subject, so Sarah sat down on a hard wooden chair while Beth politely enquired where Tessa had lived when she was married.

'Paul and I rented a cottage over by the quarry, but since he took everything but the sofa and the proverbial kitchen sink, there seemed little point in staying there.'

'Why didn't he take the sofa?'

'Because it reminded him of the necking sessions we had on it. And the time I caught him with someone else on it.'

'Oh dear.' Beth thought Tessa barely seemed old enough to have had so much experience of life but the girl cast her a wry grin.

'Don't worry. I won't bore you with talk of my pending divorce. I'm a free spirit at heart. Lone parenting holds no fears for me.' She shaved the apricot gunge from James's chin and stuffed it in his mouth. The baby smacked his lips and opened his mouth for more, rather like a small plump bird.

'Just as well,' said Sarah, grimacing.

'The only thing I really miss is the telly. Meg doesn't have one.'

'What a pity!'

'I was using it for my Open University course,' Tessa replied, not rising to the dryness of Sarah's tone. She finally scrubbed the baby's face clean then lifted him from his chair and cuddled him close. James beamed, round face shining. 'There we are, cherub. I'll just put him down. Then we can talk.' She paused at the door and looked from one to the other of the two girls. 'Would you share a room or prefer to be separate?'

The twins exchanged a quick glance. They hadn't shared a room since they were small and didn't much care for the idea. Tessa picked up their sense of unease.

'It's a big room, at the front. Separate beds. You won't fall over each other.'

'Sorry. It's just that everybody expects us to be bosom pals, because we're twins,' Beth explained. 'Only we're really quite different. Not identical in any way.'

'And actually hate each other's guts,' Sarah laughed. Tessa waited for Beth to disagree with this blunt indictment of their relationship. When no argument came, she offered to make up beds in separate rooms and dashed off to settle her son in his cot.

'We can't say life isn't interesting, can we pet?' she asked him as she tucked in his sheet. 'Never a dull moment.'

Half an hour later Meg and Tam arrived, bursting into the room in a swirl of fresh air and energy. With a squeal of delight Beth hugged them both. Sarah pecked a kiss on each proffered cheek.

'It's so lovely to see you again. I can't quite believe it.'

'How are you? Was the journey dreadful? Has Tessa looked after you?'

'Of course.'

21

'Good. Oh, I'd kill for a cup of tea.'

'Let me do that,' Beth said, taking the teapot from her and pushing her gently down into a fireside chair. She thought how lovely her grandmother looked. The years had treated her kindly, for even at fifty-nine she was still a fine looking woman. Her skin might be weathered by an outdoor life but her face remained firm and beautiful. Her golden hair had grown pale but still shone like silk, and her grey eyes were as bright and alert as ever. But then, Beth thought, Meg loves life. 'I think you're wonderful,' she said, popping a kiss on Meg's brow. 'You know we all love you. And we're so glad to be here at last.'

Meg laughed at this, pleased by the compliment. 'And I'm delighted to have you, my sweethearts. Are we not Tam?'

'Indeed we are. Just what we need to cheer us up. And how can I object to lovely females about to wait on me hand and foot.' He arranged his long legs comfortably as he sat in the rocking chair and everyone laughed. Then Meg got up and went to put a gentle hand on Beth's shoulder.

'Lissa wrote and told me how things didn't work out. He clearly wasn't the right man for you. Someone better will come along, I'm sure.'

Beth felt suddenly raw and exposed, as if her inner feelings were on view to everyone. 'I never wish to think of Jeremy Mitchell ever again.'

'That's the ticket.'

Or of his caressing hands and soft kisses, yet the memory continued to haunt her day and night. And the picture of him in bed with someone else sent her mad with despair. 'Right now it's hard to imagine I ever will. Find someone else, I mean. I really wouldn't care to risk it. He can't have loved me at all.'

Meg kissed her cheek. 'I understand how you feel. I was betrayed too, remember, by Jack Lawson, my first love. I thought I'd never recover, but I did. I still have the luckpenny that his father gave me. And I still have Broombank. Then I found Tam and was happy. So there you are. Lakeland will make you well too.'

A soft laugh and the two were hugging and Beth was mopping up tears and blowing her nose, insisting that really she was fine. 'Sarah likes it here too, don't you Sarah? Though she wasn't too sure at first.'

Sarah thought of the empty, lonely landscape, the drizzling rain, the bleak grey-walled house they'd so briefly glimpsed and forced a smile. 'It will certainly be different,' she said. 'Mind you, a warmer welcome would have been nice.'

A stunned silence filled the room as all eyes turned upon her. Beth's heart sank. Trust Sarah to put everyone's backs up from the word go.

'My fault,' Tessa hastily put in. 'I've already said how sorry I am to have missed them at the station.'

Meg smiled, shrewdly judging it unwise to pursue whatever was causing these two to cut sparks off each other. 'Everything has seemed to go wrong this week. May in general has been a disaster. Let's hope June, with the Jubilee Celebrations, is better. We're planning a big party to which you are all invited.'

'Great!' said Sarah drily.

Meg met her granddaughter's sulky gaze with a speculative lift of one brow. 'We must try to make up for our neglect, mustn't we? Though warmth, I've always thought, needs to flow two ways.'

It was a blessed relief to everyone that the Thursday of the Jubilee celebrations dawned to a pale lacy mist that rolled off the hills, revealing a burning bright day. The scent of new grass was strong on the hills and meadow pipits feasted on the insects which flew up as the three girls passed by, disturbed by their long skirts.

This was meant to be a family day with races, wrestling, dog trials and all the usual country events, Meg had told them. 'Plus a parade of the queens. And everyone who cares to join in the fun must dress in period costume too.' Meg and her sister-in-law, Sally Ann, had been sewing for weeks for this day.

'Count me out,' Sarah had protested.

'Oh, don't be a spoilsport,' Tessa had challenged her.

They'd settled, in the end, for a vaguely pastoral look with soft muslin blouses pulled off the shoulder, flowers in their hair and about their necks, wrists clinking with beaded bracelets. Even baby James was decked out in a flowered bow tie and red dungarees. They all looked fresh and young and very lovely.

23

From down in the dale came a hum of activity on the clear fresh air. Marquees carried jaunty flags, stall holders jostled cheerily for space. Children ran about on endless errands, shouts rang out, whistles, barks and happy laughter. The farming community in their best frocks and setting-off suits were enjoying themselves as only dalesfolk can. This was as good as a holiday to them.

'They've been holding this sort of sport's day since before the war,' Tessa told the twins, hitching the baby higher on her hip. 'And the Cumberland and Westmorland wrestling for a hundred years or more. We usually have it at the end of July but we've tucked in an extra day for the Jubilee.'

'How terribly exciting,' Sarah said. 'I can hardly wait.'

'Oh, come on,' Beth urged. 'Stop grumbling. Let's have some fun.'

'You might enjoy it if you'd only stop looking down that long nose of yours,' Tessa said and stepped out more briskly, ignoring Sarah's gasp of fury.

Beth and Tessa giggled and set off at a gallop, the baby shrieking with excitement as they bounced down the hill; at great risk from toppling over as they ran, since they wore platform-soled shoes, more suited to a day in town than out on the fells. But the ground was dry and hard today with not a sign of rain and pastoral peasants or not, they wished to be stylish. By the time Sarah came running to join them, flushed and breathless, the moment of disagreement had passed.

They found Sally Ann, ably assisted by her daughter-in-law, Jan, manning a hot-dog stand serving spicy Cumberland sausages on long bread rolls. It was a lovely excuse for them each to buy one. Even James was allowed a small piece and at once got ketchup all over his snub nose.

'Nick's over at the sheepdog trials,' Jan explained, laughingly trying to mop up the dribbles, 'with Meg and Tam. You'd best go and admire their efforts later.'

The girls promised that they would.

'Meg says you're to hev a good time, all of you,' Sally Ann warned them, a twinkle in her eyes, set like bright buttons in her plump pink face. 'So leave the bairn with us old uns.'

'Don't you mind?'

'We'll spoil him rotten. You enjoy yourselves.'

Tessa grinned. 'Oh, we intend to.'

And indeed she was right for it did prove to be a most enjoyable day. They watched the hounds set off on their aniseed trail, flying through the bracken, tails waving, their owners trying to outshout each other as they urged their animals on. They marvelled at the men who were so fit they could run up the fell a thousand feet or more and return only slightly out of breath at the end of it. They admired Jan's daughter, Alice, who as Boadicea headed the long procession of queens, which represented every female monarch right up to the present day.

And of course they cheered on Tam and Nick at the sheepdog trials before going to find Meg who, sensibly clad in tweed skirt, waistcoat and trilby hat, was judging a pet show for a group of hopeful, bright-eyed children.

'Never be a judge,' she warned with a sad shake of her head and a wide smile. 'Bound to upset someone. I can only hope that these young people, who all belong to my friends, will be generous with my decision. Though somehow I doubt it.'

The girls wished her luck and as one recalcitrant pet duck escaped to be chased across the field by its young owner, they went away laughing, though with immense sympathy for Meg's plight.

And throughout the day, Tessa introduced them to dozens of people who all seemed interested to meet them.

'Hey oop, who do we have here?'

'Nay, not Lissa's girls. Well, fancy that.'

'I can see 'oo you two are. Spittin image o' your mam. How is she then?'

'How you two lasses have grown, you were no more'n bairns when I see'd thee last.'

'Stoppin' on with our Meg for a bit, are thoo? Aye, you do reet.'

And so on, until the twins were dizzy with all the questions and even Sarah felt thoroughly welcomed into the small community.

'They're all so friendly,' Beth said.

'It's being a quiet place, everyone knows everyone else here and newcomers always excite much interest. But you can consider yourself honoured. Dalesfolk aren't always so quick to make friends. They like to weigh people up first, make sure you'll fit in and not try to interfere with their way of life, or damage the countryside which they treasure above all things.'

'Oh, I'd never do that.' It made Beth feel pleased and hopeful about the future. How lovely to be a part of this world. And she still had Larkrigg Hall to look forward to.

But she soon forgot about the house as Tessa took them over to watch the wrestling.

'Cumberland and Westmorland style wrestling is reputed to go right back to the Vikings,' she explained and added with a chuckle, 'as most things do around here. No punching or bullying allowed. It's not so much size as strength that counts, and some pretty canny thinking.'

A group of men were gathering around a green sward of grass, not roped off in any way but clearly selected as the ideal spot. The older men were smart in their best setting-off suits, hair slicked back while many of the younger ones were in shirt and jeans.

'Now this is what I call talent,' Sarah said, running a practised eye over the assembled company.

'They've certainly had their porridge,' Tessa agreed, laughing.

'Good for wrestlers, is it, porridge?'

'It does no harm. Ah, there's Andrew. Andrew Barton from Cathra Crag. I'll introduce you later.' Tessa indicated one young man with fair, fly away hair that flopped disarmingly over a broad forehead. His cheerful face lit with a wide smile when he saw her and he nodded as Tessa waved happily back.

'Well, well,' Sarah said. 'Friend of yours is he?'

'We go a long way back. Went to school together. All that stuff.'

'Hm. Good muscles.'

'It's the farming which does that. If they can lift a ewe, they can "tak hod", that is, take hold or wrestle,' Tessa explained, laughing.

Beth glanced covertly at the young man from beneath her lashes, trying not to be too obvious but curious to see what kind of man Tessa favoured. Dressed in open-necked shirt and jeans he looked relaxed and friendly, the kind of man any girl would be glad to know. But he wasn't looking in Tessa's direction at all. His eyes, unsurprisingly, were on Sarah.

Oh dear, Beth thought. Trouble. And felt strangely deflated.

3

Andrew Barton stood tall and straight, lightly built but with well muscled arms and shoulders. His lean, almost boyish face and pale grey eyes were entirely engrossed in taking instructions from a small, older man with pink-tipped ears beneath a dark basin-cut hair style. As if sensing Beth's interest, he half turned and looked directly into her eyes. For a long moment their gaze held and for the life of her she couldn't break away. Then he smiled and, faintly flustered, she turned quickly away, embarrassed by her own curiosity.

He went into a small white tent and after some moments returned, dressed in a white silk sleeveless vest and pants tucked into black stockings. Over these he wore velvet briefs, very finely embroidered with swirls and flowers.

'Don't you dare giggle,' Tessa hissed into her ear. 'This is a traditional costume. Serious stuff.'

And so it seemed. Moving forward, the two opponents shook hands then grasped each other around the back, each man placing his chin on the other's right shoulder.

'This is the hold which makes this kind of wrestling distinctive,' Tess whispered. 'They rarely hurt each other. The object is to get their opponent to take three falls.'

The two men were stamping their stockinged feet, set well apart for good balance. They made strange little grunting sounds as they moved round and round.

'Good God,' Sarah said, 'They look like a four-legged beast.'

'Hm. They might only seem slim and wiry but some of these

men are so tough I wouldn't care to get on the wrong side of them.'

'I wouldn't mind a tackle.' The grey streaks in Sarah's violet eyes sparkled with interest. Beth said nothing, but her own gaze was fastened as certainly upon the two figures in their strange balletic dance.

The match lasted for some time, as several throws failed. Then Andrew slid his hip under the other man's stomach and using it as a lever, threw him over his shoulder. She couldn't help but cry out when both men hit the ground but Andrew had won the fall. He took one himself next when the other man struck his legs out from beneath him. They heaved and panted and swung about and the girls became completely engrossed, willing Andrew to win. The men rolled and bounced and Beth wondered how many bruises they suffered, despite the lushness of the green turf.

'He needs one more fall,' Tessa murmured and Beth cast her a surreptitious glance. Her first impressions must have been correct. Tessa did have a soft spot for this Andrew Barton. And felt an odd sinking of her heart as she noted Sarah's equally avid interest.

Moments later it was all over. Andrew brought his rival to his knees and down he went. A great cheer went up and the older man hurried forward to slap Andrew on his back with great gusto.

'That's William Barton, Andrew's father. Everyone calls him Billy. Was a champion himself in his time.' Lots of other people crowded round to congratulate the boy. He grinned at them all before grabbing a towel and started to vigorously rub his head with it.

Then Tessa was weaving her way through the crowd towards him. 'Hi, Andrew. Congratulations. Good contest.' She planted a kiss on his sweating cheek and laughed. 'You look in good shape.'

'I'm fine,' he said, his gaze shifting to Beth, and then on to Sarah. Beth stifled a sigh as she saw his eyes widen slightly as he recognised the full impact of her beauty. Wasn't it always so?

Tessa was busy introducing them both and didn't see. Andrew nodded his head slowly as he'd done before, by way of acknowledgement. 'If you wait while I get changed, I'll buy you all a beer.'

'You're on,' Sarah purred, managing to insinuate herself closer to his side, lifting her smiling face to his. He looked down at her for a long moment then smiled. 'Give me one minute.'

Before he disappeared into the nearby tent he again lifted his gaze across to Beth. There was interest in the glance, and a shrewd speculation. Not that she noticed. Her own eyes were fastened on the ground and she was telling herself sternly that it was entirely unreasonable to be troubled because no man ever looked at her in that way. Sarah and Tessa were welcome to fight over him, if it made them happy. She was done with men, wasn't she? Larkrigg Hall was all that mattered now. She resolved to broach the subject with Meg at the very first opportunity.

It was the Monday following the sports day and the family were assembled at Ashlea for a celebratory meal.

Meg insisted the kettle be dispensed with on this happy day. Lemonade was found for the children and Sally Ann opened a couple of dusty bottles of home-made elderflower wine for the adults. There was much relaxing laughter amidst the fetching and filling of glasses and when each held a glass of wine, Sarah and Beth, Tam, Meg and Sally Ann, her son Nick and his wife Jan, a toast was made to the Queen. Glasses were clinked and smiles exchanged. And as they sipped the wine and watched pictures of the Silver Jubilee celebrations in Windsor Great Park on the tiny television set in Sally Ann's front parlour they planned how they would light the beacon fire on Dundale Knot that evening, to link up with the hundreds of others lit the length and breadth of the land to celebrate this momentous day.

Later, the family all sat down to one of Sally Ann's famous tatie pots, rich with mutton gravy, followed by thick slices of apple pie and homemade crumbly cheese. A feast to warm any heart.

Staggering under the weight of full stomachs, Tam, Nick, Jan, and the children went off laughing to see to the bonfire and the women thankfully relaxed to talk about family and farming matters.

Meg and Sally Ann recalled the tough days of the war, of Effie, their ragged evacuee, who was terrified of cows. They recalled how Lissa had come to them and how she had stayed on at Broombank and come to terms, eventually, with her lack of proper parents. Then they moved on to the twins.

'You were no more than bairns when you left for America. You won't remember my father, Joe?'

The twins shook their heads.

'He died shortly after you left in 1965. Cantankerous to the end he was. He did have a heart but you had to work hard to find it.' Meg gave a wry smile. 'Funny how things change. Just when you imagine everything is calm and settled, all problems solved, something goes wrong and you have to find the strength to fight all over again. As I fought Kath for Lissa, and Jack Lawson for Broombank.' Her eyes clouded and even Sarah held her silence, troubled by her grandmother's bleak expression as she gazed into her wine for an endless moment. Then she lifted her head and gave them all her most dazzling smile. 'That's life, I suppose. And we shouldn't dwell in the past. We must look to the next generation to bring us the future. Nick's children, and you two, my lovely twins. What are your plans then? What are you going to do with your lives? Have you decided?'

'Nothing definite.'

'No, not yet.'

'A good holiday.'

'We do have one or two dreams,' Beth admitted, wondering if it was too soon to mention them.

'I'm sure you do. I remember the glorious optimism of youth, when you feel so strong you think you can do anything, fulfill every dream.' Meg gave a little laugh. 'It's a pity it fades away so quickly.'

'You shouldn't let dreams fade,' Beth said, quite vehemently, and Meg regarded her usually quiet grand-daughter with some surprise.

'You're right, Beth. They're too precious to lose. Well, I'll let you into a secret. Tam and I do still have a dream. We'd love to visit Lissa in America but I don't suppose anything will ever come of it.'

'Oh, but you should. Mom would love to have you,' Beth was all eagerness.

'But I wouldn't want to go for a week or two. I'd like to stay for months to make up for all the lost years, and who'd look after the farm?'

'We would.' And everyone laughed.

'You know about sheep do you?'

Beth grinned. 'Not a thing.'

Then Meg asked lots of questions, wanting to hear all about Lissa, Derry, and the two younger children, Thomas and David. They talked contentedly for an hour or more while Sally Ann nodded quietly to sleep over her knitting which she always seemed to have in hand. Meg lapsed into silence once again, her mind slipping away on to private thoughts.

Beth heard Sarah sigh, could almost feel her sister's boredom pulsing through her own blood stream yet didn't quite know how to deal with it. She so much wanted her to like it here, in Lakeland. Then to her great surprise Sarah leaned forward, violet eyes vivid with a sudden gleam of excitement.

'Right now we'd just love to see inside Larkrigg Hall. We've been here a week and not yet seen inside it and we're burning up with curiosity. Do you have a key?'

Beth stared at Sarah in surprise and whispered under her breath. 'I didn't know you were so keen.'

'Sure.' To Sarah, Larkrigg Hall offered the only possibility of interest, in lieu of excitement, in this quiet dale. It was her last hope.

'Please do say that you have, Gran,' Beth added her own plea. 'We walked up when we first arrived and saw it from the end of the drive. It looks every bit as wonderful as I'd imagined. Only dreadfully neglected of course, and so sad and forlorn.'

'Yes, I dare say it is.' Meg's mind had slipped away back to the mill, and her worries over its future. She struggled to take an interest in what the twins were saying, when really she longed suddenly for them to be gone so that she and Tam could discuss the problem openly, as they seemed endlessly to do since their visit with the bank manager. They needed to find a permanent solution. They'd gained time, a breathing space, but what it called for was long hard work to pull the business round, and Meg found her reserves of energy to be well nigh exhausted. Nick had enough on his plate with his own farm and family to see to, and they hadn't the courage to take on another manager.

'Such a magnificent setting,' Beth was saying.

'The setting is splendid,' Meg politely agreed, 'but I've always thought it a rather gloomy house with very little by way of character. I do have a key somewhere, I suppose.' She glanced about the room in a vague sort of way, as if wondering where it might be but making no move to look for it.

'Can you find it? *Please*,' Sarah begged and Meg frowned.

'What?'

'The key. To Larkrigg Hall.'

'Ah, of course.' Larkrigg. Could they sell it? she wondered briefly.

31

Lissa had never liked it. No, how could they sell, when it belonged to the twins?

'Don't expect too much. I doubt it will live up to your expectations. Your mother visited once or twice and every occasion proved a most unhappy experience.'

'But that was a long time ago,' Sarah protested.

'True. Oh dear, is it seven o'clock already? We really ought to be getting out to that bonfire. Nick will wonder where we are.' She got up and went in search of her coat.

But Sarah followed and persisted. 'Mom would never talk about it, which only made us want to see it all the more.'

Meg smiled at that. 'I expect it did. Darling Lissa. Feels things so keenly but then we are all vulnerable at times. I didn't much care for the house myself. It's never seemed to me as warm or comforting as Broombank.' Meg's thoughts seemed to shift to some private memory and the twins were forced to subside into frustrated, respectful silence.

Only this time it was Beth who broke it, her voice all excited and breathless. 'We've quite fallen in love with it,' she explained. 'And we thought if we liked the inside as much as the outside, we might restore it.' She didn't dare glance at Sarah, knowing they hadn't even discussed the idea, which was entirely her own. She blundered on, her voice rising with enthusiasm. 'We feel we'd like to make Larkrigg beautiful again.'

Sarah was staring at her, mouth open in stunned surprise, then she raised a speculative eyebrow and added her own point of view. 'We'd sell it afterwards, of course, and make a vast profit.'

'Or live in it ourselves.'

'It's only an idea.'

'We're seriously considering it.'

'But we need to see inside first.'

Sally Ann had woken with a start, her knitting falling to the floor as she and Meg gazed in open astonishment first at one twin and then the other, as in their turn they glared furiously upon each other.

After several minutes Meg reached for her hat and said, 'The bonfire. Her Majesty's Jubilee celebrations must be given priority to family matters tonight.'

So Beth and Sarah had to bite their tongues and dutifully follow their grandmother out on to Dundale Knot where the rosy glow of a bonfire already lit the sapphire blue of the short Lakeland night. Sparks flew like fireflies all about and the tangy scent of woodsmoke filled their nostrils. It made Beth sigh with contentment and inside her grew such a yearning she felt almost breathless with the wonder of it.

No further mention was made of Larkrigg Hall that day or the next as everyone struggled to get back to work after all the fun.

And neither of the twins dared find the courage to pursue the subject again.

Beth was in despair. The hot days of June were drawing to a close and soon it would be July and time to leave yet nothing at all had been resolved. And they still had not explored the house. The subject had never again been mentioned.

She sat by the tarn, bare toes curled on a cushion of emerald green spagnum moss, eyes watching the tufts of silky cotton grass which floated like flakes of white as if they were a summer snowstorm. They caught on tall thistles, bounced off rocky knolls and attached themselves to the fast growing bracken.

This morning Sarah had reluctantly agreed to help Sally Ann wind wool. Jan and Meg were at Broombank worrying over orders. Uncle Nick was with his sheep, and Beth had sneaked away for a few moments alone, to think. It felt good.

These last weeks had passed in a whirl. They'd been introduced to various neighbours including Hetty Davies, a grand old lady who used to look after their mother, Lissa, when she was a baby. She'd invited them for tea later that day as a matter of fact, and they'd promised to attend the Women's Institute meeting with her in the evening to see a demonstration on soap sculpture. Sarah said she could hardly wait. Beth giggled. But her sister had behaved rather better recently.

The holiday had been wonderful, no doubt about that. Meg had driven them around half the county, proudly showing them the sights. They'd enjoyed a steamer ride across Lake Windermere, exclaimed over pretty Lakeland villages, shopped in the nearby market town of Kendal and walked for miles over rough fell country, up mountain and down dale so that the names, Hardknott, Skiddaw, Ill Bell,

Longsleddale, gradually became real places in their mind, instead of names on a map.

On two or three occasions Andrew Barton had come with them, encouraged by Sarah of course, who declared she loved to have a man about her, as if he were some sort of trophy. He certainly didn't seem to object, Beth thought, rather ruefully. But she'd made a point of keeping well out of his way. There was enough tension between Sarah and Tessa, without adding more.

Meg had even taken them to their old home in Carreckwater and the twins had exclaimed in delight over the lake, and the tiny park where they'd used to play, which were exactly as they remembered. The shop was still there, Broombank Woollens, selling jumpers, hats and scarves in lovely bright colours.

'Your mother started the business off by persuading the dalesfolk to knit for her in their own homes,' she told them. 'It's a long tradition going back generations and they were only too happy to resurrect it. Then she put frame knitting machines in the barn and that did well too.'

'We saw the barn when we arrived,' Beth commented. 'It all seemed closed.'

'Yes,' Meg calmly responded. 'It'd been closed for about ten days while some problems were sorted out.'

'Who runs the mill now?' Sarah mildly enquired, with no particular sign of interest. Meg had sighed at this and finally explained about the missing money and the disappearing manager. 'The place was overrun with police and accountants for a while.'

'Oh, but that's dreadful. Why didn't you tell us?' Beth said.

'There's nothing you could have done. We've talked it all through with the family and there's little any of us can do at present. The police say it's unlikely the man will be caught. He'll be long gone by this time.'

'That doesn't seem quite fair,' Beth protested and Meg sighed.

'No, my pet. But then life isn't fair. We trusted the man and he repaid us by stealing our hard earned cash. And the books are so cleverly doctored we'd have a hard job proving anything. A sad indictment on society but we try to be philosophical about it.'

'What will you do now?'

'I'm not sure. The business was in poor shape in any case, to be honest. When pressure of work took Derry back to America and Lissa went with him, things sagged a bit. The business has struggled on since but never quite flourished as it should. Jan gives what assistance she can but she finds it hard going, what with her own children and the farm to see to. I don't have much time either so its become a bit of a worry. We may have to close it down, in the end.'

'That would be a dreadful shame. Mom loved that business. She's always talking about it.'

'We'll see. No need to make any decisions yet.' Meg's eyes became troubled and unfocused, as they so often were these days. Sarah and Beth had exchanged meaningful glances and quickly changed the subject. And so they had waited. Tactful, sensitive, but with barely contained patience until now with the day of their flight home drawing perilously near, there was still no sign of that key.

Beth glared bleakly down the sweep of fell into the dale below, tracing the black ribbon of dry-stone walls that circled the hills like a plump girl's sash and came to a decision. She would talk to Sally Ann. This very evening after the Women's Institute meeting, or perhaps tomorrow would be better. She might be the very one to help.

She set off home with a determined spring to her step.

Sally Ann was making clover wine when the twins called at Ashlea the following afternoon.

'Now then, what can I do for you two?' Her hands were deftly chopping and she did not glance up.

They watched as she put flowers, water and sugar into a large pan, then added lemon and orange rinds, cut into strips with the pith removed, followed by a sprinkling of ginger. The small kitchen was at once filled with the most heavenly scents. Even the cat leapt softly from the rocking chair and began to rub itself ecstatically against the back of Beth's legs.

'Soft old lump. Only got one eye, hence the name, Nelson. Meg's a dog person a'course. Usually has two or three about her. I still remember old Rust. Now there was a dog. Niver had one like it since.'

Beth was anxious to get to the point so did nothing to encourage these reminiscences. 'We want to ask you about Larkrigg Hall.'

'Larkrigg? Eeh, your mother hated the place. Didn't hit it off with her grandmother one bit. Old Rosemary Ellis blamed her for being born the wrong side o' the blanket, d'you see?'

The twins knew all of this and had no wish to dwell on the past today. It was the future which concerned them.

'Do you know anything about it? The hall I mean,' Beth pressed. She couldn't quite decide how to broach the subject of Meg's reluctance to part with the key, not without seeming rude and ungrateful. But desperation was making her brave. And reckless.

'What sort of thing?'

She half glanced at Sarah. 'We don't know. Whatever there is to tell.'

Sally Ann was stirring gently, staring into the pan as it came to the boil. 'Now why would that be?'

'Curiosity.'

'It's our inheritance.'

'Is the land any good?'

'Does the house have dry rot?

The questions poured out and she put back her head and laughed. It made her plump chin wobble delightfully. 'Eeh, I doan't know. It's niver been a happy house. Built by Rosemary Ellis's great grandfather, I do believe, beginning of last century. Charles Barnabas Ellis. Ay, fancy me remembering his name. Right old tartar he was, apparently. He passed it on to his son, and his son after that. My dad worked for the family, at the quarry, till he had his accident. Told me all about the Ellises my dad did, and Rosemary was definitely a chip off the old block.' She set the pan to simmer then eased herself into the chair by the fire. The cat at once jumped onto her lap and she stroked it idly with her plump fingers, giving a rich chortle of laughter, always content to chat and recall days past. 'Old Charles Barnabas was the one who moved the stoanes, a' course.'

'Stones?'

'Aye, them what stands by the gate. The Gemini Stones.'

Both girls glanced at each other, then curled up at her feet, all attention.

'Tell us, Sally Ann, about the stones.'

'Apparently t'owd chap had a load of stoanes shifted that he shouldn't. Standing stoanes, cairns, that sort of thing. Been there for centuries they had. Upset the locals no end. Then no sooner was the house completed than there was a terrible storm and one huge stoane which stood by the entrance to the drive and had been too big to move was struck by lightning and split in two. And so it stands to this day. Well, a'course everyone said it was a bad omen and no two people of the same blood would ever be able to live in harmony within Larkrigg's four walls, not ever again.'

The twins stared at her in astonished silence.

'Do you believe all of that?' Beth asked at last, her voice soft, hoping she would pooh pooh it.

Sarah only said, 'What absolute tosh.'

'Not for me to say.' Sally Ann shook her head. 'What would I know about such things? Trouble is, the prophecy would seem to be holding up. The Ellis family has niver done aught but bicker and fall out ever since then, by all accounts. As your own mother, and her mother in turn, would testify.'

'They probably let the superstition bother them,' Beth jauntily remarked, wanting to sound scornful but not quite succeeding.

'Aye, happen.'

'Anyway,' Sarah continued. 'Beth and I are sisters, so naturally have never got on. Sisters don't, do they? So how could an old house make us any worse? And we do so want to see inside.'

'Why don't you then?'

Beth dropped her voice, trying to disguise the enthusiasm that pulsated through her. 'We've almost decided, you see, to stay, for a while at least, and do it up. But we worry about Meg's reaction. She won't even lend us the key to take a proper look inside.'

'Adventurous types, eh?'

Sarah said, 'We'd sell it and make a vast profit.' There, said the fierce glance she shot in Beth's direction, that should set the record straight. Beth went bright red.

'Aye, weel. She mebbe has her reasons. Upsetting time she had there once. But she'd enjoy having you two close by, I know that. I'll happen have a word wi' her.'

'Oh, would you?'

Sally Ann stood up, brushing the cat from her lap. 'Now then, are you going to help me strain this wine, or sit there like a pair of book ends?'

*   *   *

'So why won't you give 'em that key then?' Sally Ann faced Meg with a wry smile on her homely face.

Meg glared down at her from the seat of the tractor, her own face darkly silhouetted against a cloud-flecked blue sky.

'I've work to do, Sal. Several acres to cut before it rains. Can we discuss this some other time?'

Sally Ann chuckled. 'I've fetched your dinner. You'll be cooming to eat that, I dare swear. It's cold pork today.'

'I'm not hungry.'

'Doan't talk so daft. You can't work on an empty stomach. Anyroad, those lasses has ivery right to see Larkrigg, if they wants. It belongs to them, or so I've been told.'

Meg tightened her lips. 'Rosemary Ellis hurt their mother beyond endurance.'

'Rosemary Ellis is dead, Meg.'

'She only left it to them to spite Lissa.'

'But it is theirs, like it or not.'

'It's a miserable inheritance.'

'That's for them to decide, not you.' For a second Meg's grey eyes blazed, but Sally Ann continued, unperturbed. 'Aye, you know in your heart that it is. You niver took notice of what your fadder said, now did you? So why should these two bairns listen to you? Let 'em be, Meg. It's their life, not yourn.'

'And I suppose you'll grumble at me for ever if I don't agree.'

'Aye, I reckon I might.'

Beth and Sarah turned the key in the lock and pushed open the door. It creaked so loudly that they both jumped, then clutched at each other in a fit of the giggles. They'd almost given up hope when Sally Ann brought them the key, her soft face shining with triumph. 'Doan't expect too much, that's all, Meg says.'

'We won't.' But Beth did. She expected everything. Certainly the answer to her dreams.

'It's like something out of a movie,' Sarah said. 'I hope Frankenstein isn't lurking inside.'

Beth peered through the gloom. 'Oh my God, what's that?'

Sarah flashed her torch at the opposite wall and caught the glint of amber. 'A stag's head with glass eyes. Handsome fellow, wasn't he?'

'How cruel.'

'How English.'

'We should have left it till the morning. We can't see a thing in this gloom.'

Sarah stepped over a pile of rags, screwing up her nose in distaste and led the way down a long, dark passage, its walls covered with peeling red flock wallpaper, damp with mildew.

'It smells dreadful. Of damp and old wood fires and something even less pleasant.'

Beth said, 'At least we're inside at last, in Larkrigg Hall.' There was deep satisfaction in her tone.

Their boots echoed mournfully on the bare wooden floors. Austere, dark and empty, it seemed anything but welcoming.

Somewhere in the distant depths of the house a door banged shut and both girls jumped.

'Oh, lord. Let's get out of here.'

'It's only a gust of wind we brought in with us,' Beth said, laughing.

'Nevertheless, we'll come back tomorrow, in the daylight. OK?'

And when something scampered over her feet Beth felt bound to agree. All in all their first view of the house had been far from encouraging. But she wasn't in the least bit discouraged. Oh, dear me, no.

4

Larkrigg Fell was one of those tracts of land which went unnoticed, except by the most discerning. Hidden away from all the main tourist routes, its rough grass untrodden except by the foxes and sheep who knew it intimately, it had no dramatic crags and no precipitous summits. The stony sheep trod which the twins followed the very next day, climbed slowly and lazily, winding between juniper bushes and knuckles of rock which formed knolls and hollows.

The fell had been shaped at the dawn of time by ice overflowing from glaciers formed in the clefts of surrounding mountains, scooping out pockets here and there and tumbling rocks into them as if with a careless hand. One such hollow was deeper than the rest so had filled with water and formed the tarn by which they lingered for a moment before hurrying on to the crest of the ridge where the house stood, a shelter of oak and yew clustered about the rectangular stone building.

But the beauty of this fell lay not in its own topography but in its setting and Beth found herself catching her breath as she let her gaze travel over the panorama of surrounding hills and mountains. Smooth, crisp and green, looking deceptively easy to climb in the foreground but with jagged blue-grey peaks in the far distance.

Swirls of fine mist wreathed these higher peaks, flimsy as a bridal veil, and utter contentment flowed into her heart as if the land itself had opened its arms and embraced her. As if she had come home. Now, in the house at last, that sensation was reinforced.

As they walked from room to room, their footsteps echoing on bare boards, she found herself easily setting aside Sally Ann's superstitions and how everyone insisted upon this being an unhappy house. Though it certainly looked unloved. There wasn't a stick of furniture to be seen, and grubby walls showed lighter patches where pictures had once hung.

They stopped in what had obviously been the library, the oak panelled walls and shelving now empty of books but where, oddly enough, a seed box still sat, upturned, in the open fireplace. The windows were netted with cobwebs, the frames black with rotted wood and a piece of ceiling had fallen in one corner, revealing the floor above.

Sarah's lips curled in disgust. 'And you say we could do it up?'

Beth cast her sister an anxious glance. 'Don't you think it a good idea?'

Sarah examined her surroundings, taking time over her reply. 'I can see it has potential and I'd have no objection to making pots of money out of it. If someone else did the actual work.'

'Would you really want to sell it?'

'Of course. We'd make a killing. Once it's made weatherproof and tarted up a bit, we could sell it for a fat profit.' Sarah rubbed her hands together, grinning. 'You weren't serious about wanting to live here, surely?'

Beth walked to the window and stared at the glorious view and once again her heart lifted. How could a house be unlucky? She flicked the faded velvet curtains that still hung there and a cloud of dust flew out, making her cough. 'It seems so much in need of love and care. I feel as if it's asking me to stay.'

'You live in a fantasy world,' Sarah said, rolling her eyes in mock despair while checking she hadn't collected any dust on her perfectly manicured hands, or on her new boots. 'I saw it in your eyes the minute you saw the place on that first day. Dreams! OK, so we could get the roof fixed, stop the rain coming in, redecorate and stuff. But you wouldn't get me living here. Not in a million years.' She shoved her hands in the pockets of her jeans and gave a half shrug, wrinkling her nose at a pile of newspapers in one corner. 'Do you think tramps have been in?'

'How could they get in? We couldn't.'

'True.'

Beth returned to her argument. 'You do so love to exaggerate, Sarah. You like it too, admit it.' The more Beth thought about it, the more the nut of excitement grew inside her. She'd hardly been able to sleep last night, couldn't wait to get back here. She'd become entirely gripped by the possibility of restoring Larkrigg Hall, as if by pouring all her energies into the house she could banish for ever her yearning for Jeremy.

And she wanted to do much of the work herself. To clean and scrub and paint, the rest she could learn as she went along. She wanted to live in these hills, be a living part of this landscape.

Beth had other dreams too, only it was too soon to mention those yet. First came the task of convincing Sarah. It was vitally important that they didn't quarrel over this.

Somewhere in a far corner of the house came a distant rustling.

'Ugh, those mice again,' said Sarah. 'We'd be pestered to death with all sorts of weird creatures out here.'

'We could get a cat.'

'You've got it all worked out, haven't you?'

They came to the kitchen, the green-tiled walls and painted shelves empty of their collection of shining copperware which must once have resided there, the pride of some cook's heart. A solid fuel range, rusty with neglect held one black pan, as if someone had set it down to make a milk drink and then forgotten to return for it. One wall comprised a long built-in dresser and most of the floor was filled with a huge, pine table, not clean and scrubbed as Broombank's was but coated with filth and littered with dirty newspapers, left there probably because it was too large to remove. Everything else had gone.

Scullery, meat larder, dairy, held nothing but cobwebs and an odd assortment of stone and wooden vessels, used for some long forgotten purpose.

Beth drew in a deep breath. 'What else could we do? We're not trained for anything. We neither of us wanted to go to college. Surely we could do something with this house? Make it pay?'

Sarah gave a disbelieving spurt of laughter. 'How? Like taking in tourists? Yuk.'

'I didn't say so.'

'Good. Skivvying in this kitchen isn't my idea of fun.'

'There must be something we can do here to earn our living.'
Beth felt almost desperate for Sarah's approval. 'Look at these.' She
pointed to a row of bells on the wall of the passage. When she tapped
them, each one gave a different sound. They were labelled parlour,
drawing room, library, dining room and bedrooms, numbered one
to six. Sarah tried them out too and soon they were ding donging
as merrily as silly schoolgirls.

When their childish sense of humour was sated they went on into
the next room. But the game had eased the tension between them.

'You're running away, that's all this is,' Sarah said, half regretting
the moment of weakness yet at the same instant fighting against the
seductive allure of escape from her own problems, stuffed deep in the
recesses of her mind. Perhaps it wasn't such a bad idea after all.

'Running away from what?'

'From Boston, and failure to find either a decent job or a loyal
man,' said Sarah with casual brutality.

'What if I'm running *to* something?' It was astonishing the impact
Lakeland had made on her, Beth thought. She really belonged here.
Every day that passed brought her closer and closer to her roots. It
had revitalised her, made her realise she could start again, build a life
with her own hands without the requisite man at her side, even if she
wasn't as captivating or as beautiful as her sister.

The ebony curls sprang wilfully back from Sarah's brow, chin
resolutely tilted, full ripe lips smiling with confident assurance. Even
in shirt and jeans she looked elegant and lovely, whereas Beth simply
felt dusty and rather unkempt. She pushed the unflattering clip
more firmly into place with fidgety fingers. 'It would be a new
challenge. Do us both good.'

'Hmm, maybe,' Sarah conceded.

'We don't have to go back to Boston. Not yet. Do you want to?
Honestly?' She thought of returning home the following week, of
facing the pity in the eyes of her friends, of being that dreadful object,
a jilted bride. And she thought of Jeremy with another woman in his
arms and shuddered. It was unthinkable, more than she could bear.
'I certainly don't. What is it you have to get back to?'

It was true, Sarah thought. What did she have to return to?

She wondered what Beth would say if her sister knew that she
too had once been embroiled in a passionate affair, only with a

married man. Oh, she'd fancied Jeremy like mad once, could have taken him off Beth if she'd wanted to. But that would have been too easy. Frank was a greater challenge, and far more exciting. He'd never intended to leave his wife so it had all seemed like glorious fun. But look what the outcome had been? Disaster. Pregnancy and abortion last year, at just seventeen.

No, she didn't want Beth to know all of that. She didn't want anyone to know. They'd only condemn her and it took enough of Sarah's courage not to hate herself.

Even so, to stay at Larkrigg would be an enormous commitment. 'Where would we get the money?'

Excitement tightened Beth's voice. 'Derry sent money for our stay which Meg put in the building society. He'd lend us more, if we asked him.'

'He'd tell us not to hurt Mom by staying on here.'

'No, he wouldn't. And Mom isn't like that.'

'He couldn't afford to give us much of a loan.'

'Then we could ask the bank for a mortgage.'

Sarah rolled her eyes in mock despair. 'Will you listen to yourself? Mortgage indeed. How could we two kids get a goddam mortgage? How would we pay it back, idiot?'

Sarah was always so practical. She saw life as it really was, not how she wanted it to be but Beth's innate stubbornness took hold. 'We'd find a way if we put our minds to it. Get a job for a start. Earn our own living.'

'Oh, sure. Most ways of earning the kind of money I need are either unreliable or illegal.'

'We could do much of the work ourselves.'

'Can you see me up a ladder? Or scrubbing floors?' Sarah pulled a face and made a rude noise.

'I don't see why not.'

'And I don't see why.'

They seemed to have reached an impasse. Beth gazed out over the hump of fells, the morning mist rolling off, revealing them in all their serene splendour. She opened the window and let in the sweet smell of damp earth, wild thyme and bilberry. Her longing to stay had become a physical pain in her heart. 'I feel I have to do this,' she said, very softly. 'As if it were my destiny.'

Sarah came and snapped shut the window and Beth's despair dipped deeper.

'I thought you wanted a home and a family?'

'I do.'

'Presumably it's this burning need you feel to nest build that makes you want all of this stuff.' Sarah's voice was cold and angry. 'What's the point of a nest with no man, or babies, to put into it? A person could die of starvation here.'

'Don't be silly, we could grow our own food.'

Sarah groaned. 'I'm talking about sex, not food. Idiot.'

Beth winced. 'Maybe I just want to do things a different way round. Make the house first and find a man later. You never know, I might be lucky. And I'm too young to think of babies yet. I want to do something useful with my life. As Gran did. Maybe this is it.' She gave a little smile but it looked more contrite than confident. As if she were still apologising for something, a feeling she hated. Sarah often had that affect on her.

'You'd be hiding from reality, stuck out here.'

'What's wrong with that? And why are you so angry? The change would do us both good. You haven't been too well lately. A good, healthy life might help you get fit again.'

Sarah turned and strode out of the kitchen and along the passage, running up the stairs on light steps, her tight jeans making her legs look longer, her buttocks firm and round. 'Can you see me living here?' She leaned over the bannister, adopting a falsely social tone. 'Do come up, darlings. Afternoon tea is being served in the drawing room.'

Beth couldn't help but giggle. 'We don't have to live that way. I know it's quite big but it needn't be a smart sort of house. It's only a big old farmhouse after all.' She saw it filled with soft furnishings and chintz sofas, polished brass and bright woolly rugs, dogs and wellingtons in the kitchen, the sound of children's happy laughter everywhere. Her heart contracted and she hurried up the stairs after Sarah.

But when she reached her sister, Beth discovered that there was indeed a drawing room upstairs. Small and perfectly proportioned with turquoise wallpaper inset with cream silk panels, shredded with age. It seemed somehow out of keeping with the rest of the house.

'Oh, how lovely,' she breathed.

'Very elegant.'

Sarah flopped down on a small Edwardian couch that stood in the centre of the room and looked about her. A matching chair stood by the marble fireplace and a walnut desk against one wall. There were one or two small tables and a sideboard still bearing a tray of glasses and a decanter, as if the lady of the house might return at any moment and pour herself a small sherry. There were even ashes in the grate as if from a recent fire. 'Why isn't this room empty, like the ones downstairs?'

'Perhaps the bedrooms are all still furnished too.'

Exploration proved this to be the case, though not in the same style as the pretty drawing room. Each room still held a bed, huge wardrobe, chest of drawers, rugs and an occasional chair, most covered with dustsheets, some looked almost lived in with rugs lying about and a glass with a half full jug of water on a bedside table.

'How marvellous.' Beth was entranced. 'I feel like Goldilocks expecting the three bears to turn up at any moment.' She giggled. 'I expect downstairs was cleared because prying eyes might encourage unwelcome visitors, burglars even.'

'In this remote spot? More likely this furniture was considered too cumbersome and old fashioned to sell.' Sarah ran her fingers with distaste over a gargoyle decorated mirror. 'I mean, look at it, solid Victorian at least. Horrendous. And this mirror is cracked. Do you think the seven years bad luck is over by now?'

'Who cares? I love it. Can't you just see me sleeping in that lovely Empire bed in the blue room next door?' If I can't sleep with Jeremy's arms tight about me. No, I won't ever think of him again, not here in Larkrigg anyway, she decided, making a private and very fervent vow.

Sarah rolled her eyes heavenward. 'Clown. Though I wouldn't mind this four poster myself.' It reminded her of the old Colonial bed at Frank's house. They'd had some fun in that while his wife was out at one of her Ladies' Guild meetings. And with the memory came a view of the pity in his eyes when she'd told him about the baby. It'd been his idea to get the abortion and he had readily paid for it. She'd

47

almost hated him for the casual way he'd dealt with the matter.

But Beth was right, she hadn't been at all well for some time afterwards. Reaction, she supposed. Yet she'd been too besotted to give him up, even then.

Marriage isn't for the likes of you, he'd said. And Sarah had to agree with him. She'd no inclination to take up where they'd left off, not now she'd managed to make the break. Best to make it a clean one and show how she could manage without him.

Yet she couldn't stay here and vegetate. She had too much living to do for that.

Later, as they walked home, the sheep-cropped turf springy beneath their feet and the mew of a lone curlew circling above them, Sarah said, 'We'd die of cold come winter. There's no central heating. And this is England remember. Rain, rain, rain.'

Beth felt a lift of perverse excitement for nothing would stop her now. Not even Sarah's grumbles. She could win her round, she was sure of it.

'There are fireplaces in every room, and plenty of wood about.' The rural dream was growing in her mind. She could see herself feeding hens, making cheese, wearing long skirts and rocking in a chair by the fire with a cat like Nelson asleep on her lap as she made clover wine like Sally Ann. It would be so perfect. 'Meg says it was a big farm once, before much of the land was sold off at the beginning of this century. But there are still twenty acres.'

'You'll have me acting as a damned milk-maid next.'

'We could be very nearly self-sufficient. Try organic gardening. Keep hens and ducks.'

'They need cleaning out every week.'

'A goat perhaps.'

'Goats?' The grey flecks that radiated from the dark pupils of Sarah's eyes lit the violet like a summer storm. 'Are you mad? Goats *smell*.'

'OK, no goats.' Not at first anyway, she thought.

Beth's own, paler blue-grey eyes were alight with such a merry optimism that Sarah felt the familiar surge of affectionate irritation. Beth might be shy and awkward at times, but once she'd set her mind on something, it was hard to deny her. And she was her

48

sister, for God's sake, for all she was an impractical romantic and a raving loony. And she was suffering from a blow that would fell a lesser female. She's stronger than she looks, our Beth, Sarah thought with unaccustomed pride.

Yet how could she go along with this silly rural dream? She might agree to do the place up a bit, in order to make a profit on the sale. Money always came in handy. As for being self-sufficient? No way. 'Organic gardening, my ass,' she said.

Beth chuckled, not too disturbed by her attitude. Have I succeeded? she wondered. Can I make her agree?

As they walked down the fellside with the late afternoon sun warming their necks, they were both silent, deep in their own thoughts.

Next day they went again. This time Tessa went with them, James having been left at Ashlea with Sally Ann.

The mountains seemed hazy and far away in the summer sun, tiny blue butterflies flying up before them as they made their way up the fell, the sound of bees busy in the heather. Beth was bouncing ahead, Tessa laughingly trying to keep up with her. Only Sarah was subdued, already having second thoughts about showing an interest in the place, worrying over this new development which threatened to enmesh her before she'd had time to think things through.

As they marched along the stony drive, Beth increased her fears by pointing out pot-holes that would need to be filled in, tree branches which should be lopped, weeds to be pulled up. It all sounded very much like hard work.

They found a pile of logs already split in the yard, and the kitchen door wide open. Someone had tried, and failed, to light the range, filling the kitchen with filthy smoke and soot.

'Lord, what's happened?'

Appalled, Beth was for running into the house to see if any further damage had been done. Tessa stopped her.

'Hold on. This is a popular route for tramps heading north and that's probably all this is. But it might be someone with a more serious intent.'

'Burglars you mean?' Beth was horrified.

'We should do a recce first. Best to be on the safe side.'

They crept out the back door again and started to circumnavigate the house, peeping in windows where Beth had thrown back the shutters.

Sarah stepped over to one for a peek inside. At first she could make out nothing in the dim interior and then she gasped, bringing the other two running.

'Will you look at this.' There was laughter in her voice and when she turned to beckon them, she put a finger to her lips, dark eyes brimming with merry good humour. 'Don't make a sound. What a treat.'

Exchanging puzzled glances Tessa and Beth stepped up to the window and peered inside. They were looking into what had once been a small dining room, a fitted walnut dresser revealing the room's past purpose. The floorboards were bare and the room quite empty, except in one corner where two figures lay face down on dirty grey blankets. Clearly male, young, and entirely naked, their undoubtedly beautiful bodies glistened in a shaft of sunlight.

Beth's eyes grew round with shock and she gave a small gasp of alarm. They looked relaxed and companionable, the remains of a meal stood on the dusty floorboards among pools of water, and a black dog lay beside them, nose on paws, fast asleep.

'What on earth . . . ?'

'They've been for a swim in the tarn and come here to dry off,' Sarah suggested.

Tessa considered the firm round buttocks. 'I don't recognise either of them.'

Sarah gave a small explosion of laughter, hastily stifled by Beth who, starting to hiccup with giggles herself, slapped a hand over her sister's mouth.

'Don't, they'll hear us.'

All three girls leaned upon each other, weak with laughter, quite unable to stop the tide of giggles that threatened to convulse them.

Then suddenly the dog lifted its head, glared at them through the window and started to bark.

'Hell, they've heard us,' Tessa cried and as one, they fled.

5

Cathra Crag, isolated as it was at the head of the dale, didn't offer many opportunities for meeting girls.

Andrew Barton eased his back on the clipping stool while he waited for the next sheep to be brought to him and gazed up at the scree-streaked slopes above, shading from pale grey to pinky-purple. The farm was sound enough and had been in his family for generations, though much of the land was poor hill grazing with some allotment bounded by dry-stone walls. Thirty Galloways grazed the richer pickings but the sheep flock, mainly Herdwicks, were content to nibble what croppings they could get on the high fells.

Its isolation had never troubled him. Until this summer.

Now he couldn't get the memory of her out of his mind, though he'd seen her less than half a dozen times. Once at the Jubilee celebrations and a few occasions since on long walks, feeling a bit out of place with three females.

He could still recall that first moment he'd set eyes on her. Serene and pale with softly rounded cheeks. He remembered wondering what colour her eyes were as they were mostly shaded by the lids, fringed with surprisingly dark lashes. Apart from that one startling moment when she had looked directly at him, and he'd been too overwhelmed by the unexpectedness of his emotions to take note. Since then she'd studiously avoided his gaze altogether.

He'd heard they were staying on and the thought excited him. Should he try to see her again? Dare he? She hadn't seemed too

interested thus far. Done her best to avoid him, in fact. He supposed she was rather shy and he'd never been any good with girls.
He hadn't had much practice.

And what did he have to offer any female? A farm, with a flock
of only four hundred ewes which his father considered too small, its
future too uncertain, to spend money on modernisation, so it clung
to the old methods. As he was doing now, taking the clip with hand
shears. A long and laborious task. Not that Andrew, twenty-one years
old and anxious to be free of parental restraint necessarily agreed with
this policy but then he wasn't in charge.

Though most of the work was done by his father, the farm belonged to his grandfather, Seth, eighty-six this year. And would
remain so for as long as the old man had breath in his body. Or
so he was fond of saying. Andrew did not for a moment doubt he
would reach his century, at least.

Three men on one farm was not an easy option, even if the old one
did spend most of his day in the chimney corner sucking his pipe.
There was no doubt who held sway. Old Seth considered himself a
reasonable man but held an opinion on everything and addressed his
son at times as if he were a boy still.

Not that Billy took much notice. He was as stubborn as his father
and had gone his own way for much of his life, even more so since
the death of his wife, Emily, in 1956. Having delivered the farm
with its much needed son at the late age of thirty-eight, Andrew's
mother had uncomplainingly died. And nothing had moved forward
at Cathra Crag from that date on.

There Billy stood now, one leg hooked horizontally around the
long stick of his crook, resting a foot while he counted his sheep.
His long-sighted shepherd's eyes peered out from under the neb of
his cap, missing nothing of the scene all around him.

Andrew bent again to his task with a weary sigh. He'd get a second-
hand generator next year if he had to fight both of them to do it.

Even the clipping stool he used had been made by his great
grandfather in the early part of the last century and the shears
should by rights be in Kendal museum, for all they were still as
sharp as a razor. The distinctive smell of oily wool filled his nostrils,
his hands sore from grasping each animal, and the pain in his back
took his breath away. But for all that, he loved working with the

sheep. Not for a moment could he envisage leaving Cathra Crag, for all the loneliness biting into him right now, making him feel sour and raw.

And testing his wits and muscle against each ewe gave him good practice at 'takking hold' for the Cumberland and Westmorland wrestling contests of which he was so fond. Perhaps he did love tradition, for all he might so often rail against it.

Which brought his mind back to Beth Brandon and her sister. But what position was he in to start courting a lass? He had naught to call his own, nor ever would have, and there wasn't a damn thing he could do about it.

He knew that if they didn't go forward the farm would die. Money seemed to get tighter with each passing year. Why couldn't his father see that the old days were gone? Broombank surged forward, always making changes, keeping up with the times. They had a proper automatic milking parlour, electric shearing, hired helicopters to drop winter feed for the sheep. Why couldn't they do the same here? Why was Billy so determined to wait for the old man to die before he tried anything new?

As Andrew checked the ewe for fitness and marked it with the farm's own identifying mark he could so easily call to mind the pale oval of her sweet face, the chestnut hair clipped back behind the most delightful curl of an ear he'd ever seen in his life. Mind, the other sister was even more of a stunner. Quite took your breath away, she did.

He let the animal go, awkward in its new nakedness as its lamb greeted it with much anxious bleating. Then laughing, he reached for the next.

Oh, aye, no doubt about it, he'd have to do summat to make sure he met them again. Mebbe he could call, friendly like. There'd be naught lost by that.

'Hey oop,' shouted Billy. 'Theer's yan missing.'

Andrew looked up. 'What?'

Billy closed the pen gate on the last counted ewe and walked over to his son. 'Three hundred and ninety nine I've counted. Yan short. Wheer's it at do ye reckon?'

Andrew screwed up his eyes to gaze out over the fell, at once concerned. He did not for a moment doubt his father's counting ability. It was a skill honed over a life-time, using the old norse words of Yan, tan, tethera and so on. Each ten sheep marked on a slate. Billy was never wrong. 'Mebbe its got caught up somewhere.'

'We'll hev to gan tek a leuk.'

'Yes.' It was always worrying to lose a sheep. They knew their own heaf so well they rarely strayed. Apart from the misery and distress caused to the poor animal by injury, or worse, predatory attack, there was the serious loss of profit to be considered. A good ewe was a valuable animal, no doubt about it. 'I'd best finish this pen first,' Andrew said. 'If we'd gone electric we'd have been done by now.'

'Doan't start on that caper, lad. I'm nae in't mood. Hand clipping were guid enough for me fadder, and it's guid enough for me. We've allus managed weel enough, even in't war.'

'Labour was a bit cheaper then, Dad.'

He sniffed. 'We'll talk aboot it to Fadder some time.'

Which meant never. Andrew sighed but his own brown eyes, the mirror of Billy's, warmed with affection. His father was not an unkind man. Many would call him soft in the head. He'd been known to make a wooden splint for many an injured creature's leg that others would have put down without a second thought, or take it up to Ellen Martin, an old friend who lived high on the fell.

And he'd brought up his only son single-handed. But he was gey stubborn. No doubt about that. And set in his ways.

It took a certain kind of farmer to survive on these fells, tough, resolute, taciturn, a touch stubborn perhaps, but despite their shortcomings, Andrew felt he lived with two of the best.

'You'll have to come round to it in the end,' he warned. 'If we don't go forward, we go backwards. Losing this sheep now, proves my point. How have we time to go and look for it when we still have half the flock to clip, little extra help beyond our neighbour, old Tim here, and no guarantee the weather'll hold? We're not a museum piece, you know.'

'Cut thi cackle. Thoo won't addle a living wi' talking. And I ken weel oo's fault it is that a yow has gone missing. It were them dang trippers, leaving gates open iverywhere. They should be banned from farm land. They're a blight on 'umanity.'

54

Andrew sighed. He could not deny that visitors created problems on a farm but they brought a good deal of money to the Lakes.

He glanced up at the sky. It was a hot, dry day, not a sign of mist, perfect for the clipping. Wasting half of it hunting for a sheep that had probably got its foot caught in some rabbit hole was worse than a nuisance. Tomorrow could be wet, then they'd have to wait till the fleeces had dried off before they could start over again. Which would mean a longer delay before the wool could be sold and might well affect the price.

'We'll have to leave it and take the risk it'll wait. The weather won't.'

But Billy wasn't having it. 'We'll tek a leuk roond this e'en, afore it gets too dark.'

They found the ewe that night by the light of his lantern. Half the flesh had been mauled from her body. She'd desperately struggled to escape and been dragged several feet, streaking the ground with her own blood. Well chewed, she had plainly taken some time to die.

'Dogs,' said Andrew.

'Aye.'

Both men stared grimly down at the dead animal. The sight always distressed Andrew, used as he was to the rigours of farming life. Sheep worrying had to be treated as infectious. Once a dog had tasted blood, perhaps from an already dead carcass, the lust for killing could rise and spread. By nature a pack animal, any rogue dog would readily recruit others. It made the killing easier.

'When I catch it,' Billy said, 'Whosoever it belongs to, it'll wish it'd niver been born.'

It had been agreed that the twins would stay on for a while and work at the mill. Meg had welcomed the idea and after some transatlantic phone calls permission had been granted, along with a modest but useful sum to help finance the Larkrigg Hall project. Sarah was anxious to return to the Hall to see if the unexpected guests were still there but Jan insisted on showing the twins round Broombank Woollens. Furiously frustrating but Sarah was forced to smilingly agree.

Jan had been a good friend to Lissa when they'd been girls together, and though in Sarah's opinion she was far less stylish than their mother, and the glasses she wore did her no favours, they could hardly refuse.

Sarah pulled a wry face to Beth behind Jan's back, very clearly saying she hadn't the least interest in knowing what was what. They'd spent most of the last few days speculating about the respective owners of the bare buttocks, Tess considering various past boy friends, which had resulted in yet more hilarity.

It was hard to put the young men from their minds long enough to try and sound interested and grown up over business matters but that was the deal, so they must make the best of it.

'I thought we were only required to drive the deliveries,' Sarah remarked, trying not to let the boredom show in her voice.

Jan frowned. 'It's a small operation so you do whatever needs doing. We all have to. You might be asked to pack or fold the knitted garments, or simply fetch and carry.' She grinned, suddenly and light heartedly. It made her look surprisingly young. 'I promise not to have you knitting all by yourself on your first day.'

They both politely laughed at the joke but Sarah still wore a look of irritated concern as they entered the barn where the business was situated. As they walked in they were at once blasted by a radio playing Dancing Queen, an Abba number, and both girls laughed, putting their hands to their ears.

Beth's eyes scanned the smiling workers who comprised half a dozen women of varying ages working at trestle tables. The long crowded room seemed packed with woollen garments, piled high on the tables, on metal shelves that lined the walls, in boxes, and in heaps on the floor. The room was stiflingly hot and the smell of wool overpowering, but the women seemed quite unperturbed, singing and laughing to each other as their fingers flew. 'They seem happy enough at their work,' Beth smiled.

'Oh yes,' Jan agreed. 'They're a good crew. But don't be fooled by appearances. This may look a small cottage industry but it's a busy one. We're under quite a lot of pressure.' She pushed back her dark brown hair, hooking it behind her ears, which added to her look of harrassment. 'We have difficulty sometimes in keeping up with the orders.' Then she adjusted her spectacles on her small nose as she examined a piece of knitting.

'Has this tension gone loose again Sam?'

'Aye. That piece is no good so it'll have to be tekken back. I've sorted the machine though. See, this'n is all right.'

Jan looked at the knitting under production and nodded. 'Let's hope so. We're running behind hand as it is.'

'I'll see this batch is finished tonight if I've to do it all mesel,' he promised.

Smiling, she turned to the two girls, shouting over the sound of the music and the machines as she began to explain the process, indicating the electric knitting frames operated by two skilled men with wide grins and deft fingers.

'This is Harry and Mike. As they will tell you, getting the tension just right is the difficult part.'

'Do we need to know all this?' Sarah asked.

'I think you'll find it useful.'

'But we won't be knitting, will we?'

Jan stifled a sigh. 'True. But you should try to understand the process. If a customer mentions some problem when you're out on the road, you will at least know what they are talking about.'

'Yes but . . .'

Beth squeezed her sister's arm. 'Hush, and listen, Sarah.'

And with a grim smile, Jan continued, 'The pattern has to be set, as you can see, and the lines of knitting are automatically counted though you can do it manually if you wish. One missed stitch and you have a ladder. Then it has to be taken back on to those cones on that other machine till the mistake is found. Not that these two chaps make many mistakes, they're too experienced.' She grinned at them and they winked back at the two girls, making Beth giggle.

'You'll never know how much,' one quipped with a wicked grin.

Sarah would have flirted right back but he was at least forty. Anyway, if they were so good, let them get on with it. It all sounded far too complicated and tiresome in her opinion.

In a matter of moments a neat rectangle of knitted fabric in the required pattern had been produced and added to the growing pile on the floor. These were then passed on to the cutting and sewing departments. Lastly the welts were knitted on to neck and wrists, seams sealed and the entire garment checked, labelled and wrapped ready for packing and dispatch.

'Will the business survive?' Beth wanted to know, 'in spite of the fraudulent manager I mean.'

'If we work hard enough, and things go right for us, for once.'

Beth wondered why it was they couldn't keep up with the orders but didn't like to ask. In any case, Sarah was sending her very clear messages that she'd had enough and wanted to get away as quickly as possible. In Sarah's view there were far more interesting ways to spend their time. They agreed to be at the office door the very next morning at eight o'clock sharp, and hastily took their leave.

When the twins reached Larkrigg Hall there was disappointingly no sign of the visitors. The pile of logs still stood in the yard. Someone had attempted to scrub down the smoke blackened kitchen, with very little success since it looked blacker than ever but the small dining room, indeed every room, was quite empty. 'Which was,' Sarah remarked, 'a great pity. Just when things were really looking up.'

'I'm not sure we want strangers in our house,' Beth protested. 'Certainly not squatters. Whoever they were, I think I'm glad they've gone.' She marched out into the yard and scowled at the logs as if they were in some way to blame. 'I shall light a fire, boil some water and start the big clean up.' She heard Sarah's groan but refused to respond to it.

And while Beth struggled to light the fire, puffing and blowing the tiny flames into life, Sarah rubbed at a dirty mirror on the wall, pulled a lipstick from the pocket of her jeans and began to apply it. 'Maybe they'll be back. Can't say we haven't seen what they've got to offer, can we?'

Beth's cheeks flared to the colour of the flames she was blowing. A puff of smoke enveloped her and she turned hastily away, eyes streaming, choking for breath.

In spite of their girlish giggling, she'd begun to worry about the unknown young men. Who were they? What were they doing here at Larkrigg? How had they got in? The idea of uninvited intruders invading her house who might return at any moment, troubled her considerably.

When she'd got the fire going to her satisfaction she piled on the logs and set a pan of water to boil on top of them. 'There, we'll soon have some hot water. This is fun, isn't it?'

'Hysterical.'

'Do you think we should get a plumber to look at the old range, or a chimney sweep for the flue?'

'Haven't the faintest idea, darling.'

It took more than two hours to make the kitchen anything like decent. And as she scrubbed and bleached, mopped and scoured, Beth's usually placid disposition was put under extreme stress, for throughout it all Sarah sat on a chair, feet propped up on the corner of the table, reading a magazine.

'Will you lift your feet please? Could you move your chair?' Sarah sighed heavily each time, watching in disbelief as Beth set about rubbing the stove piping with polish and a cloth, bringing out the warm glowing sheen of copper.

'For goodness sake, you'll be washing the coal next.'

Beth's anger bubbled up, hot and unexpected.

'And are you going to sit there and watch me do it?'

'You're the one who wants to play house.'

'You promised to help.'

'Stop being such an old woman, Beth.'

'I will be an old woman by the time I've finished if I have to do up this house all by myself.'

'It was your idea.'

'You agreed.'

'I can't see us having time for housework and work at the mill.'

'Only because you're too lazy.'

Sarah pulled a wry face in mock innocence. 'Oh dear, we are in a paddy, aren't we? Get out of bed the wrong side did we?'

There were times, Beth thought, when she came close to hating her sister. She drew in a slow, steadying breath. 'I'm simply asking for co-operation. Is that so unreasonable?'

'Has it upset you because some naked but undoubtedly delicious male bodies have lain in your precious house?' Sarah pushed back her chair and flounced away from it, ebony hair crackling with a life of its own, her tone cutting. 'You're a sexual cripple, d'you know that? No wonder Jeremy abandoned you. You bored him rigid. He told me so.'

Silence. Thick and painful. 'Jeremy would never say such a thing,' she managed at last.

'I assure you he did.'

Beth's cheeks grew hot with embarrassment. 'I don't believe you.'

'Yes you do. You are far too prissy for your own good. Relax. Enjoy life, as I do.' Sarah draped herself decorously back in the chair, then caught sight of her sister's face, drained of all colour. At once she was filled with contrition and ran to fling her arms about Beth.

'Oh, take no notice of me. I'm in a foul mood. I'm sorry. I really didn't mean it.'

'I know you didn't. Why are we quarrelling, just because of some stupid squatters? We'll probably never set eyes on them again. I, for one, sincerely hope so.'

A grim laugh from the shadows by the door brought both girls whirling. 'Because being the landed gentry, you object to sharing with the peasants?'

Beth jumped in alarm then grimly faced the stranger, rather like a small tortoiseshell kitten, hair bristling with fear but ready to fight tooth and claw to protect her own territory.

'We're not gentry of any sort, as a matter of fact,' she said. 'Just as this is more of a farm than a grand house. But we do object, very strongly, to having our home invaded without our permission.' She felt Sarah's tug at her sleeve but resolutely ignoring her hisses to be silent, ploughed on. 'I would very much like to know how you got in.'

The man's eyes slid across to Sarah, roving over her body with audacious boldness. It was as if he had stripped it bare and personally fondled the taut peaks of her breasts, slid his hands into the warmth of her panties. His lips curled into a knowing grin as he watched her aristocratic brow lift with interested disdain. 'Pantry window, as a matter of fact. Loose catch.'

'And all those bloody weeks begging for a key,' Sarah drily remarked, giving a spurt of laughter.

'I shall see that it's mended forthwith,' Beth steadfastly informed the stranger, to let him know what was what. 'And if you were planning on returning, I'm sorry to disappoint you but this house is occupied and we'd much rather you left. Right now.' The open hunger of his gaze upon Sarah was making her feel quite angry. Beth held open the back door, chin tilted in brave defiance.

The man didn't move. He simply leaned against the door frame and smiled insolently at her. 'Would you indeed?'

'I'm sure you can find another squat somewhere.' If that is the best you can hope for, her tone implied.

'And do you intend to see me off the premises with your own fair hands? Or will you set your friend on me instead?' His eyes, almost black, ran over her with that same all encompassing glance, entirely sensual and provocative, lips curled in suggestive seduction. Beth stifled a shiver while Sarah merely laughed.

He held a string in one hand, the end of which was attached to a decrepit looking black and white dog. The very same who had barked at them through the window. The dog's presence made Beth hold on to her patience a while longer.

The young man's face had a craggy, lean and hungry look to it, greatly in need of a shave. He wore a printed shirt, dirty waistcoat and tight sailcloth trousers that flared out at the hem over what might have been wooden clogs. A red bandanna circled his forehead and his dark, straggly hair looked in dire need of a good wash. But there was a vital, sexual energy about him that she could tell Sarah found utterly compelling. His potent attraction was a blatant declaration of his success with women which made Beth feel uneasy. She brought her chin up higher, refusing to be bullied, not in her own house.

'Take no notice of my little sister,' Sarah said, coming forward, a brilliant smile curving her lips, one hand outstretched. 'Works too hard. Bit touchy at the moment.'

He ignored the hand, keeping his thumbs hooked into his waistband. 'Should never work too hard. Bad for you.'

'I agree.'

A long moment passed while the two openly sized each other up and Beth's discomfort grew. Then a second young man appeared and she felt her stomach turn right over. For the first time in her life Beth knew what it was to experience desire. It raged through her like a forest fire, leaving her limp and exhausted.

He was perfectly beautiful, with a superb body. Like a Michelangelo sculpture. Patrician nose, chiselled features, olive skin and the most heavenly blue eyes. Like cornflowers in a golden meadow, she thought poetically. Every line of his body was perfect from the tips of his black hair curling upon his collar, glossy as a raven's wing as it shone in a shaft of sunlight, right down to the gleaming leather of his polished boots. He carried about him a serenity and confidence of purpose that was quite mesmeric yet at the same time managed to appear vulnerable and innocent. A writer or artist perhaps, she mused. A sulky angel. Beth gazed upon him entranced, astonished and helplessly ashamed at the emotions which soared through her.

Sarah was the first to acknowledge his presence. She moved across to him, smiling in that special way she had. Beth saw the heavenly blue eyes quicken with predatory interest and she felt suddenly, desperately sick.

The one with the beard introduced himself as John Reynolds. 'Though most folk call me Jonty,' he told them.

He sauntered over to the carver chair, stared defiantly at Beth then lounged in it, propping his feet on the corner of the rusty range as Sarah had previously done. Sarah herself seemed content to watch him with smiling curiosity, like a cat.

'You seem to have made yourself at home,' Beth remarked, rather acidly.

'So? We live in your house, eat in your kitchen, swim in your lake. That a problem?'

She wanted to say that it was very much a problem but her tongue seemed somehow stuck to the roof of her mouth as every sense prickled with awareness of the beautiful young man by the door. Sarah intervened. 'Of course it isn't. Where are you heading?'

'Wherever we fancy. This here is Pietro, see? He don't talk much. Say hello to the pretty ladies.'

All eyes turned to the silent figure who hovered by the door. Except for Beth's. She simply couldn't bear to look at him for fear of what he might read in her eyes. The young man inclined his head in a deep bow but said nothing.

'Pietro? That's Italian, isn't it?' Sarah asked, moving back to him.

The young man nodded again.

'Where did you two meet?'

'On Paddington station,' Jonty replied for him. 'Six months ago. We've been hitching ever since.'

'We see the world,' Pietro added, breaking his silence at last as his whole body seemed suspended in motion, eyes riveted upon Sarah's

ace, then moving uncertainly over to Jonty, as if asking what he
would do now. Sarah flickered one humorous eyebrow.

'Sounds good.'

'It ees good.'

'And now you're here?'

'*Si.*'

'Why the Lakes?'

'I have the fancy to see the English Lake District. I hear it ees very
beautiful. *Magnifico.*'

'Indeed it is. And you must stay as long as you like. Don't you
agree, Beth?'

As Beth failed to answer, an awkward silence fell. After a moment
she gathered up the used rags and headed for the door, heart beating
like a mad thing. With healing anger, she told herself unconvincingly,
and made her shoes ring out purposefully as she strode across the
tiled floor. Outside, she lifted the lid of the dustbin and flung the
rags inside, slamming it down again with a ringing clang. She had a
great longing to throw her sister in with them. Sarah's recklessness
was beyond belief. Inviting two perfect strangers, no, far-from-perfect
strangers to stay as long as they liked. What was she thinking of? Was
she mad? No, sex mad, Beth thought, remembering with a childish
display of temper, the exchange of glances between the two.

Well she, for one, meant to ignore them. She would refuse to speak
or have anything to do with either of them. Then they would quickly
tire of this silly game they were playing, and leave. Just thinking of
the expression in Jonty Reynolds dark eyes made her blood run cold.
And as for the beautiful Pietro, he was as besotted with her sister as
was everyone who had ever set eyes on her. Damn them all.

And I'm jealous, she thought, dismayed to find tears running down
her cheeks.

63

6

Beth's agony was far from over. The next afternoon when they'd done their stint packing woollens at the mill, Sarah decided they should make the best of the good weather and have a picnic.

She dispatched Beth to make sandwiches, collect rugs and take them up to the tarn in the yellow mini. Tessa was only too willing to help since she could then meet the naked bodies in the flesh, as it were.

To all outward appearances it was a most happy picnic. James crawled about the grass, gurgling with delight in between crunching buttercups. The sun sparkled on the tarn, a blue sky streaked with feather duster clouds, a flock of pied wagtails flitting from rock to rock with lively exuberance.

Sarah sat with Jonty on a blanket, feeding him slices of apple. It made Beth shudder to see how his eyes appraised her sister with candid greed, then open his mouth for more fruit, his tongue flicking out to caress Sarah's fingertips as he took the morsel from her. Yet she couldn't tear her eyes from noting every sensual gesture.

She was all too aware that she wasn't the only one fascinated by this erotic ritual. Pietro, his head close to Tessa's, giggling like children as they watched an army of ants collect crumbs and stagger back with their prize to a nest beneath a large stone, would turn his head from time to time, and gaze longingly in the direction of the other two. That look somehow pierced Beth to the heart, making her feel more insignificant than ever. And to her utter shame, the jealousy burned all the fiercer.

She felt quite unable to speak to anyone, enduring the picnic with what good grace she could muster, while her mind busily churned over the problem.

How could Sarah cheapen herself in such a way?

They knew nothing about these squatters, nothing at all. Why had they come? How long did they intend to stay? And what would make them leave? No solution presented itself and Beth fell into a deep and uncharacteristic sulk.

What a terrible person I'm becoming, she thought, and sighing, she kicked at a stone, watching glumly as it rolled down the bank to splash into the tarn.

And how, Beth wondered, could she start work on the house, let alone move in, with squatters living here? She did not relish the idea one bit.

'Let's swim,' Sarah shouted, and in seconds had stripped off her jeans to reveal a blue bikini which left little to the imagination. She ran down to the tarn and recklessly plunged in, squealing when the cold water hit her bare stomach. 'Come on, you softies,' she yelled, gasping for breath and laughing at the same time. 'If I can do it, you can.'

'We haven't got a dinky little swimsuit,' Jonty told her, mouth twisting into a wry smile.

Sarah gurgled with delight. 'What the hell? We've already seen most of what you've got.' And laughed all the more at their startled expressions.

The confession was quickly made and Beth was forced to close her eyes as Jonty suddenly stood up, pulled off his T-shirt and dropped his trousers. She could feel her cheeks burning and didn't dare look until she heard the splash of water. Then her gaze slid to Pietro. Would he do the same? And felt a sad sense of despair at the way his beautiful eyes seemed to darken as he watched her sister and Jonty splash about and spray each other with water.

A moment later he stripped down to a pair of white shorts and ran into the tarn to join them. Something inside of Beth lurched with pain.

Tessa picked up James and followed at a more leisurely pace, calling laughingly back to her. 'Are you coming?'

Beth shook her head.

'It's hot. Do you good.'

66

'I'm fine.'

Tessa smiled. 'You could always keep your eyes closed.'

'No, thanks.'

'Suit yourself.' She touched the baby's nose gently with her own. 'Come on, cherub. We'll have a wee plodge in the shallows, shall we?'

Beth struggled to keep her interest on the baby who gurgled with delight as the water lapped over his chubby toes. But her eyes kept slipping away, fastening with deep and shaming misery upon the two young men as they splashed and chased Sarah, making her squeal and scream, revelling as she always did in an excess of male attention.

Lying on her back in the sun, desperately struggling to close her ears to the merriment and her mind to the implications, Beth started when she found Pietro had come out of the water to join her. He shook himself like a dog, flicked back the long black locks, and flung himself down beside her.

'You no like to swim?'

'Not today, thanks. But don't let me stop you. I'm quite happy here.' Her voice was admirably cool but his presence beside her made her feel oddly light headed.

'Those two are swimming,' he said, glaring fiercely out across the water where Sarah and Jonty were racing each other in an unprepossessing crawl. 'I sit here with you for a while. *Si*? You don't mind?'

He couldn't bear to see them together, she thought, any more than she could bear to watch Pietro with her sister. She could almost feel his gaze burning up the distance between them, wishing Jonty elsewhere almost as badly as she did, if for a different reason. 'No, of course not. I don't mind at all,' she assured him with forced brightness. The urge to do something completely crazy like lean against his broad shoulder, or reach up and kiss his pale pink lips, was almost overpowering. She shifted a few inches away and closed her eyes in quiet despair. Did he think that by sitting with her he made everything right. As if she didn't realise that really he only longed to be back in the water with Sarah. Then he turned his blue gaze upon her and smilingly made her agony worse.

'Your sister, she is the beauty, yes?'

'Yes,' Beth sighed, smiling quietly. 'She has always been that.'

'It troubles you?'

'Not really,' she admitted. 'It's good to see her happy.' And she did feel that, deep down, really she did. Sarah had not been herself lately and was in sore need of a holiday. They may not be particularly close but she had agreed to give up the chance of Venice for her sake. Shame washed through Beth at the thought, cleansing away the hot jealousy and leaving her feeling drained and guilty. 'She is very supportive. I really don't know how I would manage without her.'

'And you are happy?'

'Yes, I'm fine.' And she was, truly she was. If only sometimes she could get out from under her sister's shadow, or borrow some of her effervescent charm.

'You have the boyfriend, back home in America?'

Panic hit her. She really didn't want to talk about it. Jeremy was finished, over and done with. 'No, no. I'm too busy for men right now.'

'But I think you are the sweet and charming one.'

Beth looked up at him, startled. 'You do?'

He gave a soft chuckle, kissed the tip of his middle finger then placed it on her slightly parted lips. 'I do,' he whispered, and his breath on her face sent fresh quivers of longing right down her spine.

'Oh,' was all she could manage. For what seemed a lifetime she gazed into his eyes and saw surprise register in their blueness. Did he feel as she did? Would he kiss her? He turned abruptly from her.

'Come. I teach you to dive, *si*?'

'Oh, I'm not sure, Pietro. Really I . . .'

'Do not fear. I will hold you safe.'

And before she knew what was happening, she had slipped out of her frock, revealing a modest one piece bathing costume and he was taking her hand and running her down into the water. It was the most glorious moment of her life.

The next morning Sarah refused to rise in time to help with the packing and Beth went alone to the mill.

'Where is she?' Jan asked, her voice sharp. 'She hardly has to travel a million miles to work. Can't she manage to be here on time?'

'Sarah isn't too well this morning. Her health hasn't been good for some time.'

'I see,' in a voice which was neither convinced nor sympathetic.

'And she didn't sleep well last night.' Beth hadn't even heard her come in, having long since fallen asleep herself. 'It's OK, I'll do her share.' And she did, working as fast as she could. Then she was given a map and sent off in the van to learn the delivery route, which she found thoroughly enjoyable. Nothing could be better than driving through this glorious, intensely green countryside, the birds carolling so joyously, how could she fail to be cheered?

The morning passed by in a pleasant whirl and when she returned to Broombank, Sarah was taking a leisurely bath, her long hair casually knotted on top of her head, soaping her beautiful body as though there was all the time in the world.

'Wouldn't it be more sensible to take your bath after we've finished the day's work?'

'Jan doesn't need us this afternoon.'

'Then we could start stripping the walls at Larkrigg.'

Sarah screwed up her nose and sank deeper into the hot bubbles. 'You're becoming a bore, sweet sister.'

Beth swallowed a burst of impatience. 'How long are we going to let them stay?'

'Do we have to decide now? Let's take things as they come.'

'But . . .'

'Not now, Beth.'

In the days following, the two uninvited guests made no move to leave and Sarah was clearly revelling in their attentions. She took them food, begged some old blankets off Sally Ann, flirted outrageously with them both and spent hours wandering off alone with Jonty.

Beth didn't care to imagine what her twin got up to on those walks, though it worried her enormously. Sarah was so reckless. Often the whole group of them would go, Tessa and Pietro too, but Beth always refused, excusing herself on the grounds that she had work to do on the house. But then, perversely, she would resent it when they took her at her word and left her. All she could do then was try not to think about him, or her sister.

At other times Beth would do her best to join in, and not be a spoilsport. Sarah would plan barbecues or pasta parties and beg to borrow Beth's best shoes or favourite perfume and they'd try each other's clothes on and giggle together as true sisters should. But she couldn't help worrying, and again ventured to express her concern.

'Do be careful you don't start getting too keen on Jonty Reynolds.'

'What did you say?'

'I said . . .'

'I doubt it's any of your business.'

'They'll be off on their travels soon. He's only using you, Sarah. Have sense. Behave yourself.'

'How should I behave? All standoffish like you, I suppose? No way. It's a free country. I can do what I like. We're like chalk and cheese, or Callaghan's Lib–Lab pact. Who cares? Life's fun, enjoy it.' She smiled challengingly at her twin. 'I'm a big girl now, you know.'

'This isn't politics, this is real life. What happens when it collapses, as this Lib–Lab pact will eventually? What then? You haven't . . . ?'

'Haven't what?'

'You know.'

'Had sex you mean?' The chin came up and the blue eyes grew hard as sapphires. 'What if I said yes?'

'Then I'd say you were an even greater fool than I imagined.'

'*Damn* you. It really isn't any of your business, Miss Butter-Wouldn't-Melt. Be honest, you'd give your soul for the gorgeous Pietro to ravish you.'

Beth flushed bright red. 'Don't talk such utter rubbish,' and flounced off to expend her frustrated energy scrubbing sinks, but Sarah followed her, chortling with delight.

'You spend enough time talking to him. Don't deny it.'

'He likes to practise his English. Besides, he's different from Jonty.'

'How different?'

'He's kind and thoughtful, doesn't take advantage of people.'

'You're jealous.'

Beth savagely attacked the worn stonework of the sink with her scrubbing brush. 'Don't be silly. It's a simple friendship, that's all.' In truth, friendship was too strong a word. Beth couldn't quite make him out. He seemed oddly restrained, almost secretive at times, perhaps rather shy like herself, which made conversation strained and difficult.

At other times he would readily offer to help her clean windows, or scrape paper off the walls, telling her how wonderfully clever she was to decorate a big house by herself. Though he never did very much himself, at least he offered. No one else ever thought to, so Beth appreciated his kindness.

He'd told her very little about himself, except to say he'd tried several jobs but hadn't yet found the right one. And his eyes still constantly strayed to Sarah and Jonty, thus increasing her own jealousy to fever pitch. Her feelings for Jeremy had been nothing compared to this, which had hit her like a tornado, quite out of the blue.

'Hasn't he even tried to kiss you?' Sarah teased.

Beth flinched, hating the implication that no man would want to kiss her. 'I've no wish for him to do so.'

'You're desperate for him, deep down.'

That was the worst thing about having a twin, Beth decided, even one you didn't get on with. She could read your mind, 'Oh, shut up,' she said. And much to Beth's annoyance, Sarah burst out laughing.

Jonty Reynolds, in Sarah's view, was the most exciting man she'd met in a long while. Not as good looking as Frank admittedly, but with a potent undercurrent of danger which excited her. And she rather liked his cragginess, his arrogant manner, and his pulsing energy. She couldn't keep her hands off him. Nor, satisfyingly enough, could he his from her.

They took every opportunity to slip away into Brockbarrow Wood. Sarah would have liked to take him upstairs into the big four poster bed, had it not still been so filthy, and Beth hanging around all the time. Escaping her sister's eagle eye was the hardest part of it. She constantly had to think up some excuse to explain where she had been and why. Not that they were ever gone long, for they were both so highly charged it took no time at all.

The excuse today was the need to exercise the dog. But in no time they'd lost him, as usual, and since the weather looked uncertain, they went to the small bothy that stood by the tarn.

Once inside it took no more than moments for him to thrust her against the wall and rid her of her restricting clothes. But then if he wasn't fast enough she did it for him and, frantic with desire, pulled him greedily inside her. His grip upon her was punishing, pounding into her so hard her head banged on the rough stone wall, but she loved it all the more for that. Foreplay, kisses, soft words didn't interest Sarah. Clasping his head to her breast she threw back her head while he suckled her, moaning with sensuous agony. He was a man with energy and skill and Sarah liked that.

But then she wasn't seventeen any more. And she was on the pill.

It was on the eighth day that Pietro made his revelation. They were again by the tarn, their favourite place these lazy summer days.

'Do you like travelling?' Beth asked, trying to make conversation.

'No, not at all.' His reply surprised her.

'Then why do you do it?'

He shrugged. 'Perhaps I did like it, at first. Now it is very tiring. I am glad for a rest.'

'Glad *of* a rest.'

He looked down at her. 'My English is good, yes?'

'Very good.' She rolled over on to her stomach and propping her chin in her hand gazed thoughtfully up at him. He seemed more relaxed somehow, today. 'Is that why you came to England, to improve your English?'

'It is one reason. This land, it is very beautiful, is it not?'

Beth agreed and smiled at him, and something about his answering smile startled her, melting away all her misgivings and petty jealousies, filling her with uncertainties. The sick feeling was back in her stomach and with it the smallest degree of hope. 'Are you really Italian?'

'Yes, and no. Part of me feels English. Now that I am here, there will be no more travelling.'

Beth blinked. 'You can't stay, not in our house. Not for long anyway,' she added, trying to be fair.

Pietro's lower lip jutted. 'It is my right.'

'Your what?'

'My right. My grandfather, he tella me about all of this. He was born here, so I have the English blood as well as the Italian. Is good, *si*?'

Beth sat up very straight. 'Born here? In Larkrigg Hall? He couldn't have been. It belonged to my great grandmother and her family before that.'

'Not here in thees house,' Pietro conceded, 'Close by.'

Beth relaxed again with a small smile. 'So that was why you came to Lakeland? I see. You too are visiting your roots. How lovely. Seems to be fashionable. Everyone's in the library these days searching out their family tree.' She lay back on the cropped grass and closed her eyes again, the sun warming the lids, aware of every movement of his body close beside her. She'd probably been worrying unduly. Sarah would flirt for a while. Then she'd quickly tire of the game as she usually did. Willing captives soon bored her. The boys would visit one or two places, search out some ancient ancestry and then leave, like all the other tourists. But did she want Pietro to leave? Or did she want him to stay and be more to her than a friend?

No, she really mustn't think of him in that way. And at least she could stay for ever, if she so wished. Beth felt a warm glow kindle deep inside.

'My father was robbed of his inheritance,' Pietro was saying. 'It was stolen from him.'

'Oh dear.' Her lids felt far too heavy to open so she didn't bother to try. 'How very sad.'

'His papa let himself be beguiled by an ambitious woman. And so now it is lost to my family for ever.'

'I'm so sorry.'

'You know of it, I think. It is called Broombank.'

Her whole body jerked and her eyelids flew open. 'What did you say? Did you say Broombank? *Our* Broombank?'

He was nodding and smiling at her, as if it were a great joke. 'Funny, huh? Thees house of your grandmama's, it should be mine, you understand? So why should you not let me stay in your house for a while? It is only fair, yes?'

*　　*　　*

'Why didn't you tell us right away?'

Sarah had been brought over, and even she looked stunned by this revelation. Tessa sat quietly playing with James, not taking part in the conversation, considering it none of her business but staying close by in case the girls should be in need of moral support. Jonty, still sitting on the blanket by the edge of the tarn, brought out a mouth organ and started to play, 'When I Need You'.

'Not now,' Sarah snapped. 'I want to understand what's going on here.'

He ignored her and continued to play. The beautiful sounds echoed over the water and down to the valley below. Somewhere above a curlew cried, as if in response to the haunting melody. After a while Pietro lifted his eyes to his friend and the notes died away.

'There is no mystery,' he said. 'I am telling you now, am I not? I feel shy to speak of it. It take me time to strike up – no, pluck up the courage. I wish to stay in your house for a leetle while. That is all.'

There was a small silence. 'It is not that I wish to take it from you, you understand?'

'Then why have you come?'

'To fulfill a dream. I wish to see what I have lost. Is wrong?'

Beth found it hard to condemn him. She knew about dreams.

'Why do you say Broombank should be yours?'

'My grandfather, Jack Lawson, was born at Broombank. It should, by rights, have been his and in time, mine.'

'Well, not necessarily . . .'

'Instead, his papa, Lanky Lawson, he leave it to your grandmama, Meg. He expected her to marry Jack but in the end they did not marry. Jack married my grandmother instead. Do you see?'

Sarah said, 'You've lost me, brother. Oh, my God. Yes, I do see.' She turned to stare at Beth.

'What? What is it?'

She turned back to Pietro. 'No wonder you've kept your family background and your surname very quiet. You're Pietro Lawson?'

'I am.'

'Then if Jack Lawson was your grandfather, you must be some sort of distant cousin. Half anyway, on his side of the family, because we know that our mother was the child of his relationship with Kath, so he must be our grandfather too. How terribly complicated.'

They all stared at each other for a long moment and then Sarah burst out laughing. 'Well, would you believe it?'

It all seemed somehow to be a great relief. One moment they'd been surrounded by strangers, now one of them had turned out to be very nearly family.

Meg was mending a thorn hedge when the twins brought Pietro to meet her. She greeted them with a smile, one hand raised to shade her eyes against the sun.

'Mrs Margaret O'Cleary?'

No one had called Meg by her full name since the day she'd married her darling Tam. She shifted her position to get a better view, blinking at the familiar face, wondering where she had seen the man before.

'I am so pleased to meet you at last,' he said, stretching out one fine boned hand. His voice held the trace of an accent Meg couldn't quite place.

She rubbed her grubby palm on her overalls, smiling as she took his hand, looking straight into his blue eyes. Then it came to her, all in a rush, and she felt an odd little chill run down her spine. 'The hotel. You were in the dining room of the Cock and Feathers when Tam and I were having lunch once.'

His eyes widened. 'You have the good memory.'

'It was the day the twins arrived. We were sorting out a business problem.'

'*Si.*'

'It's a small world.'

'Smaller than you think.'

'Indeed?'

'You do not know who I am? Your good memory not stretch so far back?'

Meg frowned, struggling to catch a thought at the edge of her consciousness.

'My name is Pietro Lawson.'

A small silence, followed by a breathless whisper. 'Lawson?'

'My grandfather tell me you would remember him. I'm sorry you do not seem to. Perhaps because he was not important to you.'

Meg inwardly flinched but let the remark go. This young man was arrogant, as the young often were. Clearly imagined he had all the answers. And then his words fell into place, like a jigsaw forming a familiar picture she'd much rather not see, and the years slid away. Jack on Kidsty Pike promising to love her for ever. No, he hadn't quite done that. Asked her to wait for him. Given her a ring, certainly. And her best friend his baby. 'Ah yes,' she said, becoming aware of the coolness in the breeze. 'I remember Jack very well. Very well indeed. So you are his grandson? Well, well.' Then she turned her back on him, making him wait while she weaved a pliant strip of hazel in to the hedge she was layering and set the billhook safely away. It gave her time to collect herself, and to wonder why he had come. 'He went to Italy after the war, if I remember correctly.'

'That is so.'

Meg looked fully into his smiling face. 'And you have come to find your roots?'

'It was time, I thought.' He laughed and looked confidently about him, at the hills and the lime-washed walls of Broombank farm, at the twins, Sarah close by, Beth sitting hunched on a log. 'It seems to be fashionable these days.'

'Indeed.' A small, strained silence. 'Did your grandfather talk much about the Lake District?'

The smile widened as he shrugged his fine shoulders. 'Of course. He talk about it all the time. He say it is his home. He also say you took over his house, this Broombank. *Si?* That is so?'

Meg ignored the question, wishing suddenly that Tam hadn't chosen this particular morning to drive into Kendal for fresh supplies. Pulling off her hedging mitts, she massaged her aching hands. 'I dare say you've heard the story many times so I won't bore you by repeating it.' She managed a bright smile. 'Let me see now, you must be some sort of distant half cousin to the twins.'

His eyes were on the house. 'Broombank looks a fine and prosperous farm.'

Meg turned, her gaze upon its white walls mellow in the sun, and felt her heart swell with pride. 'It has always been a warm family home, though not so prosperous when I first took it over. Rather neglected, in fact.'

'And you were ambitious to be the sheep farmer, yes?'

Meg, feeling oddly reluctant, admitted that was the case. A faint stirring of disquiet made her wonder if he meant anything particular by this interest. 'It was all entirely legal,' she said, and could have kicked herself for sounding almost defensive.

'I do not doubt it. You must have been pleased to acquire such a fine farm.'

'It wasn't so fine then. Jack was never interested in farming. Too much of the wanderlust in him.' She laughed. 'And there was a war on.'

'And you were to be married, is that not so?' Meg had no wish to resurrect the past, or to pick a quarrel with Jack's grandson, though he seemed to be twisting the facts somewhat. It was too late now to explain how things had worked out the way they had, all those years ago. For all his excessive courtesy, a part of her did not like this young man, who clearly had a very high opinion of himself. Perhaps it was in the stillness of his face, the glint in his eyes that reminded her too much of Jack. And such a deep blue, so very like Sarah's own that it made her shiver with foreboding.

What was he doing here at Larkrigg Hall? Should she say something? What could she say? So far as she knew he meant them no harm. And they would only tell her they had their own lives to lead, that it was none of her business.

'Life moves on,' she said.

A small silence, then a flicker of eyebrows and a half shrug of the shoulders. 'Of course. And a new family created. How can I object to that? You let him down so he left.'

Meg felt herself flush as if she were again that young girl riddled with guilt. 'You have it all wrong,' she said, lifting her chin.

'Pietro didn't mean it as it sounded, Gran.'

She patted Sarah's hand and said nothing more, yet deep in her heart knew that he had meant every word. But if Pietro Lawson wanted a fight, then he'd come to the right place. She'd never backed away from one yet.

Sarah was saying, 'Why don't we all go indoors and have tea? It's turning chilly. And Pietro can see Broombank properly at last. You don't mind, Meg, do you?'

'No, of course not. I don't mind at all.' Oh, but she did. She minded very much indeed.

* * *

There was no question now of sending them away. Even Beth was able to forget her ambivalent feelings and be content to let them stay. How could she refuse such a small request when Pietro had every right to visit his roots, which were, after all, the same as their own. Their relationship might be tenuous but real enough. And he seemed to have so little and they had so much. He told them how he was on a student's visa, studying and touring Europe, in particular the old home of his family here in Lakeland. It all sounded perfectly reasonable. And secretly she was pleased it had all turned out so happily. At least this meant she could stop worrying and enjoy the pleasure of his company a little longer.

7

The days of summer passed pleasantly enough, apart from Jan's constant urging for them to give more time to the mill. Beth did her best but Sarah always complied with ill grace, constantly complaining of ill health or sleepless nights, managing to avoid work whenever she could.

'You go, darling. I have a headache.'

Or she would stroll in hours late, declaring she hadn't slept a wink, with not a word of apology.

'You do realise the importance of all this?' Jan would say and Sarah would smile radiantly at her and promise faithfully to be more diligent in future.

'If you're fit enough to swim in that tarn, you're fit enough to work,' Jan retorted and was rewarded with a brilliant smile by way of response.

Letters would come from America exhorting the twins to be 'useful' and for a while Sarah would arrive on time and work hard and all would be well.

But if she did put in a full day's work she would go at once to bed on her return to the house. 'Bring me some coffee, Beth darling. I'm too exhausted to help with the meal. Do you mind?'

As a consequence there were times when Beth felt thoroughly drained. What with working hard at the mill, looking after Sarah, and doing up Larkrigg. An activity which was proving far more exhausting than even she had anticipated.

* * *

One afternoon in late August when the heat haze shimmered on the stubbled fields, Andrew Barton called at Broombank, ostensibly to ask if Tessa had any odd jobs she needed doing.

'We're on our way up to Larkrigg, as a matter of fact,' Tessa told him. 'You could always put in an offer there. The twins are doing it up and would be glad of any help they can get.'

'Right.' He looked almost pleased to be asked and Beth thought it must be because he had a soft spot for Tess. Which would more realistically explain the reason for his call. He certainly seemed happy enough to play with James, tossing him up in the air and making the baby squeal with delight. He walked up to Larkrigg with them and the girls chattered on, telling him about their two visitors.

'What do you know about them?' he asked, frowning slightly.

'Quite a lot,' Sarah said, with a wry smile.

'And one of them is distantly related, would you believe?' Beth found herself explaining, without quite knowing why.

'Why, who is he?'

So Andrew had to be told the whole story, and his cautious farmer's nature forced him to issue a warning. 'I'd take care, if I were you. Happen he's here for a reason.'

'Of course he is, to discover his roots and where his grandfather was born. Rather as we are,' Sarah said.

'Aye, but why? Bit suspicious, I call it.'

'Oh, Andrew, don't be such an old misery-boots,' and she fluttered her eyelashes at him, making him flush with bashful embarrassment.

The explanations and arguments continued until they were met by the sight of Jonty and Pietro, chopping more logs in the yard.

'Getting ready for winter,' Pietro said, grinning at Beth.

Andrew intercepted the glance and prickled with angry disappointment. 'Winter?'

Blue eyes shifted from Beth to Andrew and perceptibly cooled. 'You have the objection to that?'

'No, no. Naught to do wi' me, I reckon.'

'Indeed not.'

Beth hastily stepped in and introduced the young men properly to each other. Nods all round but no one offered to shake hands. A slight awkwardness developed which she didn't fully understand.

'You've coom to stop for a lang while then?' Andrew mildly

enquired, in his slow, quiet voice, the double vowels rolling broader, the consonants more clipped than ever. And watching him she couldn't help but notice that beside the sleek Pietro, he looked sadly like a poor peasant talking to a god.

'We like it here. And we're in no hurry to leave, OK?'

'Move about a lot, do you?'

'When we feel inclined,' Jonty said, grinning. 'Free spirits, that's us.'

Andrew's frown had deepened to a scowl and Beth tried to soothe tempers by scurrying round with cans of beer. This gave a few moment's respite while everyone found a log or dry-stone wall to perch on, can rings were pulled, drafts of cooling ale supped. Then Andrew pointed to the brown and white dog at Pietro's feet. 'That your cur?'

'He's not a cur.'

'He's considered so in these parts. What breed does he reckon to be then? Bit of terrier in him, is there?'

Jonty's angular face grew dark as thunder. 'He doesn't reckon to be anything. This is Dart. He's a mongrel. I found him in London.'

The animal glanced up at the sound of his name and Jonty's hand reached down to pat it.

'Best keep an eye on him then. We don't like stray dogs round here.'

'He is not a stray. He's mine. A city dog, right? You farmers don't have a monopoly on caring, or owning bloody dogs.'

The two young men glared at each other for a long, chilling moment, looking very much as if they'd like to tear each other apart. Over a scruffy dog? Beth thought, amazed.

Then Tessa jumped up, jiggling James up into the air on a squeal of delight. 'Can I show Andrew round?' Something had to be done, she decided, about this unexpected crackle of tension. A guided tour was as good a way as any. She felt rather sorry for Andrew, out of his depth with these two. But her offer only seemed to make matters worse, making her wish she'd kept in the background as usual, for Sarah at once bridled.

'You do like to make yourself at home in other people's property, don't you? First Broombank, now Larkrigg. You'll be wanting a free trip to the States next.'

'*Sarah*, that's not fair. Tessa is a good friend and of course she can show Andrew round. Enough of this, everyone. We should all be friends not squabbling like infants.'

So Tessa showed Andrew over the house, though he expressed only polite interest. Sarah and Jonty went off for another of their long walks, and Beth started to stack logs.

The rain was coming down in horizontal sheets, beating against the windows. The sunny days of summer seemed an almost forgotten memory as September came in blustery and wet. Out on the fells the red deer were being stalked and culled as weak and surplus to stocks. Too many would damage their habitation, jeopardise them all. Grey clouds cloaked the hills and rain dripped from the trees, filling the hanging valleys, seeping into the ground, emerging to fill the becks and erupt over Whinstone Force and gush through the dale below in a torrent.

But inside Larkrigg Hall all was cosy and warm as a bright fire burned in the small drawing room grate. This was still the most comfortable room in the house, the only one with a chimney not blocked by bird's nests. Beth spent the day sanding orange paint off some old cupboards and felt exhausted. She would have liked to take a shower but there was still no hot water at Larkrigg.

'I'm going for a bath.'

'You're mad,' Sarah said. A remark which proved justified as Beth stood in the old cracked bath tub and scrubbed herself all over with a loofah and breath stopping cold water. Her skin was tingling by the time she'd finished.

She emerged from the bathroom surprisingly warm and glowing, swathed in a towel, and bumped into Jonty hovering on the landing. His presence outside the bathroom door so startled her, she couldn't think what to say.

Completely unperturbed, he grinned at her and strolled off, whistling.

Her skin crawled. Had he been peeping at her through the keyhole? She glared at it, set low in the old door and made a mental note to block it up with soap next time. His presence reminded her that they were not alone to enjoy their home in peace.

Hurrying to a bedroom she quickly pulled on her patchwork cotton skirt and T-shirt, bundled her dusty overalls into a carrier bag and headed for the small drawing room. Home, cocoa, and bed still sounded good.

But Sarah wasn't ready to leave. It was always the same, dark by the time they left. Beth didn't object because it felt lovely and grown up to sit about eating pasta, and drinking red wine. Besides, there was a quiet peace walking on the fells in the late evening, listening for the hoot of an owl, the bark of a fox. Tonight though, because of the weather, they'd been tempted to leave it even later than usual. Hence the necessity for the cold bath, to make her at least feel human but the momentary glow had gone and Beth huddled by the fire to warm herself, tucking her skirt close about her knees, staring into the hot coals.

'What about the washing up?' Tessa murmured, without much enthusiasm.

The hearth was still scattered with dirty plates from supper. The thought of boiling all the water that would be needed to wash them up was more than she could face right now. 'They can wait till morning.'

'Good idea.' Tessa lay curled on the rug playing patience, while James slept peacefully beside her, thumb in mouth, exhausted after investigating the entire top floor of the house on his bottom.

Andrew had left long since. He called on them occasionally but never seemed comfortable in their presence. Tessa said he was so edgy because he had little in common with the other boys and it hurt his pride when they teased him. Privately, Beth thought him a bit too touchy and proud, and wasn't sorry when he found some reason to leave early.

She glanced across at Pietro. He was completely absorbed sketching a pencil drawing of the baby and had not spoken for half an hour, at least. Not that Beth minded. She could have sat and watched him for hours, admiration at his care and interest in the infant swelling hugely within her.

Her feelings for him were confusing for he wasn't proving an easy man to get to know. One moment all charm and easy smiles, the next crisp and distant, cool as marble or cruelly indifferent. But then all artists were sensitive and complicated. She'd been right about that in him from the start, which pleased her. His beautiful features were beginning to stray into her dreams at night, relaying images which excited and alarmed her all at the same time. All things considered, despite the rain, Andrew's moody pride and Pietro's unpredictable moods, she was enjoying life enormously, and felt perfectly content.

The only discordant note was Jonty Reynold's sprawled body which filled the length of the elegant sofa. Sarah sat on the floor, her head resting against his knee and his fingers entwined in her long, curling hair. Every now and again his eyes would open and he would stare across at Beth, smiling in that disconcerting way he had, as if he knew a secret he'd rather not share and she wondered again if he'd been spying on her.

'We really ought to be going,' she said, knowing she would be ignored.

The fire crackled, throwing sparks out on to the old rug so that Tessa had to squash them quickly with her foot. The sudden movement sent a flicker of shadows on the ceiling.

'It's almost dark. James should be in bed by this time?' she persisted.

Sarah let out a heavy sigh. 'I don't see why we should go home simply because it's baby's bed time.'

Beth fell silent, feeling faintly foolish.

After a moment, Jonty said, 'Why bother? Stay here. We could all live together. Form a commune.' He glanced down at Sarah, lips curving into a half smile as he tweaked her hair. 'Could be interesting.'

'That's a great idea,' she agreed.

'You mean like the hippies in the sixties? This is the seventies now,' Beth said, alarmed that Sarah might agree.

'What's wrong with being a hippy?' Jonty protested, patting his bandana with affection. 'Or at least a bit bohemian. Anyway, there were communes before the sixties. After the Second World War, for instance, when some blokes couldn't settle back to work, getting your own house was a near impossibility and rationing still in operation. Life was pretty grim. So groups of young people often decided to live together in one big house, everyone mucking in with the work and the kids and the expense of it all.'

'You seem very well informed,' Sarah commented.

'My ma was brought up in one. And it did her no harm. But if your sister doesn't agree . . .'

'Oh, take no notice of Beth, she doesn't have opinions, none worth knowing anyway.'

'Thanks for that,' Beth retorted. 'Anyway, we might not get on.'

'Why not? We're all consenting adults.' Sarah jumped up and went to put her arms about her sister. 'Oh, please do say yes. It would be such fun. And we could all take turns with the chores.'

Beth gave a disbelieving laugh. 'I'll believe that when I see it.'

'No, really, I mean it. It's not fair of us to leave everything to you. Poor sweetie.' She kissed Beth's cheek. 'We could make a rota.'

'We'd have our own separate quarters,' Jonty added. 'There's plenty of room here.'

'What about Tess, and baby James?' Beth wanted to know, not quite liking the idea of being one part of a pair of couples. Not at this stage.

'Fine by me. What have I got to lose? Depends whether you can tolerate a baby around?'

'I like to play with the beautiful *bambino*. Baby James is my favourite model.'

'There's Andrew. We couldn't leave him out.'

Before Tessa had time to express an opinion on the subject, Pietro intervened. 'Not good. Andrew will not wish to leave his farm. He is too serious farmer. A dull young man.'

Tessa protested. 'He isn't at all dull. He may be a bit quiet but he has his good points too.'

'Then he keeps them well hidden,' Jonty said.

Beth felt suddenly very sorry for her. Husband deserted her, left to bring up a child alone or on charity, now everyone was criticising the man she fancied. 'Whether or not to invite Andrew must be Tessa's decision, not ours.'

'Hardly,' said Sarah, in scathing tones. 'This isn't her house, is it?'

Tessa glared at Sarah, considered combating the accusation that she was constantly after a free ride and thought better of it, biting back on her hurt pride which she really couldn't afford to have. If Sarah liked to stick pins in people, let her. 'As you say, its not my house,' she said, with all due reasonableness.

'We could take a vote,' Jonty suggested, eyeing Beth with a sideways grin.

She got up and walked over to the window. The rain had eased a little but the sky remained dark and lowering. 'It's a big decision. Perhaps we should all sleep on it.'

'Yes, here.'

And Beth turned and met his teasing smile without expression.

'Not tonight. Sarah and I should talk this through first. I'm very tired and intend leaving right now before it starts raining again.' It was the most decisive remark she had made in some time and it brought heads swivelling in her direction.

'OK,' Sarah agreed, deciding that to play along could only be to her advantage. 'We'll go home and talk.'

But as she turned away, Beth's attention was captured by a flicker of movement on the hills. After watching with interest for a moment she cupped her eyes and pressed closer to the glass for a better view.

'What is it?' Tessa was beside her.

'I'm not sure. Some men, I think. Spread out in a line across the fell tops. What are they doing?'

Tess bent closer for a better look. 'Hunting. Deer, or foxes maybe. Are they carrying guns?'

'Might be.'

'Then that's what they're doing. They don't ride about on horses in these parts to chase a rogue fox. A horse would break its leg on these fells. They walk, and after the dogs have flushed it out, shoot it dead. Civilised as they can make it, and necessary for their livestock.'

'I'm sure it must be.' Even so she shuddered.

Tessa laughingly took hold of her arm and gave it a gentle squeeze as she whispered in her ear. 'If you don't care for the idea of a commune, then say so and I'll back you up, but please don't take Sarah's line. I really don't want to get in the way or be a burden to anyone.'

'I know, Tess. Don't worry. Your friendship means a great deal to me.' And the two girls grinned at each other in perfect understanding.

'I'd do my bit. I'd work hard.'

'Let's sleep on it, shall we?'

Jonty was at the door, shrugging on his coat. 'Come on. I'm bored with sitting about. It's early yet. Let's see what they're up to.'

'Ooh yes, let's,' echoed Sarah.

'Prowl about in the dark you mean? Hunting the hunters?' Beth was appalled by the very idea.

'Why shouldn't we do some hunting of our own? It'll be fun. Come on.'

Beth telegraphed silent messages to her sister which were steadfastly ignored.

'Count me out,' Tessa said, gathering James in to her arms. 'We're off home. It's past our bedtime.'

'And mine I think. I'll come with you.' Beth stifled a yawn.

'You mean you're too chicken,' Jonty challenged her.

Pietro came and put his arm about her shoulders, as if for protection. 'No, no. Beth is very brave, are you not, little one? If she does not go, neither will I.'

So how could she refuse, after that?

There was nothing quite so black as an empty fellside and Beth stumbled through the darkness, not feeling at all happy about this expedition. What was Jonty up to? The old trees in Brockbarrow Wood creaked, sounding unnaturally loud in the silence of the night. Somewhere in the distance an owl hooted, making her glance back over her shoulder, then laugh shakily at her own nervousness. 'Where exactly are we going?'

'We won't catch up with those men,' Sarah protested. 'They'll be long gone by the time we reach them.'

Jonty's teeth glinted in the light of the half moon. 'We're not even going to try.' He whistled softly and the small dog left a hole he'd been inspecting and bounded to his heels. 'Good lad, Dart. Let's see what we can sniff out, eh?'

'What we look for? *Non mi piace.* I don't like it.'

'Shut up, Pietro. We're looking for some fun, a good game to play. I like games.' Then the two boys put their heads together for a whispered conversation which brought many stifled shouts of laughter.

Beth stumbled on in the darkness behind them all, not understanding, trying to peer through the gloom and not trip over tree roots or make any sound since Jonty had told her sternly not to. And remembering how he constantly watched her, she felt just a little afraid of him. After a while he stopped to pick up a long stick, testing it for strength. Pietro did the same and she wondered

87

why. They continued to creep through the woodland, Jonty keeping a close watch on the ground, as if he was most particular where he put his feet. He was probably right to take care. The rain had stopped but it was treacherous underfoot and Beth kept slipping and almost falling in the mud.

She shivered in the night air, feeling tired and longing for her bed even more. She'd almost decided to turn back when Jonty stopped and gave a small grunt of satisfaction.

'I knew it. Look, a well trodden path and droppings, plain as plain. There must be a sett around here. A whole colony probably in this ridge.'

Sett? *Sett*. Something clicked inside her head. 'You don't mean badgers?' Beth pushed Sarah unceremoniously aside as she came forward to look.

Jonty didn't even trouble to glance at her, only laughed at the shock in her voice. 'And you can shut up too, Beth. This is man's work. Yep, we'll try this one.' He started to poke down a hole with the stick. 'Go on, Dart. Fetch.'

And to Beth's horror the terrier leapt down the hole, scrabbling madly with its front feet. After a few seconds of this it disappeared into the black depths.

What followed next would, she knew, live with her for the rest of her life. No one paid any attention to her protests, not even Sarah who, though she covered her eyes, was too concerned with Jonty's good-will to show her disapproval as Dart found his quarry. Dog and badger began to fight. The badger fled from its sett in a bid for freedom from the terrier's jaws only to find itself surrounded, cornered by humans with sticks who made sure it kept within the bounds they had marked out.

'*Stop it*,' Beth screamed but no one heard her, or if they did, paid no heed. 'Let him go. Call the dog off.'

'Dart's only doing what's natural. So's the badger,' laughed Jonty. 'Place your bets folks, who do you reckon'll win?'

It was sickening. The terrier brought the badger down on to its back time and time again, sinking his teeth into its rump and the screams which rang out were so heartrending she covered her ears, yet still couldn't blot them out. Bile rose in her throat. The badger's glossy coat was slick with blood but still he fought. Tenacious, fearless, eyes glistening with a fierce terror in the moonlight. One small ear was almost ripped off and Beth had had enough. 'I'll stop them. I will, I will.' She leapt forward but never reached the sparring animals as Jonty grabbed her and yanked her cruelly back.

'You stupid bitch. He'd only turn on you. Stop being so bloody sentimental.'

She struggled furiously in his grasp, wanting to strike him, almost as fearless as the badger and desperate at her own impotence. 'Stop them. Stop them,' she screamed. 'Don't let Dart kill him. Oh please, don't.'

Jonty laughed out loud, a sound that chilled her blood. Then somewhere above their heads a shot rang out. The terrier was so startled it stopped fighting instantly and scooted away, tail between its legs to disappear in the undergrowth. The badger's instinct for survival was such that even with its awesome injuries it attempted to crawl back into its sett. Perhaps for the dignity of a quiet death. It didn't quite make it and collapsed in a bloody heap, inches from its sanctuary.

'What the hell d'you think you're doing?' Andrew's voice rang out, cold with anger. Beth almost collapsed with relief.

'Having some sport. What does it look like?' Jonty faced him, a cynical twist to his mouth.

Andrew jumped down from the ridge, the gun still in his hands. 'You bloody swine. Don't you know that badger baiting is illegal?'

'So what? Everyone does it.'

'Everyone doesn't do it. Not here anyway. Does it give you a thrill to see a fine animal die for your pleasure? Maybe we should put you through a similar process.' He raised the gun slightly and Beth's heart contracted. Surely he wouldn't actually shoot Jonty? She stepped quickly forward.

'Thank goodness you've come, Andrew. Never mind about Jonty. What about the badger? It's injured.'

Andrew glanced down. The animal had got as far as the entrance to his sett, barely out of sight but too exhausted to go further.

'For goodness' sake,' Sarah said. 'It's just an old badger.'

Andrew and Beth both looked at her and said nothing. There seemed nothing appropriate to say.

'We should perhaps not have let the game go this far,' Pietro muttered and Beth rounded on him, eyes glittering.

'No, you shouldn't. Why didn't you try to do something? Why didn't you stop him?'

Jonty snorted. 'Because he was as willing as me.'

'He knew he couldn't stop you,' Beth responded. 'He probably didn't understand exactly what you were up to. Did you Pietro?'

Pietro looked at her sadly, then shook his head. 'No, no. I not understand.'

'There, you see?' She turned back to Andrew. 'What will happen to the badger? Can we save it?'

'Probably a goner but I'll tek it to old Ellen. If she can't save it, no one can.'

Beth didn't ask who old Ellen was, but she was intrigued and concerned, feeling somehow responsible. 'I'll come with you.'

'Lot of fuss about nothing,' Jonty grumbled. 'Why do you, a farmer, try to protect the bloody thing? Badgers are thieves and they infect cattle with TB.'

'It hasn't been properly proved. It's only a theory.' Andrew was hunkering down beside the hole, reaching for the badger, easing it out. 'Their diet comprises largely of voles and earthworms, though much of the time they're vegetarian. They don't touch cows and do no real harm these gentlemen of the woods. Which is more than can be said for men like you.' He cradled the animal in his arms, then as he rose, he slid the barrel of the gun beneath the jut of Jonty's chin. 'Any animals which do need to be culled should be dealt with humanely, right? Not torn apart by a bloody dog, or a madman. Now go on home, peaceable like, or I might forget my manners and treat you the same way.'

Jonty tensed forward but the gun pressed tight against his throat, and though his eyes blazed hatred, he deemed it wise to stay silent.

'If I ever catch you or that dog o' yours harming an animal again, you know what you can expect, don't you?'

Andrew led Beth unerringly through the darkness to a part of Brockbarrow Wood she had not so far discovered. He swung along at such a pace she almost had to run to keep up with him, her feet slipping on the damp earth, tripping over stones. And then suddenly he stopped.

'We're here. Go quiet now. We don't want to upset the residents.'

'Residents?'

Down in a small hollow, with the sound of water from the force ringing in their ears, was the dark huddle of a cottage. All about it was a clutter of small compounds wired off into sections, from which came a cacophony of unidentifiable barks, squeaks, whistles and grunts.

'She lives here, with her animals.'

'Oh?'

They slid and stumbled down a slippery path and came at last to the front door. Andrew tapped softly on it. 'It's me, Ellen. I've a patient for you.'

A light came on inside and then the door opened and a woman stood on the doorstep, looking down upon them, a storm lantern held in her hand. She glanced at the bundle in his arms and with a jerk of her head, ushered them inside.

The smell which hit them as they stepped into the cottage almost knocked Beth out. Of badger and bird and dog. Several dogs, in fact.

Two spaniels and a collie jumped down from a narrow bed and came over to investigate, tails waving like flags, drooling to be patted. Beth obliged. A tawny owl sat on a perch, one wing strapped down with what appeared to be a pad of foam rubber, and in a basket by a glowing fire sat a grey goose, apparently completely healthy and content, save for the fact that it possessed only half a beak.

The hurricane lamp in the woman's hand revealed the kind of stark tidiness which seemed to indicate she had little regard for material possessions and no interest at all in comfort.

As she bent to her patient, Beth studied her. A tall, rangy woman in her late sixties, her features could only be described as embattled, with the deepest brown eyes Beth had ever seen, with squint lines at each corner. She wore her grey hair in a plait around her broad head which gave her a rather medieval look, a sort of other-worldliness. Several layers of woollens covered a check shirt and green corduroy trousers, signifying that, late as it was, she had not yet gone to bed. Around her neck was tied a dirty blue scarf but her hands, Beth noticed, as they set the animal on a small table, were surprisingly clean if brown and weathered and criss-crossed with scars.

'Badger, eh?'

'Aye.'

'Thought I could smell its fear.' The hands were sure and firm as she silently and methodically examined the injured animal which seemed none too happy with her probings yet miraculously permitted them, as if it guessed this was for its own good. 'I reckon he's had it.' The prognosis was issued with complete lack of sentiment in a sharp, cracking, no nonsense sort of voice. It cut Beth to the heart, yet she could sense compassion in the bleak statement. Even so . . .

'You can't mean you'll let him die?' The words burst from her before she'd had time to think and keen eyes turned consideringly upon her for the first time. The question, when it came, was addressed to Andrew.

'Who's this?'

'Beth Brandon, from Larkrigg.'

The eyes widened perceptably. 'Not Rosemary Ellis's grand-daughter? No, great granddaughter you'd be, eh? Well, well.'

'Never mind about me. What about the badger?' Beth was incensed suddenly. 'Can you do nothing at all for him?'

'Feeling guilty, eh? Your friend's dog was it, who tore him apart? Thought you'd have a bit of fun, did you? Well, I can't cure 'em all after you've had your bit of a laugh, much as I'd like to. They have feelings, badgers do, same as you and me, and they get depressed and give up when they're in pain.'

'But you mustn't let it.'

'Beth,' Andrew touched her arm. 'Don't get upset. He'd probably die of blood poisoning no matter what Ellen did.'

'I only save what can be set free,' she said, gazing again upon the inert badger. 'If it can't live a normal, useful life, better it be dead. It'd only mourn for its own kind if I shut it in a cage. Social animals, badgers are. They like to be together.'

But Beth wasn't for giving up. She was the one fighting now, for the badger's life. 'You've kept that goose, yet how can it feed itself without a beak? And what's the matter with the owl? Broken wing? Why don't you shoot it?'

'It might get better.'

'Or be killed by a larger bird when you let it go?'

'Aye, that could happen too.' After a long moment, Ellen spoke again. 'You weren't in on it then, this game?' The eyes were so deeply hidden beneath the thatch of eyebrows that Beth couldn't read their expression. But she recognised something of the wild creature in Ellen too. Reserved, a bit prickly, not trusting people too easily. Probably been given no reason to. Trust had to be earned. And man probably destroyed her work every day.

'No, I was not,' she said. 'I tried to stop them as a matter of fact, but they took no notice.' She reached for a sack lying near. 'If you won't help him, then I'll take him home with me. Tell me what to do and I'll do it.'

Another small silence, broken at last by a cackle of laughter. It erupted onto her face like sunlight on a dry-stone wall, smoothing out the folds and cracks to a craggy radiance. 'She's got spirit, this one, eh?' and as she met Beth's furious gaze, there was merriment now twinkling in her own. 'I'll fetch my herb chest and we'll see what we can do. But I make no promises.'

'Do you think he'll live?'

Dawn was breaking, pink and clear in the eastern sky and the three of them were sitting with huge mugs of tea, relaxing at last.

'Fate and good medicine will decree that.' Ellen sipped noisily at her tea.

'I think you're wonderful. You must be very gifted,' Beth said, remembering the way the woman had mixed herbs and dealt with the badger with a deft skill born of years of experience.

But the affect of this simple statement was alarming. 'Utter poppycock,' Ellen exploded. 'I do what I can and it's pitifully small at times. I'm not the hand of God, you know. Nor Mother Nature.'

Beth looked rather startled by the outburst. 'I never meant . . .'

'Do a bit of good every day, that's my motto. There's plenty doing the opposite.'

'You're right there,' Andrew put in.

'Never failed in that philosophy, ever since the outbreak of World War Two. Kept busy with the VAD while my Hugh was incarcerated in that damn concentration camp. Then when he came home and he wasn't too good, we started a smallholding which grew into taking in lodgers of the animal variety. Never made much money but it added a bit to his pension. Then he went and died.' She made it sound as if he'd done it on purpose, to spite her.

'How sad,' Beth murmured.

'All those years in the damned service. Missed being killed by the skin of his teeth more times than he cared to count, then he gets taken by a double dose of pneumonia and malaria. Never left him, that malaria.' She tossed a dead, day old chick to the owl on the perch behind her, who took it greedily. Beth averted her eyes. 'Lovely man he was, but weak you understand. I always did all the hard work. But he never got over whatever it was they did to him. After he died, I gave up the lease on the smallholding and came here. That was more than twenty years ago and I've never regretted it.'

Andrew grinned engagingly at her. 'And how would the wild creatures on these fells have managed without you? Come on, admit it. You're more than a mite flattered by Beth's faith in your skill.'

'If folk didn't interfere with 'em I wouldn't have half so much work to do,' she barked. 'Damned tourists pick youngsters up, owls, kestrels, lambs even, thinking they've been deserted by their parents which usually they haven't; without the faintest idea how to feed or care for 'em and they end up fetching 'em to me, sick or dying.

'It can take months to get a young animal healthy and properly rehabilitated to go back into the wild. Took me two years once with a young peregrine that had been imprinted with the smell of humans. And what's the point of all that effort of making it well again, if it can't enjoy life? So I have to make choices. Survival of the fittest. Besides which, I'm not made of money.'

'Yes,' Beth said, fascinated by the fierce passion of the woman, and full of admiration. 'I do realise that. I'm sorry if I was a bit sharp with you last night.'

Ellen rubbed at her red eyes with a finger and thumb. 'Aye well, it was late. We were all tired. Think no more of it. I'm off to feed that lot outside then get me head down for a few hours' shut-eye.'

'Can I see what you have here?'

'Another time, Beth,' Andrew said, getting up. 'I have some animals of my own to tend and Ellen is all in.'

'Of course. I'm sorry. Thanks for saving the badger.'

'I haven't saved him. Not yet.' A sharp reminder, bluntly given.

Beth swallowed and asked, very tentatively, 'May I call and see how's he's getting on?'

Brown eyes regarded her quizzically for a moment. 'So long as you're prepared to be disappointed. I can't do with a fuss, waterworks and all that, if nature decrees otherwise. This brock will either have the stamina to survive or it won't.'

'I do understand. I promise to be sensible.'

Seemingly satisfied, Ellen agreed she could call any time. And as she walked away up the path with Andrew, the stentorian voice called after them, 'Don't fetch them friends o' yourn. They've done enough.'

Beth made no reply. She knew exactly what Ellen meant.

8

The commune, in Sarah's opinion, proved to be a great success. At least in the beginning. Life at Larkrigg Hall was fun and she came very quickly to the conclusion that this was the only way to live. It was amazing how life had changed since discovering their delectable squatters.

Meg objected of course, which didn't surprise her.

'It's all quite innocent good fun,' Sarah told her. 'Separate quarters and all that.'

'And Pietro Lawson amongst them?'

Beth lifted her chin, mirroring Meg's own stubbornness. 'Yes, Pietro included.'

'We're big girls now,' Sarah said.

'Even so . . .'

Tam sent Meg a warning glance and went over to kiss both his granddaughters. 'Don't we trust the pair of them?' Against which Meg could find no argument and the subject was closed.

Beth naturally drew up yards of charts to show who was responsible for which chore on any given day, but Sarah found it easy enough to avoid most of these by a little diligent absenteeism. And those she did do, she made sure didn't tax her too greatly. Particularly since she insisted on being partnered by Jonty. They would hide away in the woods or even the woodshed, since private corners were everywhere, without feeling the least speck of guilt. If the two of them took twice as long as everyone else to wash up or chop logs, what did it matter so long as the task was done?

The advantages of commune life were legion. As well as finding easy opportunities to sneak away during the day, there was the ready access to the lovely beds every night. No more creeping across the fells in the dark. Instead, Jonty would pad along the landing and slide between the sheets in the great bed and they'd have to stuff them in their mouths to stop up their giggles as they thought of the others in their chaste beds.

Sarah was always ready for him, an aching moistness between her legs, a pain in her belly and feverish with impatience for him to come to her. If he was late she would punish him by making him wait for her surrender.

She would straddle him and stroke the hardness of his stomach, tease the velvety skin till he had an erection then laughingly hold him away as he groaned in his agony, begging for release. She would rub the hard peaks of her breasts against his chest and into his mouth, then draw enticingly away. Only when she chose did she let him pierce her right to the centre of her own yearning. Then she would ride him and bite him, the passion in her rising to a furious anger, driving him to satisfy a craving which could not be sated.

'Let Tessa help with the heavy work,' Sarah told Beth when, much to her annoyance, she'd been caught lying in bed one fine afternoon, ostensibly taking a nap and Beth accused her of not pulling her weight. 'It's a good way for her to pay for her keep.'

'We none of us properly do that.'

Anyone else would have thought to look beneath the bed, discovered a half naked Jonty, issued a stinging lecture about there being a time and a place for everything and left it at that. Beth, being Beth, simply tightened her lips, fidgeted with that dratted hair slide and told Sarah she wasn't being quite fair.

'Fair? What are you talking about? I do my whack like everyone else. I can surely take some free time.' Sarah jumped off the bed and started pulling on jeans.

'But there isn't any free time. Not yet. We have to aim to be self-sufficient. You could at least dig the garden or tie up the raspberries when you have a spare moment.'

'What do I know about raspberries?'

'What I mean is that you shouldn't simply follow the rota and nothing else.'

'You want me actually to look for work?' Sarah tried to hide her astonishment.

'Yes, I do. This commune was Jonty's idea, remember, not mine.' Beth plumped herself down on the bed, making the springs squeak and sag so much Sarah almost burst out laughing as she thought of poor Jonty in imminent danger of being decapitated beneath. 'You don't think that dreadful prophecy is coming true, do you?' Beth continued. 'We seem to do nothing but quarrel these days and really it should be all for one and everything, shouldn't it, as Jonty suggested.'

And Sarah hooded her eyes and meekly agreed. 'Yes, Beth. Of course, Beth,' which was always the quickest way to get rid of her when she had her organising hat on.

'And you will help a bit more?'

'Of course, sweetie. When have I ever let you down?'

The moment the bedroom door clicked shut behind her, Jonty crawled from beneath the four poster, beside her in a second, stifling his laughter as he pushed Sarah back on to the bed.

'Your sister is becoming a real drag,' he said, tugging at the zip on her jeans. 'Someone should loosen her up. Drat it, I can't get these damned things off. Why do women wear so many clothes?'

'Perhaps we should join a naturist commune? That would really save a lot of time.' And they both dissolved into peals of laughter and thrusting, sweating sex, which was much more fun than digging gardens, or weeding the raspberry patch.

Beth took to visiting Ellen's cottage on a fairly regular basis, drinking in every scrap of information she could wring from her new friend that might help with her own smallholding.

Every visit seemed to lead to a fresh discovery. For all Rowan cottage looked as if a puff of wind might blow it down at any minute it had a cultivated garden, filled in every corner with fruit or vegetables. The ubiquitious raspberries of course, rhubarb, gooseberries, black and redcurrants. Then there was mint, sage, rosemary and other herbs which Beth didn't recognise. Leeks, cabbages, potatoes and onions by the score.

'Can't grow carrots, more's the pity,' she mourned. 'Don't grow well in this stony soil.'

And the birds could feast as much as they liked on whatever Ellen didn't eat. No nets in her garden.

'Share and share alike,' she said. 'They were here first.'

There was a bee hive in one corner, its occupants humming loudly.

'What a fuss when they swarm,' she told her young visitor. 'Chase 'em half across the fells sometimes, I do. But beautiful honey. Feed on heather, d'you see?'

'How wonderful.'

'Know how to take honey from a hive, do you?' And when Beth shook her head, she laughed. 'Don't look so feared. I'll show you one day.'

But, best of all, Beth enjoyed watching the animals.

The badger made steady progress and Ellen began to drop her reserve little by little, as she took note of Beth's genuine interest in her simple country pursuits.

'I build boxes for some of the owls which I release. They have a hard time of it with all the barns that are being turned into holiday accommodation. The red squirrels come and pinch bits of coconut I leave out for them. I like to watch 'em play, proper little acrobats they are. Have you known Andrew long?'

The abrupt change in conversation caught Beth off guard. 'Tess introduced us, at the Jubilee Sports Day. We watched him wrestle.'

Ellen nodded. 'Oh, aye. He likes his wrestling, does Andrew.' She glanced sideways at Beth, trying to appear not to pry as she plucked a thorn from the heel of one thumb. 'He's a quiet lad but strong, and with a heart as big as a mountain.'

Beth felt rather amused by these compliments. Perhaps Ellen saw him as a surrogate son. They certainly seemed old buddies. 'Yes,' she said kindly. 'I can see that he is. Very steady.'

'And reliable.'

'Yes, of course. Absolutely reliable.' And no doubt utterly boring with it, she thought. Poor boy, the description was almost as damning as the 'Beth is such a nice girl' which the old ladies of Boston used to say about her.

Ellen turned away, ostensibly to mend a hole in the compound fence with a bit of bailing twine from her pocket, half watching

Beth at the same time. 'He's a good lad. I'd not see him badly done to. His future isn't too certain.'

Beth was surprised. 'Isn't it? I thought his father owned Cathra Crag.' She cut off the twine with a knife where Ellen indicated.

'Nay, old Seth owns it, and the silly old fool is as stubborn as a mule. Terrified of doing aught new, he is. And Billy, Andrew's father, don't like change of any sort. Proper pair they are. Andrew has his hands full, I can tell you.' She turned laughing eyes to Beth. 'And the poor lad is itching to modernise.'

'I'm sure he'll manage it, if he's as sound and reliable as you say.'

The brown eyes sharpened momentarily. Was the girl taking the mickey? But Beth maintained her expression of bland innocence and Ellen relaxed. 'Aye, course he will. All he needs is a good wife to help him along the road.'

So that's what this was all about. 'And I'm sure he'll find one. Lovely steady chap like him. Now I must be off. See you soon.'

Match-maker Ellen was running on the wrong track so far as she was concerned, Beth thought, chuckling to herself as she climbed back up the fell, the happy sounds of the birds and squirrels still whistling and chattering in her ears. It was perfectly plain, even to her, that Tessa was the one he had his eye on. Why else would he keep popping in whenever she was around?

'Let's hope Tessa feels the same way. She deserves a bit of good luck.'

Beth was delighted to find that Pietro talked with her much more freely these days. He seemed to have got over his bout of diffidence and was always ready to offer his help with whatever she was doing. Not that he was particularly practical. He would start a job eagerly enough, whether it be cleaning out the hen hut, or painting the living room walls. But if she didn't keep a close watch on him, she would return to find he was making patterns with the paint instead of applying it smoothly, or sitting sketching the hens instead of feeding or cleaning them.

'What a dreamer you are.'

'I am the artist. My thoughts are bigger than these simple tasks.'

'Yes, but we have to eat. And we must be clean and tidy.'

'Why? We can live without plaster and paint on the walls, buy food at the supermarket. We must lift our mind to greater things. I wish to be the great artist like the great ones in the museums and galleries of my home town of Florence. It is a proud and noble thing to be.'

'I agree, but we'd run out of money eventually, wouldn't we? And the whole point is to be as self-sufficent as possible.'

And he would look at her with his melting blue eyed gaze, making her insides churn. 'Ah, do not scold me, little one. I am the silly boy, yes? And you Beth, you are so wise. What is it you wish for me to do?'

Then he would reach over and place a soft kiss on her lips or stroke her wayward hair from her cheeks with such a tender touch that Beth would shiver with longing. Once he pulled out the slide and tossed it away in to the long grass and she gave a little gasp.

'Why did you do that?'

'Because the hair is too beautiful to confine. Discipline is bad for you. Let your hair be free. Let yourself be free.'

'Oh, Pietro. If only I could. Sarah always does exactly as she pleases but I have this need, this compulsion almost, to do always what is right.'

'You are the good girl, and she the bad?'

Beth giggled. 'No, nothing so simple as that. I'm screwed up, that's all. But I promise, I don't mind your not working. Do your sketch, I'll finish this job.' She couldn't help being soft with him, for all he was every bit as lazy as Sarah. How could she when he was so entirely charming and beautiful? And she was falling so helplessly in love with him.

Later that autumn he went home to Italy on a visit to see his family and replenish his funds. He was most careful with money, she knew that, and contributed his share to the general housekeeping fund. She watched him go with an ache of longing in her heart, wondering about his family, what they were like and whether they missed him when he was here in England.

The long days while he was away would be an agony. What if he didn't ever come back? What if he had a girl back in Italy? One he'd never told her about. A wife even. She paled at the thought. No, he would have told her. And he would be back soon, wouldn't he? Otherwise how could she bear to live without him?

She busied herself more than ever. Every day she went to the mill and spent hours on the endless chores around the house, visiting Ellen and the badger, now recovering well, working till she was exhausted and could drop into bed and sleep without the torment of longing for him.

And as she worked, Beth found herself becoming more and more a part of this landscape. She knew the dip of every hill, could name every pale and distant peak, the fold of every mountain. Kentmere Pike, Ill Bell, High Street as far as Scafell and Great Gable. And to the east the softer line of the Pennines and the Howgills. She loved them all. Loved this vista which never seemed quite the same two days together. Even the sky seemed to produce a magical new colour of pink, topaz, turquoise and blue, each and every day.

She loved the soft rain on her face, the drifts of mist that veiled the hills, the wind that tore up the valley and shook every chimney and door, reminding them all of the power of nature.

She was a country person at last, living her rural dream. And each day her resolve to stay grew ever deeper. When the house was finished she would fight Sarah tooth and nail to stop her selling it. It must never happen.

It was Ellen who sold her the goat.

'She's a good clean animal. A good mother. She'll serve you well. You'll have to watch her, of course,' she told Beth in her usual brisk manner. 'She's young still, with a mind of her own. As all goats have.' And proceeded to give a lengthy list of instructions.

'I'll take good care of her.'

Beth took it home without mentioning it to anyone, except Tess of course. The goat rode in the yellow mini beside a delighted James who kept tickling it under its chin. But after the goat threatened to eat the little boy's jumper right off his back, Tessa had to stop the car so Beth could squash herself between them and try to keep the animal's mouth shut, which proved far from easy.

It took some time to extracate it from the small car, particularly as they doubled up with laughter.

Sarah was standing in the drive staring at them, appalled. 'Are you quite mad?'

'I thought it might help to keep the grass down,' Beth said, her voice unusually defiant.

But the goat, named Lucy, proved willing to eat anything but grass, which largely she scorned. Young trees she enjoyed enormously, and the leeks which Beth had so painstakingly planted. Several items from the washing line mysteriously disappeared and Jonty lost a dozen nails he'd been about to hammer into the fence.

Learning to milk her was another trauma. She would eye Beth with suspicion, stamp her foot and move away at precisely the wrong moment. And even when Beth managed to keep her standing still, milk squirted anywhere but in the bucket.

Not that there was much milk in the first place since they couldn't afford to feed her on the high concentrates necessary. And she absolutely refused to stay in the little house which Beth and Tessa painstakingly built to keep the rain off and save her from chills. They seemed to spend much of their time chasing the obstinate Lucy over hill and dale.

'Poor Beth,' Jonty said, surprisingly sympathetic.

'She'll settle. Give her time,' was Beth's response to every complaint.

'Don't put me on the goat rota,' Sarah warned. Advice which Beth took very seriously.

And then there were the ducks and geese. These she bought from a local farmer, clipped their wings in the required manner, and settled them in a nettle patch by a small pond.

'They'll keep off intruders. Geese are good for that.'

'We never have any intruders. And we'd see them coming a mile off if we did,' Sarah protested, rather sharply in Beth's opinion.

'Leave the kid alone,' Jonty protested. 'Let her keep a goat if she wants one,' and for once Beth warmed to him.

She fed them on corn and barley and after a while the birds started to lay eggs, the ducks every day, the geese once in a while. Some of the geese proved good mothers, the ducks less so, and Beth set the spare eggs beneath broody hens.

'When they hatch, we can sell the young birds on and make money,' she explained, relieved to find they had a use after all.

'As well as fattening some for the Christmas table,' Jonty agreed. 'Good thinking, Beth. You're coming on. Not such a silly goose after all,' and she forgave him the awful joke since he'd taken her side for once.

When Pietro returned, tanned and refreshed from his holiday, looking more gorgeous than ever in Beth's eyes, he wasn't too keen on the goat either but reluctantly agreed to carry the bucket for her when she went to feed and milk Lucy.

'How were your family? Tell me about them,' she asked, breathless with excitement at seeing him again and wanting to keep him to herself for a while.

He perched on a nearby stone to watch her, seemingly in a contented mood. 'Ah, my family, I must admit they care very little for me. I am, what you say, the cuckoo in the nest. They think I am not very bright.' He tapped his head with one finger, making her laugh.

'I don't believe it.'

'It is true. I am not good at making the money as they are. My parents they divorce and Momma marry again. My stepfather, he never forgive me for not making much money like him. He has the good restaurant and little hotel, a *pensione* in Florence, near the Pitti Palace. He make much money, and my half brothers, they too have businesses. I keep changing the jobs which he not like. He say I no good. My mother was pleased to see me but he not miss me while I am in England, I think.'

She stared at him, round eyed. Hadn't she guessed there was deep sorrow in him? 'Oh, but that is so sad. What about your own father?'

'He say since I chose to go with my mother, he doesn't wish to know me as his son any more.'

'But that is dreadful.'

'And here too I am resented.'

Beth was astonished. 'Resented? Why on earth do you say that?'

'Because you all think that I have come to steal the Broombank from your grandmother. You do not trust my love for the Lakeland hills. Is that not so?'

'No, of course it is not so.' The urge to put her arms about him and nurse this raw vulnerability was almost unbearable.

'Your friend, Andrew, he think so.'

'Andrew is not my friend,' she stoutly and recklessly declared, then bit her lip, feeling guilty at denying him. 'Well, not as you are my friend.'

He smiled at her then, and her heart lit with the radiance of it. 'Oh, Pietro we love having you here. We all love you.' She stumbled over the word, cheeks flushing hotly, wondering if he guessed her real feelings for him. Then he laughed, and kissing the tip of his finger placed it on her tip-tilted nose as he had done once before.

But he found it difficult to disguise his disgust as Beth started to wash the goat's teats. He started to pace about, half watching her, half absorbed in his own thoughts.

She had missed him while he was away, he could tell, which was surely a good thing. He was winning her over, he thought, little by little. But she was shy still and it would do no good to rush her or he would spoil everything. Assuming that is, he had definitely decided she was worth pursuing. For there was still the matter of Sarah and Jonty. Where was that relationship leading? And more important, how did he feel about it?

He studied the ground, kicking at stones and bits of turf as he brooded over the problem while Beth worried over how he felt about her, and how she should explain to everyone that if the supply of milk was to continue they would need another goat. A billy.

'Don't let your stepfather bother you. There are more important things in life besides making money,' she soothed, dragging her attention back to his family.

'Of course there are. Who cares about an old man.' He brightened. 'Let me draw you. With your hands busy with the goat and your cheeks all pink, you look quite delectable.'

The colour on her cheeks deepened as she ineffectually protested. 'Oh, no, I'm far too plain to be an artist's model. Sarah would make a lovely one, don't you think?' She longed for him to deny it, to say that really she had a quiet, pastoral beauty far greater than her more flamboyant sister.

But he kept his eyes on the small pad of paper he had pulled from his pocket and gave a disarming shrug. 'One does not draw only what is superficially beautiful. I see into your soul.' When he smiled at her, a brilliant, beautiful smile she thought her heart would stop. Even so, disappointment was tight in her throat and his words did little for her fragile ego.

But what else could she hope for? That he would see what wasn't there? She was indeed plain and dull, a milkmaid, as Sarah would no doubt say. A grubby one too after a day's work. And he was a true artist, sensitive and kind, trying to make her feel better.

Beth sat as obediently still as she could, holding on desperately to the fidgety goat, longing to be able to flirt or pout or flash her eyes, as Sarah did. She wished she dare dress in bright colours that didn't quite match and still look stunning. She ached to be able to behave recklessly for once, and have Pietro fall at her feet with passion in his eyes.

'There, it is done.'

'Can I see it?'

She forgot for a moment that she held a bucket between her knees and a goat at her fingertips as he leaned closer. For one heart-stopping moment she thought he might kiss her properly at last, but he half turned away to lift up his sketch pad and show her the picture, as if the thought of kisses had never entered his head.

'It is perhaps not my best work but shows how you have a beautiful soul, I think.'

'Oh, what a wonderful thing to say.'

Her hands flew to her face and thinking she'd been released, Lucy darted forward, put her foot in the bucket, knocked it over and sent milk streaming all over Beth's feet then stomped away, bored by the whole process.

'Oh no, Sarah will kill me.' They both ran after the goat laughing, and Pietro managed at last to catch Lucy before she'd escaped too far. But the rare moment of intimacy had been lost which, Beth thought, was a great pity.

If Pietro showed disappointingly few signs of returning her love, Beth nonetheless grew more content with each passing day. Her skin glowed, her hair had grown longer and she enjoyed the sweep of it upon her shoulders, the burnished chestnut blazing to an autumn fire whenever the sun shone upon it. Some of her youthful plumpness was smoothing out to a new slender strength as she worked on the land, honing her muscles with regular exercise day after day. Working at Larkrigg was proving healthy and immensely satisfying.

Her life felt rich and fulfilled, needing only for Pietro to notice these changes in her to make her happiness complete. She lived for that day. But there was no hurry, she told herself. And he did seem to quite like spending time with her. Almost as important, she was learning about the countryside.

She loved to watch out for redstarts and wheatears, nesting in niches of dry-stone walls. Sometimes she would see a sprightly merlin cruise by on a passing windstream, and there were always the yellowhammers, tits and wagtails busy with their own affairs. Her favourite was the mistlethrush which Ellen called a throstle.

She could see her dream beginning to take shape before her eyes. Rural life, a smallholding, Larkrigg Hall coming to life with warmth and comfort.

Had it not been for Tessa, she might have worked till she dropped and not even noticed. Wherever Beth was, whatever she was doing, Tess was beside her offering help and support, lending her not inconsiderable muscle.

Then one morning Lucy ate Sarah's favourite cashmere sweater and her fate was sealed. The goat had to go. Beth returned her to Ellen who looked startled for a moment, and then burst out laughing.

'I warned you. Goats have a way with them. A mind of their own. Never mind. Come and look at old Brock.'

The badger was curled up in a homemade sett, fast asleep with another badger.

'He's got a mate.'

Ellen grinned. 'A new friend, you might say. I'm letting 'em both go off together tonight, back where they came from. They're good chums now and I reckon they'll do all right.'

'Oh, I'm so glad.'

'You were right. He did have stamina. Happen you have too, the quiet sort, and that's why you recognised it in him.'

'Me? Lord, no. I'm a little background worker, that's all. More a beaver than a badger.' She laughed, relaxed and happy as she always was when visiting Ellen.

'Aye, well. There's some as say that a bit of hard work never hurt anyone. But don't overdo it, lass. Let others do their whack too. And don't put yourself down so much.'

Overhead they heard the cack-cack of geese and both women looked up through the oakwoods, watching the vee formation swoop across the open sky. 'Aye, the year's drawing on. Can't you feel the pulse slowing a bit? There they go, heading south on heaven's M1.'

That night she helped Ellen set the two badgers free, quite close to their home sett. Nothing had ever given her more satisfaction than to see them disappear safely together into the earth. The badgers at least were safe and content.

9

The next morning at breakfast, invigorated by the successful return of the badgers and deeply missing the goat, Beth stuck valiantly to her dream and tried to persuade everyone to let her buy a cow.

'Cow's milk tastes better,' she explained. 'A cow will eat grass, doesn't run off at every opportunity and we can make our own butter and cheese.'

No one seemed at all convinced.

'A cow is central to self-sufficiency,' she persisted, chin high.

But they simply sat around the huge scrubbed table and stared at her, as if she'd suggested buying a camel.

'Someone would still have to milk the damned thing every night and morning. Which wouldn't be me,' Sarah protested.

'No one would ask you to.'

'I don't mind helping,' Tessa said.

Whenever the sisters became embroiled in an argument everyone else tactfully held back and left them to it. Tessa had overstepped the line on this occasion and was rewarded with a fierce, violet-eyed glare from Sarah, for what was meant only as a generous offer. 'I don't suppose you would mind. You enjoy getting free milk for the baby. And this is between me and my sister, right?'

'Sorry.'

Stung to defend her friend, Beth spoke more spiritedly than usual. 'I'm not so sure that's correct any more, Sarah. This is a commune, remember, so everyone should have a say.'

'We can take a vote,' beamed Pietro and Beth sent him a grateful smile.

'Good idea. A vote. But do remember that a cow is a beautiful, docile creature. Nothing like a goat. Wouldn't you just love to own one? Perhaps a Jersey with soulful eyes.'

Sarah managed a dry smile. 'I can't say it's a burning ambition. It would need feeding. Hay and stuff.'

'We've plenty of grass and could grow some hay for next winter.'

Sarah sought new protests. 'There'd be calves to dispose of.'

Beth dug her heels in. 'We could sell them at market or grow them on ourselves, so we could make even more money. Start our own dairy herd. I've got it all worked out.'

Sarah thought she might pass out. 'What! Dairy herd? Stop it, Beth, you're going too fast. And where would we get the money from?'

Beth flushed bright red. 'Sorry, I do tend to get a bit carried away.'

'It's that stupid old woman you hang out with. You'd probably end up losing the damn creature, anyway. You've no more idea of how to look after a cow or help it give birth than – than I have.'

Beth could not argue with this and stared morosely at her plate. 'I wonder if Ellen knows anything about cows? And Jan has complained that we're not doing enough work at the mill. I feel quite guilty about the fact I've missed quite a few times recently. I tried to explain how busy we'd been, how there always seems so much to do here, but she didn't seem convinced. Perhaps you could go in and help a bit more, Sarah, or Jonty could, since I'm so busy with the animals?'

Sarah frowned but grudgingly agreed that she'd see what could be done. Jonty made no comment at all.

'Talk to Andrew,' Tessa suggested and Beth snatched at the idea. 'Of course. Why didn't I think of that? I'll go and see him first thing in the morning.' And experienced an odd lifting of her heart at the prospect of seeing him again, which she put down entirely to the fact that this time she meant to take proper advice and buy the right animal. Then she could finally realise her dream for complete self-sufficiency.

Beth went alone to Cathra Crag since she was the one who wanted a cow, and found it was not at all as she had imagined. She expected all

112

Lakeland farms to be like Broombank, rambling, well proportioned and beautiful. Up-to-the-minute machinery standing in its yard, neatness and efficiency the order of the day.

This one was small and squat, standing right at the head of the dale in a circle of high fells which probably hadn't looked much different in medieval times. The outbuildings were old and decrepit, covered by tin roofs and leaning drunkenly against the farmhouse which itself seemed to huddle beneath the crag whose name it bore.

The September day was mild but with a flurry of rain on the wind as Andrew led her into the farm kitchen, his clogs ringing on the blue slate floor.

Most of the narrow space in the room was filled with a huge table, but this one wasn't scrubbed to a bleached whiteness as the one at Broombank was. Instead it was covered with a check cloth spotted with brown sauce and egg yolk. Dirty plates and mugs stood among chips of plaster which had obviously fallen from the ceiling. Beth didn't dare glance up to check how safe it was. She was too appalled by the sight of a rather grim old man, broad faced with a hook nose, shaggy eyebrows and several days' stubble on his chin. He looked every bit as unkempt as his surroundings.

He sat in a chair by a huge kitchen range which showed more red rust than black lead, the cracked hearth was filled with used mugs and a large brown tea pot. The huge range itself held an oven and a boiler, and in the centre a small fire grate where a few pieces of coal burned fitfully. A long mantleshelf ran the length of the room, cluttered with unwashed cups, spills for lighting the fire and tins marked tea, Swan soap or Best Ginger Biscuits and, as Seth was to tell her later, 'owt what coom's in handy like.'

'Hey oop, 'oo hev we here?' He gave a toothless grin and the creases in his face seemed to lift and slacken, taking years off his age. He set down his pipe to lean forward on the creaking rush seat for a better look at her. 'Thoo's a nice little lass.' One hand, hard as horn, grasped Beth's and she found herself pulled towards him. He wore grey trousers stiff with dirt and held up with string, and to her horror, gaping wide at unbuttoned flies to reveal none too clean underdrawers. She could feel her cheeks start to burn as she tried to regain her hand.

'Hello, Mr Barton?'

'Aye, that's me. Not quite as lish as I once were, but still in one piece,' and he cackled softly at himself. Beth gave a self-conscience little laugh.

'I'm sorry to disturb you like this, without any warning.' What a silly thing to say, she thought. As if he might have cleaned the place up and baked a cake if he'd known she was going to pay him a visit.

Andrew stepped forward and spoke in a loud, clear voice. 'This is one of the twins, Granddad. I told you about her.'

'Oh, aye? One o' Meg's girls?' His faded eyes twinkled with an unexpected merriness. 'I can see why you've fetched her, lad. She's gaily fair. I wouldn't mind an armful meself were it not for me arthritis.' Beth looked startled for a moment then burst into peals of laughter. She liked this old man, smelly or not.

Andrew grinned and reached for the kettle that sat on the fret-worked hob, whispering in an aside to Beth as he rinsed the pot and scalded the tea. 'You mustn't mind him. He still thinks he's seventeen instead of near eighty-seven.'

'Oh, I don't mind at all. How are you, Mr Barton? Keeping well, I hope.'

'I keep thrang. Only way to stay young.'

Laughing, Beth turned to Andrew for a translation.

He means he keeps busy. He carves handles for shepherd's crooks. Does some gey fine work.' Andrew pointed to a selection on the wall beside him. There were deer heads, foxes, and every conceivable variety of bird.

'Why, they're wonderful.' She was most impressed.

'And for your benefit,' Andrew explained, 'lish means active. He may not get about as he once did but he misses little, I can tell you. Isn't that right, Grandad?'

'Aye,' he said with satisfaction and started to pour tea from his cup into his saucer and suck it up noisily through pursed lips.

'Oh.' Beth smiled, accepted her own mug of tea and pulled her stool closer. She then proceeded to enjoy the most fascinating afternoon she'd ever had in her life. Half of what old Seth said was quite unintelligible to her ears, despite Andrew's frequent translations but the old man was nothing if not entertaining. He told her all about the war, the hired men they'd once employed, the POWs from the local camp, and the ploughing they'd had to do.

'On this thin ground, would thoo believe it? Kept hens too. Lovely eggs. Don't get 'em like that these days.'

'I've got some hens.'

He grinned at her. 'Well thoo can fetch me two or three dozen eggs a week then. We've none here now. Women's work, hens.'

Beth hid a smile. 'I can see you must have enough to do without worrying about hens.' She glanced significantly about the room, trying not to catch Andrew's eye.

He told her how his mother used to clean these very slates on her hands and knees with a scrubbing brush and a tin of soft soap, and how ten bairns all slept in one small back room.

'And she did all the washing by hand, tha knows. I had to wind the handle on t'mangle for her. Do you mind what a mangle is?'

Eyes brimming with laughter, Beth confessed she did not.

'Nay, they teach 'em nowt in schools these days.'

'Did you go to the school in the dale, Mr Barton?'

'Aye, when me dad could spare me from the farm work. I niver 'ad much education though, so I've had to make do wi' me brains instead.'

Beth chuckled, bringing a smile to the crinkled face. 'Then if I want to know anything, I'll ask you.'

'Aye,' he said, gripping her hand very fiercely, 'You do that.'

Later, as Andrew showed off his small herd of Galloway cattle he apologised again for his grandfather. 'He lives in the past naturally, since there's not much future left to look forward to. Mind, it doesn't stop him bossing us about and keeping us on our toes.'

'I can imagine.'

She listened with interest as Andrew spoke with pride about his young steers, watching how his face came alive as he talked, and realising that he wasn't dull at all, not if you paid attention.

'They do well on very little, which is what you need up here, and they don't mind the cold or the wet because as we say in these parts, they have a top coat and a waistcoat. The long outer hairs shed the rain well while the thick pelt beneath keeps the beast warm. You can't beet 'em on these hills.'

'I want to hug one, they look so delightfully hairy.'

Andrew laughed. 'I wouldn't recommend it. Wild they are,' he said.

'Not soft like dairy cows. Nearest thing you'll get to an untamed animal on a farm these days. Proper young rebels. If you see a wee Galloway calf out on the fells, niver touch it. It's mam'll have summat to say on the matter.' He spoke with such affection and warmth that Beth found herself laughing with him.

'You like them better than the sheep?'

'I wouldn't say that, but I'd like to keep more, specialise a bit. Do a bit of cross breeding with Shorthorns. There's money to be made there.'

'I don't think we'll try beef cattle,' she said, very solemnly.

When he smiled, his grey eyes twinkled delightfully, lighting his face into boyish delight.

'No, I reckon they'd prove a bit of a handful for your lot.' And they laughed together as if it were a great joke.

In the cow byre he introduced her to a couple of friesian house cows who provided the farm with milk. Beth scratched one at the root of her horn while rubbing the other's chest. The animals shifted closer.

'They'd stand and let you do that all day,' Andrew chuckled. 'Right pair of softies they are.'

He talked for a long time, telling Beth all she would need to know, demonstrating how to milk them. With his hard hands on hers, he showed her how to pull on the teats and get a good froth of milk in the bucket.

'Cleanliness is everything, of course,' he explained. 'You don't want no infections.' And he painstakingly went through his morning drill while Beth listened and watched with close attention, trying not to feel overwhelmed by the list of tasks.

'It's a matter of practice, I suppose. I dare say I'd soon get used to it.'

He studied her carefully. 'What about the others? How do they feel about the idea? Would they help? You can't look after a cow all by yourself. I've watched them lot, they let you do far too much already.'

'I'd have to ask them.' Wishing one of them could be as capable and practical as Andrew.

'And one cow wouldn't keep you in milk all year. You'd need a couple for that, at least.'

'I think one would have to be enough, to begin with. And it's true

I don't yet have everyone's permission to buy even that.' She glanced shyly up at him. 'Would you come and tell them about it, as you've explained it to me. Tell them you'd find me a lovely quiet one. It might help.'

She had to tilt her head back to look pleadingly up at him and he seemed to be studying her face for a long while as he carefully considered his answer. Beth waited, knowing he was never one to hurry and besides, she was content to wait. The warmth of the byre, the lowing of the animals was oddly soothing, somehow making her feel languorous and safe, cocooned in a soft web as if nothing at all could harm her.

'I'll give it a try if you want me to,' he said finally.

'Great. And I'm sure Pietro would help me. He's very kind,' and he stepped away from her, breaking the spell.

By the time Andrew had finished telling the others all about cows even Jonty was calling him a wet blanket.

'Come on, they can't be all that difficult. You're saying cows are beyond we mere townies, is that it?'

'They're hard work and a tie, not to mention being a live animal that has to be tekken proper care of.'

'And you of course know all about them.' Jonty's harsh tone was condescending.

'Aye, as a matter of fact I do.'

'And we couldn't learn?'

'I wouldn't know. It's not for me to say.'

Beth inwardly groaned. This wasn't at all how she had meant it to go. Andrew was supposed to give them the facts and help her enthuse them. This was merely putting their backs up.

Jonty, and even Pietro were merciless in their teasing whenever Andrew called. She couldn't understand why they seemed to derive so much pleasure from it. Admittedly he was very different from them. They were city bred and fashionable. Andrew's clothes looked as if they'd been passed on from father to son, and smelt strongly of cows and animal feed. On his large feet were a pair of clogs, no doubt excellent for keeping out the wet but hardly appropriate for an afternoon visit. And his plain country face was more gaunt and weathered than sculptured and beautiful. His fair hair flopped across his broad forehead, instead of springing back in tight black curls.

But he'd been kind and informative, had helped to save the badger, and if sometimes his dogged patience and pride irritated her, she really should be grateful to him. She was sure he only put up with this sort of plaguing because of Tessa. Today though, must be entirely her own fault. She had asked him to come and he was suffering because of that request. She should have known better and it was really up to her to protect him.

'Let's change the subject shall we?' she tried, but the others were beyond listening. Were all young men so combative?

'You might know about the cows and the stupid sheep but what do you know about music, books, politics, art?' Pietro was asking, his face a mask of polite enquiry.

Andrew took his time answering. He stood, hands clenched, fidgeting with unease. When he did speak, his voice was low and rough. 'Nowt.'

'What did you say?'

'*Nowt.* I know nowt aboot art or politics, except how it applies to farming. Nowt aboot music and books. But I do knoaw about cows.' The accent had thickened, as it always did when he was distressed.

'And cows are far more important,' Jonty jeered.

'They are to me. And they're not to be tekken on lightly.'

'Ah. The know-it-all peasant farmer has spoken. There shalt be no cow at Larkrigg Hall because the commune idiots couldn't cope with one.'

The fists clenched tighter, tensing his whole body. 'I'm nae a peasant farmer. My family hes farmed Cathra Crag for generations.'

'And nae doot one day it'll all be yours,' Jonty continued, mocking his accent.

Hot colour fired the round cheeks. 'Mebbe. Mebbe not. I doan't know.'

'Ooh dear, not trouble at t'farm, eh?' He put back his head and laughed, loud and harsh and Pietro and Sarah joined in. For all his awkwardness and sad appearance, Beth's heart went out to him. 'Stop it,' she said. 'Stop it, stop it. That's enough.' Then in a gentler tone, 'Thank you for your advice, Andrew. We'll give it our most careful consideration.'

His eyes upon hers were hurt and angry. 'Aye, weel, it's thy decision, not mine.'

Beth turned to Jonty, shame filling every part of her. 'I think an apology is called for, don't you? Andrew was only doing what we had asked, to give us the facts about a matter we know nothing about.'

Jonty met her challenging gaze and held it with an insolent lift to his brow. Or you'll do what? it seemed to say. A threat which Beth struggled not to heed. She hated bullying of any kind and had no intention of standing by and saying nothing while this quiet young farmer was made to look a fool.

She turned briskly to Andrew. 'By way of recompense you shall stay to supper,' and hearing stifled groans from her companions, offered her most warming smile. She was rewarded with a brightening of his expression and instinctively put out a hand to touch his. 'We're having a lovely broth tonight. And we could open a bottle of wine to cheer us all up.' She hoped he wouldn't notice that Jonty had not done as she'd asked and offered any sort of apology.

The evening began with a limited success. The food at least was delicious and Tessa made some garlic bread to go with the broth which Beth had prepared. Sarah opened some wine and they all dressed up in their brightest long skirts and danced to Stevie Wonder and Fleetwood Mac.

But Andrew studiously made no further effort to take part in the conversations which centred mainly on fashion and books, when *Star Wars* might come to the local cinema and whether the latest craze for skateboarding would last.

Only once, when Tessa made an idle remark about the increasing number of visitors who came to the Lake District did he for a moment, become quite animated.

'Aye, and they're all daft enough to leave every gate open, drop litter for t'cows to choke on and go up t'same hills and wear away the footpaths. You'd think they'd have sense to spread out a bit, wouldn't you?'

Everyone looked at him in startled silence, astonished by his unexpected outburst.

'I think they go up the most famous hills,' Beth gently pointed out. 'You can see their point. They want to prove they can do it, and of course enjoy the view.'

Pietro and Jonty spluttered with laughter and Andrew cast them a fierce glare. It was so sad, Beth thought, to see the contrast between them.

'Aye, and they let their dogs run out of control. Proper nuisance they are.'

'Farmers do nothing to spoil the countryside, I suppose?' Sarah sweetly enquired, while lifting one perfect brow.

'We make the countryside what it is. Our sheep keep the grass short and stop the bracken encroaching. It'd be a wilderness without us to tend it.'

Jonty gave out a loud crack of laughter as he opened another can of beer. 'What about your friend, old Ellen and her junk yard? She's a local and doesn't do the countryside any favours with her mess, does she?'

'She does no harm to it, and makes contributions in other ways.'

'Like saving old badgers that'd be better off dead?'

Andrew's jaw tightened. 'Aye, summat of the sort. At least she protects what rightly belongs here.'

'You mean we don't.'

'Not for me to say.'

'Farmers have only themselves to blame for the tourists,' Pietro put in. 'They do the bed and breakfast, have the caravans on their farms. They are as greedy as everyone else, I think.'

Andrew appeared enraged by this attack. 'We have to do summat to add to our income, don't we? There's a limit to the improvements you can make on a hill farm. Geography, climate, the land itself puts limits on you. You've more choices, happen, in arable farming. Here, there's only so much you can get out of a Swaledale ewe. Bad weather at the wrong time and your lambing season is ruined and so is your income for the year. And farmers have their livings to make, same as everyone else.'

Jonty gave an exaggerated yawn. 'We seem to be managing very well without,' and all three of them collapsed into gales of laughter while Andrew's face suffused in red from his neck to the roots of his hair.

Beth put up a hand. She'd been quite impressed by the strength of his argument and his ability to put it so effectively. She'd learned a good deal about Andrew today, most of it surprisingly likeable, and she felt again the shame of her friends' treatment of him. 'No more arguments. Not tonight. Let's just have fun, shall we?'

Gradually the giggles subsided, more beer was opened, wine glasses were refilled and a silence sank upon them all. After a moment, Sarah said, 'So what do we do then? We can't talk about music or films as Andrew knows nothing about either, nor dare we discuss the apparently controversial subject of the countryside or tourists as he gets upset, so what do we do?'

'Play monopoly?' Tessa suggested with a grin.

It was then that Jonty made his most outrageous suggestion yet. Perhaps it was the excessive amount of wine they'd drunk which accounted for it but he suddenly got up and came over to sit by Beth on the small sofa. 'I enjoy games and you said we should have fun, so why not a game of the more adult variety? Why don't we do a bit of partner swopping? That'd be good for a giggle, eh?'

'What?' Sarah sat up straight in her seat, all amused calm gone, bristling defensively. 'What are you talking about?'

His arm had somehow crept around Beth's waist and he was pulling her against him. 'You are so beautiful,' he said in mock dramatic tones. 'How about it?'

He winked outrageously at her, making her giggle though half aware of a frozen expression on Pietro's face. 'Don't be silly. We don't even have partners,' and at once realised what a dangerous defence that was.

'We can soon solve that,' he said, nuzzling into her warm throat. 'Fight a duel or something,' and she couldn't help but laugh more than ever.

'We could draw lots,' she suggested, playing along with his wicked teasing as she revelled in the burning jealousy in Pietro's eyes.

'I know.' He wagged a wobbly finger. 'Tessa can have Pietro. See how she gets on with him and Sarah can have Andrew. That should liven the peasant farmer up a bit.'

Andrew got to his feet, ears pink and almost seeming to stand out from the side of his head, hands clenching and unclenching by his side as he struggled to contain himself. 'I've told you before, I'm no peasant farmer, and you shouldn't talk about women in that cheap way.'

'Joke, joke,' Jonty said, airily waving a hand. 'Calm down, Sir Galahad.'

Andrew drew in a deep breath. 'Happen Tessa'd rather have Pietro. Beth can come wi' me. I'll see she's kept safe if you lot want to play that sort o' daft lark.'

'Heavens, Beth, you've found a protector.' Sarah chortled with glee and fell back into the arm chair, legs waving in an apoplexy of delight while Beth simply stared at Andrew, astonished.

Jonty took this momentary lack of attention on her part to nestle Beth closer. 'She doesn't need nursemaiding, do you love? I'll take good care of you. And Sarah can give you just the education you need, farmer boy.'

Pietro was by this time glowering quite furiously at them, and something inside of Beth sang with joy to see it. Could he fancy her after all? Tension crackled in the room, the joke threatening to turn ugly. Trouble was the last thing she wanted.

'Don't I get a say?' Tessa protested. 'I'm not against a bit of fun but I'll make my own choices, thanks very much, if a choice there is to be,' and cast Andrew such a fierce warning glance that Beth thought he should rightly have been burned to a crisp. Poor Tessa. How dreadful to feel so neglected and jealous.

'Let's stop this now,' she said, managing at last to prise herself free of Jonty's several hands and sit on the arm of the sofa. 'Andrew's right, this joke has gone far enough.'

Then suddenly Sarah went over and plonked herself on Pietro's knee. 'Personally, I'm all for it. Why not? Only I'll have Pietro.' Eyes glittering with anger, furious that Jonty should embarrass and betray her in this way, Sarah meant to show him that she too could play games. Scarlet lips curved into a sensual smile as she stroked his smooth cheek with a lingering fingertip, then lowering her mouth she kissed him, with a smooth sensuality that held everyone in thrall.

Beth saw him jerk as if with shock and her heart sank with misery. So now he had Sarah, as he had no doubt wanted all along.

He didn't move again but the kiss seemed to go on for ever and Beth could do nothing but helplessly watch. Swamped by hot humiliation, she wanted, in that moment, to curl up and die. How could Sarah do this to her? How *dare* she? Was she entirely blind? Hadn't she even noticed how she felt about him? Then she heard Jonty's soft voice in her ear, 'Take no notice, love.' Then out loud, 'We could toss a coin,' as if it were all of no consequence. 'How about that?'

'No thanks,' Sarah said.

'Pietro?'

Pietro was still otherwise engaged.

It was Andrew again who settled the matter. 'Let Beth decide.'

Jonty grinned. 'OK, why not? Go on, Beth sweetheart. You choose. Who do you fancy? The clod-hopping country yokel, beautiful but fickle Pietro or myself, all male and satisfaction guaranteed.'

Beth could hear Tessa start to giggle and she couldn't help but laugh too. Jonty could really be very funny. 'I think I'd need notice of that question,' she quipped, eyes brimming.

'Pity.' Dark eyes teased. 'I can't persuade you to choose me then?'

She shook her head and Jonty put one hand to his heart in exaggerated self-pity. 'I've been spurned as a lover. How will I survive?'

A spurt of laughter bubbled up in her throat.

'Stop it, Jonty. You're incorrigible.'

'Incorrigible?' he shouted. 'What a wonderful word. What does it mean? Does it mean this?' Then before she had time to anticipate his move, he'd snatched her from the arm of the sofa and pulled her into his lap, kissing her long and hard. Seconds later she emerged flushed and flustered with embarrassment while he called for more, more. But no one else seemed in the least amused.

'Leave Beth alone.' It was Andrew who spoke but Pietro who moved first. With Sarah still in his arms he strode over to the sofa and dropped her unceremoniously upon Jonty's lap. 'You stick with this one, OK? You want her, you got her. I will make my own choices from now on.' Jonty suddenly glared up at Pietro and the air became charged with unspoken emotion while Sarah slid to the floor in an undignified heap of squealing fury.

Then Pietro put his arm protectively about Beth and she willingly leaned against his shoulder, looking up at him with eyes swimming with gratitude. And as she did so, she did not notice the flicker of pain which passed across Andrew's face.

'Come on,' Tessa said, tugging at Andrew's arm. 'Let's disappear. We're not wanted here. Let them sort it out between them.'

Beth didn't even see them go.

Then Jonty got up and walked to the door where he turned and winked at Beth, then glanced challengingly back at Pietro. 'Take care of her now.' And to Sarah, still sprawled on the carpet, he said, 'Are you coming or not?' And she dusted her hands, pushed back her hair and followed him quietly out of the room.

Pietro remained motionless as he watched them go, Beth, gratitude for Jonty's cavalier assistance bright in her eyes, lay content in the warm circle of his arms. She could feel the beat of his heart and loved him in that moment, more than she could have ever imagined.

10

She sat on the edge of the sofa, her hands clasped in her lap and gazed at him. He was so beautiful and she longed for him to love her so much that she could hardly take in what was happening. Was he disappointed that he hadn't got Sarah? Did he really like her? Did he want to talk or have sex? And how did she feel about that? How should she handle it? Would he mind that she had no experience and was still a virgin, that she was unused to the kind of grown-up games Sarah took for granted?

'More wine, or a beer?' he asked, holding up her glass, and she shook her head.

Beth dropped her gaze, not watching as he went to refill his own, feeling suddenly very young and awkward, and oddly reluctant to take this any further. Where were Tessa and Andrew? Were they in another room? Were they making love? The thought somehow made her feel uncomfortable but then they were meant for each other, weren't they? And Tess had been married before, had the kind of attitude to life which Beth could only envy.

In her mind she saw herself lounging back enticingly upon the sofa cushions, beckoning the beautiful Pietro to come to her with a bewitching smile. He would tremble as he took her in his arms and place his soft lips to hers. He would breathe words of love in her ear and she would cradle him against her breast. Then he would gently peel away each layer of her clothing, kissing every part of her and she would give herself to him with joy and he would tell her she was the only woman he had ever loved, ever could love.

In reality she sat with her knees jammed together and felt more tongue-tied and shy than ever in her life before. And very slightly afraid. How very shaming and degrading this all was. Not in the least bit romantic. What was she doing wrong?

Should she tell him right away that she wasn't on the pill, she worried? Or would that make him laugh, think her even more stupid and naive?

'You look most uncomfortable sitting there,' he said. 'Why don't you have another drink?'

'No thanks, I think I've had enough.'

'Never enough.'

'You'll have to tell me what you want me to do.'

'Don't you know?'

She shook her head, smitten into silence by her longing for him.

'What makes you think I do?'

She smiled at that. 'You're a man.'

'Yes,' he said thoughtfully, his heavenly blue eyes on hers. 'I am, aren't I? And you do not quite know why you are here, playing this stupid game?'

'Oh, no, I really don't mind.' She could have kicked herself. How juvenile that sounded, as if she were a schoolgirl who'd been told to report for some special duty. She couldn't help but smile. 'I'm sorry. I'm not very experienced at this sort of thing.'

He came and sat beside her on the sofa, pulling her towards him. There was an awkward moment as somehow her nose bumped against his and she gave a nervous giggle. 'Why don't you leave it to me?' he said. 'Let me make the decisions.'

'Oh, yes, of course.' Beth thought she might die of happiness. Wasn't this what she had longed for?

He pushed her back against the sofa cushions and putting his mouth to hers, started to kiss her. His lips were not soft as she had imagined but hard and rather moist and surprisingly cool. She'd been kissed before of course, by young men at the school dances but this seemed different somehow, as if it were merely a ritual, a prelude for what followed after. His tongue had invaded her mouth and she wondered what she ought to do with her own which seemed dreadfully in the way. She could taste the red wine he'd drunk which wasn't unpleasant, because in a way it made her feel drunk too.

126

Then his fingers began to methodically unbutton her shirt and her heart gave a little flip of alarm. So soon? He slipped one hand inside and as he grasped her warm breast Beth gave a tiny squeal. She hadn't at all been prepared for the pain of it as his hand massaged the soft flesh. He smelled of garlic and seemed to be breathing very hard but she really didn't mind, she wanted only to do everything right and not to put him off. She risked putting one hand to the nape of his neck and began to caress his hair.

'Don't be shy,' he murmured and began to nuzzle below her earlobe but somehow missed and kissed her shoulder instead. 'Drat, a bit too much wine. Sorry.'

She was almost relieved. Perhaps he wouldn't be able to manage it after all. Sarah said men couldn't perform properly when they were in their cups. She giggled as a wave of mild hysteria hit her at the quaint phrase which had come to mind. Then his mouth closed over hers again and she forgot everything but the dark need growing in the pit of her stomach. His hands were at her waist, pulling her beneath him. What would happen next? Would he manage to take off all her clothes, drunk as he was, or should she do it for him?

'Pietro?'

He didn't answer, seeming to be concentrating hard on her bra strap.

'I'll do it,' she said helpfully and yanking at the hook and eye, slid out of it. Her breasts felt suddenly wonderfully free, exciting her as they seemed to fall into his hands. But ignoring their ripe plumpness he reached instead for the hem of her skirt and slid his palms along the length of her thigh.

Dear God, she thought, starting to panic, when would he ask her about precautions? When were these things usually sorted out? Should she ask him if he'd brought something or would that sound too much like an invitation? Oh, dear lord, why hadn't she listened more carefully when her sister had talked about lovemaking?

His breathing was a rasping sound in her ear, his hand now fumbling with her panties.

Was she expected to take those off too? And what if she did? His fingers made the issue irrevelant and she gasped, startled by the sensations he was creating in her even as she blushed at her own daring. Now his mouth was at her breast, swearing softly as he sought the nipple. He was pushing his body on top of hers and something hard throbbed against her thigh.

And in all this fumbling he had not spoken one word to her. Did he think her pathetic?

Oh, dear God, she must say something, this couldn't go on. Yet all she longed to do was to close her eyes and not think at all, only experience the strength of his love. Beth was quite certain that Sarah would never have found herself in such a predicament. How stupid to want to be as reckless and sexy as her sister without using the same common sense beforehand.

He wasn't even kissing her now, hardly seemed aware of her at all as he struggled with the zip on his jeans. She could scarcely focus on anything but these new, intoxicating sensations that robbed her of will, and the growing needs of her own body like a raging thirst within. She could feel herself slipping beyond reason and common sense, no longer caring what he did, so long as he quenched that thirst. She was gasping for breath now, crying out his name. Tell him soon. Now!

He slid his hands beneath her bottom and pulled her to him.

'I'm not on the pill.' The words came out too loud, almost as a shout.

'What?' He jerked, his knee knocking against her shin, bringing a sting of tears to her eyes. 'What did you say?'

'It doesn't matter. I – I shouldn't have spoken. I want you to go on – I really do. I love you so much, Pietro.'

His whole body seemed to freeze. 'You are the virgin?'

She almost giggled then, but it was no more than hysteria. 'Yes, I suppose I am.'

He said something indistinguishable in Italian, then he was pulling away from her, trying to get his jeans back over a painfully swollen portion of his anatomy and Beth didn't know whether to laugh or cry, or wish herself quietly to die of shame there and then. He banged out of the room and she lay as if in paralysis while tears spurted from the corner of each eye and ran down her cheeks into the ear he hadn't quite kissed.

Sarah lay in bed still, showing no inclination to rise, for all it was past eleven. Beth shook her awake and told her they were wanted at the mill.

'Drat the woman. Why can't she leave us alone?' She sat up, hair a tangle about her head, eyes blinking in the bright sunshine as Beth flung back the curtains. 'Where's Jonty?'

'Probably up long since.'

A suspicious glint came into her eyes. 'He never gets up early. Where's Tessa? Have you seen her this morning?' Before Beth could reply, Sarah was out of bed and storming across the room clad only in her sleeping shirt. She ran out on to the landing and flung open the next bedroom door. A surprised figure sat up in bed.

'Has Jonty been here?'

'What?'

'Don't play the innnocent with me. He has, hasn't he?' Sarah glared ferociously as Tessa smilingly picked up the grizzling infant from his crib and pulling aside her nightdress, set him to her breast. At once the sound of greedy sucking filled the room. 'Go and get dressed, Sarah. You look as if you've had a hard night.'

What a tangle of emotions, Beth thought, as they bounced along in Meg's old van. They were starting on the long journey to Keswick to deliver woollens, Jan having laid the law down fairly fiercely this time.

But first they had to drive down the long lane that wound through the dale, passing limewashed farmhouses with squat chimneys, drystone walls padded with moss and verges thick with parsley, spleenwort, and the mountain fern that grew so vigorously in this damp region.

It would be funny, Beth decided, were it not so very serious. Sarah jealous because she imagined Tessa fancied Jonty, when really she was pining for Andrew. And apart from a burst of valiant protectiveness, Andrew hadn't seemed too interested in anyone, apparently going home early last night, saying he must get up at five for milking.

Then there was Jonty making a play for herself, and Sarah resentful and sulking. And having torn into Pietro this morning, he'd gone off whistling with blithe unconcern as was his wont, completely uncaring that his 'game' seemed to have caused so much upset.

But Beth only wanted Pietro, and having miraculously got him, making a complete mess of her chances. And who did Pietro want? Herself or Sarah? She sighed. What a muddle.

As if reading her mind Sarah said, 'There was hardly any necessity

129

for you to throw up your hands in virginal horror last night. Jonty didn't really want you. He was only saying it for fun, and to annoy me. He likes to play games with people.'

Beth felt herself cringe, crashing the gear stick to change down as they approached the school. 'You mean no man would wish to make love to me? I believe you told me so before, several times.' Oh, give me just a little of your confidence, she thought. Let me not see myself as the complete idiot you see.

Sarah cast her a sidelong glance from beneath long lashes. 'Did anything happen between you and Pietro?' And when she saw the flush creep up under her skin, she laughed. 'As I thought. You messed it up, didn't you? Played the virgin. Am I right?' And shaking her head at her sister's stricken expression, laughed again. 'I know you too well.'

Beth was spared from answering this cruel taunt as a figure stepped out from behind the old stone schoolhouse and flagged them down. 'That's Andrew. What does he want?'

She drew the van to a halt and leaned out of the window. 'Hello. Problems?'

Andrew glanced from one sister to the other and Beth could hear his clogs shuffling about on the rough stones. 'I heard the van coming along the track so I thought I'd – well – have a word. I wondered how it went last night.'

'How it went?'

He knew he shouldn't be saying any of this but couldn't quite stop himself. The thought of Beth in Jonty Reynold's arms was more than he could bear. He had to know what happened. 'I tried to save you from him, you see.'

'Save me?' She couldn't quite believe what she was hearing.

'Aye, from that daft game.'

'I can look after myself, thank you very much.'

'I'm not so sure.'

She heard Sarah almost choke on a giggle and Beth too tried to laugh. 'What is this, an interrogation?'

He looked hurt and she felt a wave of panic. Surely he wasn't falling for her? Oh, but that would be too dreadful. Didn't they have tangles enough? It was Tessa he was supposed to fancy. 'I really don't think . . .'

'Jonty Reynolds was making a real nuisance of hissel. It were a daft idea anyroad.'

'It was only meant in fun,' she said more coolly, feeling she should make an effort to discourage him from the outset.

Andrew flushed. 'Too much drink, and too cocksure of hissel that one. He needs bringing down a peg or two.'

Beth rather agreed but didn't consider this quite the moment to say so. Andrew would only read more into it than she meant. 'He has a flippant sense of humour, that's all.'

'Why are you defending him?'

'I'm not.'

Again she heard Sarah's stifled snort.

'Did someone have the sense to stop him before proper hurt was done? That's what I want to know.' Andrew was glaring at her now as if she were in some way to blame and Beth felt an unexpected spurt of anger. Was he suggesting she was wrong to sleep with Pietro? What absolute cheek! Not that she had slept with him, strictly speaking, for nothing had happened. It had been a complete failure. Or was he suggesting she'd slept with Jonty Reynolds? Dear God, his opinion of her must be pretty low.

But she had no intention of letting Andrew Barton know anything of her business. She certainly wouldn't give him the safisfaction of being able to say it served her jolly well right.

'As a matter of fact we had great fun. I hear *you* went home early.'

She saw his face change colour, go oddly white then deep red, right to the tips of his ears. 'I had t'milking to do.'

'Of course. As you said, cows are so tying.'

She heard Sarah's stifled hiccup, threatening to choke her, and for a moment felt a twinge of shame. There was no really need for her to be unkind to Andrew, for all his clumsy interference. Nor should he try to interfere. Beth revved impatiently on the accelerator, then spoke in her sweetest, but nonetheless most cutting voice. 'Thank you for your enquiry but I'm fine, thank you very much, and I really don't think it's any of your concern. OK?'

As she put the little van into first gear and drove off, wheels sending up a cloud of dust she could see him in the wing mirror, still standing in the middle of the lane. And with Sarah's laughter ringing in her ears, rich and throaty, it all added up to a very real sense of guilt.

* * *

Meg was seated by the empty grate when they arrived back at the mill, banging doors and shattering the silence with their stifled giggles and chatter. They took off their coats and dropped their voices to a few whispered words.

Their grandmother seemed strangely still and inactive, half aware of their concerned glances but yet in a world apart. It had not been a good day for Meg. The tractor had refused to start, some ewes which had taken them all of yesterday to count and contain in the intake land had escaped through a gate left open by some unthinking walker. She felt exhausted, and tomorrow they'd have to start collecting them up all over again.

Then she and Jan had gone through the order book, looking in fact quite healthy, which should have made her feel better. Only it couldn't replace what they'd lost and the effort to do so filled her with weariness.

Having the twins here had helped, but she couldn't expect them to stay for ever. For the first time in Meg's life the silence of the fells filled her with depression.

Beth made a pot of strong tea and slid a mug of it into her grandmother's cold hands. 'We've done the deliveries. Are you all right?'

Meg smiled her thanks and took a grateful sip. Then the words burst from her, the idea still only half formed in her mind, unprepared.

'Tam says I need a holiday. I can't remember the last time we had one. Or if indeed I ever have. Farmers, as a rule, don't take holidays. But what with all the business worries lately . . .' She stopped for a moment before continuing, 'I feel strangely worn out. Probably my age or something but Tam thinks a break would do me good.' She smiled weakly and Beth went and sat on the arm of her grandmother's chair and held her hand.

'I think that's an excellent idea. Where would you go?'

'To America? Where else? We nearly went once, Tam and I. Got passports and everything.'

Beth gasped, then laughed with delight. 'But that would be wonderful.'

Meg nodded, grey eyes starting to smile. 'I think it would be wonderful too. Perhaps I'm not too old for dreams, after all. As I told you, I've always held a longing to go, to see my darling Lissa again, and Derry and the boys of course.'

'You don't want to waste your time over those two scamps,' Sarah teased, referring to her young brothers.

'Mom would love to see you.' Beth spoke with enthusiasm. 'But I thought you were worried about who would look after the sheep and the farm?'

'Nick has said he would. But it'd put more work on Jan of course, helping him, which would leave Broombank Woollens almost entirely in your hands. Sam, the foreman would take the brunt of the work, but you'd have to do much more than you do now. Is it too much to ask?'

'No,' Beth said firmly, before Sarah could reply. 'It isn't at all. Broombank Woollens will be safe in our hands.'

'Of course it will,' Sarah agreed. 'Why shouldn't it be?'

Meg's stomach fluttered with excitement at the prospect of their trip and she could already sense the pressures of everyday life slipping from her as they sank back in their seats and felt the thrust of the engines.

'Isn't this grand?' she whispered and Tam clasped her hand tight in his.

'A second honeymoon, to be sure.'

Meg gave a low, throaty laugh. 'Wicked man.' But she was not displeased. She couldn't wait to see Lissa again and chat away with her, as they had once loved to do. She couldn't wait to see the two young boys who she hadn't seen since they were bairns.

Broombank was safe in Nick and Jan's hands, ably assisted by young Bobbie who had already set his sights on farming. And Alice and the two younger ones, of course, who never liked to be left out of anything.

As for the mill, well, it would do those two girls good to take on a bit more responsibility. Keep their minds off that Pietro Lawson maybe.

Tam said she was prejudiced against him and he was probably right. Lissa trusted her two daughters so why shouldn't she? They'd be fine. What could go wrong in a few weeks? And she gazed out upon the wind-tossed clouds in a blur of contentment.

* * *

Several days later Beth cornered Pietro in the kitchen, desperate to set their relationship on a more secure footing.

Outside the rain lashed against the windows and the wind rattled the shutters like a mad thing trying to gain entrance. Summer was a distant memory and the mild days of autumn were passing too. While some leaves still hung on the trees, tenaciously clinging to life, most lay in sodden heaps throughout Brockbarrow Wood, like heaps of bright jewels.

Soon it would be winter and too cold to go upstairs and sleep in the bedrooms, certainly in the ones where the roof leaked. What they would do then, Beth couldn't imagine. Even now, in the places where the roof was at its worst and chunks of plaster hung free it was almost as wet inside as out. Water seeped in and dripped off the lathes into the many bowls and buckets they'd set about the landings and bedroom floors. Even on the so-called dry parts, mould decorated the ceiling, spreading like evil black lace over the cornices and plasterwork.

The money in their building society account was growing worryingly low. She couldn't think how it had been spent quite so quickly but there always seemed to be something they needed. And it would take thousands to mend the roof. She'd had two quotes and both were too frightening to contemplate.

But here in the kitchen, lit only by the light of a lamp it felt cosy and warm. If only Pietro would forgive her for spoiling everything the other night and say that he loved her she would be the happiest girl alive, and leaking roofs wouldn't matter a jot.

'Have you forgiven me?' she asked, in a voice fearful and nervous of rejection. 'We were interrupted the other day and never finished our conversation. I know I'm not like Sarah. I do wish I could be more like her, instead of all conventional and shy and hopeless.' She couldn't meet his eyes, kept her own firmly fixed on the envelopes she was addressing for the mill. She'd asked him to help her, it being the only way she could devise for them to be alone.

She slid a catalogue into another envelope, damped it with a sponge, pressed down the flap and dropped it into the box set for the purpose while waiting for his reply. It was a long time in coming.

'I do not blame you, little one. It was unfortunate that it ended as it did between us, but the game was a foolish one. We should not have played it.'

Or he should have taken Sarah up on her offer, he thought, which might have proved even more entertaining. His emotions that night, however, had quite startled him. That he'd been ready and able to sleep with Beth without any difficulty whatsoever, for all the fierceness of his jealousy had quite startled him. Yet how could he toss it aside, like an unwanted bottle of sour wine? Perhaps he thought that taking her would somehow eradicate it. Scowling a little, he thrust a catalogue into an envelope. Some people were not sincere. They liked to tease and plague a man.

'I should have mentioned my problem right away,' Beth was saying, aware that anxiety made her voice sound high pitched and wobbly.

Pietro smiled abstractedly at her, not quite listening. 'I should have thought to ask. Always set out the rules first in any game.' His lips curled into a half smile. 'But my mind was on other things.' He reached out and touched her hand, not wishing, at this juncture, to have her guess exactly where his mind had been. It was good that she liked him, and that she believed he felt the same about her. Wasn't that the whole reason for his being here? She was not so attractive as Sarah, this small girl, nor so captivating in other ways but neither was she half so plain as she imagined. One day, when she lost the puppy fat, as she was already beginning to do, she might even be considered attractive. Though never as stylish as an Italian girl of course.

He had won her with a look, with a smile and his supreme Latin charm. Too easily in a way. But not so with her sister, which annoyed him. Perhaps he should take care not to risk losing Beth too. That could spoil all his plans.

'You must think I'm absolutely wet,' she was saying. 'So pathetic. Most girls are having sex like mad and I'm all hung up with complex inhibitions and anxieties. Aren't I stupid?'

In that moment she longed for him to take her in his arms and kiss her passionately, to tell her he was glad she'd kept herself specially for him, declare for ever his undying love.

'It is good for me that you do not so easily give yourself to a man,' he said and her face lit with such a radiance that it quite threw him off balance for a moment. 'I am glad.'

'Are you?'

'Of course. I think you very – very sweet and quite delightful.'

'You do?'

'I do.' And now he did kiss her, a soft kiss which was gratifyingly close to what she had hoped for. And if it didn't quite light with passion, that was only because of the proximity of the box of envelopes, Beth told herself, annoyingly getting in the way.

She felt dazed with love when he broke away. 'I'm going to get everything sorted out soon, so you won't have long to wait,' she promised and frowned. 'Though I'll have to see a doctor first, I suppose,' then flushed with fresh embarrassment as she saw the look of horror on his face, wishing she'd never broached this very personal subject.

'I would not presume to tell you what to do. That would not be right.'

'Oh, you are so lovely and kind to me.' Beth smiled softly at him, flattered by what she took to be his concern for her. 'But we can't go on like this. I need you so much, Pietro. And I know that you feel the same.'

'I do.' He only just stopped himself from lifting his voice into a question. 'Of course. Yes, of course I do. How could I not?'

'So there's really no need for us to wait, is there?' Beth could hardly believe she was saying all of this. What had come over her? But she desperately wanted to be like Sarah, free and fun-loving, the kind of girl who excited a man.

'If you say not,' he said kindly.

'Oh dear, I've never talked like this to a man before in my life. I'm not being too pushy, am I?'

'If you are, it is very sexy.'

'Really?' She was entranced. 'It isn't as if anyone will know, is it? I mean, with Gran and Tam gone. No adult lectures.' She pulled a wry face, meant to be amusing, nudging aside a small sense of guilty betrayal. She was an adult now, wasn't she?

She longed to feel that pulsing passion which true love was supposed to bring. To banish the awkwardness that had so ruined their first effort, and feel at last this man moving inside of her, as he was surely meant to be. 'I shall be able to enjoy it when I don't have to worry about, well, you know . . . accidents.' She flushed again.

'Poor little one. So confused. So many scruples.' He touched one hot cheek with his cool lips. 'You must know that I am very fond of you. You are special to me. I would not have you hurt. So, do not rush with this – this plan of yours. You are too sweet and giving.'

'Am I?' The ache in her breast grew so badly she could hardly bear it. A long pause as she gazed longingly into his eyes, blissfully unable to read the thoughts whirling through his mind.

'There is of course, another solution.'

Wide-eyed and trusting, she gazed at him still. 'What is that?'

'I do not know why I didn't think of it before. It is obvious. We should marry. That would be the very best solution for us all, would it not?'

She became very still. 'I beg your pardon?'

His voice strengthened as his thoughts clarified, surprisingly clearly in his head. 'I stopped the love-making not because I dislike the idea of a bambino by accident, you understand. But because when I have a fine son, like little James, I want for him to be born into a proper family. I wish to be married to his mother.'

'Oh.' All colour had drained from Beth's cheeks as she stared at him, stupefied. 'You don't mean it. Please don't say it if you don't mean it.'

'I do mean it.' Half an hour ago he would not have done. Now he saw clearly that this was the right move for him. A decision had been necessary and he had made it. It was really exceedingly wise of him.

Pietro took her hand to hold it in both his own, adopting the expression he thought most suitable for an ardent lover. He had seen a play once, back home in Florence, where the young hero had almost died for love. He must have looked something like this. 'I adore you, my little one. How can I pretend otherwise? I long to take you home and show you off to my family.'

Then she squealed with such delight everyone came running, and were astonished to find that Beth had swept all the envelopes on to the floor, her arms were tightly clasped about Pietro's neck and they were both laughing and dancing about like silly children.

11

'You have to be mad.' Sarah stared at her twin as if seeing her for the first time.

'I'm not at all mad. Don't be jealous, Sarah, be happy for me, please. Pietro loves me.'

'Has he told you so?'

Beth ignored the sudden stab of disquiet as she realised that he had not actually said as much. 'There are more profound ways than mere words,' she said, rather naively.

'Don't be a little fool.' Sarah had dragged her in to the small sitting room for a private, sisterly chat, which Beth correctly interpreted as Sarah doing her elder-sister-by-seven-minutes-bit. 'Listen to me. Just because a man takes you to his bed doesn't mean . . .'

'Please don't lecture me. Innocent I may be, but I'm not quite such an idiot. In any case, Pietro agrees I should remain a virgin until we are married.'

'*What*? You mean you still haven't . . . ?'

'No.'

'I don't believe it.'

'We're good friends. That is what is important,' and Sarah let her go with a sigh of exasperation.

'Have it your own way. But what about Meg? And Mom? How do you think they'll take this news? You hardly know him. It's much too soon to think of wedding bells. Look what happened the last time. I'd hate you to be hurt in that way again. Oh, I know we quarrel like cat and dog, but you're my sister, for Christ sake, I care about you.'

139

Beth had never heard Sarah sound quite so sincere. 'Thank you,' she said, and put her arms about her, hugging her close. 'It's kind of you to be so concerned but you needn't be.'

Sarah pushed her impatiently aside. 'I mean it. Live with him for a while. Sleep with him. Get to know him, but don't commit yourself. It's too soon.'

'Why so cynical? I was the one who was jilted.'

'Do you want that to happen again?'

'Pietro wouldn't do that. He's kind and sensitive. Unlike Jeremy, he's a man of honour.'

Sarah gritted her teeth. 'There's no such animal. No man is kind out of the generosity of his heart. Nor can he be entirely trusted. Think what you're doing here. I do care for you, Beth, and have no wish to see you hurt.'

'That's very sweet of you to say so.'

It also galled her to think her plain 'little' sister might marry before her, despite a dramatically declared intention to scorn marriage which she'd no intention of keeping. Of course she had Jonty, a flawed lover perhaps, but never less than exciting or entertaining. 'Look at Tessa, grasping for handouts, but can you blame her, stuck with a kid and no husband? You wouldn't want to end up like that, now would you?'

A new viewpoint which brought pause for thought. 'I – I suppose not.'

'You should never rush into marriage. Worst thing a woman can do.'

Beth began to see some sense in her sister's words and nibbled thoughtfully on her lower lip. 'But it wouldn't feel right simply to live with him.'

'For God's sake it's not the Dark Ages.' In Sarah's eyes it seemed incredible that Beth still had these scruples, not to mention her virginity. Losing both might bring her down to the realms of the rest of we poor mortals, she thought. So long as her precious conscience was salved. 'We could have a ceremony, if you like?'

'What?'

'Why not? A homemade one.'

Beth started to laugh. 'What good would that do?'

'It would make you feel better. Sort of dress rehearsal. And practice makes perfect, or so they say.' Then they were both laughing and hugging each other and making plans as Sarah so loved to do. 'But first, my lass, you must pay a visit to the good old doc.'

A new excitement seemed to light the commune over the next few days. Sarah took charge of the arrangements as she so loved to do. Everyone was delighted by the news, even if it was no more than a homemade celebration.

Only Pietro seemed less than enchanted by the idea.

'We'll have a real wedding one day, when Meg and Tam get back from the states,' Beth promised.

'You should write to your mamma now.'

'Not quite yet. Sarah's right. We have to get to know each other a bit better first.'

'But it will not be the same. I want for you to marry me properly, at once.'

'Pshaw. Marriage,' Jonty said, his hand idly stroking the dog as he lay on the rug at Pietro's feet. 'It's only a bit of paper. Paper won't keep a couple together if they're sick to death of each other. It won't pay the bills or bring up kids. It didn't keep my dad at home. It's what you two decide, what you promise each other, that's what's important.'

Beth looked at him in astonishment. 'That's true, Jonty. Absolutely. Thank you.'

'Don't mention it.' He grinned at her. Since he'd championed her over the doomed goat and helped make Pietro jealous, Beth had quite warmed towards him. Wild and wayward he may be but he still had a heart, evidently.

Pietro's displeasure subsided slightly, which was a relief. And though she was excited about the plans they were making, Beth couldn't help but feel guilty about keeping her 'wedding' secret from her family. She did mean to tell them, of course, and would write to Mom soon. But not quite yet. And she resolutely dismissed the matter from her mind.

Tessa found an old Edwardian dress in a chest and started to alter it to fit her. 'You'll be a beautiful bride.'

'Non-bride.'

Tessa chuckled. 'Whatever. You're doing the right thing. If I'd tested the waters a bit first I could have saved myself the cost of a divorce.' She mumbled through the pins held in her mouth while adjusting the dress to fit Beth's slim figure. 'They used to have "bidden weddings" in the Lakes in the old days.'

'What on earth was that?'

She took the last pin out and slid it into the folds of frayed silk. 'Where the bride used to ride on a horse to church and one person was appointed to call on friends and neighbours along the way, and bid everyone to attend. Then after the ceremony the bridegroom would throw pennies to the children, before they would unlatch the lych gate and let him free with his bride. You can still see the groom doing that to this day as he and his bride come out of church. Mine didn't have any change of course, daft fool, and we were stuck there for ages until someone found him some.' She rolled her eyes in despair. 'Typical. Anyway, in the old days everyone would race back to the reception, with prizes for the winners.'

Beth giggled. 'Sounds great fun but I can't ride and we haven't got a horse. And we aren't even going to church.'

'We can at least have a party, and maybe a race? And we could go and "bid" Andrew come. I'm sure he wouldn't want to be left out.'

Beth recalled their last meeting and how they had quarrelled, and felt an odd reluctance to confront him with the information that she was getting 'married' to Pietro, though why it should matter she couldn't imagine. He was apparently convinced it was Jonty she fancied, which amused her greatly for he had no right to object to anything she did. Worryingly he seemed to think that he had, which didn't auger well for his future with Tessa.

But Tessa was obviously very fond of him, which was why she wanted him there, and Beth felt it important that she find happiness too. Everyone must be happy, as she was. And little James needed a good father so the friendship should be encouraged.

'Of course we must invite him. How could we not? But I don't want any trouble with Jonty over it.'

Jonty, in fact, promised on his word of honour to be as good as gold. 'Well, tarnished brass perhaps,' he chuckled and Beth suddenly hugged him on a surge of emotion. Everything was going to be quite perfect.

'You're all right, Jonty.'
'You're not so bad yourself, princess.'

The air was crisp and dry as they bounded through bracken a foot high, taking a short cut over the hills to Cathra Crag, giggling and laughing like children let loose on a school outing. There was something about a clear autumn sky that made it seem more intense and wider than a summer sky so often fussed with cloud. The rich splendour of Brockbarrow Wood cresting the peak below them was a joy to behold with its rich aura of rust and gold, and Beth made a mental note to call and see Ellen soon. The coming of winter to Rowan cottage must be a bleak prospect indeed.

Beyond the bracken came the heather, a vast pallette of mauves, violets and purples and then they were running and skipping over turf cropped as short as a bowling green. A stoat ran out suddenly between their feet, startling them so they all stopped to roll on the ground with laughter, and afterwards to lie and catch their breath.

When they were rested they set off again at a more sedate pace.

Autumn leaves and fruits circled her hair, since they were all they could find, and she carried a bouquet of nasturtiums. But it didn't matter because the cream silk gown felt wonderful flowing against her legs for all it was moth-eaten and shabby, as if she were truly a bride. Beth tucked the warm shawl which Tessa had lent her close about her shoulders and glanced shyly at Pietro.

He walked by her side, vigorous and handsome in white trousers and crisp jacket over a blue roll neck sweater. He was always impeccably well dressed. Typically Italian.

Beth loved simply to gaze upon him, drinking in his beauty, and thinking how he would soon belong entirely to her. She could hardly believe her good fortune. They were both young and full of love, bubbling with passion. And in a way this was even more romantic than a real wedding because it was private and secret, done in the old country way.

He bent his head to whisper in her ear, 'The dress suits you. It make you look pretty. *Bella*,' and her heart melted with love for him. No one had ever called her pretty before. 'This is only the beginning. Soon as it is possible, we will marry properly, *si*?'

All her love was in her eyes as she told him that yes, she would marry him in a twinkling, the moment Meg returned home. 'You know it is what I want too, when the time is right.' And deep in her mind a small voice added, when I am entirely sure of you. At least she wouldn't be jilted at this wedding.

It was Jonty who saw the men first as he strode alone, way ahead of them. 'Look, lined up across the fell. Hunting foxes again?'

'Obviously,' Tessa agreed. 'Come on, cherub, you're getting heavier every day,' she said, addressing young James who was tucked on her hip as usual, his small plump legs clad in tartan dungarees, round cheeks glowing pink in the brisk breeze. 'Let's go and find Andrew, shall we?' and he happily showed two white teeth as he gurgled with pleasure.

They found him cleaning his gun.

'Decided to end it all have you?' Jonty joked.

Andrew glared at him, and at Pietro, but made no comment. Then his eyes fastened on Beth.

'We've brought you some news,' she said, feeling suddenly dreadfully conspicuous and for some reason, rather silly.

His eyes widened as they scanned the length of her, taking in the whole image, decked out in the pretty dress and flowers. She was now so overcome with shyness she found herself flushing furiously, but before she could explain he'd turned away to attend to his gun. 'We've got a job on. I haven't time to talk.'

Tessa shielded her eyes and scanned the fell tops. They were quite empty and barren, not a sign of life on the skyline. 'Is it something to do with the men on the hills?'

'Aye. There's a rogue dog about. Killing sheep. He's had three of ours, two from Ashlea.' He glanced at her. 'Nick's up there, wi' his gun, along with me dad and most of the other farmers from the dale. The dog has to be found and stopped.'

'What, shoot him you mean?' Beth was appalled.

'We can't lay down poison, now can we, or we'll kill summat we shouldn't?' Andrew hooked the open barrel over his arm and started to fill his pockets with boxes of cartridges. 'It's got nine lives that one, I'll tell thee that. Nick had a go at it last night and it still got away and killed another ewe. I'm glad to see you've sense enough to leave your own dog at home,' he said to Jonty, who made no reply. Then he nodded at them all and started to walk away.

Suddenly the idea of their 'bidden' wedding seemed terribly frivolous.

But before anyone had time to say anything more, a shot rang out, a clear loud crack in the empty air. Andrew stood stock still for a fraction of a second then he began to run.

'Stay where you were,' he called back over his shoulder and the baby started to scream, startled by the bang and the anger in his voice.

'I'll take him in to old Seth,' Tessa said, trying to soothe him as the others, hardly pausing to glance at each other, started to run up the hill.

Only one of them had spoken. Jonty, shouting, *'Dart'*.

'Isn't he safe at home?' Pietro demanded, as he gasped for breath with each pounding step.

'Couldn't find him when we set off.'

To which he muttered something unintelligible in Italian. No one required a translation.

It was hard going up the fellside. The ground was uneven in this part, pitted with holes and slippy with dewy turf. Here and there the ground split wide open, falling away into crevices or sheets of rough scree. Above their heads buzzards and carrion crow circled, scenting fear on the air, waiting and watching.

'You stay below,' Andrew shouted, more fiercely this time, but they ignored him. Jonty was determined to reach the dog before the men did, and Pietro kept close by him, the two girls trailing a long way behind, struggling to catch them up.

Again a shot rang out and they could see the group of men now, faces grim and tight-set, surrounding the rim of a ravine. Then they saw the dog. It had cornered the ewe on to a ledge and had its teeth fastened into its neck. Still warm and twitching with the last remnants of her strength, a mess of blood gave testiment to a battle royal as the dog snarled and growled, shaking the almost dead animal with such a tenacity that its own body looked in danger of snapping in two.

'Gan roond back on it,' one farmer softly called. 'Doan't scare it or t'booger'll git loose and run off. If I miss wi' this shot you hit it as it runs.'

'Reet.' The farmers took up their positions, barrels were loaded, preparations made.

'Dart?'

For a moment the dog looked up, ears pricked, face bright and trusting. 'Leave it to me,' Andrew shouted. He lifted the gun to his shoulder and fired. There was no question of the dog running now. It lay dead, sharp fangs still bared and dripping with blood.

The punch hit Andrew full in the face, knocking him off his feet and backwards down the hill. Jonty flung himself after him and the two men locked together, rolling down the fellside, over and over, as one.

'The gun.' Sarah was the first to move, setting off after them, screaming at the top of her voice. 'Stop them. Stop them. Get the gun.'

Pietro reached it first, abandoned on the grass. He picked it up, broke it and ran on down the hill. Jonty's cry curdled the blood in their veins.

'Damn murderer. You killed my dog and I'll bloody well kill you.'

The fight continued right to the bottom of the hill. They were all exhausted by the time they reached the farmyard, the two men's faces both covered with blood as they staggered about, aiming punches that missed more than they connected.

'The dog had to be killed.' Andrew's words, punctuated by painful gasps. 'He'd have gone on killing. We can't afford to lose valuable stock.'

The sound of a shout came from the fell above but both men ignored it as Jonty hit out again.

Andrew ducked and punched him in the ribs, doubling him up.

Jonty responded by grabbing Andrew around the neck, trying to twist him around and floor him. But Andrew was too used to such tactics in his wrestling contests. With one easy movement he flicked Jonty over and sent him sprawling.

'And you can keep your filthy hands off Beth,' he growled, moments before she reached them.

'This has got to stop,' she cried, running between them but Jonty knocked her aside, beside himself with fury, beyond any sense of reason.

'Leave it, Beth,' Andrew urged. 'I can handle him, the arrogant coward.'

And he may well have done so had it not been for Pietro, who came upon him unexpectedly from behind. And grabbing his arms, pinioned them back with a grip of steel.

'Stop. Enough,' she cried. Nobody heard her.

'You bastard.' Jonty wiped the blood from his mouth and made a fist, hitting out again and again till Andrew's head rang with each blow.

'We could have – taken – the – dog – away,' he shouted above Beth's screams, punctuating each blow with a word. 'Kept him from your bloody sheep. You could have given him a chance.'

Andrew lifted his head, glaring his hatred of the other man through eyes puffy with pain. A dribble of blood ran from his mouth and he knew at least one tooth was broken. 'What chance did the cur give the poor ewe?'

'How do you like to be cornered?' Pietro coldly enquired, easily quelling Andrew's exhausted efforts to be free. Jonty lifted his fist again while Pietro held on, tightening his grip on Andrew's arms the more he struggled to be free.

'*No,*' Beth screamed, hands slapping at them both. 'Stop it, stop it. Sarah, do something, don't just stand there.'

Jonty tossed her aside as he might an irritating fly.

'OK, OK, we'll let your precious yokel go, but we can have some fun with him first, eh? We'll teach the cocky bugger a lesson he won't forget.' Jonty lifted his head to look about him, then laughed. 'You said you liked cows? The young peasant farmer's an expert on the subject, right? Then let's see if you enjoy sharing a midden with one.' He flashed a message to Pietro who laughed too, then both men picked Andrew up. Pietro by the arms, Jonty by the legs, and they swung him up and over a low wall into an open pen where a young steer and his mother had been nervously contemplating the scene. Andrew fell in the stinking slime with a grunt.

The twins both froze with horror.

It was Tessa, who had been rooted to the spot by the farmhouse door who acted first. Hastily depositing James safely by the horse trough she ran over to Jonty and yanked at his arm. 'What the hell are you doing? Get him out of there.' She could hear her child protesting vociferously but for once ignored him, praying he'd stay put.

'To hell with it.' Jonty jerked his arm from her grasp. The twins came to in the next instant. They ran to look over the wall, where Andrew lay sprawled in the straw and liquid mire on the floor of the open pen. One animal stood reasonably quiet but the other was starting to fidget, looking close to panic, eyes rolling back in terror.

'Those aren't milk cows,' Tessa was yelling. 'That's a young bullock.'

Jonty laughed. 'No more'n a calf, it looks harmless enough to me.'

'With his mother, a Galloway. Beef cattle.'

Beth looked at the shaggy coated cow with her calf and recalled how Andrew had told her about the Galloways. *'The nearest thing you'll get to an untamed animal on a farm these days.'* But it was all right, she told herself with relief, Andrew was on his feet, staggering to the low wall.

'For God's sake get out of there,' Tessa said. 'And watch the gate. Don't let them escape. Heaven knows how far they'd run now they've been spooked.' She half glanced over her shoulder to check on James. He was starting to crawl in her direction, pleased to show off this new skill. Fear clutched her breast.

'Stay there, cherub. Wait for Mummy.'

He took no notice.

What happened next seemed to go on for ever but in fact probably took no more than seconds. As long, in fact, as it took for the farmers to get down from the felltops and view the dire result of the fight which had at first only amused them.

One minute Jonty and Pietro were reaching over the wall, teasing and laughing at Andrew covered in filthy slime, pushing and thumping at him to prevent him from climbing out. The two animals, almost crazed by this time, threshed about and bellowed in terror. Then Jonty somehow slid over the wall and was in the pen with Andrew, swearing he'd kill him if it was the last thing he did.

'Don't be so stupid. Get back,' Tessa shouted, again glancing back over her shoulder as she heard James's gurgle of delighted laughter. Perhaps it was because everyone else's attention in that moment was likewise diverted by the innocent James, now perilously close to the pen, that they didn't anticipate what was about to happen. Almost as wild-eyed as the animals, Jonty swung round and thumped what he believed to be Andrew out of the way. 'You and your bloody cows.' But it was not Andrew at all. It was the calf.

'Jonty,' Sarah's scream echoed over the fellside as she realised the danger at last. But it was too late.

The calf was half demented already, and somehow Jonty had got himself between the calf and his mother. It was perfectly plain to everyone that she did not like it. Before anyone could move or do a thing to prevent it, she'd lowered her head and shoulders and begun to pummell him against the wall of the pen.

Sarah lay on the big bed she'd once shared with Jonty and let herself sink into deep depression.

It wasn't as if she'd loved him, she told herself. They'd had fun together, that was all. Sex. Teasing. Fun. Games. I won't grieve. I refuse to. But the image of the scene tortured her, filling her mind, waking and sleeping. She saw the blood spurting, forming scarlet splashes all over her skirt and Beth's cream 'wedding' dress as they'd struggled to drag him clear. She woke sometimes in the night in a hot sweat, screaming and trying to brush the stains away, then she'd go to the bathroom and fill the old bath and scrub herself raw to rid herself of the memory. But it was impossible. She would remember those sickening moments and the crack of bones splintering, for as long as she lived.

'It was you, Beth, and your bloody cows,' she said, violet eyes big as bruises in her pale face. 'If you hadn't fussed so much in the first place about a dratted cow, Jonty would never have thought to tease Andrew with one. He never meant to hurt anyone. It was all a joke. If you hadn't been so prissy and just enjoyed sex with Pietro instead of wanting flowers and wedding bells, this might never have happened.'

No matter how much she might run up and down stairs with comforting cups of cocoa and calming words, she couldn't alter that fact. The horror of it all was too much to bear.

Beth had no strength to argue. She sat shivering, arms wrapped about herself as she stared at the floor, not wanting to hear Sarah's words.

'And now I have no one,' Sarah wailed. 'What a goddammed mess.'

'He's not *dead*,' Tessa screamed, standing up and facing them all in furious despair, fists clenched, tears running down her face. 'Stop talking about him as if he were dead. Stop thinking of yourselves. They say he'll never walk again. Think about *him*.' Then she ran from the room, leaving Beth to pick up and console baby James, reduced to sobs by the emotion in his mother.

And despite her best intentions Sarah turned her face into her pillow and wept too.

To Beth's great astonishment in the days following, Tessa cried even more than Sarah. Great gulping sobs which threatened to overwhelm her by their anguish. At first she thought that it was Tessa's fears for baby James, who'd been so dangerously close by. But later it came out how she'd secretly cared for Jonty all along, without saying a word to anyone. Finding the right words to comfort her seemed a near impossibility. Tessa kept saying how unlucky she was with men and Beth could only wonder at her own misjudgement.

What a terrible muddle.

It hadn't been Andrew who Tessa had wanted at all, but Jonty. That must have been what had driven the two apart, and why he'd appeared to have taken a liking to her. Obviously in an effort to get over Tessa.

And Andrew's jealousy had finally overwhelmed him. No wonder the fight had got so quickly out of control.

Questioned endlessly by the police about the accident, seeing two of his best cattle sold off cheap because he couldn't bear to have them on the place, and now to lose the woman he loved. Poor man. Beth could hardly bear to think of it.

12

No one felt much like work during these long, nerve-wracking days, so Beth begged time off from Jan. She was surprisingly unsympathetic.

'I knew no good would come of this commune business. What your mother will make of it, I really daren't imagine. I hope to God she doesn't blame me.'

'Why should she? Don't be silly, Jan. This has nothing to do with the commune. It was an accident which would have happened anyway.' But would it? she wondered. Was Sarah right about it being all her fault? If she had never become obsessed with her rural dream and the idea of owning a cow, would Jonty still be well and whole to this day? Beth tried to tell herself that the under-currents of tension had been there from the first between Andrew and Jonty. They'd taken an instant dislike to each other and there'd been nothing she could do about that.

But perhaps these tensions had been made worse by trying to live together, had become so heated they'd finally exploded, in the most terrible way.

The weather worsened, growing wet and bitterly cold and the fells were taking on the silence of winter. November was here, Christmas on the horizon.

Even the curlew had deserted them for milder climes on the coast. And Beth felt very much alone.

They took it in turns to visit Jonty but he never spoke. He lay, sometimes faking sleep, sometimes genuine, surrounded by drips and trollies and unimaginably frightening medical equipment. Despite their vigilance he resolutely ignored them all.

The nurses tried to reassure them.

'He's doing fine.'

'He'll be starting physiotherapy as soon as his ribs mend and his internal wounds are healed.'

'He'll be able to lead a pretty full life from a wheelchair. People do these days. Don't despair.'

But they did despair and Beth suffered an intolerable level of guilt, more than she had ever imagined possible.

Once, Jonty opened his eyes and glared straight at her as if saying that yes, it had been entirely her fault. But he didn't speak and after a long moment holding her anguished gaze he closed them again. As long as she lived she would never forget the accusation in that pain-wracked stare.

She tried to bury her guilt and misery in work. She spent hours digging and weeding the garden, cleaning the duck pond, mending dry-stone walls, chopping logs. Anything which would exhaust her and help her sleep at night.

When she wasn't working she took long walks over the fells, gratefully breathing in the cold crisp air, trying to come to terms with what had happened, trying to convince herself that she was not the cause of this disaster.

But it did no good. Sleep eluded her and if ever the accident did slip from her mind for a moment, a mere glance in her sister's direction brought all the terrible anguish rushing back. However unfair and illogical, Sarah held her entirely responsible, and made no attempt to disguise that fact.

Everyday reality returned with the drop of a letter on the mat. It was from the bank manager. Beth read it in disbelief and hurried at once to Sarah.

'Did you know we've spent all the savings, and Derry's loan too. Every penny we have in our bank account? This letter says we're overdrawn.'

Sarah lay in bed. She never rose before lunch these days which invariably was brought to her on a tray by Beth, and she would pick at it in a perfunctory way. 'What does it matter?' she said, sleepily pulling the bedclothes over her head. 'There's more in the building society.'

'For how long? You have to get up, Sarah. We have to sort this out.'

'I don't give a damn about the goddammed account. *OK*? What the hell does money matter?'

'We have to face life, Sarah.'

But Sarah blankly refused to speak to anyone, even the bank manager, however reasonable he sounded. She stayed in her room day after day, not crying, not sleeping, simply lying on the bed and staring at the ceiling or sitting on the window seat gazing out over the fells. Every now and then she'd storm about on the bare boards, and everyone would lift their heads and listen until she'd go quiet again.

Tessa moved about the place like a zombie, going through the motions of feeding and caring for James automatically, with no conscious thought, but spending more and more time at the hospital. She said at least she could be of some use there, keep Jonty company. And no one could quarrel with that.

It seemed perfectly ridiculous to Beth that Pietro should fall into a sulk because she'd told him their wedding must be indefinitely postponed.

'Postponed? But why? This was all very tragic but it is over. Life must go on.'

'No one is in the mood for weddings, or playing games and pretending.'

'It would cheer us all up.'

'I don't think so.'

He put his arms about her. 'You can at least come and share my bed,' but Beth eased herself free.

'I'm sorry, I know it might sound foolish but I really don't think that would be right, not yet. How could I think of love-making when Jonty is lying in bed, partially paralysed. It would be too callous. Perhaps when he begins to recover . . .'

'But that could be weeks, months.'

Beth looked bleak. 'I'm not saying we have to wait quite that long, but I can't help the way I feel. And I'm worried about Sarah and Tess. How can I be selfish and think only of myself? It wouldn't be right. You do understand, don't you?'

For a moment Beth thought the quarrel would errupt into something worse as Pietro glowered at her from beneath dark brows. And then he put his arms out and gathered her close, stroking her hair and kissing her brow. 'But of course. I am being selfish, wanting you too much. What you must do is to write and tell your mamma that we are engaged. Tell her to come over quickly, then in a month or two, when Jonty is feeling better, we can have the proper wedding. No more silly games.'

She turned away from him, not ready yet to consider the future. 'This isn't the time to make plans, Pietro. Please try to understand.'

'I think you do not love me,' he pouted.

'I do, I swear I do.' But she could not, would not give in. She settled the argument with an indisputable fact. 'In any case, we can't afford a wedding. We have no money.'

'What you mean, no money?'

'We're not rich, you know. We must work and save. This place is costing a fortune to do up, more than I realised it would. And I've had this letter . . .'

He gave a careless shrug. 'Poof, what is money? I can get whatever we need. How much would a little wedding cost? Peanuts.'

'I'm not simply talking about financing a wedding. I'm talking about our future life together. Even the roof still leaks.'

'You can borrow money for the roof from your family, from Jan or Meg. Then we will be cosy and can marry, yes? My family always help each other. They will help me, yours will help you. *Si?*' He reached for her again but Beth pushed him away, very slightly irritated by his inability to comprehend fully how she felt. Her head ached and she wished she could go to bed and someone bring her cocoa for a change.

'You make it all sound so simple. My family have their own problems to deal with. And I've had this summons to see the bank manager. Problems.' She pulled a face, trying not to show her very real concern.

'Go put these problems right quickly, then we can marry soon.' He took her in his arms and kissed her with such ferocity she melted in his arms and forgot all about her headache. 'See how you want me. You come to my bed tonight and I will kiss you some more. Yes?'

'No.' She tried to laugh, to show that she wasn't really cross with him. But he walked off in a huff, leaving her shaking her head in loving despair.

And since no one offered to go with her, it was left to Beth alone to visit the bank and sort everything out. She didn't even ask Tessa for a lift but walked down the lane as far as the Broomdale Inn and caught the bus into town. She was really quite proud of herself.

When she got back to Larkrigg it was to find Tessa packing her bags.

'What are you doing? You're not leaving?'

'I'm taking James to my mother for a bit. See if she remembers who I am.' Still the same jokey Tess but with a sad edge to the quips. 'It will be easier to visit Jonty from home. He needs me more than you do, Beth.'

'Yes, I can see that.' Beth sat on the edge of the bed, watching her fold baby clothes and felt suddenly, desperately alone. With Tess gone there'd be only the three of them left.

'I'm sorry, kiddo,' she said, reading Beth's mind. 'I know he's entirely unsuitable, and won't be any better tempered in a wheelchair, but I think I must love the bastard. I'm not going to abandon him now, not when he needs me.' Her eyes filled with tears and she dashed them angrily away. 'Not till I've given it my best shot.'

'You'll come back and see us?'

'Try and stop me.' Kisses and hugs and brave words but they both knew that even if she did come back, it wouldn't be the same. The dream had been tarnished, the innocence savaged. The commune had been Jonty's mad idea and for all he'd been difficult to live with, they'd miss his energy about the place, his acerbic comments and dry wit. The game was over.

But then it would probably have ended soon in any case, Beth told herself, remembering all the tensions that had sprung up between them. And with Tess beside him perhaps Jonty could find some sort of salvation. 'He's a lucky man.'

'Tell him that.'

'You'll write.'

'Of course.'

And Beth helped pile her luggage into the small yellow mini. 'I'll miss you, Tiger,' she said, hugging baby James as she tucked him into his car seat. Then she found Pietro in the kitchen drinking coffee, dragged Sarah out of bed and insisted they both come and see Tessa off.

Pietro hugged her and tickled James under the chin, making the child giggle ecstatically.

'Given up on us, have you?' Sarah said, shuffling across the yard in dressing gown and slippers, her raven hair flying wild and free in the brisk afternoon breeze. For all her declared grieving and the grubby, uncared for clothes, Sarah looked, as always, absolutely stunning. She could wear a potato sack, Beth thought with a twinge of envy, and still look beautiful. 'Now we've no money left.'

Tessa flinched at the cruel taunt but turned away and climbed into the driving seat without a word. Sarah's face remained grim as she closed the door after her.

'He was only using you, you know. Any woman who'd open her legs was fair game for Jonty. He didn't love you.'

Tessa turned empty eyes to meet Sarah's fiery gaze. 'Nor you.'

'He'll use you and hurt you and show not a morsel of gratitude.'

'I don't want his gratitude.'

'You're a fool.'

'Maybe he'll change.'

'Maybe hell will freeze over.'

Both women faced each other for a long, tension-filled moment and then Sarah smiled coldly. 'We're both losers, it seems.'

'Not me,' Tessa said, turning to wink at James who gave a shout of laughter and began to kick his fat legs and drum his heels on the seat, oblivious of everything but his own joy at riding in the motor. 'Depends how you judge success. Come on, cherub, let's go see Grandma.'

'Drive carefully. Don't stay away too long,' Beth called.

'Don't worry, you haven't seen the last of me yet,' and the mini coughed into life then drove serenely out of the yard, the painted eagle on the bonnet a defiant blaze of colour.

Beth stayed in the yard until the little car was nothing more than a yellow blob in the dale below, then she shivered as a chill wind struck through her sweater right to the heart of her. The mountains had never looked more bleak and blue with the cold of a coming winter, clouds gathering grey and heavy with the threat of rain.

'I think we might be in for a storm,' she said. But she was talking to herself. Pietro and Sarah had gone into the house long since.

Later that evening as Beth fastened up the hens and checked that the geese and ducks were safe, the wind was even worse. The outhouse roofs rattled ferociously, doors slammed and she was almost knocked from her feet as she ran back and forth, putting abandoned garden tools away, tying dustbin lids down, anything which might be sucked away by the ferocious wind and spewed up miles away across the fells. A house on a ridge was all very well with its panoramic views and clean, fresh air, except in bad weather.

She clung to a dry-stone wall for a moment and watched the black storm clouds foaming about the heads of the mountains, back lit by a translucent blue. It made her feel small and insignificant and she shivered, for the first time apprehensive about the future.

Was she doing the right thing by postponing her marriage to Pietro? She'd known him for such a short time but she did love him, and had no wish to lose him. But was it possible to fall in love so quickly and would it last? Why did she have any doubts at all? Why wasn't she dragging him down the aisle as fast as she could?

She'd certainly behaved with unusual impulsiveness during these last few weeks. Buying the goat for one thing, which had proved a total disaster. Buying hens, ducks and geese which she kept largely as pets and for the few eggs they provided. Still seeking some pastoral dream. Then without heeding anyone else's advice she'd decided on a cow and set off a whole chain of events which had ended in horror.

Now Beth felt that the accident had left her even more unsure of herself, filling her with uncertainties.

And Larkrigg would seem so empty without Tess. She would miss her, if not Jonty. But however irritating he could be with his odd games and weird sense of humour, she'd never have wished this terrible tragedy on him, never. Nothing would be quite the same ever again.

There were tears rolling down her cheeks, the first she had cried since it happened. Somehow there hadn't been time with everyone else's problems to see to. For a long moment she allowed herself the luxury of self pity and let the sobs come, cupping her face in her hands like a child. If only she could turn back the clock and they could all be happy and carefree and young again.

After a while she wiped her wet cheeks with the flat of her hand and lifted her face to the wind, letting it finish the cleansing process. The tears had eased her tension and she felt a little better. No regrets, she decided. The decision is made. We'll see what life brings.

The rain started as she ran to the rectangular stream of light spilling from the kitchen door. Sarah was standing by Pietro at the kitchen range and they moved smoothly apart as Beth entered. Poor Sarah, she thought, seeing the glint of tears in her sister's eyes. She was suffering too, and how kind of Pietro to comfort her. Beth kept her voice bright and cheerful as she struggled to close the door against the wind.

'There's a real gale blowing up. I hope everything's battened down properly or we'll have no poultry left in the morning.'

'Stop worrying about the bloody poultry. They'll survive without your fussing,' Sarah said sharply. 'We all will.'

'Shall I make cocoa?' Beth suggested brightly, as everyone stood about in the kitchen, not quite knowing what to do or say next.

'For goodness' sake, not everything can be cured with a cup of cocoa. I'm going to bed.'

When Sarah had gone, slamming the door behind her, Pietro took Beth in his arms. 'Now that we are alone, you will come to my bed tonight, yes?'

She pushed him away, laughing. 'No, of course I won't.'

'Why not? I need you.'

'We've been through all of this countless times.'

'Why should we not comfort each other?'

'There's Sarah, just a few doors away, grieving for Jonty.'

'She could have had him, if she'd had half of Tessa's courage,' he said, and knowing he was right, Beth felt almost embarrassed for her sister.

'Sarah is very sensitive,' she hastily explained, 'and she doesn't find it easy to give of herself or deal with difficulties of that nature. I've no wish to sound disloyal but I wouldn't call her a naturally caring person. She finds it hard to show her feelings.'

'You mean she thinks only of herself.'

'I mean, she doesn't have Tessa's depth of compassion, or admittedly, that kind of strength. But she has others.'

'Such as?'

'Can we leave it please?' It didn't seem right to be talking about her twin in this way. It was true that Sarah imagined every difficulty in life was a personal slight against herself. Mom was constantly telling her that it couldn't all be ice cream and pink candy floss. But then she'd managed, more often than not, to prove Mom wrong there, somehow getting her own way in most things and doing precisely as she pleased. Sacrificing herself for a permanent invalid was, therefore, quite beyond her capabilities. Even so, while Beth felt able to criticise Sarah's weaknesses, she couldn't bear anyone else to do so.

'Have you decided yet when we are to marry?' Pietro was saying as he pulled her close, nuzzling into her neck. Instinctively Beth turned her face away but he only kissed her neck, making her giggle.

'Stop it, you're tickling me.'

His arms tightened about her and the kiss became more passionate, leaving her weak with longing, her resolve in grave danger of slipping.

'You see how I can make you feel any emotion I wish.'

Beth eased him gently away, pushing back her hair with a trembling hand. 'I dare say you can. But we must be patient. Please.' Determined to ignore his sulks she persuaded him up the stairs to his own room. 'We'll talk about this another time. There's really no rush.'

On the landing they parted with a last lingering kiss. He could feel her need for him in every tremor of her body and exulted in it. 'What a waste,' he said. 'You will not change your mind?'

'No.'

'You are too cruel. You like to hurt me.'

'Go to bed,' and extricating herself from his arms, escaped laughingly to her room and firmly closed the door.

Curled up in her own warm bed Beth turned her mind deliberately away from Pietro to the worries over their financial situation and the efforts they must make with the mill. They seemed to have achieved little. They'd been so busy with the house which was costing far more than they'd expected. Beth could feel her dream slipping away and she sighed, plumped her pillows and turned over, annoyed with herself for worrying.

The wind moaned and howled about the house like a live thing, and she could hear the drip drip of water into the buckets and bowls that stood about her room. Finally these sounds lulled her to sleep, or else she slept from sheer exhaustion. She dreamed of herself and Pietro, a clutch of children at her knee, living in a beautifully restored Larkrigg Hall. It was all utterly delightful.

Sometime in the night a sound woke her and she padded out on to the landing. What could it have been? Should she go out and check on the animals? Rubbing her eyes she went to Pietro's door and listened. Was he asleep? Perhaps he would go down with her. It was dark and lonely outside. She lifted her hand to tap gently upon the panel and then stopped. Sarah would accuse her of fussing again. It was only the wind moaning after all. Nothing else. Hugging herself against the cold she hurried back to bed.

'She's afraid to take the risk of course, because of Jeremy. And she's a born worrier. Worrying about what other people might think or feel. Afraid of her own shadow at times, our Beth.'

'I think she neglect me.' Pietro slid a hand over the length of Sarah's thigh and sighed. 'Why cannot she be more like you? Determined and strong,' and he kissed the corner of Sarah's mouth where a smile lurked.

'Bloody selfish and insatiable you mean,' and the smile burst into a laugh as she pulled him on top of her. 'Beth hasn't an ounce of confidence in herself. A dull little waif, no use to you at all. I've always been the one to make all the decisions, answer questions for her even, when we were small.'

'Is that why you and she do not get on? Because you think her so hopeless?'

'Oh, she likes to quietly boss and organise me, and can be incredibly stubborn, but she has her head in the clouds much of the time. And is far too proper for her own good. Don't you think so?'

'I think she is all these things you say, but also sweet and kind and very loving. Why cannot I love you both?'

Sarah gave a low throaty chuckle. 'Ask her that, not me.'

'I do not wish to upset anyone, you understand? Not Jonty or Tessa, or Beth.' He slid a hand between her legs and began to rub. 'I want only that which I deserve.'

Sarah arched her back, giving a low groan. 'You deserve me, darling. Didn't I always say so. To hell with Beth.'

This seemed to amuse him, laughing as if it were the funniest joke in the world, and Sarah laughed with him.

Moaning softly and moving her body to an instinctive rhythm, she pushed her fingers through her hair, lifting it back from her face, revealing the perfect line of cheekbone and brow. 'And I am much more exciting, wouldn't you say? Without any hangups whatsoever.'

And as he turned her over and thrust himself inside her, Pietro heartily agreed.

As the days passed, Beth felt no reason to regret her decision. If sometimes Pietro sulked and moaned she regarded this merely as his Latin temperament, telling him how young they were, how they had all the time in the world.

As a blustery autumn changed into a cold December, life at Larkrigg grew tough. She had never realised how quickly a fire could consume logs and how difficult they were to get dry in a freezing house. She'd thought that Jonty and Pietro had made ample provision for winter but they were disappearing at such an alarming rate that more logging expeditions had to be planned. With no other form of heating they desperately needed the warmth. And it was worth the effort. Beth did so love the scent of pine and the acrid tang of oak, even if the smoke did billow out from the damp logs and make their eyes sting. It was all part of country life.

Whenever the weather permitted they would spend hours in the woods, chopping and sawing whatever dead wood they could find lying about, fitting household chores in on wet days. Occasionally they would make the long journey to the hospital at Lancaster to see Jonty. He never seemed to welcome their visits and relations between Sarah and Tessa continued to be strained. But Beth insisted it was the right thing to do.

'We can't forget him. He's our friend,' and Sarah would widen her eyes at such remarks and make some pithy comment of her own, making Beth blush with fresh guilt.

And there was Andrew too, to consider. They seemed to see less of him these days. Probably because Tess was no longer with them, Beth assumed. But Christmas was almost upon them and she'd managed to find a few eggs for Seth, so one fine morning she set out over crisp grass bleached with hoar frost to visit Cathra Crag. It crackled beneath her booted feet and the air was so cold it almost hurt to breathe it in. But she didn't mind, just looking around at the beloved beauty of the mountains reminded her again how lucky she was to be living in such a magnificent place.

Taking the eggs, which she couldn't really spare at this time of year, would serve as a good excuse for the visit. That way there'd be no embarrassment for either of them. Then she'd tactfully check out whether Andrew was getting over Tess.

Besides, Beth thought, Seth would be glad of a visitor. This cold weather must keep him confined largely indoors, carving his crook handles. He'd probably welcome a bit of crack, as he called it. The prospect made her sing as she strode out over the fell tops, but she was very certain that it was only because she liked this old man who lorded it over everyone at Cathra Crag.

He was exactly where she expected, seated on his rush chair in the chimney corner, sharp knife whittling a piece of wood which he told her was ash, nature's best, the image of a stag's head coming to life in his hand.

'Hey oop, lass, you're leuking a bit peaky. You're not on one of these daft diets, are you?'

Beth placed the mug of tea she had made into the old man's bony hand and sat down beside him on the three-legged stool by the fire. 'Your eyes are too sharp by half,' she laughed. 'I haven't been sleeping too well but I'm fine, really. How about you?'

'Oh, they'll not kill me off so quick.'

Beth smiled. 'I don't suppose they will.' She sipped at her tea, the homeliness of the old house warming her, soothing her heartache. Perhaps in time she would look back on all of this and laugh. She didn't feel much like laughing right now but self pity would do no good. If Sarah wished to blame her for the accident, there was nothing she could do about it. Certainly rushing into marriage with Pietro was not a solution, sulk as he may.

'Have you always lived here?'

'Since 1886.' He frowned. 'Or was it 1885? Aboot then, anyroad. I were born upstairs in t'front room and I'm still here. Not a traveller am I? But t'house isn't worn out yet.' He grinned at her, showing his few front teeth, yellowed with age and stained from his baccy.

'No,' eyeing the ash from the fire scattered over the rag rug, and the peeling paper on the pock-marked walls. But it was Andrew she was concerned about. 'I can see it's good for a few years yet. What about Andrew? Was he born here too?'

'Aye. His mam tried a few improvements to the place but mainly give it up as a bad job. She were allus sickly, poor soul.'

As Beth searched her mind for a way to ask after his grandson's health, she heard his clogs scrape on the step and then stamp hard, as if knocking off the worst of the mud. Then the sound of them ringing on the slate floor as he approached. When he saw Beth his face went bright red and she smiled, her heart suddenly racing with nervousness. But he wouldn't blame her for the loss of Tessa, surely? Would she have to bear the guilt of that blighted relationship as well?

'Hello.'

'I didn't know you were here.'

'I came to see how you all were.'

'She's tekken a fancy to me, hes this little lass,' Seth informed him, dropping one wrinkled eyelid in a huge wink.

There was a small tight silence as Andrew took off his jacket and hung it on a peg at the back of the door. When he turned round, Beth searched his face for any clue of his feelings but could find none. There was nothing else for it, she decided. I'll just have to take the risk and ask.

13

'Have you seen anything of Tess lately?'

'No, why should I?'

'I only thought . . .'

'That's your trouble, Beth, sometimes you don't think. You dream dreams, not necessarily the right ones.'

She bit on her lip, wishing the floor would open and swallow her. 'You're probably right. Sarah calls me a dreamer all the time. She says I'm a romantic loony.'

'So you are at times.'

'Sorry.' The pain was clearly still too raw for him to even bear the mention of Tessa's name. Beth decided she must change the subject, take his mind off her blunder. 'I came to see Seth, and you of course, as I'm in need of advice over what best to do with my twenty acres?' She glanced from one to the other of them but no such advice seemed to be forthcoming. Andrew had turned his back to her and Seth was paying excessive attention to cleaning out his old clay pipe.

'I would've thought you had plenty of folk to ask advice from,' Andrew said, the faintest hint of mockery in his tone.

'Who?'

'Nick.'

'He's very busy. And neither Sarah nor Pietro know anything about farming.'

'No,' Andrew said dryly. 'They wouldn't.'

Something hurt in the back of her throat but she swallowed it and battled bravely on. 'And you're the expert on farming, right?'

He pulled off his dusty overalls and tugged his shirt over his head preparatory to having a wash, to stand before her bare chested, clad only in trousers and his clogs. 'I thought you were content with it as it was. With your few birds.'

The muscles of his chest were strong and firm and rippled almost with a life of their own, calling to mind the day she had watched him at the wrestling. Beth would have turned away embarrassed, but was too aware of the challenge in his grey eyes. She felt slightly breathless, and believing he was deliberately trying to unsettle her, her next words came out sharper than she intended.

'I want it to be a proper smallholding. I may not have been too successful thus far but I'm at least willing to learn, and listen.'

'Eeh, I remember Meg when she were just starting out on t'farm,' Seth reminisced. 'Drank in every word, like she were thirsty for aught you could tell her.'

'I've always admired Gran. She knew what she wanted from life and went for it. I'd love to be like that.'

'And you don't know what you want, do you? Is that what you're telling us? Seems you're always changing your mind.'

Beth bridled. 'What makes you say so?'

'I thought it was Jonty Reynolds you had your eye on, but mebbe I was wrong. Mebbe you don't mind which one of 'em it is.'

'I beg your pardon?'

'Or now he's no longer a man, you've had to look elsewhere. Either way, I hear you're living with the Italian now.'

Beth felt the colour drain from her cheeks then flood back in again, stunned by his words and the acid in his voice. She half glanced at Seth but the old man was concentrating on his whittling, gone suddenly deaf. 'Pietro is still at Larkrigg, yes. So? What, exactly, are you suggesting?'

'Nowt to do with me. Live with whom you choose.' He turned the taps full on, letting the noise of steaming water gushing into the sink drown any reply she might have made. He dipped his head in and sluiced himself over head and chest, scrubbing vigorously with a large block of soap while Beth struggled with her rising temper. She was waiting with a towel when he had rinsed himself clean with cold water. His eyes met hers, solemn and questioning while hers told him very decidedly that he had no right to judge her, no right at all. Then he shook back his wet hair and buried it in the towel.

'I'm obviously not the only one who can make wrong assumptions,' she said tartly, and turning to Seth, continued more briskly, 'I wondered about Christmas trees.' She went back to her stool and locking her arms about her knees, fixed her eyes upon the old man's face, studiously ignoring Andrew for all she was aware of his hovering presence. She wasn't at all interested in Christmas trees any more, but not for the world would she let Andrew guess as much. How dare he speak to her with such contempt? What had she ever done to offend him so?

Her heart was pounding and deep inside she felt quite sick. 'I've been reading up about them,' she continued with false brightness. 'If I plant a thousand this year, and every year for the next four years, by then the first crop should be tall enough to sell. What do you think? Am I right? Will I make a profit?'

Seth gave a bark of laughter. 'I'd say you're a chip off the old block right enough. You'll do all right, little lass. What do you think of that, Andrew lad? She's going to grow us a forest.'

'Fox cover,' said Andrew sourly and reached for a clean shirt from the rack above the fire. Beth got to it first and handed it to him, a fiery challenge in her blue-grey eyes.

'You don't approve? Why not? If it'll make money and save the house from falling down around our ears. And we need to eat. It's worth trying. Unless you have any better suggestions?'

He shrugged on the shirt and started to button it. Her eyes clung stubbornly to the glimmer of naked flesh rapidly disappearing behind crisp cotton. 'Do you intend keeping sheep?' he demanded, making her jump.

'I'll need to keep a few, if only to keep the grass down, won't I?'

'Aye, well they'll eat any young whips of trees you put in.'

Beth hadn't considered that possibility. 'I could fence a section off.'

He laughed. 'That'll get rid of your profit then. Play at farming if you must, but don't expect to make much money at it. There's little profit in the land these days.'

'I could at least try.'

'You asked for my advice and I gave it.'

'Thank you.' Her tone was cool. 'But it seems rather negative.'

'It's your land, suit yourself.'

'Yes it is,' she said loftily. 'Thanks for your help. Or lack of it.'

She turned her back on him then and chatted with Seth for some time, struggling to digest his advice on what and how to plant, when she might hope to lift her crop of trees, and his suggestions for marketing. Time flew as he enlivened their conversation with numerous anecdotes from his long farming life which took an age to tell, but at least Seth's advice was positive and truly beneficial.

Andrew stayed silent throughout, sitting in the chair opposite and never taking his eyes from her face, nor offering one word of comfort or information which might be of use.

Then he glanced at the clock on the mantleshelf and got up to reach for the frying pan. 'One o'clock. Bacon and black pudding, grandad? Dad'll be in soon.'

Beth wrinkled her nose. 'Black pudding?' and the old man cackled with laughter again.

'Sliced and fried theer's nowt to better it. D'you want a piece? It's an aphrodisiac, tha knows.'

Beth chuckled and kissed him on his brow, acutely aware of Andrew moving about around her, slicing bread, laying plates out. A rough and ready meal for three lone men. 'No, you old rogue, I'll pass, thanks. But it's obviously doing you a power of good. I'm off now, take care. Thanks for the advice.' This last to Andrew, with an ironic twitch of her brow.

'Aye,' he said and when she walked to the back door, he followed her. The sight which met their eyes when he opened it left them both bereft of words for a whole half minute. She had been in the house for no more than a couple of hours, Andrew half that time, yet the open fell was now covered in a thick coating of snow. And more flakes were falling even as they stared, soft and silent, blown by a cruel east wind.

'This looks like sticking,' Andrew said. 'You'd best get a move on or you'll get stuck. D'you want me to see you home?' Offered hesitantly, she noticed, and with obvious reluctance.

'No thanks, I'll be fine.'

'I don't mind.'

She longed instantly to accept, but stubborness wouldn't allow her to do so. He hadn't offered her one drop of courtesy this morning, let alone the advice she'd asked for, and all because of her mistake in mentioning Tessa. It wasn't her fault if Tess had left him for Jonty, and he had lost her. It didn't give him the right to pick her life apart.

The sky was grey and lowering, heavy with snow, not pretty as a Christmas card as it was supposed to look at this time of year, but she could manage very well. As she stepped out in it, her boots sank two inches or more through the crisp layer. 'I'll be home in no time,' she said, trying not to show her reservations. Snowflakes crowded her head and face, settling in seconds on her snug coat.

For the first time that afternoon Andrew seemed to show a genuine concern for her. 'Watch where you're walking, won't you? It's easy to get lost. It could turn into a blizzard.' Then as if having finally convinced himself of a genuine emergency he reached for his coat and started to tug on his own boots. 'I'm coming with you.'

'There's no need, I can manage perfectly well on my own, thank you very much.' She was startled by the quick flash of fury in his eyes as their gazes locked.

'Don't be daft. You could fall in a snow drift.'

'I won't.' She was appalled to find tears choking her throat. 'I know the way and I'll keep to the track. I don't need you. I don't need anyone.' And she stomped off, determined to show she was her own woman.

'Suit yourself,' he yelled after her. 'Don't send for me if you fall in a ditch.'

'I wouldn't dream of it.'

'Good.'

And she heard the door slam shut.

'Damnation.'

Andrew stared out of the window at the gathering swirl of snow. There was going to be a blizzard, no doubt about it. What the hell had he been thinking of letting her go off like that? Why did women have to be so damned stubborn? He must be out of his mind.

Was it her fault if she fell in love with the wrong chap? Happen if he'd spoken up sooner about his own feelings for her, she might have looked at him different. Instead of which she had it fixed in her daft head that it was Tessa he fancied.

He watched her small figure quickly being swallowed up by the whiteout and came to a swift decision. Wrong words between them or not, he had to make sure she was all right. He could follow her at least. Keep his distance and see she got home safe. He began to tug on his big wellington boots and reach for his waterproof. His dog was at his heels in seconds.

It took him no more than moments to explain the situation to Seth, even so the snow was already forming ramps against the dry-stone walls, sculpted by the wind into strange formations by the time he set out. He couldn't see the sky, could see little beyond the bouncing, swirling flakes and a few feet in front of him. His boots sank deeper with every step. At least it wasn't freezing. Yet.

Andrew struggled to keep a brisk pace, his eyes searching for a bright spot of colour which would tell him she was on course for Larkrigg. But as he trudged onward, sweating slightly beneath his waterproof he saw no such reassuring sign. He swept his gaze wider, in case she had wandered off track.

He remembered an accident the previous winter when two girls had set off to walk a very short distance, over Coppergill Pass to the dale below, on a crisp winter day with a blue sky and sun beaming upon them. It had seemed safe enough but they had stepped on to a drift of snow that had given way and dropped them into eternity. Nothing could be trusted in weather like this.

'Seek, Toby.'

He could kick himself a million times over for not stopping her from setting out alone. Why hadn't he insisted on going with her? He would never be able to live with himself if anything happened to Beth.

He stopped, the snowflakes crowding him, turning his face and shoulders to that of a snowman. He loved her so much. Why couldn't she see that?

If she wasn't as sweet and innocent as she appeared, and how could she be with the way she'd been hot for Reynolds and was now living with that Italian lout in a manner he'd sooner not think of, he still loved her. He couldn't help himself.

Andrew quickened his pace and started to call her name, panic in his voice.

The journey home was a nightmare for Beth. Several times she almost panicked as she felt sure she had wandered from the track, quickly swallowed up by the billowing snow. She felt alone in the world, blanketed by the silent snow falling cold and melting on her cheeks to slide down her neck and make her colder than ever. Her gloves and knees were already soaking from the number of times she had slipped and fallen. Pads of it had slid inside her boots and she could barely feel her toes. Somewhere ahead was the comfort of Larkrigg and she must keep her head, concentrate on where she put the next foot, only too aware there were parts of this landscape which dropped precipitiously away, where she could slide down into a crevasse and never been seen again.

Why had she been so stubborn? Why hadn't she let Andrew walk her home? Why had they quarrelled in the first place? What she wouldn't give now for the sight of his smiling face?

The snow seemed to get deeper and deeper, far quicker than she had imagined it would, slowing her with every step. The guiding lines of the drystone walls had disappeared in a blur of white. She stopped to catch her breath and look about her, realising with a dreadful certainty that she was lost. Nothing but virgin whiteness met her eyes. No landmarks, no hills, not even a fox's footprint to follow.

She must find shelter. A dry-stone wall to hide behind, dig herself a cave in the drifting snow. She tried not to think of all the dozens of sheep who sought the same kind of shelter every winter and perished in it. What alternative did she have?

She knew she was sobbing because she could feel her tears hot on her frozen cheeks. By nightfall it could be well below freezing. No, she shouldn't stop at all. She must keep moving. Doggedly Beth pulled one foot out of the deep snow and then the other, her breathing growing more laboured with each step. Her legs buckled beneath her and she collapsed in the snow, too tired now even to cry. She would rest for a moment. Gather her strength to carry on.

She must be hallucinating. Someone was calling her name. Was it Sarah? No, not Sarah. Pietro?

'Beth.'

There it was again but she really couldn't find the energy to call back. Why were they disturbing her? Somehow her soft bed no longer felt as warm and cosy as it should, even so she couldn't somehow raise the energy to leave it.

A warm breath on her cheek, a wet nose against hers. Someone was licking her face. A dog? In her bed? Reality returned to her in a rush. The blank whiteout, the freezing cold snow piling fatally upon her. And a dog's excited nose snuffling into her cheek. She'd never been so pleased to be so comprehensively licked in all her life.

'Hello, boy. Am I glad to see you,' she managed, voice weak and cracked with fatigue.

A dark figure bearing down upon her, lifting her, strong arms holding her, the rasp of a warm cheek against hers. Thank God, it wasn't a mirage. She could hardly believe her good fortune. She was safe.

'Andrew?'

'Don't worry, love. You'll be all right now.'

And she knew that she would be. She leaned against him, clung to his solid form. 'Oh, Andrew. I thought I'd never survive this. I'm so sorry for being stubborn.'

'Don't talk. Save your breath for walking. You're way off course. You can thank my dog Toby here, for finding you.'

'Thanks Toby.' She rubbed the dog's head and it barked a joyous welcome, pleased by his own cleverness.

Andrew half carried her the rest of the way, and even that was a strain. She really had been well off track.

Then suddenly a rectangle of light was spilling out on the ground before them and she knew she was home. A figure stood in the doorway, dark against the light.

'What is it?'

'Beth. Got lost in the snow.'

'I'll take her now.'

'Let me at least bring her inside.'

'No, you can leave her with me.'

A second pair of arms were taking possession of her and she whimpered at being deprived of the warm safety of her rescuer, but really she was beyond protest. She turned to thank Andrew, to invite him in for a warming drink but the door was closing and she couldn't seem to stop herself from collapsing in Pietro's arms.

Yet much later as she lay at last in the safety of her warm bed, she held a vision in her mind of stunned disbelief on Andrew's face. She thought she would remember the agony in it for as long as she lived.

By morning she woke feeling half way human again. She went to the window and found the weather was worse, the snow raging across the fells, blotting out everything. Did Andrew get home safely? She must find out.

She showered and dressed as quickly as she could and ran downstairs. Pietro and Sarah were at the stove, giggling over some joke and cooking bacon and eggs. They both turned to smile at her.

'You look better.'

'Silly Beth, in trouble again.'

'Thank you, sister dear, for those few kind words. Have you heard from Andrew? Did he get home OK?'

'I am sure he must have or we would have heard,' Pietro said with a shrug, breaking two eggs into the pan.

'You didn't leave him outside yesterday, did you?'

'Do not fret, little one. You were the important one.'

'But you could at least have given him a hot drink.'

'He would not have wished to intrude.'

No, Beth thought, he probably wouldn't.

'Whatever possessed you to go out in such dreadful weather?' Sarah asked. 'Are you absolutely loopy?'

'It wasn't snowing when I set off.'

Pietro snorted with derision. 'That man should not have let you try to come home alone. He is, as I said, a peasant, a fool.'

Beth swallowed, feeling guilty over her refusal to accept the offer of Andrew's guidance. 'It wasn't his fault.' But Pietro wasn't listening. He expertly flicked the eggs over and reached for the plates.

'I think he want for to cause trouble for you, for us all. I never like the man.'

'And you missed all the hard work yesterday,' Sarah put in, in her most complaining voice. 'We spent hours in the woodshed sawing those damned logs, didn't we, Pietro? You can do your own logging next time.'

Beth forebore to mention that chopping logs was nowhere near as difficult as being lost in a snow drift. 'You shouldn't pile the logs so high in the grate, then we wouldn't need so many.'

'Skinflint,' Sarah retorted.

'Someone has to count the pennies.'

'And it must be you?'

'Apparently.'

'Nag, nag, nag. You're no fun any more, Beth.'

Beth bit down hard on her tongue. She felt far too weary for another battle right now.

There was no hope of them going anywhere that day, let along to check on Andrew at Cathra Crag. The wind battered against the windows, piling the snow right up to the sills. The roof creaked ominously and it took every ounce of her energy to plough through the terrible drifts to check on the poor soaked hens and geese to replace their frozen feed and water. They were all snow-bound, locked up together in this old house.

What a strange trio they were. How would it ever get sorted out?

Something had woken her. Beth opened her eyes to find her room still dark. She lay still for a long moment, wondering what it could have been. Was it the wind? It came again, a terrible grinding, creaking sound and then an enormous crash. She was out of bed like a shot, reaching for her dressing gown. A barn must have fallen down, or perhaps the geese were announcing intruders.

Confused, she tripped over a bucket, sending dirty water splashing all over her feet. Cursing silently for not having emptied it for ages, she sought the light switch. Nothing happened. Oh, lord, the snow must have brought some wires down, or part of the fragile roof. She scrabbled in her bedside drawer for a torch.

It was freezing cold on the landing, making her shiver, and her bare toes ache on the wooden boards. The wind rattled the small window ferociously, blowing along the landing as if there were no glass at all to stop it. The snow would be drifting worse than ever in this howling gale. And somewhere in the depth of the house a disaster had taken place, she was sure of it.

Shivering with cold she hurried to Pietro's door and pushed it open without knocking. Beth called his name in a soft whisper but there was no reply. The bed was empty. Where was he? Not still drinking wine in the kitchen, she hoped. She hurried out of the room and was at the top of the stairs when she heard the next sound, like a cry in the depths of the house.

At first she put it down to the fierce north-easterly and started down the stairs. It came again and this time she returned, to look thoughtfully back along the landing.

She found herself walking along it, like a ghost in her pale dressing gown, bare feet making no noise on the cold boards.

The sounds were clearer now. The cry again, and a soft moan. Could it be the wind? Or Sarah, still grieving for Jonty? Beth could hear her own heart beating loud against her ribs as gently she turned the handle of her sister's door and pushed it silently open.

A single candle glimmered on the bedside table, giving off very little light but sufficient to halo in its glow the pale flesh of two entwined figures in the great bed. A gust of wind lifted the curtains, making it gutter and die, but not before the two had both turned towards the door and seen her.

Beth lay like a stone in her own bed for the rest of that night. She had hurried back to it like a frightened rabbit into its hole and knew nothing on earth would persuade her to confront them right now.

It was as if a part of her had been waiting for this to happen, as if this unspoken fear had been the true reason why she'd hesitated at committing herself to Pietro. As if she'd needed to be absolutely certain it was herself he wanted, and not Sarah.

Now her doubts had been proved justified.

It wasn't the small and rather plain sister he'd wanted at all, but the tall, sophisticated, sensual beauty. She'd simply been fooling herself to believe otherwise.

If she slept that night, she had no recollection of it and got up next morning feeling rather as if she too had been padded all over with sound-proofing snow. Nothing quite penetrated her sense of unreality.

Beth found that the weight of snow had indeed brought a portion of roof down through the ceiling in one of the back bedrooms. Splintered lathes and plaster were everywhere. Bed, furniture, ancient carpet, everything was blanketed in a rapidly thawing mound. Through the cross beams could be seen a gaping hole, open to the rafters and the glimpse of an innocent blue sky.

Yet even this disaster seemed as nothing compared with the greater one which had taken place this night. A hole had been punched in her heart and through it shone her sister's happiness.

'You don't really mind, do you?' Sarah chattered, as she generously buttered a slice of toast. 'You and Pietro were pretty well finished, weren't you? He says you'd completely lost interest in him.' She was bubbling over with suppressed excitement, her face alight with a lovely radiance.

'Did he?'

Beth sat with her own piece of dry toast untouched, trying to take in the full implications of everything which had occurred these last few days and nights, and not quite getting to grips with any of it. Everything she touched seemed to turn sour.

'You do understand how sorry I am? But it's best out in the open, don't you think? We've been wanting to tell you for simply ages. You've only yourself to blame, darling. You've ignored him for weeks.'

'Have I?' Beth marvelled at the steadiness of her own voice when inside she still felt numb with shock. She welcomed the numbness for she knew the pain would be worse when it faded. And what exactly did Sarah mean by – *wanting to tell you for simply ages*? She opened her mouth to ask but Sarah interrupted her.

'Pietro says he really cannot bear any more of your squabbling.'

'Squabbling?'

The violet eyes were luminous. 'Refusing him all the time. He is human, darling. He needs love and attention or he'll wilt away. All men are the same, sweetie. Why can't you realise?' She gave an expressive shrug, her beautiful mouth curving into a smile of mischievous delight. 'What a pretty coil though, eh? Pietro says he can't help loving us both, because we are twins. Isn't that sweet? And since you clearly no longer wanted him he came to me.'

'You mean you took him.'

Sarah pouted. 'Don't be a poor loser. And don't blame Pietro, the poor darling couldn't help himself. Neither of us could.'

Something inside of Beth finally snapped and she stood up, white and shaking. 'This isn't a piece of jewellery, or favourite dress you've commandeered, Sarah. This is the man I love.'

'Oh, phooey, don't play the drama queen. You're only pretending to be cross, I can tell.'

The callous audacity of the selfish act was bad enough, Beth thought, but Sarah's absolute certainty that she wouldn't mind was utterly breathtaking. Yet she knew that Sarah never thought of anyone but herself. If she didn't recognise any hurt except her own, that was the way she was, the way she had always been. To expect Sarah to be any different would be to go against the laws of nature. 'You know nothing about the way I feel. Perhaps you never have.'

'Silly child, I understand you perfectly.' The lilting voice took on a plaintive note. 'I'm not like you, darling, all self-sufficient, sensible and contained.'

Beth gasped. 'Is that how you see me?'

Sarah pouted. 'You can be very bossy you know, in your own quiet little way. You could have had Pietro if you'd truly wanted him, as I could have had Jonty.'

Beth wondered if that were true.

'And besides, the whole thing is your fault from start to finish. If it weren't for your appalling silliness and romantic nonsense I'd still have Jonty, wouldn't I? The accident would never have happened. And you know how I need a man. I must have one. It's essential to my health and wellbeing. And you owe me. You do see that, Beth darling, don't you?'

14

Christmas was a misery. With no hope of reaching Broombank they had to make the best of it on their own.

There seemed nothing to be done either about the roof, not until the thaw came, so Beth closed the door on it and hoped for the best.

No carol singers came to their door. Few Christmas cards arrived since even the postman couldn't get through. And the food they held in the larder was poor and not very festive. Beth put up a small tree and decorated it with scraps of coloured paper and tin foil, but it did little to cheer her.

And night after night she could hear them making love. She buried her head beneath her pillows but still she could hear them, if only in her imagination. Her ears strained to catch every gasp, every cry of release, every creak of the old bed springs. Her eyes grew hollow and dark ringed through lack of sleep. Often she would pace the floor of her bedroom for hours until she was too exhausted to stand up and would then fall into bed and sink into oblivion. Blissful relief.

How could she bear to go on living in this way? And what would she do when the thaw did eventually come? If she left, she would lose everything. She had already lost Pietro. Was she prepared to give up her sister too, who was still dear to her? And Larkrigg Hall – her inheritance?

She couldn't bear to leave and she couldn't bear to stay.

It was a bleak and lonely time. One night she thought she heard tapping at her door and very nearly went to answer it. But then realised it must only be the constant drone of the wind and snuggled down again beneath the warm sheets, forcing herself to relax and sleep.

During the day it was almost worse.

The snow lay in great drifts, banking up against dry-stone walls, glittering with frost on their outer surface but deadly soft beneath. Where the wind had scoured the grass of thick snow, her feet made prints in the crisp hoar frost, disturbing the tiny icicles which feathered every blade of grass. The world looked so pure and white and beautiful while she felt dark and muddied and ugly.

Every morning Pietro and Sarah would go off to play in the snow like children. Beth could hear their squeals and shouts of laughter as they sledged and threw snowballs and stuffed the icy snow down each other's necks.

'Come with us,' they urged. 'We've made skis with bits of wood. We're going to try cross-country skiing. Come on, Beth. Don't be an old misery-boots.' But as politely as she could, she always declined.

And in Larkrigg Hall itself the cold bit deep with iron jaws. The water, which came from a private spring nearby, froze in the ground. And snow continued to fall from time to time through the hole in the spare bedroom ceiling. Life was impossible, yet what could she do?

Larkrigg belonged as much to her as it did to Sarah. More in a way, for Sarah would not have stayed on had she not been persuaded into it. So how could Beth risk abandoning it? All she could do was grit her teeth and be prepared to carry on.

She dressed in layer upon layer of her warmest clothing, and as far as possible confined herself to working in the kitchen where the restored range now gave off a radiant heat.

One morning she was digging out the hen arks from beneath feet of snow, stacking broken spars of wood, inspecting damage, thankful that at least the poultry remained safe and well. Pietro came to stand beside her, saying nothing. She ignored him, as she had done for over a week now. At last he spoke.

'It was no good for us, was it?'

'I see that you thought so.'

'You didn't love me enough.'

Beth felt the curl of restoring anger deep inside her and welcomed it as the land would welcome the sun. 'You think not?'

'You were infatuated with me, and I with you. But it could not have lasted. We are too different.'

'And you discovered this fascinating fact in Sarah's arms, did you?'

'You are angry with me. I deserve your anger. But Sarah, she needs me.'

Beth gazed at him, stunned. 'And I don't?'

He held out his hands, palm up in a helpless gesture. 'You are sensible and strong. You will survive.'

'*What?*' How could he say such a thing? How could he ever imagine that she, Beth Brandon, the shy, awkward twin could ever be the strong one? Wasn't it enough to be jilted once, very nearly at the altar, let alone twice? Why did it always have to be she who was the loser?

'See how you build this place with your own hands. You have the dream and you go for it. I admire that in a woman.'

'Yet there must be something wrong with me. I get the house and Sarah is the one who wins you. Is that how it goes? Funny how Sarah always seems to get everything she wants.' Beth was proud of the way she was holding on to her dignity with not a threat of a tear. Her calmness was really quite astonishing, as if a mist had gone and she could at last see everything quite clearly.

'Sarah is the weak and feminine one. She cannot manage alone but needs someone to take care of her. And she love me very much. As I love you both. In different ways. You understand?'

'Sarah? You think *Sarah* is weak and feminine?'

'But of course.'

The idea was so preposterous and he looked suddenly so boyish, and pathetic, and sorry for himself, that a spurt of rebellious laughter bubbled up in her throat. 'Yes, Pietro. As a matter of fact I do understand. More than you realise.'

He looked pleased. 'Then we are still the best friends.'

'Well, not quite. Not as we were.'

'Ah yes, but you are the sweet, forgiving one. Did I not always say so? *Ciao.*' Then he brushed a kiss upon her brow and smilingly walked away, as if he had made everything fine and dandy between them now. Beth let him go without protest, her mouth tight with her determination not to cry, not after she'd done so well.

Freda Lightfoot

* * *

The trees of Brockbarrow Wood were like black sticks in the snow, back lit by the brilliant glare of a low winter sun.

A thaw had at last set in and Beth's wellington boots sloshed through puddles and lumps of melting ice as she made her way down the hill. Her spirits were lifting at the thought of calling upon Ellen. It felt good to be at last out of the house and this morning, with the sheep trods at least passable and running with water, was the first opportunity she'd had.

She carried piping hot soup in her basket which Beth meant to offer tactfully as a lunch for them both. She guessed it might prove to be the most substantial meal Ellen would have tasted for some time, since most of her money went on her animals and birds.

When she reached the clearing, Beth was relieved to see everything as normal. The cottage seemed to have stood up to the weather well. Ellen was moving about in the garden, attending to her chores as usual. Two of the dogs and the old grey goose trailed behind her, while a kestrel perched lop-sidedly upon her shoulder. Dressed in wellington boots, a thick knitted hat and a man's raincoat with a padded waistcoat over the top, she looked like a cross between a latter-day pirate and a tramp.

'Hi, everything OK?' Beth called, setting the basket down on the doorstep. Ellen half glanced at it then turned quickly away. So, she hadn't eaten too well recently. As suspected.

'Fine. Why shouldn't I be?' she barked. 'Bit o' snow don't bother me.'

Beth was used to her prickly manner and didn't remark upon it.

'We aren't fine.' Should she tell her the whole truth, ask if she could move in? 'A whole chunk of our roof is sitting on the spare room bed. It had to happen one day. I would've had it fixed before now if I'd had the money. Never mind. We'll find it somehow, I dare say.'

'How?'

'You tell me.' She went over to the compound, seeking sight of a young barn owl she knew to be in there. Ellen came to join her.

'Looking for Barney? He's inside. Not too keen on this bright sunlight.'

'Will you be letting him go soon?'

'When spring comes and I can arrange a new home for him. His last barn is now four holiday bedsits.'

'Ah.' Beth looked sad. 'Evicted, eh? Poor old Barney.'

'That's why he was brought to me. His parents apparently panicked when their home was ripped apart and they deserted him. I've had to be his foster mum. Why some folk are so insensitive to breeding times I cannot think. Amateurs. This one won't be again. I gave him a piece of my mind.'

Beth chuckled. Ellen always managed to help her put things in perspective. 'I'll bet you did.' She watched with interest as Ellen tended a roe deer that had injured its foot, and laughed as a group of red squirrels squabbled over a bowl of peanuts. 'You're always so busy, and happy,' she added wistfully.

The old woman cast Beth a keen glance. 'Don't be fooled by appearances. I have me worries too. This isn't paradise. I could be evicted, just like young Barney here.'

'Who would do such a thing?'

'It's your land, you tell me.'

Beth beamed. 'There's no problem then. Look, I don't know about you but my stomach is growling with hunger.'

'I can feed meself, thanks very much.'

Beth sighed. 'I know. Nettle soup and chickweed salad. Well, I've leek and potato soup, wholemeal rolls and cheese in the basket. You couldn't force yourself to share it with me, I don't suppose?'

Ellen's craggy face broke into a grin. 'I might be persuaded.'

As she turned to enter the cottage, she suddenly stopped and glared at Beth. 'You look a bit washed out. Are you all right?'

'Fine,' Beth lied, and then mimicking Ellen's earlier sharpness, 'Why shouldn't I be?'

A thoughtful pause then, 'Aye, well that's all right then.' But as Ellen collected dishes and spoons, she didn't feel too convinced. There was summat wrong with the little lass, and she'd find out what it was or her name wasn't Ellen Martin.

As January passed and winter wore on, spring seemed further away than ever. Beth escaped often to Rowan cottage and Ellen's compound. Sometimes she would help with the wild creatures, at other times the two of them would sit and chat or simply watch the animals at their antics. Even watching a tit struggle for a taste of the fat from Ellen's hanging bird pudding that she made for them was never less than entertaining. It was peaceful in the woods. And it soothed Beth's troubled spirit.

But she didn't forget old Seth. The old man looked forward to her regular visits, even if the hens weren't laying and she had no eggs for him.

He loved to talk about the way life had used to be in the dale, 'when I were a lad. Niver fought in either war but I've had me hard times all the same,' he told her. 'Poverty and hunger I've known, and still brought up a clutch of childer, scattered half over Westmorland and Cumberland.'

'It's called Cumbria now, Seth, since government re-organisation,' Beth reminded him but he fixed her with a fierce glare.

'It's Westmorland to me and allus will be. Government can say aught they want, they can't tell me what to do, any more'n me own bairns hes that right. Though they'd nae doot like to. Allus shoving bits o' paper under me nose to sign. Pester me to death they do.'

'I'm sure they don't mean to.'

'Aye they do. Naught they'd like better than to knock me off me perch. But I'm going nowhere. Not yet, I'm not. I'll not sign their dratted papers. You can be sure o' that. I'll do as I please.'

'Quite right,' Beth gravely agreed.

He folded his lips as if having won a great battle and Beth was unsure quite what she had to said to upset him. It seemed to put him in a bad mood for the rest of the afternoon and she vowed to take more care in future.

On occasions Andrew would be at Cathra Crag when she called. At other times not. She never objected when he wanted to walk her home across the fell now. She owed him her life, so how could she refuse?

Once or twice he had happened to call upon Ellen while Beth was there and the three of them would enjoy a merry hour, working on Ellen's chores, playing with the dogs or teaching Beth all about the wild life in the area.

Beth's favourite place was by the tarn, listening to the ice crack and creak as ridged waves frozen in motion by the fierce winds finally split and heaved apart. The sun sparkled upon the resulting shards, glinting to pink and palest turquoise and ice blue.

'See,' Andrew pointed out the footprints of a passing fox, visible on the shore. 'As the weather worsened he'd have to walk further to find food. Mebbe resort to eating frozen grass if necessary.'

'Poor thing.' There was always something to watch, something to talk about in this ever-changing landscape. 'I love a clear, crisp day like this. It's so calming.'

'Aye, winter is what I'd miss most if I couldn't live in this dale,' Andrew told her. And she understood perfectly.

'You wouldn't ever leave though, would you?'

He shook his head vehemently but his eyes were troubled. 'Not if I can help it. But who knows what's in store for us, eh? Farming is a tough life. Mebbe it'll give up on me before I'm ready to give up on it.'

'I hope it doesn't.'

He looked down at her and for a moment neither spoke, then he turned up her coat collar, holding it close against her chin as he smiled at her. 'Come on, before you freeze over like the tarn. Let's beg some of Ellen's terrible coffee.'

These were the best times. The relief of a few hours away from Pietro and Sarah was huge, and of not seeing them in each other's arms. How much longer she could bear things to go on as they were, Beth couldn't imagine but gave no indication to her new friends of her troubles.

Sometimes she wondered if Ellen and Andrew watched her. They would exchange glances, transmit silent messages to each other and she would tense, ready to rebuff any probing. Then they would turn away and say nothing, after all.

Only once, when Andrew was crossing the fell with her, a playful breeze at their backs scudding them along, did he comment upon the situation at Larkrigg. 'I hope you're not being too soft with that sister of yours.'

'Why?'

'You look tired, as if you've been working too hard.' He put out a hand and catching her arm, brought her to a halt, his grey eyes keen and shrewd. 'Don't let her, Beth. There's no reason why she should put all the work on to you.'

'She isn't. She doesn't.' Feeling faintly flustered by the intensity of his gaze Beth tried to break free of his hold, but found she couldn't. 'I'm fine. Really.'

'Is it Pietro then? You'd tell me if he was being a nuisance, wouldn't you?'

'Tell *you*?' She stared at him, astounded. 'Why should I tell you? Not that he is a nuisance of course. But if he was, why should I come running to you?'

'Because I'm your friend. I know we've had our differences and I probably spoke out of turn that time, but I reckoned we'd put it behind us. I'm trying not to interfere in your life. But that doesn't mean I don't still care about you.'

She saw the wounded expression in his eyes and felt a quick burst of shame. There she went again, pushing him away, inflicting her hurt upon him, when he meant only to be friendly. 'I'm sorry, Andrew. I didn't think. It's only that I shy away from . . . I like to look after myself.'

'There's no shame in needing a bit of help now and again. From a friend.'

She slanted her gaze up at him, not quite sure how to respond. His face held a calm strength, and she envied that in him. The only times she ever felt calm these days was when she was with him. He seemed to be intently studying her face. For any sign of problems? she wondered. Yet he could still be touchy at times, which made her prefer to avoid all conversation connected with Tessa or Pietro, or even Sarah. It made their meetings difficult, sometimes awkward at times, since these people were so much a part of her life.

But she hated to see anyone hurting. She knew about hurt. And Andrew must have suffered deeply when Tessa went off with Jonty. He needed time to get over losing her, as she must get used to the idea of being without Pietro. It seemed an almost impossible task.

'You'll be leaving soon, I expect,' he said.

'Leaving?'

'Aye. Back to America. Back home. You and Sarah, and your boyfriend. I was wrong about Jonty, wasn't I? It was the Italian you fancied all along, wasn't it? I realise that now. Bit dim in these matters, I am. It was Tessa who was hot for Jonty Reynolds, eh?'

'Oh, Andrew.' Filled with pity, she didn't know what else to say.

'Well, now you've got him, so that's all right.'

Beth had to summon every ounce of courage she possessed to keep a smile on her face, though allowing a swathe of silky fine hair to fall forward and hide its falseness. 'Now who's talking daft?' It was a struggle to still the tremor in her voice, but she managed it. 'Whatever makes you think the beautiful Pietro would even glance in my direction, when there's Sarah around?'

Deep furrows of doubt clove the thick brow as he frowned down at her. Then lifted and cleared on a sudden burst of incredible joy which entirely transformed him. He put out a hand to lay it on her arm with a tremulous touch. 'Are you saying that there's nowt between you?'

She wanted to shrug away the hand, turn and run from him as fast as she could. 'I'm saying, for a man who claims he has spadefuls of common sense, you do jump to hasty conclusions.'

Andrew considered her face for a long moment, the way she flicked at her hair with a fidgety hand, pretending to laugh and studiously ignoring his gaze. His voice, when he spoke, was soft and gentle. 'So that's the way the land lies. I'm sorry. I should've realised.'

'What? I don't know what you mean?' she said, the brittle spurt of laughter threatening to errupt into tears.

'Happen you do, happen you don't.' He saw it all now. Loved and lost, wasn't that how they described it? A surge of hot anger soared through his veins. If he ever got his hands on Pietro Lawson, he'd make him sorry he'd ever set foot in this dale. 'You've had your problems then? With your sister and that chap?' His voice was quiet, soothing, and she responded with a weak smile.

'You could say so, yes. But then so have you.' Determined not to wallow in her own self pity. 'Let's not talk about it.'

'No, we'll leave it at that, shall we?'

'It would be for the best,' she agreed.

'Right.'

They stood and stared at each other, the wind lifting her hair and whipping it across her flushed cheeks. With one finger he pushed it back and hooked it behind her ear. 'You never wear that nice little slide any more,' and her eyes flew to his, startled and questioning.

'Sarah says it's awful.'

'What does she know?'

She was so moved by the warmth that emanated softly from him, that without thinking she tipped up on to her toes and kissed him swiftly on the mouth. His lips were soft and warm and for a fleeting second she felt suddenly, unexpectedly happy, as if a black dam of muddy water had burst and she was cleansed and free.

The gesture seemed to startle Andrew every bit as much, and for a long moment they stood and gazed upon each like startled children, captured in a shaft of sunlight.

'You could always marry me instead,' he said.

Beth blinked. 'What did you say?'

The words had surprised him as much as they had Beth, but having spoken, he made an instant resolve not to retract them. 'I've not a lot to offer but I reckon I could make you happy, Beth. There's the farm a'course, though it's small, and farming isn't as safe a job as it was. I'd work hard though, look after you. I'd be good to you right enough.'

Embarrassment washed over her. What had she done? Feeling sorry for herself had made her careless. It wasn't fair to involve Andrew in her problems. Hadn't he been hurt enough by losing Tessa? Now she had to extracate herself from this mess without making matters worse. She drew in a quick breath. 'I'm sure you could make any girl happy, Andrew. But there's no need to go so far, just because you feel sorry for me.'

'Who said I felt sorry for you?'

'What I'm trying to say is, I understand why you are doing this but are you sure it'd be such a good idea?'

'You mean you don't fancy me.' His eyes, the very tautness of his body became stiff with pride. Beth searched her brain for the kindest words she could find.

'You are a great friend to me, Andrew. But for us to – for you and me – I'm not sure it could work, are you? Too much lingering hurt. Marriage on the rebound isn't such a good idea, is it? For either of us.'

A long silence as a pained stain of colour rose in his neck, and in which Beth would have done anything to take back this conversation. Fists clenched at his side, his voice thick with injured dignity, he mumbled, 'I shouldn't have asked. It were too soon. Clumsy idiot that I am.'

'No, no, I don't mind, really. I'm flattered that you should ask me. Thank you.' She couldn't bear to look at him.

'It weren't meant as flattery,' he burst out, angry at himself now. 'I meant it.'

'I don't doubt that you did,' Beth said, as gently as she could. 'And I'm very – very fond of you but . . .'

The unfinished sentence hung between them.

'I've got to go,' she said at last, unable to bear his unhappiness on top of her own. What a dreadful mess. She hadn't realised quite how lonely he must be. Living out at Cathra Crag with two old men must really get to him at times, and losing Tessa had obviously been the last straw.

Stuffing both hands into her anorak pockets she turned and ran across the fell. Andrew did not move until she had crested the ridge, then as she stopped to look back at him and wave, he simply turned away without responding, and strode off down the hill.

'Oh, God. Now what do I do?' Only the wind answered.

As she continued her climb up to Larkrigg Hall her heart grew heavier and her feet slowed with each step. How could it be otherwise when she must prepare herself for the prospect of spending yet another night with Sarah and Pietro's bliss ringing in her ears.

15

Pietro had begun to worry that he might have chosen the wrong twin, despite all his careful considerations. However fascinating and beautiful Sarah might be, she was completely self-centred and, to his great distress, not at all interested in marriage as a good Italian girl would be.

Somehow or other, he meant to compensate his family for their great loss all those years ago, to take revenge on their behalf. But if this plan did not succeed, then he must think of another. He knew not how or what, but something. Meg was the key. An independent lady who had much power over his twins.

He had imagined it would all be easy, but these silly girls thwarted him at every turn. He must persuade Sarah to stop the work and marry him. Otherwise, he would be forced to use his charms again upon the little Beth.

And so he watched Beth, saw again how appealing she was, how amenable and compliant. She might be too proper, too honourable for her own good, and certainly for his, yet the more she was forbidden to him, the more delectable she became.

If she brushed past him he could smell the sweet scent of her hair, burnished bright about the delicate oval of her face. He'd scarcely noticed before how the long dark lashes so often drooped to fan her pink cheeks. If only his impatience had not got the better of him, they might have been married by now. And he would then be closer to possessing his heart's desire.

Perhaps, he thought, it was not too late.

Freda Lightfoot

And so he strived to come home early, or to call in during the day, looking for any opportunity to be alone with her, to try to coax her to forgive him. And to his great delight she seemed confused and bewitched by his attentions, though he sensed her struggle with her conscience in every delightful tremor of her body.

Even when Sarah was at home he took calculated risks, freely offering to help Beth with the chores, seeking any moment he could to be alone with her.

Whenever she turned round he was at her side, putting his arms about her and kissing her neck when she was washing up or cooking their evening meal. Capturing her in the wood shed and slipping his fingers inside her blouse to seek the bud of her breasts and excite her even more. Or hiding behind the hen hut to jump out and capture her in his arms when she returned from feeding and watering the birds inside.

To Beth it was a blissful, torturous nightmare as he stole kisses, caressed her, brought her to the brink of a passion which threatened to engulf her and was then forced to slip silently away for fear of discovery.

He told her how he loved her. What a blind fool he'd been. So contrite and humble was he, and she so entirely besotted by the wonder of this astonishing declaration, that how could she not believe his every word?

It was shocking, wonderful, irresistible and quite impossible. He could hear the creak of her bed springs and knew she lay sleepless through the achingly long hours of darkness, wondering how she could find the strength to resist him. And how she could ever face her sister again if she did not.

She woke in some confusion. It was still dark but something had disturbed her. Was it that same tapping on her door, or a tree branch against her window? All her senses came alert and Beth became aware of Pietro standing by her bed. A moment later and he was kneeling beside her, gently stroking her hair.

'Did I wake you?'

'Yes.'

'You look like a child tucked up in bed.'

She gazed at him, a stream of light from the open door highlighting

192

the sculptured lines of his high cheekbones. Her eyes begged him to go away and leave her, for if he stayed she could not resist him. 'I'm not a child, Pietro, and you shouldn't be here, in my room.'

He kissed her cheek, and the corners of her mouth, softly and seductively and then her neck, his voice blurred and sleepy. 'Do not scold me, little one. I am a mere male and you know that I love you. How can I lie in my cold room alone when my body tells me you are so close. I miss you. I need you. Let me stay. Let us make love together.' He was peeling back the covers and cold air touched her flushed skin for a second as he slid in beside her. Her mind told her to protest, to stop him from this outrageous act but her lips refused to obey. She made room for him in the narrow bed.

His movements were swift and fluid, unbuttoning her nightgown with urgent fingers, covering her in soft kisses all the while. And as excitement rose hot and fierce in her breast she felt all sense of wrong slip from her. She wanted him to go on kissing her, wanted him so very badly her body ached for his touch.

Longing only to be a part of him, her body arched instinctively, revelling in painful ecstasy as his fingers located a rosy nipple and rubbed it between finger and thumb.

Then he pulled her down beneath him in the bed, pushing her into the soft pillows with his own weight as he drew her thighs apart.

'I want you, Beth. I have always wanted you. I mean to have you.'

She felt suddenly light-headed and terribly happy, and she moaned his name, delirious with need, thrusting aside the small voice at the back of her head which urged her to stop. Her desperate need to submit was too great to ignore.

'You have taken care of those little matters?' he asked, lifting her nightgown and clenching his hands about her buttocks. She gasped out weakly that she had.

'Good.' The weight and scent of him was overpowering, her mind slipping out of control. She could see the glint of his teeth as he smiled in the darkness then he traced the outline of her mouth, flushed rose from his kissing, with the tip of one finger and she responded with a whimper of desire.

Her body seemed consumed by wanting, willing to do anything he asked of it.

'Please,' she begged. 'Don't do this to me.' But she didn't want him to listen to her. She would die if he stopped now. All thought of Sarah was gone from her mind.

His mouth was somewhere about her breast, his hands busy with her nightgown, soothing, kissing and talking to her as he removed his own clothing. She could hardly bear to wait another second for him, but he seemed to feel it necessary to go on talking, persuading, soothing her, saying something about the three of them.

'So we can live happily together. The three of us. Why not? Not so terrible. These days anything is permissible, *si*?' His fingers grasped the soft mound of flesh and sank into soft moistness and she gave a yelp of shocked pleasure.

'W-what did you say? Three of us?'

'You, my sweet little one, me, and your so exciting sister. We make the perfect team, do we not?' And his tongue pushed between her teeth, rasping against hers.

It was as if she'd been drenched with ice, as if she were once more back in that snowdrift, frozen in pain. *Three*. Pietro, herself and *Sarah*? She felt every muscle tighten against him.

What was she thinking of? *This was her sister's man.* If she went through with this, if she let Pietro make love to her she would have betrayed Sarah as surely as her sister had stolen Pietro from her. She would have sunk to Sarah's most lowest and selfish level and be as without scruples as she.

'Let me go. *Let me go.*' But it was too late. The fullness of him was inside of her, thrusting and pulsing, his body grinding against hers and everything vanished from her mind in a torrent of shameful sensation. It was all over surprisingly quickly, a matter of seconds before he reached a shuddering climax and shouted something loud in Italian.

Then Beth was pushing him from her, tears rolling down her cheeks, and her body ached with pain as she desperately searched the tangle of bedclothes for her nightdress. Failing to find it she struggled out of the bed to stand shivering with cold and shame and terrible despair in the aftermath of this unwise coupling, on the bare boards of the damp bedroom.

'Get out,' she said, as calmly as she could manage.

He gazed serenely up at her, eyelids drooping with langorous fulfillment, and laughed. 'What you say?'

'I said get out. *Get out.*'

She continued to shout at him, her voice rising dangerously close to a scream, until swearing comprehensively and unintelligibly in fluent Italian, he gathered up his clothes and strode from the room. Then she collapsed on to the bed in a storm of tears.

'*No two people of the same blood would ever be able to live in harmony together within Larkrigg's four walls.*'

The prophecy seemed, all too terribly, to be coming true.

She had never meant it to happen. But it had, and she ached with guilt and shame. There'd been little pleasure in it, so hurried and furtive had it been. She should never have permitted him into her bed. How could he have taken such a risk?

But she could hardly blame Pietro. Hadn't she almost encouraged him by not protesting enough about his stolen kisses and caresses? Beth burned with shame and humiliation.

She daren't even imagine how Sarah would react if she ever discovered what had taken place.

What Sarah did to others was permissible, to have it done to herself was not even to be contemplated. Beth groaned in agony. Sarah might speak very grandly of being a free spirit, of Pietro loving them both, but in reality her sister would tear her limb from limb, pluck out her eyes and feed her to the birds if the truth came out. And it would be no more than she deserved.

Yet however exasperating and selfish Sarah was, she was still her twin and Beth knew she should not have hurt her in such a deeply intimate way. It was a terrible betrayal for which she should be punished.

Even so Beth had no wish to give him up. It was in her eyes, in the way her fingers strayed to touch him at every opportunity. If the love-making which had taken her virginity had been less ecstatic than she might have wished, the reason was obvious. How could they possibly be true and ardent lovers with such guilt upon them? The torment of their situation had marred their love. But dare she face her sister's wrath? Certainly not yet. Perhaps not ever.

She must never let him love her again. A vow fervently made, even though she doubted her strength to keep it. She must do whatever was necessary to avoid temptation.

*   *   *

'May I come and live with you?'

Beth gazed with pleading eyes at Ellen as she helped her feed the squirrels. Spring was always her busy time with a new crop of fledgling orphans to take care of. She didn't answer immediately, didn't even glance at her.

'I could help with the animals and I'd pay for my keep.'

'I raised these two nippers myself, started with warm milk and sugared water, now they're on full squirrel diet of peanuts and all the acorns I can root out for them. Their mother died as a result of acting as decoy to save them from a dog. Lost her life in saving theirs.'

'How dreadful.'

'It's what mothers do.'

'I suppose so. Sisters are rather different.'

Ellen chuckled. 'I reckon they are. Not getting on then?'

'Not much.'

Then after another long pause. 'There's a small bed in the spare room. You're welcome to that but it has no bedding.'

'I could bring some sheets and blankets from Larkrigg. And I'll pull my weight around the place. I won't be a nuisance.' Relief, and a valiant attempt to be cheerful about an impossible situation.

Ellen merely sniffed. 'You'd better not be. I've enough lame ducks about the place already.'

And so it was agreed. That afternoon Beth swept out the one other bedroom in Rowan cottage, made up the old iron bedstead with clean sheets and prepared to face Sarah with some sort of explanation, well removed from the truth.

In the event it proved remarkably simple. Over a carefully cooked chicken dinner, Beth explained her decision to leave.

'It's only for a little while. Ellen hasn't been too well lately,' she lied, crossing her fingers beneath the table, 'and she has a new influx of patients. Only yesterday she took in two squirrels, a stoat and a clutch of baby wagtails.' She was babbling, Beth warned herself. Mustn't overdo it. 'I'll stay with her till she feels more herself.'

Sarah thought her mad of course, and said as much, but put it down to Beth's foolish obsession with animals. 'And how am I supposed to manage?'

'I'll still come and work in the mill.'

'I mean here, at Larkrigg. I can't look after this place on my own. It's your pet project, remember.'

Beth promised faithfully that she would continue to do her bit at Larkrigg. Pietro scowled at her but judged it wise to make no protest.

The next day she moved in to Rowan cottage and felt an almighty sense of relief. Here she would be free from temptation, free from the nightly horror of hearing Sarah's throaty laughter mingling with Pietro's deeply caressing and much loved voice.

And free from the daily temptation of falling into his arms.

One day in early spring Meg and Tam arrived home and Beth and Sarah hurried along to greet them, wisely leaving Pietro at home.

They both looked happy, relaxed and tanned, and could hardly stop talking for a moment. There were long letters and presents from Boston. Family news to exchange. Meg and Tam were full of their trip, the children, Lissa and Derry and what a wonderful time they'd had together.

'We even visited some farms. It was fascinating to compare notes with American farmers. Their farms are so big.'

Then they listened with sympathy to the tale of the accident.

'You mustn't blame yourselves. It wasn't anybody's fault. Except perhaps the dog's. Andrew had no choice but to put it down. Once they have the blood lust on them, that's it, there's nothing you can do. There's no cure. I've known a farmer be forced to shoot his own dog, and silently cry about it afterwards, for all they claim not to feel any great affection for a working animal.'

'Jonty was furious and then it all got out of hand,' Beth explained.

'I wasn't too happy about the idea in the beginning,' Meg said. 'It's unfortunate that it should all end in this sad way but you mustn't blame yourself, any of you. Accidents happen, particularly on a farm where everything is so unpredictable. No one can guess how an animal is going to react.'

'It all happened so quickly,' Beth said. 'Tess rang the other day and she says Jonty's still flat on his back, will be for months yet. He has movement in his arms, is eating like a horse and telling everyone what to do.'

'That sounds healthy enough.'

Beth smiled. 'She also says they've given him a shave, cut his hair and he looks a different man. Long hair and bandannas are not allowed in hospital, apparently. But he has a long way to go. Broken ribs to mend, lots of painful physiotherapy ahead.'

Meg put a consoling hand on her arm. 'I'm sure he has the strength to pull through. And he has Tessa.'

Beth half glanced at Sarah. 'Yes, he has Tess.'

'It is entirely in keeping with her character that she should devote herself to him. What strength that girl has. You wouldn't believe how she suffered at the hands of that feckless husband of hers. I do hope she and Jonty find some happiness together. She deserves it. I've told her, if there's ever anything we can do, Tam and I, she has only to say.'

'I'm sure she knows that,' Sarah drily remarked.

Meg looked at her for a moment, considered challenging the tone of voice and then opted for a change of subject.

'And how are you both?' She gazed shrewdly at the twins, particularly Beth.

'Blooming,' Sarah laughed.

'Me too. I'm fine.'

'You don't look fine.'

'I've been working hard. We both have. At the mill and on the house. What a winter we've had. You wouldn't believe.' And she told about the roof falling in, and of being lost in the snowdrift, making it all sound like a merry joke.

Tam intervened as he saw further creases of worry gather on Meg's face. 'This can surely wait till another day. We're too tired for any more news right now. Jet-lag, you know. We oldies need to sleep.'

'Oh, but we've quite caught the travel bug,' Meg laughed.

'Aye, we might try a trip around Europe next, eh Meg?'

'Absolutely. Flying was wonderful. I wouldn't mind having a go myself.'

'Oh, Grandma.'

'What have I said?'

'Is there nothing you couldn't do?' Tam teased and Meg grinned.

'Not if I set my mind to it.' And they all burst out laughing.

It was a lovely, chattering afternoon and when it was time for them to go, Meg and Tam stood at the door and waved until the twins had climbed the hill.

'What do you think of all this then?' she said. 'Commune indeed. It wasn't like that in our day.'

And grinning, Tam tucked his arm about her waist. 'No,' he agreed. 'I had you all to myself. The way I liked it.'

Meg looked up at him startled, and then burst out laughing. 'Go on with you, you old romantic.' And they closed the door on a star-filled night, content to be home.

Pretending to Meg that everything was fine had been the hardest thing Beth had ever had to do.

Throughout the long days of winter she had nursed her sorrow alone. Silent tears had blocked her heart with pain as she'd wished she could sob or rail or cry. But what good would that have done? Sarah was right. She had refused Pietro on more than one occasion. First she'd messed up their love-making and then had put off the wedding upon which he had apparently set his heart.

No wonder he'd grown bored with her shy indecisiveness, as most of the male sex did in the end. It was all entirely her own fault. She didn't sparkle as Sarah did. She couldn't be witty and vivacious. She wasn't *wickedly* exciting. She was dull and rather childish.

And she was also incredibly stupid, because on top of everything else, she'd upset Andrew as well. She hadn't seen him since his crazy proposal that day by the tarn, but she'd sometimes wished that she could love him. He was exactly the kind of man Mom would choose for her. Steady, reliable, kind and gentle. Good husband material. And there was something she liked about him. He had pride and courage, a sense of humour and . . .

But he wasn't Pietro. How could she ever love anyone after Pietro?

How could she ever explain to Andrew how she truly felt, and how this terrible mess had all come about? That Sarah blamed her for Jonty's accident, so therefore decided this gave her the right to claim Pietro as her own. Sarah without a man was unthinkable. And Beth knew from long experience that any further protest would only make her own agony worse. So she'd faced her grandmother with what good grace she could muster. And thankfully Meg had seemed satisfied by her answers.

But she should have known better.

* * *

The following morning Meg came to see them, with that familiar light of determination in her clear eyes.

'Now about Broombank Mill,' she began. 'I have to admit to a sense of disappointment.'

Beth listened without argument to Meg's justifiable complaints of their negligence, and to Sarah's excuses. She made none herself. She felt almost as if this conversation were taking place a dozen miles away and her head was a soft squashy ball that could absorb none of it.

'Sam is fine at the knitting,' Sarah was saying, 'but he has far too much say in the way things are run generally. And Jan doesn't have the time. I think she's tired of it.'

'I agree Jan has too much to do.'

'I've been giving this some serious thought and if you gave me my head, Meg, I could do things so much better. I'm not short of ideas.'

What was she saying? Beth struggled to understand.

'But I wouldn't be happy simply driving a boring van about. We could employ a young lad to do the deliveries. Or Pietro would be glad to do it. He's already offered to help.'

Has he? Beth thought. When was that?

Meg was looking very thoughtful. 'True,' she said. 'You're very quiet, Beth. What's your opinion?'

She felt cold in every limb, her lips too stiff to form the words correctly yet she must have managed it, for they were coming out of her mouth. 'I really couldn't say. I admit I've spent far too much time working on Larkrigg. And looking at the state of the roof after this winter's snow storms, I reckon it was all a waste of time. You were right, Gran. We should have left well alone.'

Meg looked troubled. 'Dear me, this isn't like you, Beth, to be so defeatist. You said yesterday that you were fine.'

Sarah cut in, 'She's tired. She fusses too much about the hens and the house, the roof falling in completely, which no doubt it will in the end.' She smiled her radiant smile. 'We've none of us got much sleep this winter.'

Beth stared at her but did not make any further comment.

'Then it looks like you'd best start working in earnest, to pay for a new one.' Meg turned back to Sarah. 'We'll have to call a board meeting of course, but you have my vote. I certainly don't want any more responsibilities.' And it might do you some good, young lady, she thought. This was exactly what she had hoped for. 'It's time for Tam and me to take things a bit easier and let you younger ones take the weight. I've always believed that responsibility is good for people. We'll put it to the family this very afternoon that you, together with Beth of course, should take complete control of the company. And be properly paid for your efforts.' She smiled, and somehow Beth managed to smile back.

There was surprisingly little resistance to the plan, except from Jan who made the point that better time-keeping would be required. Sarah had the grace to humbly apologise and agree.

'You'd have to learn the business from the ground up,' Jan said.

'We'd want to,' Sarah smoothly agreed.

Beth could hardly believe what she was hearing. Events seemed to be running away from her.

Why on earth had Sarah suddenly taken it into her head to run Broombank? She hated work, everyone knew that. Jan too wanted to know, but unlike Beth had no qualms about asking.

'What's in it for you?'

'Money.' Sarah's lovely face was quite open and frank. 'We are financially embarrassed at the bank. We still need to finish the renovations before we can even think of selling Larkrigg. We need money. Isn't that right, Beth?'

She could hardly deny it.

And so, with little more discussion from anyone, the motion was carried. Sarah, with Beth to help her, would be entirely responsible for the day to day running of Broombank Mill, while remaining answerable to the family at the regular monthly board meetings.

Each morning Sarah put on her smartest suit and went off to work at the Broombank. You'd think she was working in the city of London to see the fuss she made, Beth thought.

'What do you think of this blue? No, too severe.' Ripped off and tossed aside on to the bed with the other discarded items. Later, Beth would have to put them all away, of course. 'The green then? No, not really my colour. No idea why I bought the thing. You can have it, if you like.'

'Thanks.'

'On second thoughts, forget it. Why would you need such a smart suit, for God's sake?' A gurgle of girlish laughter.

A performance which might once have amused Beth, but now only served to fuel this hateful feeling of jealousy and resentment.

Sarah had bought a small, nippy Renault and every weekend went off to Carlisle or Kendal, seeking yet more outfits commensurate with her new business image. Her newly increased salary wouldn't last long at this rate, Beth thought, somewhat uncharitably.

On that first morning, she too arrived at Broombank Mill early, dressed ready for a day's work.

'I don't think so, darling,' Sarah protested, shaking her head and making the ebony curls dance merrily about her lovely head as she laughed. 'Helping with deliveries is one thing, but you'd be absolutely no good in an office. You know how scatter-brained you are. And someone needs to stay here and look after those dratted animals.'

'We only have a few poultry.'

'Hens, geese. Whatever. They need care, haven't you said so a hundred times? And what about all those tasks around the place you're always going on about? Fixing this kitchen door so that it shuts properly for a start. Finishing the decorating. Building those new shelves in the study. You'll love having us out of the way, so you can get on with them in peace.' She stuffed a packet of sandwiches into a fashionable leather satchel and smiled vaguely in Beth's direction as she continued, 'I'll ring someone about the roof. We can't go on with half of it on the spare room bed.'

'We have no money.'

Sarah slung the satchel on to her shoulder and headed for the door, high heels tapping on the slate floor. 'I'll speak with the bank manager. Surely even he will be able to see the sense in having it fixed, otherwise our investment in this house will be ruined. We can get a mortgage to do the rest of the repairs. Get some professionals in. Even your DIY schemes aren't quite up to re-roofing, darling.'

'Would you like me to see him?' Remembering how Sarah had refused to speak with him about their small overdraft.

'No, sweetie. I'm a businesswoman now. I can deal with it.' She opened the door and called up the stairs. 'Pietro, are you ready? We're going to be late for heaven's sake.' The sound of her heels died away in the hall and the front door closed with a crisp click, echoing through the empty house.

Beth stood where she was for a long moment until, blinking furiously, she turned to the stove and poured herself a fresh cup of coffee.

She took a sip of the scalding black liquid, which was so hot it brought a sudden sting of tears to her eyes.

She was glad to be alone, she told herself resolutely as she cleared the table, scrubbed now to a pristine whiteness. She turned on the taps, swishing soap suds in the bowl. And she'd no wish to become a modern businesswoman, none at all. The animals and the land were much more her province. Dare she risk any more animals? Perhaps not. Yet Beth felt she really ought to do more to justify her existence, her dream.

She could try her Christmas tree project. But somehow the fun had quite gone out of everything and the prospect of day after day alone on this empty fell, in this empty house, seemed strangely daunting.

She dried the dishes and stowed them away in the neatly painted dresser. She folded the tablecloth and napkins, placed the fruit bowl back on the table. Positive thinking, that was the key. Establish a routine.

But what should she do today? She glanced about the tidy kitchen. Through the open kitchen window she heard the joyous notes of a carolling song thrush, and from somewhere deep in the heart of Brockbarrow Wood, a cuckoo's throaty call. Beth put back her shoulders and made herself smile. She could start on the spring digging, feed the hens, ducks and geese, mend some walls, replenish the log store. Then she'd check out jobs needing attention in the house.

Yes, she told herself with steadfast resolve. There was plenty to occupy her. She needed no one, no one at all.

16

The days stretched out longer than Beth had ever expected, her once seemingly endless chores now failing to fill the emptiness, no matter how hard she tried.

With the last two hundred pounds in their building society account, she bought a thousand christmas trees.

'Now's the time to plant them,' the nursery told her, giving full instructions. She spent the rest of that week slicing rows of grooves in the thin soil and treading in the young whips.

'There,' she said, the wind lifting her hair and her spirits in a burst of energy. 'And if I do the same each and every year, in a few years I can market them.' It gave her some sense of satisfaction that she too could make a useful contribution.

But the energy quickly evaporated. The silence of the fells seemed deeper, the skies somehow wider, the wind colder and less friendly. Despite the busy activity of a group of hedge sparrows squabbling over territory, and the return of the house martins carrying fresh mud to patch up last year's nest in the eaves of the old house, despite her very real progress with her garden, she was lonely.

In the evenings when Pietro and Sarah came home from the mill she would thankfully escape to Rowan cottage with Ellen and steadfastly refuse to mourn.

But Ellen, in fact, needed little help and with not enough to fill her day, and the aching loneliness of the nights, in desperation Beth once more presented herself at the mill.

✳ ✳ ✳

'I've told you to keep away. There's nothing for you to do here,' was Sarah's greeting.

'There must be something.'

'Yes, keep out of my way.'

Sarah made it quite clear that Beth's presence was not required, which made her feel more inadequate than ever. Yet stubbornly refusing to take no for an answer she helped with some packing. Unfortunately that didn't take very long. Then she swept the floor and tidied the stock shelves which brought sly glances and mumbles of resentment from the young girls whose job it usually was. Beth next asked to be shown how to use one of the machines but this too was refused. Eventually, one of the older women told her she was unsettling everyone, making them feel that their jobs weren't safe.

'They think if you learn to do it, they'll be out of work.' Horrified by this, she scurried back to the office only to be met by Sarah's furious glare.

'I thought you'd gone home? You should stay there.' She almost added – where you belong, but managed to restrain herself in time.

Beth ate her sandwiches at lunch time outside on the wall, quite alone and in complete despair. Nothing she did seemed to go right. Having interfered with everyone else's work that morning no one would be friends with her. Besides, they saw her as part of the management and not one of them. Sarah saw her as a nuisance.

By late afternoon, desperate for any occupation, she was back in the packing room, checking the stacked boxes in readiness for Pietro to collect the next morning. It was quiet in here and at least she was out of the way. Then she heard voices raised in anger, one of them Sarah's and she stood quite still, unashamedly listening. The voice carried clearly through the fibre board inner walls.

'I've told you before, you are not, on any account, to defy my instructions. I specifically promised that the order would be completed by the end of this month.'

'You should have checked wi' me first. There's no way we can meet that deadline. We're already full to busting wi' work.' Sam's voice, steady and firm.

'But we have to, you silly man. I promised.'

'Only way we could manage it would be for you to take on extra staff. Nay, that'd be no good neither, not without more machinery and space to put 'em.' Beth could almost hear him thinking, chewing over the problem in his steady way. 'And Foster and Son have been waiting two months too long already, we hev to see to them first. I can't see any way out. You'll hev to ring 'em up and put 'em off for a week or two. They'll understand.'

The slam of a fist hard upon the table. 'No, they won't understand. They'll think we've let them down. That *I've* broken my promise.'

'Nay, I'm sorry Miss Sarah, but if you will risk giving such short delivery dates, this is bound to happen. You hev to give us time to knit the damned things.'

'Don't you swear at me.' Sarah's voice rose with such fury that Beth started to tremble on Sam's behalf, all her sympathy going out to him, for he was surely only trying to do a good job. 'You're fired. Do you hear me? *Fired.*'

All sound faded away. All chatter ceased, every machine stopped working. Only Radio One continued to blare out the cheerful sounds of 'Take a Chance on Me', though there were no longer any voices joining in with the words.

'Nay lass,' Sam, almost disbelieving but not at all conciliatory. 'I've worked here since we first set off, near fifteen years ago.'

'Then perhaps it's time you had a change.' The chilling words rang out clear, drowning the happy voices of Abba. Beth crept to the door and peeped in to the big room. All the women and girls were standing about, mouths agape, and Sam was white-faced, stunned by what had befallen him.

'You wouldn't like to talk this over with your gran first?' he suggested.

'I'd like you to collect your cards from the office at four o'clock sharp, and leave.' On that, Sarah spun round and fixed everyone with such a glare they all scurried back to work. Then there was nothing but the tap of her heels on the slate floor and the slam of her office door.

Beth went at once to Sam and tentatively touched his arm with the tips of her fingers. He looked shrunken, diminished, as if his whole world had fallen in upon him, which in a way it had.

'I'll talk to her, try to get her to change her mind. She might, when she cools down.'

He turned grateful eyes to meet hers but they were old suddenly, and empty. 'Aye, I'd appreciate that. Only I don't reckon much to your chances.'

Neither did Beth but she could at least try.

Sarah was sitting behind her desk staring sightlessly at order books and balance sheets when she heard the door open and saw her sister slip in. She drew in a deep breath and waited for the lecture to begin. It came, as expected.

'You can't sack Sam. He's kept this place going for years.'

'It won't fall apart just because one employee is given the push for insubordination.'

'He's only eight years from his pension and he'll never get another job at his age. It would be too cruel to let him go.'

'He should have thought of that before and worked a bit harder. He thinks we're still in the playful sixties not the late seventies with a new decade round the corner. We have to compete. Times are hard.'

Beth considered her sister across the desk and frowned. 'You sound as sour as old Miss Philips at the Academy. For goodness' sake, what's come over you lately? You're not usually so callous. What has Sam done that's so terrible? Told you the truth perhaps? I do sympathise, Sarah, but if the order can't be ready in time then that's the way it is. Accept it, apologise to the customer and take more care in fixing dates in future.'

'Which shows how much you know about business. We wouldn't have got that order at all if I hadn't promised delivery in three weeks.'

'Three weeks isn't very long. Perhaps we're not geared up to such quick deliveries. Why take the risk?'

'Why don't you stay home and play with your dratted hens?'

Beth flinched but held her ground. 'Is there something else worrying you?' she ventured and held her breath. Such as my behaviour with Pietro? She almost felt giddy as she waited for Sarah's response.

'Now what could possibly be worrying me? Because this business is falling apart at the seams maybe? Because however hard I try, the work doesn't get done quickly enough? Or there isn't sufficient money in the account to buy the wool they need to keep up with the orders? Now why should that worry me?'

Or because I'm out of my depth for the first time in my life, and daren't admit it? came the unwelcome thought into Sarah's mind, a fear that ate away at her constantly at times. Quickly outshone today by a certain sense of triumph at seeing her sister's stunned expression at her list of problems. That would show her.

'I'm sure it isn't as bad as all that. The business isn't in serious trouble, is it?'

Sarah sighed, trying to avoid her shrewd gaze. Her twin could be strangely perceptive at times and she'd no wish for her to know quite how serious the problems were. 'No, Beth, we're not in serious trouble. The business is basically good, once I have implemented some changes. If I am permitted to do so without interference, that is.'

'We need more capital, is that it?'

Sarah widened violet eyes in mocking disbelief. 'At last, you've realised the problem. Welcome to the real world,' and laughed when Beth flushed. 'Yes, of course we are under-financed, having expanded too rapidly in the past, I dare say. And that light-fingered manager didn't help. Added to which, you and I are living in a house that has half fallen down around our ears and is costing a small fortune to restore. And we know who to blame for that, don't we?'

If they could only sell the dratted thing, that might solve everything, Sarah inwardly grieved. But they'd never get a good price for it, not the way it stood now. Even if she persuaded Beth to agree.

Beth pulled a chair up to the desk and sat down, propping her chin in her hand and regarding her sister across it with a brave smile. 'I know you can solve this. I have every faith in you. You've always been the clever one. Don't worry about Larkrigg. Tell me what you want done and I'll do it. You can forget about paying builders, I'm not afraid of hard work.'

Sarah had scarce the patience to take any more of Beth's stalwart good will. There was only one solution. She'd known it all along. 'Come on. Get your coat on.'

'Where are we going?'

'To see that friendly bank manager of yours. A mortgage on Larkrigg might just solve the problem.'

'A mortgage?'

'We have discussed it before, and it was your suggestion in the first place, remember?'

'So I did. Do you think we'd get one?'

'Why not? We're both working now.' Spoken with wry good humour.

'What about Sam?'

Sarah paused at the door, recognising the mulish set of her sister's mouth and gave in. 'Fine. OK. Sam can have his job back so long as we get all the money we need out of that dratted house to set this business on its feet.'

Beth beamed her delight. 'Just show me where to sign. Wait for me in the car. I'll tell him right away, then he doesn't worry.'

It proved surprisingly easy to arrange a mortgage on Larkrigg Hall, since there was none on it at present and Sarah felt quite light-hearted with relief as she climbed into the big four poster that night.

She watched Pietro move about the room, carefully folding his clothes. It was one of the things which delighted her most about him. His style and his fashionable expertise. His naked body too was pretty good, firm and supple as a god, and her fingers itched to touch it.

'We're going to make pots and pots of money. Won't that be fun?'

He laughed. 'Yes, I suppose it will.'

'You don't sound too sure.'

He came towards her. 'I am sure, if it make you happy.'

'You make me happy.'

'*Prego.*'

'You like Beth too.'

'Of course.'

'I see you looking at her sometimes.'

'Not as I look at you.'

'Love me?'

'You know that I do. I wish you to be my wife.'

Chuckling, she flung back the covers and spread wide her legs, tantalising him by letting him see every part of her. 'Prove it then.'

And he did indeed do his utmost to show how comprehensively he loved her until he fell fast asleep, sated and exhausted.

Sarah lay watching him for a long while, smoothing her fingers over the perfect swoop of his brow, the high-boned line of his cheek. Her last waking thought was that if perhaps he was not quite so vigorous as Jonty in his love-making, at least he adored her and belonged exclusively to her. Jonty would never belong to anyone. The dreadful Tessa had got the worst deal after all. And snuggling into her pillow she concluded that perhaps she had got the right man in the end.

Better still, she now had the finance she so badly needed. Nothing could stop her. She meant to be successful. And very, very rich. Nothing and no one would stand in her way.

During the weeks that followed, Sarah discovered a surprising fulfillment from her work at the mill. She made sweeping changes and kept a strict eye on wages, installing a system of piece-work which meant the women had to work all the harder in order to reach a bonus and make a decent wage. This, she felt, had been most beneficial as it kept them on their toes. They didn't waste half so much time on tea and lunch breaks now, which must be all to the good. It had admittedly caused some friction for a while but she'd solved that in the end by a change of staff.

Out went several of the older women who she decided were too difficult to deal with and in came younger girls who were so afraid of her they did exactly as she told them. Which was how she liked it. Above everything she hated disagreeable employees who thought they knew more about how the operation should be run than she did.

She laid off the cottage hand knitters as she decided they were too slow and inefficient and bought in new knitting machines, which meant there was less space to operate in and Sam complained about this, saying the Factory and Shops Inspector would not approve when next he called.

'Damn the inspector,' Sarah said, and met Sam's stubborn expression with such a fierce one of her own that he was compelled to back down. Admittedly he might have a point but if she was willing to take the risk, what business was it of his? It could be years before anyone troubled to investigate them way up here on the high fells, and she would have taken her profits and gone by then.

He wouldn't complain again, she knew that. His job was far too precious to him. She had won, as she usually did.

She sent Pietro out round the shops as a representative which proved to be a brilliant move. The women proprietors were so captivated by his good looks and Latin charm that they ordered far more stock than they'd meant to. And if Sarah worried sometimes that he might take advantage of these situations she shunted them aside. Their love-making was proving most satisfactory, much more inventive now that Beth had gone and they were entirely alone each evening. He'd taken her on the kitchen table last night, right in there among the remains of dinner. She laughed to think of it. It was good to have him all to herself, exactly the way she liked it.

Yes, everything was progressing well. The orders poured in and with more machines and staff to operate them, plus her competitive bonus schemes, delivery dates were much better kept. Which proved that her methods were working. Let the women grumble. It was profits which counted at the end of the day, or they'd all be out of a job.

By the end of the year she felt quite confident that the business would be pulling out of its difficulties and she could start to relax.

By the following year she meant to make even greater profits. She hadn't quite worked out how yet, but knew that she would. It was imperative.

Large sums of money had been spent on Larkrigg Hall repairing the roof, making the structure sound and fitting out a new kitchen which Beth had resisted for a time but Sarah had insisted upon.

She'd had two new bathrooms installed since the ancient Victorian one had been quite inadequate, and had the whole place rewired and refurbished by experts, sweeping away all of Beth's homemade efforts. New carpets covered the bare boards, the walls were papered in tasteful designs, the pine woodwork gleamed and new curtains hung at the windows. You really wouldn't recognise the place, she thought with satisfaction.

And their lives had opened up so much more. She and Pietro had collected a group of friends and acquaintances among the more select of their neighbours and built up a most entertaining social life.

They had several people in to dinner at least once a week and frequently they would throw an impromptu party, when they'd consume tons of food and the wine would flow freely. Sarah loved to party. Really, she was almost grateful for Beth's insistence that they stay and renovate Larkrigg Hall, for it had proved to be the ideal house for entertaining. Everyone remarked upon how beautiful it was, and how clever she was to have made such a good job of it.

The only problem was that she was growing bored. Sarah

considered that she'd achieved what she'd set out to achieve and was beginning to lose interest.

What was the point in working too hard, if you could make enough money without? Her wardrobe was filled with enchanting dresses and smart suits. A new car stood in the drive.

True, Gran was always trying to interfere and make her keep things the way they'd been for years, wittering on about tradition. The bank manager grumbled at her from time to time, and sent her not very pleasant letters, but she didn't trouble herself over either of them, old fuddy-duddies that they were.

So long as her workers kept churning out the goods she would go on spending the profits, and darling Pietro would help her.

'You're too soft with her. If Sarah says jump you jump. Tell her no for a change.'

Beth gazed mournfully at Andrew and conceded that he might have a point. Sarah seemed to grow ever more demanding and wild. After the last party she'd thrown, they'd all danced so wildly to 'You're the One that I want', pretending they were John Travolta and Olivia Newton-John it'd taken Beth the best part of a week to get the wine stains out of the carpet. 'I can't help it. It's always been this way.'

Particularly since I betrayed her by sleeping with Pietro, and have to seek ways constantly to salve my conscience, night and day. She did her utmost to avoid him, but it wasn't easy, for he continued to court her good will and seek her love.

He brought her small gifts and bunches of wild flowers to express his need for her, begging her to let him make love to her; once demanding they run away and marry. But she would not.

'She asks and you provide,' Andrew said.

'Something like that.'

They were sitting on a tree stump at the edge of the wood eating sandwiches, having spent the morning walking the fells to check on his sheep and this season's crop of lambs, now fat and harassing the life out of their mothers. From deep in the dale came the whirr of machinery on the sultry air as the harvesting had begun at Broombank, but up here all was peace and quiet, except for the drone of bees in the sweet scented heather.

Beth always loved to walk on the hills and Andrew, as their

nearest neighbour, was good company. He never minded her tagging along, almost seemed to welcome it. Since the day he'd found her in the snow their friendship had grown steadily, though he had never again repeated his offer of marriage for which she was most grateful. He'd only ever asked her out of pity, because they were both hurting. But it wouldn't have worked. She could never imagine any sort of romance between them.

He made a rude sound in his throat. 'Even when she steals your fella you do nothing. I am right, aren't I? She did take Pietro because you wanted him?'

'Because she needed him. I had my chance. I asked him to wait and he couldn't, not then. He thought I didn't truly care for him.' If there hadn't been the accident, if I hadn't made him wait, we'd be married now, she thought. Instead, she'd been thrown into the hateful roll of the 'other woman'. She'd betrayed her own sister and could barely live with herself as a result.

'So how come you still moon after him? Have you no pride?'

Beth flinched at his harsh words, so unlike him. Why was he being so disagreeable? 'I don't moon after him.' Oh, but she did, which Andrew really ought to understand. Wasn't he still agonising over the loss of Tessa, even after all this time?

Andrew was a good man but not for a moment could she consider telling him the whole truth about her relationship with Pietro. And a part of her was afraid of losing his respect.

He was still quiet and difficult to talk to at times, keeping his own council in a way she found hard to deal with but he'd come to be an important part of her life. There had even been times during these last months when she'd wished they could have fallen in love with each other, instead of with other people. Life would have been a good deal less complicated for them both. But you couldn't plan the way you felt about a person.

Pietro made her feel good. With him, all her shyness evaporated and she felt happy and alive, never silly or awkward. Pietro said that if she agreed to continue their affair the twins would simply be sharing him, as twins should share things. So far, she had managed to resist these persuasions.

'You're obsessed with him. You both are.'

Beth bridled. 'Absolutely not. Anyway, even if it were true, is that such a crime?' She bit down hard on her sandwich, not tasting it. She must never tell Andrew what she had done. Not ever. It was her own shameful secret, her private guilt.

'Do you still go to the mill?'

She shook her head. 'I had to give that up. Sarah won't hear of my working in it.'

'There you go again, letting her push you out of what you have every right to be a part of.'

Beth had made no protest when Sarah had taken complete charge of everything, including the final restoration of Larkrigg. But then how could she? She owed her too much. So it had seemed petty to fight over who controlled the mill.

'It's probably just as well. We get on better if we spend as much time as possible apart. Sad but true. Anyway, I'm happy enough looking after Larkrigg and my poultry, and helping Ellen of course.'

'Skivvying,' he snorted, and Beth felt bound to protest.

'Not at all. I love working at Larkrigg.'

Hard work was her refuge, for there were still those oh-so-painful moments when she couldn't rid her mind of the picture of Sarah and Pietro together. And when work failed her, she was glad to escape to the hills, alone or with Andrew, anywhere to avoid the torment of her own thoughts or the sight of the two lovers.

And so it must remain, for the present at least. Until Sarah let him go.

'It won't last.' She'd spoken the thought out loud, before she'd had time to stop herself. Andrew glanced at her.

'What won't last?'

She flushed deep pink but continued, 'This affair between Sarah and Pietro.'

A long tense silence grew between them. 'And then you imagine he'll come back to you, is that it?'

Beth bravely met his accusing gaze with a steady one of her own. 'I know that he will. Sarah grows bored with everything in the end. She always has. And Pietro still likes me. H-he's said so.'

Andrew made a sound now that quite shocked her and standing up, threw the sandwich as far as he could. It bounced down the hill and fell at the feet of a surprised ewe. She'd offended him again. He seemed peculiarly sensitive today.

'Damn it, Beth. Do you intend to spend your entire life picking up your sister's leavings? Why, for God's sake?'

'Because I won't have stolen him then. She'll have given him up of her own free will and it won't have been my fault.'

She thought for one terrible moment that he might hit her. When he spoke again, his voice was hard as granite.

'I see that you demean yourself with this sort of talk and I'll hear no more of it.' Then he picked up his crook and strode away down the hill, not glancing back once to wave, as he usually did. Beth watched him go with a deepening sadness in her heart, then put her head in her hands and began to cry.

17

Life had once seemed so sweet. A game to play and enjoy. A dream to pursue, friends around to share it. Now everything had gone wrong. She was being torn apart. What should she do? Give up all hope of happiness? Or snatch at whatever love she could find with Pietro, as he begged her to do?

Tears spurted and ran between her fingers. Beth had never felt so desolate, so low, and she continued to sob as if her heart would break.

When her tears were quite spent she lay for a long time exhausted, curled up by the roots of the old ash tree. Like a small mouse in the silence of the woods.

After a time she slept, then she watched a stoat emerge from the undergrowth with a pheasant's egg, its long sleek body glinting in the sun. It rolled the egg patiently with the tip of its nose through the long grasses and disappeared with it down a hole only to return seconds later for the next.

Patient, methodical, a thief stealing what didn't belong to him. Was she like that? No, Sarah was like the stoat. Sarah was the thief. She had stolen Pietro in the first place. So if he now wished to return to her of his own free will, hadn't he every right to do so? She only had to be patient.

Was that why Andrew was upset? Because no matter how long he waited, he could never have Tessa, never know the happiness which one day she would enjoy with Pietro?

Sarah would no doubt return to America, or go on that continental tour she'd kept promising herself for years. Running the mill would soon pall, and country life had never appealed. Then she would tire of Pietro too and leave him for the bright lights and seek a new man to flatter and wait upon her.

Beth hugged herself, and not seeing any flaws in her own reasoning, felt better with each passing minute.

Wasn't such happiness worth waiting for?

By the time the stoat had hurried away with its last prize, she felt quite able to stand and gaze over the majesty of the landscape, laughing as a tiny vole, startled by her sudden movement, scurried into the undergrowth. The sun blinked at her through the branches, and the warmth of the earth seemed to have seeped into her soul and calmed her.

Perhaps she would talk with Sarah, in a general sort of way. Try to test the true nature of her feelings. Yes, of course. Why hadn't she thought to do so before? Sarah might be contented at the moment but she always tired of everything, in the end.

And with this new and fragile recovery, she set off across the fell on a lighter step.

Pietro too was in Brockbarrow Wood, on the opposite side from Beth's situation. He lay beneath a low canopy of hazel, well hidden from sight.

From here he could see right across the dale. He could see Broombank below, nestling in the cleft of the hill. He saw Sarah drive up, in a temper again, he thought. She'd ruin the clutch on her new car if she didn't calm down.

He could see Meg moving about in the farm yard, calling to Tam to come inside and he felt a burning resentment for their obvious contentment, envied them their comfortable life. Why should they have so much and he so little? That could have been him down there. Those could have been his sheep. Instead of which he'd been forced to suffer his stepfather's scathing remarks, constantly telling him how useless he was.

And he was not useless, he was deprived. He had been deprived long ago of his true heritage, to live here, in these beautiful green mountains and learn the land of his forefathers. Family is all important, every Italian knows this, and his parents' marriage had been destroyed because his grandfather had given up everything which should have been his, to this ambitious, avaricious woman.

He heard Meg laugh at something Tam had said, as if she had not a care in the world. Then he put his arms about her and kissed her cheek as if she were a girl still.

This woman was happily married yet his mother had known nothing but trouble. How could she, such a beautiful lady, have been expected to be content with life as a simple baker's wife, struggling to find every penny? She was a woman of great pride. His father had failed her, as his father, Jack, had in turn failed them all. No wonder she had left him for another, richer man. But it had ruined all their lives. The moment she left them, his father had become a broken man, the family was in ruins.

And the source of these great troubles lay here, at Broombank, in their past.

His mother would have been happy here, with much money and family about her. With space and beauty and good air to breathe, instead of the poverty in their poor village, the small overcrowded house and long hours of grinding hard work. No wonder she left with the first man who offered her freedom and a comfortable life.

And so he must take his revenge. For the sake of his father who had lost everything. For the sake of his mother, who had been so forced by deprivation to take the course that she had. For the sake of himself. And at the same time, Pietro would enjoy proving to his stepfather that he too could be a man of action, and perhaps substance, one day.

'What d'you think you're doing?'

He started at the soft voice in his ear, then rolled over in the grass and looked up into Ellen's curious, brown-eyed stare.

'Stalking?' he said, grabbing the first idea which came to mind. 'Watching for the deer.'

Ellen frowned her disbelief. She'd watched this young man often while she went quietly about her business in the woods. Not that he'd ever noticed he was being watched, but there was something about his behaviour that didn't ring true. She could always smell suspicious behaviour in an animal, a man wasn't much different.

219

'You don't get many deer so near to habitation at this time of year. You've no glasses? You won't see much without a good pair of binoculars. They like to keep their distance.'

She sank softly to her knees beside him in the long grass and gazed out across the fell tops, eyes studying the skyline, combing the craggy outcrops, the sheep cropped turf. 'Where is he then? Stag is it, or hind with a young un?'

'He's gone.' Pietro got quickly to his feet. 'And I must go too.'

'He must've gone quickly.' A movement caught Ellen's eye. Meg and Tam moving about some distance below in Broombank yard, their voices carrying with easy clarity on the soft breeze. She watched them for a moment then her eyes slid back to Pietro and as their gazes locked an understanding dawned. 'You get a good view of Broombank from here.'

'Yes,' he said, holding her gaze. 'So you do.'

'And you watch.'

'So? Is it the crime that I watch the twins' family at work?'

Ellen got stiffly to her feet and brushed her hands on the seat of her trousers. 'Depends why you're doing it. And what you were thinking as you watched.'

'I think nothing. What should I think?'

Still Ellen held fast to his gaze, studying him with the same keen observation with which she studied her wild creatures. 'Good folk, the O'Cleary's. Friends of mine.'

'Of course. Mine too.' He half turned away, dropping his gaze, avoiding the knowing gaze that seemed to peer right into his soul. 'I must go. I have the work to do. I should not even be here.'

'No, you should not.'

And with a brisk nod he hurried off in the direction of Larkrigg. But Ellen was thoughtful. He'd not liked her curiosity. It'd caused him great discomfort. Were she a more fanciful woman, she'd imagine his expression in the second before he'd broken that telling gaze, to be one of enmity.

When Beth reached Ellen's cottage about an hour later, after a long and healing walk, Ellen asked if she had seen Pietro.

'No, should I have done?'

She shrugged her shoulders. 'I wondered.'

220

Beth shook her head. 'He's out on a long delivery run today. He won't be back until late, he said.'

'Ah.'

'I saw Andrew.'

Keen brown eyes pierced her. 'How was he?'

'Fine.'

'You two speaking, are you?'

'Why shouldn't we be?'

'You're picking up my phrases a bit too handy, I reckon.'

Beth grinned. 'Andrew and I are good friends. There, will that do? But don't start your match-making with us. We're not a couple of your strays. We'll organise our own lives, thanks very much.'

'Aye, and a right mess you'll make of it, an' all.' Ellen turned away, briskly changing the subject.

'Are you free to help an old woman then?'

Beth glanced teasingly about her. 'I don't see any around.'

'Flatterer.' Ellen laughingly handed her a bag of scraps. 'Injured swan, settled on the tarn. He won't stop long, probably lost his mate but he needs a bit of feeding up to help him mend. Take care now, he's not a pet. They can go for you, can swans.'

Beth took the bag and went happily off to the tarn. The greylag goose, dubbed Georgie Girl by Ellen, started to waddle along beside her and she stopped, confused. 'Oh dear, I don't know if you're allowed to come.'

Ellen cackled with laughter. 'It's all right. Take her with you. She enjoys a swim and she'll come back when she wants to.'

Scarcely a ripple marred the glasslike surface of the tarn, save for the swan serenely swimming across to Beth the moment he spotted his dinner. Georgie Girl made a dash for the water, keeping her distance from the tarn's new occupant and began to flap about and bathe the dust from her wings. Laughing, Beth kept one eye on her as she fed the swan, now padding about on the shore, opening his big black beak in greedy anticipation.

'OK, OK, I'm coming.'

When the scraps were all gone and the corn with it, she sat on a hummock of grass and watched him preen. Ellen was right, he must once have been a fine looking bird but was now a bit haggard and thin, and walked with a limp. Perhaps someone had taken a pot-shot at him

221

as well as killing his mate. Sad, when you think that swans mate for life. Which again turned her mind back to her own problem. Pietro was as sleekly handsome as the swan but with man's complexities. He loved two people, a fact that for the moment she must accept.

'We'll have to call you Pegleg,' she told the swan, and as if mortally offended by the very idea, he turned his back upon her, wagged his tail with displeasure and sank smoothly back into the water.

Beth laughed. 'Don't take the huff. I think it a splendid name.'

From somewhere in the distance came the sound of a car engine, revving as it wound its way up the track. Surely it couldn't be going to Larkrigg? They rarely had visitors.

Beth shifted her position for a better view. It was a large, blue car, rather official looking. Oh dear, whoever it was would find no one at home. She got up and started to hurry towards it, hoping Georgie Girl wouldn't choose to follow. No, Ellen said she'd go home when she'd enjoyed her swim and Beth felt she really should see who was calling.

She began to run and was quite out of breath by the time she reached the lane and managed to flag the car down. She held her chest for a minute, all hot and bothered from the unusual exertion, laughing at herself.

'Sorry, running uphill isn't my thing. I'd be no good in a fell race, would I?' Inside the car was a small man in a dark suit. He did not smile at her little joke.

'Miss Sarah Brandon?'

'Beth, as a matter of fact. Can I help you?'

'I'm looking for Broombank Mill.'

Beth pointed in the general direction of Broombank. 'Oh, you've overshot it by a mile. What a pity. It's actually a big barn at the farm down in the dale. No distance over the fell, but a couple of miles by road, I'm afraid. You'll find my sister in her office I expect.'

He thanked her for her help, manoeuvred the car to turn it round and returned the way he had come.

'Now who could that be?' she wondered. 'Not a cheerful soul,' and made a mental note to ask Sarah when she came home later that day.

Sarah felt anything but content as she seated herself at the end of the big kitchen table and glared across at Meg. She considered

Broombank's kitchen to be a most unbusinesslike place to hold a board meeting but it was apparently a long-held tradition which everyone insisted on keeping. How could you speak your mind when the table was littered with delicious slices of home-cured ham and pickle, huge hunks of cheese and great loaves of bread all muddled up amongst her business papers. It was too ridiculous for words.

'I really don't think we should even consider buying any more new machines at this stage,' Meg repeated and Sarah felt her ire rise again, tightening her throat.

'I understood that I was to have complete control of the mill.'

'Indeed you have, Sarah, love. While remaining answerable to the Board, of course.'

Sarah bit down on her lip and held on to her fast disappearing patience. 'If we don't replace old machinery and change our style we can't move forward or hope to compete in the market place. We need to get more fashionable.'

Irritatingly Meg merely smiled. 'This trade is built on centuries of tradition. I don't think we particularly need to be fashionable. And I don't see the necessity for new machinery at all. You've already bought some, why do we need more?'

'We do too much by hand. The days of old-fashioned hand-knitting are gone. Automation is the key to greater profits.'

'We've done rather well with our old-fashioned hand knitting over the years, as a matter of fact. Can we afford to abandon these traditions?' This from Jan, who, since she and Sarah had never seen eye to eye on matters, including the new improvements, hardly deserved the bother of a reply. Sarah chose to ignore her.

But Jan was a practical, no-nonsense sort of person. Tough enough to have brought up a family of four and still find time to work with her husband on the farm. She was not easily put off. 'Well? Does tradition count for nothing any more? And do we have the funds for this so-called modernisation?'

Sarah drew in a furiously stifled sigh and shuffled a few papers to prove how busy she was. 'Would I suggest it, otherwise? Could we please come to a decision, I have a great deal to do this afternoon. Now, let me point out . . .'

A knock on the door stopped her and Sam stuck his head round it. 'Sorry to interrupt but . . .'

'I told you we were not to be disturbed.'

Unperturbed by the ice in her tone, Sam continued, 'There's a gentleman to see you, Miss Sarah. He says he can't wait and won't be put off.'

'Oh, very well.' Perhaps a break would give them time to come to their senses. She stood up and faced the family. Meg, Jan, Tam and even Nick had come to the board meeting today. Ganging up on her? 'Think about it. We aren't making sufficient progress the way we are at present. Our competitors have the edge. It's up to you.'

Then she gathered up her papers and swept out of the kitchen.

When Sarah had concluded the difficult interview with the man in the dark suit and watched him drive away down the lane in the direction of Broomdale and the main road, she decided against returning to the kitchen. She was thoroughly sick of their arguments. Besides, they'd probably all got bored by this time and wandered off back to their dratted sheep.

She stuffed various papers back in to the drawers of her desk, shoved a letter under her blotter and was almost out of the door when Meg caught her.

'Can I have a word?' Closing the door so that Sarah had little choice but to comply.

'I'm rather busy.'

'Then I'll come straight to the point. I'm not too happy about the way things are going.'

'Oh?'

'Pietro in particular. Don't you think you are giving him a bit too much of his own head? Doing the deliveries was fine, and he has some skill as a salesman, I'll grant you. But yesterday I heard him instructing Sam, in no uncertain terms, which order to deal with first. Sam did not take kindly to this sort of interference. He has been organising the rota of orders for a long time.'

'Then perhaps it's time things changed.' Sarah walked to the door and took a firm grasp of the handle. 'I'm sorry Meg, but Pietro has my backing, entirely. He is the one who meets the shop owners on a day to day basis, so he must have a say in what is required, and when.'

Meg was hating every minute of this discussion. She really felt too tired to deal with youthful rebellion and Sarah's arguments did have an edge of reason in them, and yet . . . 'I do understand what you say but Pietro does get a bit above himself at times, sounding quite proprietorial. He really went for Sam, in front of everyone. As if he owned the place, which I must remind you, Sarah, he does not.'

Sarah's mouth twisted in to a wry smile. 'He's Italian, a little volatile at times. I'll speak to him when he returns from his deliveries. Was there anything else?' Cool and distant, pleased to see how this unsettled Meg.

'Well, as your grandmother, in lieu of your mother not being present, perhaps I should ask where all this is leading?'

'All what?' In a tone meant to freeze.

'With you and Pietro.'

'You mean you disapprove?'

'I-I'm not saying anything of the sort. I'm not sure what I feel.'

'You object to him. But then you'd be bound to, wouldn't you? Him being Jack's grandson.'

For the first time in years Meg felt herself grow pink with embarrassment. 'Yes, I suppose you may have a point there. I am trying not to be prejudiced against him.'

Sarah smiled sunnily as she opened the door, anxious to escape. 'Don't worry, I'm not heading down any aisle to the altar yet but keep on trying to like him, Gran. You never know what might happen in the future.' And she walked to her car, got in and tore off up the lane without a backward glance. She'd had enough work for one day. She'd take a long, hot bath and as soon as Pietro got back from his deliveries they'd go to bed with a bottle of wine.

To hell with the lot of them.

But when she came banging into the kitchen while Beth was chopping vegetables for supper, she was very plainly in a tearing temper. Beth decided that perhaps her discussion with Sarah could wait for another day.

The summer seemed to pass in a whirl. Bleached hot days out on the fell, or battling with the garden Beth was growing at Larkrigg, a battle she sometimes lost in her endless tussle against the wind and weather, every small success was a joy. Her garden was sheltered by a drystone wall and tall oak trees bent by the wind.

There always seemed so much to do and even in the depth of

summer one eye must be kept on the winter which would surely follow. As July turned into August and September approached, the log store had be replenished and dried out thoroughly, vegetables grown and stored, onions and beetroot pickled, and preserves of every colour, taste and hue boiled and bottled and ranged upon the larder shelves. Beth spent long stifling days over the kitchen range and had never worked so hard, and felt so fulfilled in all her life.

During the long sunny afternoons she and Pietro would often sit together high on the fellside alone, where the buzzards and curlew flew, where they could talk endlessly over their problem. Very occasionally she would allow him to hold her and kiss her, within certain set boundaries of course. Boundaries which at times strained her to the limits of her endurance. She had no intention of permitting any repetition of that night when she'd let things run out of control.

And if sometimes the voice of conscience still pricked, she pushed it resolutely aside, for she saw her love for Pietro as inevitable, beyond her control. So long as they kept to these rules she was robbing Sarah of nothing. It was the nearest Beth had ever come to recklessness and while the old part of her was shocked, the new Beth revelled in this show of defiance.

And so these afternoons became a vital part of her life. Long, lazy moments of stolen ecstasy in secret hollows with no one to spy upon them but the solemn-eyed sheep. It seemed the safest place, far away from both Broombank and Larkrigg, and any risk of Sarah coming upon them together and misconstruing the situation.

For these short periods Pietro belonged entirely to her, a wonderful compensation for all her hard work and sacrifice.

Such meetings were fraught with danger though, which perversely made her want them more than ever, particularly since he so often assured her of his love. Sometimes, with his hands in her hair, or driving her to distraction as he caressed her breasts she believed she might die of need for him. Then she would push him away and laugh it all off and he would sulk and complain that while both twins were content to love him, and who could blame them, for was he not a god among men, neither one of them would agree to be his wife. 'Why are you so stubborn? You refuse to share me or let me make love with you. You do not love me, I think.'

'Oh, but I love you very much, Pietro. So much I need you all to myself.'

'Then why you not fight for me?'

Beth sighed. 'Because Sarah is my sister, and for all our disagreements, I still love her. How can I agree to marry you until we have solved the problem of Sarah? I don't want to hurt her. I feel guilty enough.' It did not occur to Beth to ask why Pietro could not leave Sarah. She accepted, unquestioningly, that he loved them both.

'You say she steal me from you, so why you feel guilty?'

And Beth would frown. 'It may be the modern way not to worry about such things, but I do. Either we face her and explain, or we wait. She must grow bored with you soon,' and Pietro would say how could any woman grow bored with him? And they would both giggle with delight at his vanity and wickedness.

'Do you wish for me to go away? Do you want to give me up?' he would ask and Beth would squeal with agony and say she couldn't bear even to consider such a possibility and then she'd have to let him kiss her again, just to prove she still loved him, putting off the moment of decision.

18

Summer was passing and the mellow golden days of September were upon them. The Lakeland scenery was a blaze of colour, the air filled with the hard, dry-throated cough of stags as they staked out their territory for the coming mating season. Down in the woods goldenrod and white hemp nettle bloomed, and blue harebells where it wasn't too wet. And out on the fells the bracken grew thick, a never-ending nuisance for the farmer but for secret lovers, even relatively innocent ones, a blissful mattress of seclusion.

On two separate occasions Beth thought she saw the dark blue car again. Once she mentioned it to Sarah and her sister told her it was simply a supplier bringing her the extra stocks of wool that she needed. Sarah never cared to be cross-questioned and Beth had no wish to annoy her. Certainly not right now. It could unleash all kinds of trouble between them.

Often, alone in her bed, listening to the snorts and barks of Ellen's animals through the open cottage window, Beth thought how the old Gemini Stones prophecy had come so terribly true.

But how she missed Larkrigg. Leaving the house she had devoted so much of her time and dreams to, had torn her apart. Continuing to live with her sister within its walls had proved quite impossible. Any other woman but Sarah, so full of her own pride and self-importance, would have guessed the real reason behind her decision to move. As it was, they kept up a façade of politeness, managing to communicate about practical matters appertaining to the mill or the house, while underneath the air positively crackled with tension, yet neither spoke of it.

229

* * *

It was a relief always to get away, and Cathra Crag remained one of her favourite jaunts, though she'd been avoiding it lately, because of Andrew.

On this particular afternoon the sun was shining and Beth felt happy and content. She'd gone over to Cathra Crag with four dozen new-laid eggs, as she often did on a Friday. The three men each enjoyed two every morning with their breakfast. Beth collected the weekend milk from the dairy then settled for an hour's chat and a cup of tea with old Seth. She'd brought newly baked scones too and he was telling her the story of his boyhood again, so it took a while. Later, she helped Andrew's father feed the calves, and the afternoon light was waning by the time she'd bid her goodbyes and was ready to set off back up the fell.

'If you see Andrew, tell him it's his job to make supper tonight,' Billy said.

Beth grinned. 'Right.'

'We need a woman aroond t'place. Time he got wed,' Seth said, and Beth laughed and quickly escaped.

She met Andrew, as expected, working on the endless task of repairing dry-stone walls. She stood and chatted with him for a while, watching him work, his movements methodical and slow, carefully choosing the right stone for the job, putting it back together like a complicated jig-saw without resource to a scrap of mortar.

A double wall of stone narrowing towards the top, the centre filled with rubble, through stones holding the whole together. It leaned slightly into the prevailing wind while on top were the cams, smooth and flat. Fascinated as she always was to watch this grand old craft in action she found herself also oddly fascinated by the easy rhythm of his body, the muscles rippling in his back as he worked in shirt sleeves despite the gathering coolness of the autumn evening. The sight of him brought to mind the memory of his strip wash in the kitchen and her cheeks flared on a rush of embarrassment. What was the matter with her?

He half turned and caught her studying him and her colour deepened, as if she were a schoolgirl still. She could have kicked herself.

'Who taught you?' she asked, desperate to cover her confusion, for

230

of course she knew well enough that the craft had been passed on from father to son through the generations.

Perhaps for this reason he didn't trouble to answer her question but took a step towards her, his grey eyes luminous in the evening light. 'Beth, there's something I need to say. Something I think we should discuss.'

'Oh?' She felt oddly flustered and half turned away to glance at her watch. 'Make it quick then. I have to get back. Sarah and Pietro will be home from the mill soon and there'll be hell to pay if there isn't food on the table for them.'

'For God's sake. Can't you forget them for a minute? Can't they look after themselves? I thought you'd moved out?'

She looked astounded. 'We're still a team. We each have our own job to do. I promised mine would be to look after Larkrigg and the animals. I love it. Sarah has all the real worries with the mill every day. I can hardly expect her to cook her own meal as well, it wouldn't be fair. I must go.' She started forward but he grabbed her arm and held her fast.

'I need to talk with you, Beth. There are things I have to say, things I must get off my chest or I'll go mad.'

She laughed, pushing back her hair with an impatient hand as she avoided direct eye contact with him. 'Heavens, how very serious you sound. Get on with it then! I've told you, I haven't all day.' She realised her tactless mistake as soon as she saw the flicker of pain cross his face but it was too late, the words had been spoken. She couldn't call them back. He released her arm and stepped away from her.

'Another time perhaps, when you're not in such a hurry.'

'Look, I'm sorry, I didn't think.'

'No, Beth. That's your trouble, you don't think. And you don't see what's in front of your nose either.'

'What's that supposed to mean?'

'Never mind.' He ran a grubby hand over his face, a gesture of such weariness that her heart went out to him. Something had upset him badly. Whatever could it be? Why had he never married, she wondered? Did he still mourn for Tess?

'If there's something troubling you, tell me.'

'What's going on? That's what I'd like to know,' he burst out and her heart began to pound. So that was it. They'd been discovered.

231

They'd been seen together, out on the fell. And that it should be Andrew somehow made it worse. Oh, dear lord.

'I – I don't know what you mean.'

'Aye, you know well enough. I'm not blind. You're mad for him, I can see that. That's why you moved in with Ellen. But you're still seeing him, and he isn't right for you, Beth. Believe me, he isn't. We need to talk.'

Anger rose in her chest. How dare he tell her what was right or wrong for her? And why did he always have to be so damned sure of himself, so touchy and mysterious. She backed away from him, lifting her chin in haughty disdain. 'I have no wish to quarrel with you Andrew, but really I think this is my business, not yours. I can't bear any more of . . .'

Whatever it was she really couldn't bear, Andrew never discovered as they both heard the sound at the same instant.

It was Ellen, shouting and waving to them, and she sounded in considerable distress.

A scene of devastation met their eyes. The boxes that had served as setts and homes, the perches and wire cages and compound which had once safely held the birds and animals were now smashed and empty. Kestrels, owls, badgers, deer, squirrel, had all gone, dispersed, probably in fear from the wanton destruction. Andrew and Beth stared in horror at the scene then Beth flew to Ellen and wrapped her arms about her. For once she did not shy from the close physical contact, rather seemed to welcome it. She was shaking with shock.

'Sit down. You look dreadful. Let me get you a cup of tea.'

'Bugger tea. What about my animals?'

'Are they dead?' Beth gazed fearfully at the heap of rubble.

'I haven't found any bodies. Yet.'

'Thank goodness for that at least.'

Andrew said, 'Who do you think did it? Have you seen any strangers about?'

She shook her head. 'I've been out and about most of the day but I saw only a few tourists down in the dale, walkers mainly heading over Dundale Knot. They'd be hardly likely to be interested in my little set-up.' Her mind was busy, had been ever since she'd walked in upon the destruction, and a theory was growing. But she held her own counsel. What proof did she have?

'What about the cottage?'

Ellen sighed. 'That's in a pretty state too.'

'Oh no. Look, we can't do anything now, its almost dark. We'll stay at Larkrigg tonight and start clearing this mess in the morning. I'm sure it won't look half so bad by then.'

But it did. It looked a hundred times worse. In the tiny kitchen every plate and cup had been smashed. The living room had been ripped apart, Ellen's few books and pictures torn to shreds.

'It could have been worse,' she said, but the brown eyes looked more bleak than optimistic.

Andrew soon appeared, having got up especially early to deal with his chores, and the three of them worked solidly till lunch time. It was an arduous, heart-breaking task. They were glad to sit and drink the hot soup Beth had brought in a flask, and eat the home-made ham rolls.

After lunch, assisted by Beth, Andrew finished mending the compound and it stood, empty and forlorn, silent testimony of Ellen's patient care now in ruins.

'Half of them weren't yet fit enough to live on their own. That's what hurts the most,' Ellen mourned. 'Some, like the cheeky squirrels, will do all right. They could have gone long since, but I still hadn't found a home for Barney. I was hoping to find him a mate. Now he's gone. Even Georgie Girl has disappeared.'

Beth's soft heart sank with gloom. She could find no words to express the misery she felt. Who could be so utterly cruel and callous?

'Perhaps we should go and look for them?' Andrew suggested. 'Now we've got some sort of order restored to the place, we could search the woods, see if we can find them.' But Ellen was shaking her head.

'They'll have gone to ground. Sick creatures always do. They'll die in pain and alone, wondering why I let them down.' The tough old lady had tears in her eyes and Beth and Andrew exchanged agonised glances. What could they do? Then Beth had a idea.

'There's still the swan. He hasn't gone yet, has he? Whoever did this, wouldn't have tackled Pegleg. Let's go and see how he is. He'll want some dinner, at least.'

233

Ellen brightened. 'Of course, I'd forgotten about him.'

They gathered some food scraps and Ellen found corn and seed and they set off to find him. He was at the tarn, waiting for them as usual. But he was not alone.

'Georgie Girl,' Ellen cried, running down to the water's edge.

The goose cack-cacked and came swimming serenely towards her, full of its own importance at having found her fine friend. Andrew and Beth both burst out laughing, then glancing up at a tree Beth pointed excitedly.

'Look, isn't that Barney over there?' Now she laughed all the more. 'I think your food is so good at your hotel your guests will very soon return.'

'I think you might be right,' Ellen said, grinning.

'And they'll bring their mates with them, then you'll have twice as many to worry over,' said Andrew and as they laughed again, he grabbed Beth and gave her a jubilant hug of delight and she leaned into his arms, tears of relief rolling down her cheeks. It was as she glanced up, ready to share this joy when she found his eyes upon her, and there was raw hunger in that gaze. It so shocked her that she forgot what it was she'd been about to say. Then he abruptly let her go and walked over to Ellen, and she wondered if she had perhaps imagined it.

'Someone has it in for you,' he warned. 'And for all we know, they may try again. You'd best take greater care in future. Lock your door for a start.'

'I've never locked it yet, I'm not about to start now! What have I to lose?'

'Your home. He could burn it down next time.'

Ellen quickly sobered. She hadn't thought of that. 'I hope there won't be a next time.'

'He?' Beth queried.

'Whoever.'

'Let's not over-state the case, eh? It was just a bit of mischief, meant to give me a message. And I reckon I've got it. The point has been made.'

'What point are you talking about?'

She half smiled. 'I'm not to meddle, not to interfere in what don't concern me. Not to be a nosy old woman.' She tapped her nose and grinned, content to face anything now she knew that at least some of her birds and animals were safe. 'Don't worry. I've an idea who might have left this little calling card and if I'm right, I can sort him out myself.' And that was as much as they could get out of her.

There was a large, official looking envelope in the post the following morning when Beth went up to Larkrigg as usual. She left it propped up on the dresser so that Sarah could see it the moment she came home. Later in the morning another stranger called, tubby and fair-haired this time, and driving a van.

'Miss Brandon isn't at the mill so I was told to come up here.'

Beth had to tell the man that she had no idea where her sister was. She imagined she saw worry on his face as he drove away but was too busy wondering if Sarah was with Pietro somewhere to call him back and take proper notice of his problem.

It was a daily battle to close her mind to visions of them together but later, when Pietro did not come to her as he usually did, she had to busy herself cleaning out the cupboard under the stairs. It was tidier than it had ever been before but she felt no better for the effort. Her mind was a fog of emotion, her body aching for him, and hating herself for driving this deeper wedge between herself and her own twin.

Yet her troubles were as nothing compared with poor Ellen who, on her return to the cottage, Beth found still looking for her precious animals. Over the next several days she was so concerned with helping her, that she forgot all about the van and cut the time she spent at Larkrigg by half, since Ellen needed her more.

None of the other animals returned and they could only hope for the best for them, though some losses had to be expected. At least Ellen had her dogs, and her favourite friends, including Georgie Girl, were back.

The very next market day, Sarah invited Beth to accompany her shopping in Kendal and she readily accepted, happy to award herself a day off. There were a few essential items she needed but first they trawled the dress shops and Beth sat patiently waiting or putting on a suitably admiring expression as Sarah tried on dresses, trouser-suits, sweaters and skirts by the dozen, rejecting most of them but managing to find a few worth buying.

'What about you?' she asked. 'Don't you want something new?' glancing in distaste at Beth's ancient flared trousers and long sheepskin waistcoat which she wore over a cheese-cloth shirt.

'Why should I need anything new? Where would I wear it? In any case we can't afford it. And I think you've spent enough too.'

'Oh, don't be such an old misery. Though I agree, buying new clothes for you would be a complete waste of money,' Sarah uncharitably remarked. 'Let's go to the Wheatsheaf for lunch.'

Beth felt as if her head were spinning. She couldn't seem to get the reality of life through to Sarah at all.

'We can't afford expensive treats. A snack-bar will do.'

'Oh, don't be such an old misery-boots.' It was a short-lived argument which Sarah won, naturally, by storming along Highgate straight into the hotel, and Beth had to admit it was an excellent lunch.

But it was a silent, chilly meal and afterwards they strolled through the crowded streets, in and out of the shops, Beth buying the few items of food she needed, Sarah complaining the whole time.

'Oh, not fish again. And I'm tired of chicken, why can't we have something interesting like smoked salmon for a change.'

'We can't even afford potted beef.' A small, hard knot of fury was building inside Beth. Why could she never persuade Sarah to be responsible?

'I believe you deliberately enjoy being perverse, simply to torment me,' Sarah mourned, pouting, and Beth gave her an exasperated look.

Sarah insisted on going up through the cobbled Shambles and around Kendal market where she became fascinated by the antique and bric-a-brac stalls.

'Look at this, I'm sure it's Dresden.'

Beth took the figurine from her hand and set it firmly back on the stall. 'Don't even think of it. We're not buying anything more that isn't on my list. Our money goes nowhere these days. And they tell us inflation is under control. Heaven knows what will happen if all these pay rises we read about each day in the paper actually go through. I could do with a pay rise myself.'

'Are you complaining at what I give you?' Sarah testily replied.

'I'm merely pointing out that we've no spare cash for treats such as smoked salmon and Dresden china when we're still paying off the restoration work you've ordered. I was quite happy for us to do up Larkrigg slowly, ourselves, but no, you must have it done by experts, and experts cost money, Sarah.'

'You couldn't put a roof on.'

Beth conceded the truth of this but listed, one by one on her fingers all the other workmen they could well have managed without. 'Joiners, carpet-fitters, builders, interior decorators for God's sake? It's frightening. We didn't need a new kitchen, or a plush new bathroom suite. What has come over you?'

'We're making money at the mill, why shouldn't we spend it?' Sarah fired back and Beth struggled to stifle her concern. Was she fussing unnecessarily, as she so often did? Why did she feel this sense of impending doom?

'I got the electricity bill this morning and it made my hair curl. What have we been doing, to use so much?'

Sarah shrugged elegant shoulders, turning the figure in her hands. 'It's cold in my room. I bought an electric fire.'

Beth gasped. 'But we've paid a small fortune for central heating.'

'Yes, but you insisted on using that old range to do it with, and it doesn't seem to work very well in my room. Too many draughts from those ancient windows. I hate old houses.'

'Do you think we're made of money?' Beth could hear her voice rising to a dangerous pitch, became aware of people turning curious glances in the sister's direction. She struggled to hold her patience, and failed. 'There's a fire grate in your bedroom and we've plenty of wood. Use that, why don't you?'

'For Christ's sake, Beth, I've better things to do with my time than light fires every night.'

'You mean you want me to put lighting your bedroom fire on my list of jobs too, because you'd rather sit there than in the sitting room, is that it?' She was hot with temper now but as Sarah merely smiled, all the heat drained from her like a cold shower. It wasn't hard to imagine what she and Pietro found to do each evening in her bedroom. 'I see.'

'No you don't. You don't see at all. Oh, for goodness' sake, don't let's quarrel about money, it's too boring. Leave the bills to me.'

It was at this moment for some reason, that Beth remembered the fair haired man and the van and when she told Sarah, her face seemed to pale. 'He was looking for you. It was the same day you got the letter, the one which seemed terribly officious. Is there a problem?'

'What problem could there be?' Sarah snapped, meticulously examining the contents of the stall.

'I don't know. Your workers aren't threatening to strike, are they?'

'Don't be stupid, Beth.' Sarah handed the Dresden figure to the stall holder. 'I'll take that please. She'll look rather fetching on my dressing table.'

Beth gave an explosion of such fury that the stallholder almost reeled backwards, clinging desperately to her precious figurine as one sister made a lunge for it while the other struggled desperately to pull her away.

'I apologise for my sister's behaviour but we cannot afford the Dresden figure. Thank you.'

It was a small but very real victory.

It proved to be a difficult winter. Christmas came and went, spent at Broombank with the family as usual.

The early months of 1979 were marred by industrial dispute. Piles of rubbish lay in the streets, pickets stood outside hospitals, schools and factories. In some towns even the dead were left unburied. None of this greatly affected Beth, though she sympathised with those who were. She listened to the news on her radio as she scrubbed the winter mud from the kitchen flags, constantly stoked up the stove and various fire grates and suffered the ills of winter in a shivering Lakeland.

Freezing winds, snow filling the dale, creating havoc. The rough oily fleece of the Herdwicks and Swaledales might help them endure even the toughest winter but as the ice and snow packed down on the high fells, their source of food vanished and had to be supplemented through the efforts of man. Ewes had to be dug out, found by experienced dogs or the tell-tale signs of discoloured snow. Then the ice on their backs must be thawed out before they froze to death.

Winter always made life hard for the farmer. For Beth too it became increasingly difficult. She struggled to care for her own few sheep which Andrew had sold her, plodding through the snow to take them hay and concentrate, carefully counting them each day to check they were all well. But little help was forthcoming from Sarah or Pietro, who declared they were too busy with their own work at the mill.

Beth had hoped that by not living under the same roof as Sarah, everything would be made right between them. But really nothing had changed. They could hardly bear to be in each other's company for more than half an hour. She had never known Sarah to be in such a sour mood for so long. Usually her tempers were vicious but fleeting, followed by warm hearted flippancy. Not any more.

Beth didn't mind leaving meals to keep hot in the range for Sarah and Pietro each evening, but nothing quite suited. If she made chicken, Sarah said she would have preferred fish. If it was fish, left ready to grill or steam, Sarah could never find the energy to cook it and said a beef casserole would have been more convenient. Beth would find complaining little notes next morning or, if she arrived before Sarah left for work, be forced to suffer sniping words in silence or risk a tantrum at the least provocation, even if the poor postman did not arrive exactly on time.

'You go off to work, I'll bring any letters down to you when it comes, if you like,' Beth promised. But even this didn't seem to please.

'I'll wait. I don't need you to tell me what to do.'

And Pietro himself was so often in a strange mood. He would seem withdrawn and full of sulks, spending hours alone walking on the fells, declaring he needed time to think.

On one occasion he came home with one eye closed, the beginnings of a bruise gathering about it. He said he'd walked into the low branch of a tree and while Sarah laughed, saying it was a likely story and probably one of his wool customers had socked him one for trying it on, it was Beth who offered sympathy and packed it with ice.

The winter months churned by, quiet, cold and wet and filled with simmering, frustrated emotions and churning fear. For all Sarah's continuing ill temper, there were days when Beth could not resist secreting herself away with Pietro. As today, with icicles forming on the window outside, the roads too dangerous for him to risk, they lay curled up together beside a crackling log fire, oblivious of the very real danger that Sarah might at any moment return home early from the mill and catch them together.

These snatched moments when they could be alone were a delight and a torture for her. A part of that rural idyll of which she had dreamed. She would sink into his arms, eager to let him kiss the full softness of her mouth, and caress the taut peaks of her breasts till she was mad with need for him, very nearly at that dangerous point of no return.

'It is all right. Do not resist so fiercely. She will not come.'

'She might. I'm sure she guesses.'

'No, no. We are not the culprits. We are the innocents, yes? But if you say we must not make love, then I will respect your wishes, as always.'

His patience with her continued refusal, constantly astonished and humbled her. How he must love and respect her. If only Sarah would give him up, there would be no further need for all of this agonising restraint. Starry eyed with love for him, Beth was still the romantic at heart.

'But I grow tired of her sulks,' he was saying. 'Perhaps she need a break. We all do. A holiday would do us good, yes? In sunny Italy. I will take you both. Is good idea, yes?'

Beth had to laugh as she shook her head. 'Don't be ridiculous. Can you imagine us all on holiday together? How could we hope to keep our feelings secret then? Besides, I have far too much to do here.'

'What could be more important than spending time with me?'

'I have my animals, the hens and ducks and geese. And my little flock of sheep. And who would help Ellen with her animal hospital? Besides, now don't get in a sulk again, but I've almost decided . . .' She hung her head so that the chestnut hair fell forward over her face, hiding a shy smile. Pietro was entranced.

'What is it, my little one? Another secret? What is that you have almost decided?'

She slanted a shy smile up at him. 'I never told you but I've talked to Andrew and he's promised to sell me the cow I've always wanted, this spring. Oh, I know there was the accident but Meg has convinced me that I was not to blame. And Jonty is much better, though not likely to return. She's a Jersey,' Beth continued excitedly, paying no attention to his expression of dawning disbelief, 'and absolutely beautiful. Then I shall make cheese, and clotted cream on the Aga.'

Pietro's smile had quite vanished. 'Clotted cream? I talk to you of love and of Italy and you talk to me of a cow?' He stared at her as if she'd gone quite mad. 'I think you love your animals and your stupeed cheese more than me.'

'Oh, don't be cross, Pietro. It does not suit you.' She was giggling uncontrollably now, refusing to take him seriously, delighting in his jealousy of her love for the animals. 'I suppose it does sound rather funny, but don't you see, I could make a good little business out of it. I would like to show Sarah that I'm capable of achieving something of my own.'

'We agreed there were to be no more animals. I am tired of them all. You marry me, sell this place and we travel the world together. What you say?'

Beth burst out laughing, then kissed his perfect nose. 'What a wonderful romantic you are, even worse than me. How can we possibly run away together? We have to settle things with Sarah first. You know that you must tell her soon. It's the only way.'

'She can come too.'

'On our honeymoon?'

He grabbed her close in his arms again. 'Oh, if only bigamy were not illegal then I could have you both.' Beth so revelled in the hot kisses which followed this utterance, that she quite found it in her heart to forgive him for his apparent disloyalty.

'There's Mom and Meg to think of. We can't go on with this muddle. We mustn't hurt them too.'

He very nearly told her that it would give him the greatest pleasure in the world to see Meg hurt but managed to bite back his words just in time. How long could he keep both twins dangling? It was becoming a trial even his great skill was finding a strain. Her cheeks were rosy with love from the heat of the fire and he wondered why he was not overwhelmed with need for her. Coolly he considered her. 'There will be no more disobeying me. I will decide everything. I am the man.'

'What?' She almost laughed again and then saw the grim expression upon his face. 'You are going to tell Sarah soon, aren't you? About us.'

'I think you know me not at all. Why should I trouble myself when all you think of is your stupeed rural dream.'

She looked at him properly then and felt a gulf open up between them, as if they viewed each other from the wrong ends of a telescope. 'I–I'm sorry I've annoyed you. I thought you'd be pleased, amused perhaps, but happy for me.' A small pulse of alarm started up inside. 'You're not really cross, are you?

You are teasing?'

A small strained silence then Beth smiled at him, radiant and happy, pushing her doubts aside. 'I know what is the matter with you. You are afraid of Sarah's temper. Me too. What cowards we are. We'll wait till she's in a better mood, shall we?' And she lifted her face to be kissed.

But it took a considerable amount of persuasion and dangerously sweet loving this time, to put him in a better mood.

19

It was a blustery evening in early April when Sarah came home in a fine old temper, the worst yet. The whole house rang with it. She slammed the front door, flung her shoes across the hall knocking one of the stag's eyes out with a heel, threw her leather satchel at the wall, tossed her coat on the floor and stormed up the stairs in a veritable rage.

'*Damn* fool. Blast and damn him to hell. *Goddam-the-son-of-a-bitch.*'

Beth withdrew to the kitchen and gently closed the door. Was this it, the day she had dreaded? Had Sarah at last discovered the truth?

She quietly prepared her sister's supper tray and drawing in a deep breath of courage, climbed the stairs to her room.

She was astonished to find Sarah in her dressing gown, sitting at the foot of her bed, eyes brimming with tears.

'Heavens, what's the matter? What is all this about?'

'Oh, Beth, I'm at the end of my tether.'

'You? Never.'

'Some jumped-up little Factory Inspector has threatened to close us down, would you believe?' She clenched her fists and drummed them against the bed post. 'How dare he? How *dare* he? We had the most awful stand-up row, in front of everybody and now they've all gone on strike. Would you believe it? After all I've done for them. It's because everyone else has been doing it, they think it's fashionable. Oh, I hate them.'

'Oh dear.' Beth placed the tray carefully on the table and kept her face averted as she smothered a smile. She hardly thought it possible for the women to go out on strike on a whim. They must be in earnest, with a very different version of events to Sarah's. Their simmering resentments were almost tangible whenever Beth called at the mill, though she'd never dared say as much. But a strike could be serious for the business and must be put right. 'Why did the Factory Inspector threaten to close you down? What's wrong?'

'Nothing, in my opinion. Lots of silly regulations about so many feet between each machine, space for each worker, and such-like Victorian nonsense.'

'Perhaps,' Beth tentatively suggested, 'It is for the safety of the women.'

Sarah looked at her askance. 'For God's sake these are only frame knitting machines, not a car production line.'

'Even so.'

Then the tears were spilling down pale, beautiful cheeks and the eyes she turned up to Beth were shimmering like sapphires. 'I've tried so hard, I really have. I wanted it to be a success. Oh, Beth. I can't bear to be a failure.'

'You are not a failure, of course you are a success.' Appalled at her sister's state and overcome with compassion, Beth held her in her arms while Sarah sobbed against her shoulder as if releasing a long-held grief. It was surprising how very vulnerable she seemed, and all rather alarming. Most unlike her.

'The mill is nothing but a worry. I didn't think it would be,' she sobbed.

'You've done wonders with it. Getting everyone to work harder and keep up with the orders. You'll solve this problem too.'

'But the women hate me.'

'There, there, don't take on so. I'm sure it can all be put right. You only have to comply with the regulations. Swallow your pride and admit you were wrong.'

'I won't. I can't.'

'You must.'

'But it would do no good, don't you see? We still have to get the orders out and how can we, without the machines, without the women to work them? Oh, Beth.' And she started to wail again and

244

Beth smothered a sigh. Sarah was very like a small child when, having been found out in some fault, refused to admit to it.

'Perhaps you could ask Meg if we could borrow one of the other barns for a while. Or look for alternative premises?

Finding solutions for her, a way out for her pride, ever soothing and urging her twin to be calm, as she had done since time immemorial. Gradually the sobs quieted and when Sarah's face had been refreshed with cold water and Beth had persuaded her to eat a little of the chicken she had prepared, they talked, as they had not done in months.

'Do you blame me for all of this?' Sarah asked, still looking pale and wretched.

'All what?' Beth became very still.

'All this misery and worry?'

'Of course not. Why should I? I used to be the worrier, remember, not you. You've been working too hard, that's all.'

'And you've been so quiet lately. Keeping your thoughts to yourself.'

'I didn't wish to trouble you with them.'

'It was perfectly obvious you weren't happy living here with us. That's why you left, isn't it? Because you couldn't bear to be near me? You hate me, don't you?'

'What utter rubbish. Why should I hate you?'

'Because I'm always in such a foul temper. I don't mean to be. Life's been so hard lately.'

'I know. I don't take any notice of your temper.'

'You're hurting because Pietro left you as Jeremy did. Because he loved me and not you, you think no one will ever love you, don't you?'

'Perhaps, sometimes.'

'And because I could run the mill and you can't even manage a house properly.' Sarah rubbed away the final traces of tears while Beth gritted her teeth, making no reply. This wasn't the moment for sensitivity.

'But Pietro truly cares for me, you see. He adores me.'

Beth stared blankly at Sarah. 'I can see that he does.'

'Only he's been so sulky lately, I worry about him growing bored with me. Do you think he might?'

Beth felt her face freeze as she struggled to speak. 'How could anyone grow bored with you? Aren't you the fascinating Brandon twin?' The words seemed to come from some other mouth to her own, but were rewarded by a deep chuckle of gratitude, rich and throaty.

'Oh, Beth, you are so good for me. I couldn't bear to lose you as my own dear sister.' Then Sarah's arms were around her, kissing Beth on the cheek. 'Neither could I bear to lose Pietro. I think I'd go mad if I ever lost him. I'd just die. You do see that, don't you?'

'Yes, I do see that.'

'And you don't mind?'

This was the moment to tell the truth. The moment she should explain that it was she who Pietro loved and wanted to marry, and not Sarah at all. That he had only been pretending, waiting for Sarah to release him. Yet how could she destroy her own sister in such a way? The mill workers were on strike, the inspector threatening to close them down, letters from someone, the bank perhaps, which were clearly troubling her. Things were not too good in the country at the moment, anyone would be a fool not to know it. And Sarah seemed suddenly so weak and vulnerable, believing implicitly in Pietro's love. How could Beth take him from her at a time when she needed him most?

She put her arms about Sarah, feeling tremors of emotion shake the slender body, and recalled so many similar occasions in the past. 'I want you to be happy, that's all. Didn't I always?'

'Oh, Beth. I only have you, besides Pietro, that is. I know we've been at odds lately. Those dratted Gemini Stones got to us. You know, the ones that Sally Ann told us about?' She giggled. 'Yet you do matter to me. Very much. You *do* know that, don't you?'

Beth's heart filled with compassion and sadness at the raw need on her sister's face for approval, and for appreciation, and love. 'Yes,' she said. 'I do know that. Enough of this anguish. Get some sleep. You'll feel much better tomorrow.' She began to tuck Sarah into bed, as she had used to do when they were small. 'Pietro was talking about a holiday. Perhaps it would do you good. Sort out the strike, which I'm sure won't be serious, then take a week or two off. Why not? You deserve a rest.'

Violet eyes regarded her with open admiration and gratitude. 'I do wish I'd been born with your open heart and generosity, Beth.'

'And I your brilliance.' She laughed, picked up the tray and walked to the door, back rigid with her determination not to break down. It was over. Whatever she felt for Pietro, or he for her, must be set aside in the interests of her sister. What Sarah had said long since, remained true. She needed a man, needed Pietro. Beth could no more take him from her than she could fly. 'Go to sleep now. You'll be fit as a flea in the morning, ready to take on any number of inspectors and striking workers. You'll soon get it sorted out.'

'And be quarrelling with you again?'

Beth smiled, trying not to show her own despair. 'That too, I expect.'

And with a ghost of a smile, left her.

Beth did not return to Larkrigg the next morning. For once she felt quite unable to face her sister's demands. She played the coward and stayed with Ellen at the cottage, busying herself with the animals, trying to keep her mind as well as her hands fully occupied.

She had given her all to Sarah and made the ultimate sacrifice. Right now she could do no more, certainly couldn't face her until she had herself more under control. Ellen, as if sensing she was on the brink of despair, quietly watched and held her own counsel, saying little beyond what was necessary to perform the myriad small tasks which made up their day.

Beth waited with dread and longing for Pietro to call, as he surely would if she did not appear at the house today. One moment hoping that he would come for her and carry her off with him to Italy, the next that he would not come until the peace and quietness of Ellen's presence had given her the strength to face him. She practised what she would say to him but as time slipped by and there was no sign of him, she wasn't sure whether to be relieved, or mortified by his lack of loyalty.

Work was, as always, her salvation. She spent that first day repainting all the shabby window frames on the cottage, in a bright new green.

'They were rotting away,' she scolded Ellen. 'You should take more care.'

'They're old, like me.'

'But if you painted them, they'd last longer.'

'Oh well, you can give me a coat of that magic paint next.'

Beth actually laughed. Ellen's blunt sense of humour always cheered her. How was it she could laugh, breathe even, now that she knew she had lost Pietro for good?

On the second day Ellen took in a young fawn, brought by a woman who had found its mother lying dead on an open moorland road, killed by a speeding car. On the third they carefully released Barney, with a new mate, settling him in new quarters provided by a local farmer in an unused barn. It took the best part of the day and night, since it was a tricky business and they felt compelled to stay and watch, to be sure the owls would settle.

'We'll come every day for a while and keep a quiet eye on them. But I think the move will be successful. He's a sensible chap is Barney,' Ellen said, as if they were bosom pals.

On the fourth day, reality struck with a vengeance. Everything seemed to go wrong at once.

Beth heard a car in the lane and came out to investigate when she found the goose face to face with an adder. Georgie Girl was poking her cropped beak forward in curiosity to the creature which raised its broad flat head defensively in a strike position. She quickly grabbed a tea towel and flung it at the snake, missing entirely but the goose, far from being put off, gave a cack-cack of annoyance and poked her beak forward again.

Somewhere at the back of her head, Beth heard a car door slam and a man's footsteps approach. If the goose or snake were startled by the arrival of a stranger, one or other could make a very fatal mistake. An adder bite might rarely cause death in an adult but a small goose was quite another matter. And Ellen loved Georgie girl as a favourite pet.

'Oh, do go away, you silly snake. You're supposed to be shy and retiring.' But of course, Georgie Girl, with her insatiable curiosity was the aggressor here. Only she would come off the loser.

'I'll deal with it,' said a man's imperious voice, and the stranger strode over to the snake.

'No, don't.' But before Beth could reach for another tea towel the man hit out at the snake with a stick. At exactly the same moment, Ellen came striding around the corner of the cottage and the adder, quick as a flash, seemed to knock its head against her leg. To Beth, that moment seemed frozen in time. The goose flapping and hissing, the man cursing, Ellen looking down in surprise at the zig-zig pattern slipping hastily away through the long grass.

'Dear Lord, I think he bit me.'

Beth turned on the man, hissing almost as fiercely as the goose. 'You caused this, you stupid man, blundering about. I could have stopped it without anyone getting hurt.' It was an ungracious and unjustified attack but her nerves were stretched to snapping point without this.

'Someone had to take action,' he said, rather pompously.

'I was dealing with it. Adders won't attack unless their cornered.'

'I take it you are Miss Brandon.'

Beth was about to tell him that her sister was at the mill, and why was he bothering her when Ellen gave a plaintive cry.

'It's starting to hurt. Very badly.'

'Oh God, Ellen, are you all right?' Beth dashed over to her, calling to the young man. 'We'll have to use your car.'

'I'm not an ambulance service,' then looking at Ellen's ashen face, 'oh, all right.'

Swiftly Beth washed the wound with soapy water, making Ellen keep very still so the poison wouldn't spread. Then the old woman was laid carefully on the back seat of the Ford Cortina, a clean tea towel covering the wound and they drove off at great speed to the local hospital.

She was treated immediately and kept in overnight, to be on the safe side. When Beth could do nothing more she was surprised to find the pompous young man still waiting. He offered her a lift home which she decided he owed her, for his clumsy interference. She was too concerned over Ellen to wonder if he had any other motive. Ellen must be around sixty, Beth worried. Could she take the shock of being bitten by a snake?

As she was soon to discover, his offer had not been out of kindness or generosity on his part, at all. By the time he had dropped his bombshell and departed, Beth was shaking with shock, and it took her every ounce of strength she possessed to race up the fellside to Larkrigg Hall.

*   *   *

249

It was quite empty. Beth ran from room to room in a daze calling for Sarah, and for Pietro. There was no answer but the echo of her own voice.

'I don't understand, they should be here. It's late. Where can they be?'

Then she saw it, a letter, lying in the centre of the kitchen table.

She opened the envelope with trembling fingers and drew out a single sheet of paper. Somehow she knew what it would say even before she read it. They had gone. They had taken the Renault and gone away.

'I can't bear trouble, Beth darling,' the letter said. 'You can sort things out much better than me, without ever losing your temper. And Pietro thinks a good long holiday will make me myself again. You did agree that I should take one. And I really can't take any more stress. You don't mind, do you? Will write again when we get there. Your ever loving sister, Sarah.'

20

It was several hours later and Beth was sitting in the kitchen at Broombank, her head in her hands and facing the fact that she had lost everything.

She could still hear the pompous man's voice, droning on as he drove her home, past a cluster of farm buildings, white washed cottages and a humped back bridge.

'I'm here to talk about the knitwear business.'

'I know nothing about the mill.'

'Then I'm afraid you are going to have to learn, Miss Brandon.' And calmly, without a trace of emotion in his voice he'd told her how the bank must call in its loan and demand that it be repaid. 'If not, we will have no alternative but to declare you bankrupt, and since your sister is not around to answer the question, then I must ask it of you, Miss Brandon. Can you pay us, or not?'

Which was why, the moment he'd gone, she'd rushed up to Larkrigg, certain there must be some mistake, that Sarah would be there to explain it all, quite rationally. Yet a part of her had not been surprised to find her sister gone. Sarah did not care for difficulties.

In one short evening Beth's entire world had collapsed. Sarah and Pietro were gone. Ellen was seriously ill, and she faced the possibility of bankruptcy. The implications of which were only slowly sinking in.

'That's the end then,' Meg said, her voice bleak. She sat slumped in her chair, more weary than Beth had ever seen her. 'We can't find any more money to prop it up. The mill must close.' Then she shot up in her seat, face ashen. 'Dear God, I hope Broombank is safe in all of this.'

Beth went quite cold at sight of Meg's distress, guilt weighing heavily upon her shoulders. How could this have happened? 'He told me the farm and house were not involved. Just the mill.' Her own mother had started this business and she and Sarah had lost it.

'Thank heaven for that. And Larkrigg?'

'At least we still have that.'

Meg gazed at her in silence, her eyes saying, but for how long? Tam cleared his throat and then in his soft, Irish voice said, 'Are you sure it's safe?'

Beth stared at him in a state of defiant shock. 'Of course. We can't lose that. Not Larkrigg.' She'd seen how Meg and Tam had glanced at each other, alarmed by her vehemence but they said no more. They knew what the house meant to her, even if they couldn't quite understand why.

Sarah had never wanted to live at Larkrigg, not really wished to come to Lakeland in the first place. Never cared about the house, except as a source of profit, or as a backdrop to her own ambitions and the image she had of herself as a successful businesswoman.

Only she hadn't been successful, not at all. She knew well enough how to spend money but not how to make it. She had known how to give orders to her employers but not how to listen to their problems, or to understand what it was the business really needed. Her most fatal mistake had, Beth realised, been impatience. Sarah had to have everything now, today and not tomorrow, nor some distant time in the future, but immediately, whether it could be afforded or not.

She had drained Broombank Mill dry of profits and had now run from the resulting catastrophe, taking Pietro with her. Where she had gone Beth could only guess at. She assumed it to be Italy, to the sun, and freedom. Bags had been packed, wardrobes stood empty, money taken and Larkrigg Hall stood as empty as their bank accounts.

And Beth presumed she was expected to put everything right so that Sarah could return at the end of her holiday, tanned and lovely as ever, with all problems solved.

Meg offered her a room at Broombank, of course, but Beth declined. She wanted to be independent, not intrude on her grandparent's lives.

She wanted time to think things through, slowly and calmly. And right now she felt anything but calm. Nothing seemed quite real.

As the family grimly examined the list of Broombank Mill's debts, the full realisation of her own negligence finally dawned upon Beth.

Ignorance was no excuse. Her own lack of interest in business matters now filled her with shame. Her obsession with a romantic country dream, and with an unfulfilled love affair made her cringe with new guilt. And all the time the structures which made up their lives had been crumbling around her and she had not even noticed.

'How could I have been so blind?'

Meg stretched out a hand to console her. 'We all were. Don't blame yourself, Beth. We should all have taken more notice. I should have realised the last time I asked to see the books and was fobbed off with yet another excuse, that there was a serious problem. But then it's easy to be wise in retrospect.'

Predictably, Jan was furious. 'I guessed. It was obvious she hadn't the first idea what she was doing. No one would listen to me.'

Meg sighed. 'It's too late for recriminations, Jan.'

It was proving to be a most uncomfortable meeting. They had talked for hours and were no nearer a solution. The overdraft was enormous, the mortgage on Larkrigg Hall unpaid, there were horrendous debts with suppliers and even the women were complaining of not having received their latest wages.

The next day Beth went to the bank and again faced Mr Groves, the pompous young bank official. He courteously enquired after Ellen's health and then Beth explained, as carefully as she could, how she had no money to pay for any of these debts. No money at all.

'Then you must sell off your assets.' Which, after yet more complicated explanations, finally dawned on Beth what it was he was telling her to do. He meant for her to sell her home, Larkrigg Hall.

'They won't let me out yet,' Ellen told her, from her hospital bed. 'And I feel like I'm in prison here.'

'No complaints. You're my piece of good news,' Beth said, relieved to find her friend so perky. 'At least you're on the mend.'

Ellen pulled a wry face. 'They've decided to give me a good going over while I'm here. Talking about a bit of angina. They want to make sure that the shock hasn't affected the old ticker. Lot of daft fuss.'

'No, it isn't. Get a good rest. See, I've brought you some grapes.'
And they both laughed.

'What will you do if you lose the house?' Ellen asked in her usual
blunt manner, which for once quite took Beth's breath away. It took
some minutes before she could reply.

'Who says I'll lose it? I haven't given up hope yet.'

A small silence. 'You can stay on with me as long as you like.'

'I know.'

'Not that it's any sinecure living out on the fells in an unheated
cottage. Think what would have happened if that dratted bank chap
hadn't arrived when he did. I was in agony, you know.'

They both thought about that for a minute and fell silent. Beth
wanted to say how he had partly been responsible for the accident,
but knew that would have been unfair. He'd done his best in difficult
circumstances, as she had done. And Ellen's point was valid. Life in
such circumstances out on the fells was difficult and lonely. In the few
months Beth had spent at the tiny cottage, she'd already learned about
the hardships of country life in cold reality. Ellen was an individual,
an eccentric, content to shut herself away with her animals with little
if any contact with modern living. For all her wistful rural dreaming,
could Beth be content with so little? And for how long?

She fought the decision at first, as hard as she could, hoping for a
reprieve, praying the inevitable could be avoided.

She sold off the machinery, returned the remaining stock of wool
to the suppliers and begged them all to give her time to pay the
remainder. They asked for security, letters from her accountant or
solicitor, saying they needed assurances that it would be worth their
while to wait. They weren't going to make things easy for her.

Meg offered some of her savings but Beth gently refused. 'No,
Gran. Why should you suffer? You and Tam will need that for
yourselves.'

'We'd rather see you right. I don't want you to go down under
this.'

'It wouldn't be near enough in any case. Save it for that trip
round Europe, or your retirement.'

She visited each individual member of staff and explained the
situation, that there would be no wages, that their jobs were gone.

It was hard, but telling Sam was the hardest of all. He was sad but not surprised. He offered to work without pay and Beth had to explain tactfully how that would not help them. They were well past such tactics.

'I'm on the dole then?' he asked, the shocking indignity of it all showing in the hurt in his voice.

'I'm afraid so.'

At the door of his cottage he took her arm. 'If you ever need any help, let me know. I'll not get quickly tekken on, not at my time of life. If you start up again . . .' The words choked in his throat and Beth put her arms about him and kissed him.

'You'll be the first to know, I promise.'

But if laying off the workers was bad, dealing with the bank almost drove her to distraction. The young man called her almost daily, either by phone or in person, or sent curt little messages for Beth to call in at the bank and report on progress.

'Can't you give me even a little time? I'm doing my best here.'

But the bank claimed it had been most patient. They had a business to run and now wanted their money. Richard Groves wrote down the latest figures and showed them to her. The mortgage, the creditors, the overdraft and bank loan were still impossibly huge. If she handed over Larkrigg Hall, he said, that would about cover it.

Beth gasped. 'But I'm doing my best to save that.'

He tried to look sympathetic but failed. 'We'll get it anyway, in the end.' When she'd finally been brought to her knees. 'And you'd still be in debt because the interest would have mounted up even more by then.'

After another week, in which she saw that he was right and the debt had indeed grown alarmingly, she finally conceded defeat. 'If I give it up willingly now, would that save me from bankruptcy?'

He agreed that it might. 'The bank will find a purchaser, admittedly at far less than it's now worth with all the recent improvements and alterations, but sufficient to clear everything, if you're lucky.'

Lucky? 'I'll sleep on it,' she said, walking out of his office with head held high. But sleep was quite impossible. Alone in the empty cottage, even the sound of the animals failed to soothe her. She was finished.

The following morning she signed the necessary papers and agreed. Everything was gone now. She owned nothing, not even her own home. Larkrigg Hall belonged to the bank, but at least her debts would be cleared and she was free of debt.

All her planning and efforts seemed to have failed, and in addition to all of this was the aching loss that she never dared mention. A private pain which must be born entirely alone.

Ellen returned home in fine fettle, bossing and ordering her about, demanding to know how each and every animal had survived so well without her, complaining bitterly about being brought home in an ambulance, as if she'd been at death's door. 'Lot of nonsense.'

Beth made a cheese and celery bake for tea and they sat and ate it together by a blazing pine log fire. The scent of it filled her heart with nostalgia for those evenings in the drawing room at Larkrigg.

'I'll only stay until I've sorted myself out,' Beth told her. 'I think I've decided what I must do, but I'd like a little more time to be sure.'

'There's no hurry. Take as much time as you need.'

'I know, and I'm grateful.'

But they both knew that this wasn't strictly true. Generous as Ellen was, she was poor, living from hand to mouth. And if Beth couldn't pay her way, Ellen could not afford to feed her. If she stayed in Lakeland she would need a job, and transport to reach it. But what kind of job? And where? Work in a pub? Wait on at tables or in a shop? None of these appealed and were situated far away from Broomdale. Besides, that was not what she had come to Lakeland to do. Better to go back home and write the whole thing off as a failure.

By nine o'clock Ellen was nodding by the fire. Georgie Girl settled contentedly on her slippered feet, as if aware that it was Ellen, on this occasion, in need of consolation and comfort.

'You ought to be in bed,' Beth chided.

'Aye, in a minute. I'm enjoying this fire.'

'Well, I think I'll go. It's been a long day.'

'You do, lass. You haven't my stamina.'

And smiling, Beth got up and left them, old woman and goose, content with each other's company.

The short, sharp days of winter were growing longer. May was upon them and the breeze almost mild. The panoply of mountains stood tranquil, pale and snow-capped in the distance: Striding Edge, Bowfell, Crinkle Crags and Harter Fell, while all around the cottage, spears of green daffodils were bursting into golden bloom, and deep in Brockbarrow Wood a cuckoo called, expressing content with its lot, as Beth could not.

She'd taken her time this morning, walking round by Whinstone Force to sit for a while and watch the plunging waters fall into the gill below, enjoying the ice cold spray on her face. She cupped her hand, scooping and drinking from the crystal cold water. No water tasted quite so good as that found gushing from a Lakeland mountainside. Her hands still tingled with the cold as she walked along the edge of Brockbarrow Wood, stopping to speak to Pegleg, still in lone residence at the tarn, then across the open fell to Larkrigg. She intended to collect her personal belongings, a task she had postponed for long enough.

She walked up the long drive by the Gemini Stones and thought again how true the legend had proved to be, then smothered the thought in the more practical one of how they never had got around to pruning these old trees. Though she'd planted a few new ones.

The air had grown cooler as she climbed, whipping colour in to her pale cheeks, tossing her hair about and she recalled how she'd always used to wear it clipped back with an unbecoming slide. A feature that only Andrew had apparently approved of. Dear Andrew, she really must go and see him soon. She'd avoided him because she hated to talk about her troubles with anyone.

She trailed a hand on a lichen covered stone wall as she walked, the feel of it rough against the soft palms of her hands. And couldn't bear even to look up at the house as she struggled to blink the tears from her eyes. How far away that day seemed, the day they had first looked upon Larkrigg and she had persuaded Sarah to make it their home. As Beth let herself in the back door, her shoes echoing eerily on the tiled floor, she smiled at the now gleaming old range as if meeting an old friend. She rubbed a hand over the scrubbed pine table, the pristine paintwork, the polished copper piping, and remembered it all as it had been when they had first seen the house, neglected and dirty, unloved and uncared for.

Someone else would now work in her kitchen. Someone else would sit in the small sitting room, and sleep in her bed.

Someone else chasing the rural idyll.

She smiled to remember how they had first set eyes on Jonty and Pietro, lying naked in a shaft of sun light. The picnics, the swimming in the tarn, the fun and laughter. What a chain of events had unfolded since that day. And what had their youthful exuberance brought them? Precious little happiness. All those hopes, dreams and promise gone to waste.

Jonty was confined to a wheelchair. Tessa tied to him and his no doubt increasing ill temper. How she would welcome Tessa's lively company right now. And poor Andrew more alone than ever.

For herself, a triangle of love that could never hope to work out to anyone's satisfaction. Succeeding only in betraying her own sister.

And Sarah, run mad with money and power, had driven them to the brink of bankruptcy and escaped the consequences, as she always did.

She packed as quickly as she could, desperate to spare herself any more agony. She took only her most precious items, and absolute essentials. Even so there was more than she realised.

She loaded an old wheelbarrow and trundled some boxes down to Ellen's cottage. It took several trips, and since there was little space in the tiny bedroom she stacked them up without unpacking. She'd just have to dip in for whatever she needed. The rest were to be collected by Tam in the Land Rover and stowed away in the great loft at Broombank, probably to remain there for ever, forgotten and neglected.

She filled Ellen's larder with the countless jars of preserves and pickles, and the residue of her store of vegetables. They could live on jam, bread and chutney if nothing else, she thought, with a wry touch of humour.

The worst moment was parting with the animals. Ellen couldn't afford to take them on. The Herdwicks would be returned to Andrew but Meg took most of the hens and ducks. Jan took the geese. The rest had to be sold. It was like parting with old friends, symbolising the end of her dream. There would be no smallholding now, no Jersey cow, no clotted cream.

And deep inside she felt a rare and burning anger against Sarah. She'd behaved with complete selfishness, been recklessly careless without a thought for the consequences, or the affect upon others of her spendthrift ways. Yet even as Beth quietly seethed, guilt also played a part. If she hadn't been so taken up with her own feelings for Pietro, she might have paid more attention to what was going on.

She should have insisted on taking a full part in the mill and in earning their living, not let Sarah shoulder all the responsibility. If only they'd been like other sisters and been able to share the work and the worry. If only they hadn't been at such cross-purposes the whole time, with the kind of tension that prevented any sort of worthwhile communication.

And what was she supposed to do with her life now that everything worthwhile had vanished from it? How was she expected to pick up the pieces without Pietro or even Sarah beside her? Where was she supposed to live? What could she do to earn a living? So many decisions still to be made.

But as she locked the great front door for the last time, Beth knew that really there was only one solution. She must go home, to Boston. There was nothing left for her here in Lakeland. And she walked away from Larkrigg without a backward glance.

As the days and weeks passed she came no nearer to finding any alternative solution. Much as Beth might pretend to fight it, she nursed the memory of Pietro like a wound. His face haunted her dreams and the scent and feel of him was like a physical presence beside her throughout each long day and night.

She asked all the local farmers if they needed help, a housekeeper or dairymaid perhaps, but those days were long gone. Most had a wife to care for them and those who didn't, couldn't afford the luxury of paying for their house to be swept.

They were all of them concerned and tried to help, asking what she knew about milking, or lambing or bringing on a good calf. And she was forced to admit that she knew nothing, nothing at all. All her confidence had gone and she felt sure she'd be useless on a farm. She hadn't even managed to look after one goat. So Beth was forced to turn her attention elsewhere and discovered there was no work either at the Broomdale Inn, the local garage or the small post office run from Mrs Wilson's front room. She would have to look further afield, in Kendal or Windermere, if she meant to stay.

As she struggled to make up her mind, money became a problem and she hated to be beholden to Ellen for anything. She worked as hard as she could in the garden and with the animals, desperate at least to pay for her keep that way.

Then she woke one sunny morning to the glorious sound of the dawn chorus and decided, on impulse, that today she must talk with Andrew. Perhaps he would have some ideas to offer of what she might do. Failing that, she could at least say her goodbyes before she left for America. He had been a good friend to her. He deserved that much, at least.

She made an effort with her appearance for once, putting on a flowered skirt and plain blue blouse that brought out the colour in her eyes, and set off to walk over the fell to Cathra Crag, enjoying the briskness of the breeze in her face.

And it would be good to see old Seth again. She hoped the old man was well. She'd neglected him during her troubles.

Oh, but she would miss all of this, back in Boston. The way cloud shadows chased each other across the backs of green mountains. Those mornings when spiky black trees emerged ethereally through the white veil of a ground mist, the soaring song of the skylark and the damp, dewy smell of fresh new grass.

Through a blur of tears she gazed out across Larkrigg Fell and down into Broomdale, her eyes following the ribbons of dry-stone walls that laced the country together, and hedges full of May blossom like a rim of frothy lace edging the green skirts of the fell. Above her was the aching emptiness of the sky, lighting the distant peaks which always seemed tantalisingly closer than they actually were.

Tears rolled down her cheeks, rapidly cooling in the wind. Until this moment she realised, there'd been no time for tears. She'd been quite beyond them.

In one night she had lost her sister, the man she loved, and now her home. She had no money, no skills or training in anything, no way of earning a living. And no one at all to love her.

Not that self-pity would do any good, she told herself sternly. Nor would resentment, guilt or anger. Whatever Sarah was doing right now, she was looking after number one, herself. She must learn to do the same and acquire a little selfishness too.

Beth counted her blessings, one by one on her fingers. She had her health, her youth, and at least the sacrifice of Larkrigg had cleared the debts. She was free now, free to pick herself up and start again. Turn the page of life and go on, no matter what the cost.

Seth was not in the chimney corner where he usually was, or apparently on one of his endless walks. The partly carved deer's head that was the crook handle he'd clearly been working on, stood abandoned on the mantle-shelf. Seth himself lay fast asleep in the high Victorian bed where he'd very likely been born and where he may now be about to die, if his stentorian breathing was anything to go by. The sound of it sent shudders down her spine. He seemed too ill to even notice her presence but Beth sat with him for a while, holding his wrinkled hand.

Back in the kitchen she asked Andrew how ill he really was. He was surprisingly offhand.

'I wouldn't know. As well as can be expected. He's had flu' and he's very old. Happen he'll recover, happen he won't.'

'I'm so sorry.'

'Why should it trouble you?'

'I like him. He's my friend.'

'Then you could have come to see him a bit sooner. He's been ill for weeks.' Andrew placed a mug of strong tea in front of her and Beth hesitantly began to tell him of all that had happened to her in these weeks, why she hadn't been round to see him. 'I've had a terrible time.'

He cut her short. 'Don't tell me your problems, Beth, I've enough of me own.'

'But I've always come to you.'

'Well happen I can't help any more.'

'Ellen has been ill. She was bitten by an adder.'

'Aye, I'm sorry about that.'

'And we've only just escaped being made bankrupt. Sarah has gone, and so has Pietro.' She caught at a sob in her throat. 'Can't you see how that has been devastating for me?'

Andrew drained the boiling water from a pan of potatoes, tossed the lid away with a clatter and began to mash them with a fork. 'Good riddance to him.'

'*What?*'

'I said . . . Oh, never mind.'

261

'I heard what you said and it was unkind.'

'Happen. And up here at Cathra Crag we face the threat of bankruptcy every week. So what? Join the club.'

She was appalled by his heartlessness. They seemed to be right back where they'd started, doing nothing but quarrel. Irritated by his lack of understanding she reached for the pan and fork.

'You're making a rotten job of that, let me do it.'

Andrew obstinately held fast to the handle, trying to wrench it from her grasp but she clung on and a sort of undignified tussle took place between them, ending with a loss of a good third of the pan's contents on to the floor. 'Now look what you've done, you daft woman. I can manage on me own, thanks very much.'

She scowled at him, heart thumping with concern. 'What is it, Andrew? Why are you so angry with me? What have I done?'

'Done?' He gave a short, bitter laugh. He'd heard all her news on the local telegraph, otherwise known as gossip, long before she'd bothered to find the time to come and tell him herself. The thought of her pining for Pietro Lawson was more than he could stomach. 'You've done nowt, have you? That's your trouble. You live in a little dream world. Little Miss Innocent. You swan through life without a moment's concern. One minute mooning over Jonty Reynolds, the next over a man who, besides being completely unworthy of you, belongs to your sister.' He waved the fork in her face. 'But do you let that bother you? Do you hell. You ignore everyone else, are content to spend all the money Sarah gives you and then whinge when there's none left.' The fork flew through the air and landed by some miracle, in the sink.

Beth had gone white to the lips. 'That's totally unfair. It wasn't like that at all.'

'Oh, wasn't it?'

'No. I didn't know the mill was in trouble. Sarah never told me.'

'And you never asked? Why, I wonder? Because you were too besotted with that fancy Italian to care.'

'I loved Pietro – do love him.'

'Aye, so you keep telling me.'

'I couldn't help the way I felt – feel.'

'Spare me the hearts and flowers.' His lip curled with contempt as he started to ladle out spoonfuls of mash and mince on to a plate.

She could feel her cheeks burning now, with embarrassment and distress. 'I didn't know you felt this way, Andrew. So angry and bitter.'

He flung the pan away from him in a gesture of complete frustration then turned to face her, eyes blazing. 'How do you expect me to feel? Of course I'm bloody angry. Do you think I'm not human or something?

Do you think I haven't seen you kissing and canoodling and doing God knows what out on them fells? Do you reckon I don't care? Why shouldn't I? Because I'm the local yokel, the ignorant peasant. Because I've no heart? Damn you, Beth, I do have a bloody heart, and feelings too. I've loved you since the first moment I clapped eyes on you and you treat me like shit.'

'W-what did you say?'

'You heard. You thought I asked you to marry me out of pity. Well, you couldn't be more wrong.' And flinging Seth's dinner plate on to a tray he strode out of the room and clomped furiously up the stairs.

Beth remained exactly where she was, frozen to the spot. Then she let herself quietly out of the back door and ran back over the fell, sobbing as if her heart would break.

The next day a letter came from Sarah, full of apologies about leaving Beth 'in the soup' as she called it. How she was sure Beth had 'sorted it all out' by 'sweet-talking' the bank and how she and Pietro were travelling through Europe, taking their time, en route for Italy to meet his family.

'We'll be back before you know it,' her letter chattered on. 'When we've had a lovely rest. And what do you think? It'll be as Mr and Mrs Pietro Lawson. We've decided to get married in Florence. You won't mind not being a bridesmaid or anything, will you? It's such a lovely opportunity to enjoy a wonderful honeymoon before we return. Isn't it exciting?'

Two days after that, Beth met Andrew by the tarn and told him she would marry him.

21

There was an election that May and Mrs Thatcher came to power. It seemed to indicate a new era to have a woman prime minister, one in which women could be as powerful as they wished to be.

Beth settled for much less, a marriage without love, on her part at least, though with plenty of good will and her very best intentions. Everyone told her what a good man Andrew was and she would smile and say yes, of course he was, and her very best friend. They'd make a good life together.

She was just twenty years old and already prepared to make compromises in her life.

Beth knew she would never forget the look of brilliant hope on his face when she'd told him. She'd been entirely honest and admitted that she didn't love him quite as she should.

'You'll come to love me, in time. I know you will,' he'd assured her, which she didn't believe for a moment but knew that she could never love anyone now, so what did it matter? But when he'd stepped closer, as if to seal the bargain with a kiss, she'd backed hurriedly away and he'd regarded her with a thoughtful seriousness. 'Will it be soon?'

'Why not? Sooner it's done the better.' And the sooner I can get over my broken heart, she had thought, and escaped.

The wedding took place on the last day of June. Meg put on a splendid reception at Broombank and all the neighbours came, including old Seth who was now much recovered, though still suffering from a troublesome cough. Ellen was there too of course, looking unnaturally smart in a costume she had probably owned since the Coronation. Even Jan was smiling and wishing Beth well, and the neighbouring farmer's wives clucked and chirrupped with pleasure.

'Happen they're too much in love to wait,' they murmured, always ready to enjoy a romance and see a young bride and groom off on a new life together.

It was two years since she had come to the Lake District and everyone was slightly surprised she didn't wait for her sister to return from her own extended honeymoon. Amazing how they'd both decided to marry at the same time. Twins were so alike, were they not? Though the other one had eloped to Italy, after all that trouble with the mill. Proper bit of excitement that was.

Lissa and Derry, the twins' parents, naturally came for the wedding and Beth was so thrilled to see them. There was much laughter and kisses all round, and so much news to catch up on from home. But they were more inclined to worry over Sarah's defection.

'What is he like, this young man?' Derry wanted to know.

'Why wouldn't she wait? Why didn't she tell us? A joint wedding would've been so lovely.' Lissa mourned.

But Sarah was gone and Beth didn't want to talk about her, so gradually everyone stopped too and concentrated instead upon wishing the young couple well.

Since it was expected, the happy couple took a weekend away at a fine hotel in Ilkley. They were shown into a comfortable bedroom with a four poster bed which unfortunately reminded Beth of the one at Larkrigg where Sarah and Pietro had made love with such noisy gusto. She shuddered and turned quickly away to unpack the small case she had brought with her.

Andrew, who had seen the involuntary spasm, felt his heart sink. He hadn't expected this to be easy but right now he wondered if he could ever win his young wife's affection. Rushing her would certainly not be the way. The moment the smirking porter had gone, pocketing his unearned tip, he hastened to reassure her. 'You can have the bed. I'll sleep on the floor.'

She stared at him and he saw the gratitude spring in to the melting grey-blue eyes, even as she struggled to disguise her relief. 'Oh, Andrew. Not the floor.'

'The chair then,' giving an airy laugh, as if sleeping apart from one's bride on honeymoon was the normal way of going about things. 'Though it looks a mite small, don't you reckon? For a big chap like me.'

Beth gazed at the great bed, wondering how she would feel about sharing it with Andrew, his rough farmer's hand on her breast where Pietro's silken touch had caressed her. His mouth on hers where Pietro's sweet lips had kissed hers. She should have considered all of this before she'd agreed to marry him of course. It was too late now. She felt herself stiffen, as if already repulsing her husband's caresses, and her distress must have shown in her face for Andrew again hastened to calm her anxieties.

'It's all right. I don't mind. And no one will know, so long as we don't ask for breakfast in bed, eh?' he joked.

She looked so young and desirable standing before him that the longing to take her in his arms almost unmanned him. Did he have the discipline, he wondered desperately, not to touch her when he knew she slept so close? He must find it somehow, or risk losing his lovely Beth for ever. And he did so want to make this marriage work. All he had to do was to give her time to get used to the idea.

He took hold of her shoulders and turned her to face him. 'I want you to come to me willingly, Beth. However long that takes, I can wait.'

For a long moment she gazed up at him, eyes filling with tears. 'I do want to be a good wife to you. I want to make you happy,' she said.

'You will. Let's take things slowly, right?'

She nodded, then tipping up on her toes, kissed him gently upon his lips. It was light and insignificant, a mere whisper of a kiss, as if given by a child. 'Thank you,' she said, and picking up her dressing gown headed for the bathroom, the terms of the marriage it seemed, were settled.

So it proved, for when the short honeymoon was over and they returned to Cathra Crag, they settled for separate rooms, Andrew remaining in his old one while Beth slept alone in the main bedroom, recently vacated by Billy in her honour.

And if either Seth or Billy considered the arrangement odd for a newly married couple, neither made any comment upon it. Happen

267

this was the modern way, Billy thought sadly. Or else his son had a problem, happen caused by losing his mother so young. Time would sort it out. Best not to interfere.

Seth merely watched, held his own counsel and pondered. Summat was wrong and he meant to find out what it was, and if possible be the one to put it right. Nothing had beaten him yet.

On that very first morning when Beth walked into her kitchen, she was almost overwhelmed, not only by the fact that no one in their right minds could call it labour saving, but also by a most noxious smell. She was nervous of this new life she had embarked upon and anxious to do well in it, but this was beyond even her worst nightmares.

'Heavens above, it's like someone died. What on earth is it?'

Seth stood sheepishly fidgeting in the doorway. 'It's me 'orns.'

'I beg your pardon?'

'I've put 'em on to boil.'

'You've *what*?'

'For me crook handles, see?' He showed her a large pan in which two pieces of ram's horn reposed in bubbling splendour. 'This soften's 'em oop a bit like, then I can press them into reet shape. After that it's all in the skill of me knife.'

Beth stared at the old man, pinching her nose with finger and thumb against the stink. No wonder there was always an odd smell about the place. What had she let herself in for? Three men, three different generations, all no doubt set in their ways. 'I hope this doesn't happen often,' she said.

'Oh, no. It teks ages to carve a crook handle. I'll do yan for thoo, shall I?'

A smile twitched at the corner of her mouth. 'What would I want with a crook?'

He grinned mischievously. 'To dole in that gormless husband of yours?'

And seeing the wicked twinkle in the old man's eyes she thought for a moment he had guessed, then she burst out laughing. 'Things are going to change round here,' she warned, wagging a finger at him.

'Aye, lass. I reckon you'll have your hands full reet enough, wi' us lot.'

* * *

The very first thing she did was to throw away the stained tablecloth and scrub the big kitchen table. With quantities of bleach and hot water it came up gleaming, almost as good as Meg's. She wouldn't let herself even think of her lovely kitchen at Larkrigg. That belonged in the past. This was her home now and if it was not what she'd been used to, then it was up to her to make it better. If Ellen could make a good life for herself in that tiny cottage, then she must do as much here.

Beth was determined to make a good impression. She may have a lot to learn about her role as a farmer's wife, but she could bring some warmth and care into these men's lives. She shooed Seth off to the woodshed to press his precious pieces of horn and opened all the doors and windows to get rid of the smell. Then she cleaned the kitchen from top to bottom, scrubbing the sink, walls and window sill, scouring out every cupboard, rubbing up the old paintwork till, if it didn't exactly shine, she knew it to be clean.

After a restoring cup of tea, she set to baking a mutton and potato pie in the old solid fuel range, and on the stroke of twelve-thirty she heard the clatter of clogs coming along the back passage. Billy and Andrew back from the fells, Seth joining them from his shed.

They all hung their caps on the door peg, washed their hands at the stone sink in the back scullery, and came to their places at the table as they always did. Their noses were twitching at the delicious aroma that rose with the steam from the pie. A feast of a meal awaited them. Andrew had done them right proud in his choice of bride, their satisfied stance said. With a scrape of chair on slate floor and an eager clatter of feet the three men sat down and raised expectant eyes to Beth's.

'I think you've forgotten something,' she said, a gentle smile of reproof on her face.

They glanced uncertainly at each other. 'What's oop?' Billy politely asked.

'Your clogs. They're full of mud and muck from the fields.'

'Nay, it's a farm, lass. Hadn't thoo noticed?' Seth chuckled.

A small silence, in which Beth continued to gaze at their three shining faces through the steam of the pie, but she made no move to cut it. The smell of whatever was on their clogs was making her gag. Swallowing hard, and trying to ignore the ferocity of her husband's frown, she held to her resolve with a smile. 'The farm is outside. In here is my kitchen, which if you notice, I've just cleaned. If you wouldn't mind leaving your clogs or boots in the back scullery and change into indoor shoes, I'd be most grateful.'

For a moment she thought Andrew might explode. His face went beetroot red and he shot up from the table. 'If we're not good enough for . . .' he began but it was Billy who put out a hand to stop him.

'Now then. The lass is right. We've lived so long on us own, we three chaps, that we've forgotten our manners. I seem to recall your mother saying much the same thing, once upon a time.'

This, apparently, settled the matter and the three men trooped out of the kitchen, returning after a moment in stocking feet, some of them sporting holes through which big toes peeped. 'We'll get some slippers,' Billy promised.

'Good idea,' Beth agreed, and hiding a smile, dished out a huge chunk of pie for each of them by way of reward. Not a word was spoken as they demolished it, and the rice pudding which followed. Eating, appeared to be a serious business, yet within half an hour they had washed it all down with a huge mug of tea each and were replacing the clogs and going about their work.

'Tea at five,' Andrew told her, smiling and nodding before going on his way. He'd forgiven her about the clogs because the pie had been so good and she'd looked so pretty serving it.

When he'd gone Beth sank back in her chair with a sigh, surveying the wreck on the kitchen table. A small victory, but a victory nonetheless. She wondered whether the rest would be so easy, and somehow rather doubted it.

Tea at five? What would they expect? She'd have to bake scones or gingerbread. Jam and bread perhaps? Or some sort of meat and salad? When everything was cleared away she began to investigate her stores more thoroughly. There was plenty of flour, potatoes and vegetables, cold bacon in the larder but no eggs. She'd have to get her hens back from Meg. Neither was there any bread in the bin, and few tins in the cupboard. She thought of all the preserves she had left at Ellen's and wondered if she dare find the courage to beg a jar or two back. She'd have to do some shopping, for there seemed little food in the place. Had she time to nip down to Mrs Wilson's little shop?

She surveyed the back scullery with greater attention. There was a round bin which contained some sort of foodstuff, for the calves perhaps? Would it be her job then to feed them? Apparently so. She'd better get instructions from Andrew. There was also an old mangle that doubled as a laundry table and what she now realised was an old fashioned dolly tub and posser. Fancy these old things being left here. They should be in Kendal museum.

And then with dawning dismay she looked more closely about the kitchen, examining it more closely.

No washing machine or spin dryer, no vaccuum cleaner or electric iron. No toaster, grill, radio or TV. No modern contrivances of any kind.

She opened the door and ran across the yard. Andrew was in the barn, sweeping out the loft, making it ready for the coming season's hay.

'Where are all the plugs?' she asked. 'And the kitchen equipment?'

The awful silence and the slackening of his mouth into a shocked oval, told its own tale.

'You do have electricity, don't you?'

He gazed above her head, as if seeking inspiration, or wishing the almighty would whisk him away so he didn't have to answer this question. 'They laid the mains on right to the head of the dale here, but Grandad wouldn't have us connected on to it. He didn't trust it.'

'You've got your own generator then?'

'Well . . .'

She gazed at him, stunned. 'No electricity at all?'

'No.'

'Then what happens in the evening? Do you sit in the dark?' Beth couldn't believe that she'd never noticed this before, but always when she'd called it had been daylight, and if sometimes it'd seemed a bit gloomy, she'd put it down to old Seth's fancy not to waste money on electricity unnecessarily. Many old people were like that. It had never occurred to her that there was none.

Andrew was looking almost angry now, as if it were her fault in some way. 'We use the oil lamps, OK? I'd like electricity connected as much as you would. I bought an old generator once, for the clipping, but he wouldn't let me use it so I never really got it working.'

'Well, get it working now.'

'I don't know if I can. Or if Seth would agree.'

'Oh, for goodness' sake.'

'I know, Beth, I know. I'll speak to him, I really will.'

'Speak to your father, I'll talk to Seth myself,' Beth said and swinging about, went off in search of the wood shed, where she enjoyed a long and fruitless discussion with the bombastic old man.

'We've no money for such fancy tricks,' he told her, barely raising his head from the length of ash he was shaving to a wonderful smoothness.

'But it would make life so much easier for us all. You could have an electric blanket to warm your bed.'

She might as well have offered him a flight to the moon, so scathing was his expression, and received nothing more than a lecture on good health for her troubles.

Two days later she told Andrew that whether Seth liked it not, she'd written to the electricity board to see how much it would cost to put them on the mains.

Andrew looked stunned. 'You'd no right to do such a thing. We probably wouldn't be able to afford it, whatever it costs.'

'How do we know unless we ask?'

'Don't tell my Dad what you've done. He doesn't like interference.'

Beth merely wrinkled her nose at him and grinned. 'Oh, don't be such an old fuddy-duddy. You've said yourself this farm should modernise. Have you tackled that old generator yet.'

'It's all rusted up.'

'Then unrust it. And see about wiring up this house to it. Right?'

He gazed at her, feeling a kindle of admiration like a pain deep inside him, for all he was nervous of his family's reaction to her revolutionary talk. And in other places an ache of a different sort. How long could he go on like this? He loved the way she tossed back her thick hair, so silky and glossy he wanted to stroke it, stroke her, feel the smoothness of her skin next to his. He closed his eyes for a moment and swallowed, disciplining himself not to look at her again while he agreed to do what he could with the old generator. 'I doubt it'll be big enough to do all the work you require of it. I'll happen look for another.'

But he never got the chance to give it a try. In no time at all Seth discovered what he was about and put a stop to it.

'I'm not having no 'lectic wiring in my house. Burn the place down it will. And there's no fire brigade for ten miles or more.' And that put an end to the subject of electricity.

The lack of electricity, however, proved to be only one of her problems during that summer.

Beth felt as if she had stepped back in time. The best she could do was to scour the place clean from top to bottom, ruthlessly throwing away dozens of old newspapers, tin cans, rotting shoes, and a jumble of assorted rubbish she couldn't even put a name to.

'Ere, that might coom in handy,' Seth would protest, every time she tossed some item into the big plastic bags she was using.

'For what? Screwing a hole in your head?' She stared at the broken screwdriver. 'Good idea, might let in a breath of fresh air.'

'Saucy madam,' Seth would say, then laugh his toothless laugh, and help her with the next cupboard until he became absorbed in some treasure he hadn't set eyes on for fifty years and carried it off to his woodshed, like a prize.

But whenever she suggested the smallest alteration, even a coat of paint, there was always absolute and obdurate refusal.

Andrew didn't have the time, Seth complained it was a waste of good money, and Billy wouldn't have anything altered from the way things had been when his dear wife had been alive.

If she was ever in any doubt about this, it was confirmed when she broached the subject of the front parlour, ever cold despite the heat of summer outside.

Beth could detect the small changes Andrew's mother must have made all those years before. Brocade curtains at the window, long since faded to an indeterminate shade of brown. The fifties-style crocheted antimacassars on the two fireside chairs, and a small green tiled fireplace. But the round table was covered with a Victorian chenille velvet cloth in dull red. The ancient harmonium was cluttered with photographs of ladies in long skirts and men holding hay forks. The room smelled musty and unused, the window caked with dust.

She had to make things better. Beth felt she must make every effort to create a good life for herself here, at Cathra Crag, for herself and Andrew. She owed him that, at least. And if she didn't keep busy, her mind kept returning to the haunting image of Pietro, intruding on her need to find peace. Bringing the little parlour in to the present day would be her salvation.

'Can I modernise it a little?' she begged Andrew, afraid to attempt any more changes without permission.

A flicker of anxiety clouded his face. 'Why? What's wrong with it as it is?'

She searched her mind for the right explanation. 'It's not mine.'

'It's not mine, either. But Dad likes it this way.'

'Surely I can be permitted to make some small changes? They wouldn't begrudge me that, would they?'

'You mean you're regretting taking on two old men, my family.'

Beth bridled. 'No, I didn't mean that at all. I'm very fond of Seth, and Billy.'

'The front parlour is saved for special occasions.'

'It was once. Things are different now. We're married, and we've nowhere to call our own. Somewhere for just the two of us.'

He gazed at her bright face entranced, enchanted suddenly by the prospect of sitting in this room of an evening, alone with her. Andrew gazed into Beth's pleading blue eyes and wanted, desperately, to give her anything she asked for. And he wanted to take her up to his bed, this very minute. So badly, he thought he might disgrace himself right here in front of her. Then he remembered his honeymoon and the fact that she had openly admitted, right from the start that she didn't love him, and he felt himself go limp with fresh despair.

Marriage on the rebound, wasn't that the word she used? Oh, she was honest all right was Beth, you couldn't fault her there. 'Whose fault is that, if we're never on our own?' Feeling a miserable sort of satisfaction when he saw her blush, and hating himself for embarrassing her.

Beth did not pretend she didn't understand him. 'You promised to be patient.'

He ran work-worn fingers through the shock of thick fair hair, and it fell forward onto his brow. She had a sudden urge to push it back again. 'Aye,' he said, and the sad bitterness in his voice jolted her. 'Happen I'm regretting it. Happen I might decide to be patient for a life-time. We'll see. But if you're not content with the usual way a man and his wife find to be alone, there's nowt I can do about it.'

He didn't regret letting her see the depth of his frustration, which gave such a cruel edge to his tone, but he did regret its cause. He wondered bleakly if their marriage had any hope of surviving.

'I thought we should have some space to ourselves. It would be a start,' Beth finished, almost wishing she'd never broached the subject.

'You can ask Dad. But if he won't agree, you'll have to put up with things the way they are, won't you?'

'Thank you,' was all Beth could manage, stunned by his outburst and his sour mood. Yet he proved to be absolutely correct. Billy was every bit as obstinate as his father. He eyed her with doubtful suspicion when she broached the subject.

'Everything is just as it was when Andrew's mam were alive.'

Beth swallowed her impatience. 'That's a long time ago, when Andrew was a baby Mr Barton. Times move on.'

'Not so long in the lifetime of this farm. Nowt's worn out that I can see.'

'No, but . . .'

'I'd sooner you leave things as they are.'

And she felt too new and insecure to press the matter further. And somehow, with the picture of Andrew's sad face clear in her mind, getting to sleep in the big, soft bed was even harder on that night, which had nothing at all to do with redecorating the little parlour.

They continued to sit in the big farm kitchen, with the two old men either side of the fire hogging its warmth, while she and Andrew perched as best they could on a couple of hard stand chairs. They hardly looked at each other, let alone talked. It was uncomfortable and claustrophobic and not at all what Beth had had in mind for her married life.

She noticed too several smaller irritations. If she moved a picture or ornament, put a chair back in the wrong place, it would then mysteriously return to its original spot. Once, she went so far as to buy a remnant of fabric on Kendal market and sewed a new pair of curtains in bright blue and yellow cotton, which she hung in the front parlour, for all no one ever used it. They lasted a day before someone silently took them down and replaced them with the dark brown ones, which Beth had come to hate because they kept out all the sun, and represented her failure.

She might be married to the son of the house, and the two old men were impeccably courteous to her, but she felt no more than a visitor, politely tolerated.

The only time she and Andrew could hope to be alone was after Seth and Billy went off to bed.

At first she had escaped early to bed herself, tired from her exhausting day of housekeeping and learning the farm chores. Now she tried the very opposite. However tired she was, she determined to stay up for those few precious moments she had Andrew to herself. She was anxious to get to know him better, told herself it was her responsibility as a good wife. Even if there were no sex between them, at least they could become better friends. Or what hope did they have together?

They would sit for a while in the two fireside chairs, as if there were nothing in the world wrong between them. Often there would be long, painful silences, at other times Andrew would talk to her, though always about farming matters. And Beth would struggle to take an interest, relieved that he cared enough to share his concerns with her, when she'd so badly failed his greater needs.

'Would you credit it? Ben Cottram is selling up,' he said one evening as he read the farming snippets from the local paper. 'I never thought he'd give up.'

'Why is he?'

'Small farms are closing down every week. It's very worrying. Young men aren't so keen to take on this way of life as they once were, and won't do it at all if there's no financial incentive.'

'Yes,' Beth said. 'I can see that.'

'Without government investment, hill farming would be finished. And if it went, that would damage the whole environment. The grass would grow too long and kill all the rare flowers, then there'd be no butterflies, no seeds for the birds. The bracken would take over and you'd have a wilderness where no one could walk.' Beth listened, fascinated, beginning to see her young husband in a new light as he talked of these matters so close to his heart. She found she enjoyed watching his awkwardness fall away as his enthusiasm grew with each point he made.

'And it'd damage the rural economy, d'you see? Jobs would disappear, and a whole way of life. Everything would be different.'

He was looking so furious Beth had to laugh. 'But that scenario isn't going to happen, Andrew. The government is investing in hill farming and you aren't going to lose Cathra Crag.'

'I hope not. But I feel sorry for Ben. He put everything he had in to that farm and now his sons aren't interested. You can't trust your own family these days, can you?'

She was shocked. 'You can trust Seth and Billy.'

'Happen. Unless Seth decides to do summat daft. It's his farm don't forget, not mine. And even families can let you down.'

And remembering her own betrayal, Beth could not deny it. As her thoughts wandered, she missed what Andrew was saying next, then came to, realising he was still talking about Seth.

'But he'll do naught about it. You can't make him plan. This electricity business is typical of him. Says he's too old to be bossed about, and why should he consider aught he don't want to.'

And Beth laughed again, not thinking it mattered since they were all safe here together. And as he continued to talk, she watched him with closer attention.

How small creases formed over the bridge of his nose as he worried over these issues, so dear to his heart. How every so often he would run his fingers through his fair hair and rumple it, making him look young and vulnerable. His lean, boyish face had filled out a little but there was no spare flesh on his taut, muscled body. He worked too hard for that. And she couldn't help but admire him. He wasn't really at all bad looking, though she'd paid little attention before. And a countryman born and bred, right to the heart of him. Patient, steady, reliable, as Ellen had once been at pains to inform her.

'I resent us being so backward here,' he was saying. 'Broombank rents a helicopter to drop feedstuffs to the sheep on the high fell in winter, we drag it up on a sled in the old style. They use modern technology wherever they can, take note of scientific developments with regard to feed, injections, doses and drenches and the like. As a result they keep a healthier flock and make money, while we struggle from hand to mouth.' He began to pace about, fidgety with frustration.

'Old Seth never had to give proper attention to planning and paperwork. And Dad is pottering on to his retirement. It's no way to run a farm. The old ways are gone.'

Beth smiled her sympathy, but her mind was paying less attention to his words and more to watching his movements. 'You can't talk Seth into doing anything he's set his mind against. I've learned that much. It took me all of Friday to persuade him to change his shirt and underthings so I could wash them. It was a long fight but I won in the end. I even succeeded in getting him to change those dreadful trousers, so I could clean and mend them.'

Andrew gave a sudden grin. 'Not his cap and waistcoat though.'

'No,' she admitted on a gurgle of laughter. 'I haven't got that far yet.'

And they laughed together, eyes dancing, glancing shyly at each other and then away again. After a moment, a silence fell between them, growing to the point of awkwardness and Beth set aside the knitting she was working on and stood up. 'I think I'll go to bed now. I'm tired.'

'Right.'

'Will you be coming up soon?' She hesitated at the door, wondering if she should suggest that he come up now, with her.

She was not unaware of the need which so often flared in his eyes when he looked at her, for all he might try to disguise it. Some day soon Beth knew she should take her husband to her bed. No man should be denied a loving wife and Andrew had been good to her.

He kept his eyes on the fire as he spoke. 'I'll glance at the paper first.' And made no move to follow as she walked from the room and quietly closed the door.

22

Climbing the stairs to the big, draughty bedroom, Beth tried to erase the memory of his closed face from her mind. He had looked almost gaunt, with tired rings beneath the eyes in that second before he'd broken her gaze. How badly this way of life must be hurting him. It wasn't the sort of marriage Andrew deserved. But was she ready to face the inevitable? Was she able to offer herself to a man she did not love?

She sat on the edge of the bed and stared about her, striving to make herself feel better by admiring the small improvements she'd been able to make in her own bedroom.

She'd hung pictures on the walls, put new curtains at the small window and a rug upon the lino floor, a blue jug of flowers on her chest of drawers. Yet somehow the room seemed as empty and cheerless as ever. The big feather mattress was admittedly comfortable but did nothing to ease her loneliness as she lay in the centre of this huge bed, all alone each and every night.

Beth listened now to the sounds of him riddling the ashes in the fire grate, then going out to do his final nightly round of checking on the stock. It would take him ten minutes, then she would hear the sound of his footstep on the stair, passing her door as he made his way to his own room. Would he ever come to her of his own volition? Did she want him to?

Her mind conjured up pictures of him in his single bed, and she couldn't help but worry over the future. Was this what she had expected, to live a celibate life? Was this what she wanted? Beth doubted she had ever considered the question. And daren't, even now.

But some day soon she must come to terms with the fact that her dreams for Pietro were simply that. Dreams. Pietro was lost to her and she must make the effort to be fair to Andrew. For her own sake as much as his. Life must go on. Hadn't she told herself so a dozen times?

Did he assume she was not a virgin, she wondered? Hadn't he seen them on the fells together? If so, it somehow mattered to her that he understand it had been only on the one occasion that she'd gone so far, when things had somehow got out of hand because of the snow. Why it should matter she couldn't quite say, but knew that it did.

Sighing, she got up from the bed. There were few comforts in the bare room, for all her efforts. She hung her clothes in a cupboard, certain it must be damp and, as she did each and every night, stripped off her clothes, stood on a towel, and by the light of her candle started to wash herself from the bowl of hot water she'd set on the chest of drawers. Having a proper bathroom installed was another change Seth would probably never sanction, even had they the money for one.

She'd slicked her body all over with the warm soapy water when there came a tap at her door.

Panic gripped her and she glanced about for her old dressing gown. 'Just a minute, then you can come in.'

But the door opened before she could move and Andrew stood framed in the opening, his anguished gaze at once taking in her slender loveliness, her naked body glistening with soft soap and candlelight. 'God, I'm sorry, I thought you said come in.'

Beth stood transfixed, caught like a rabbit in the glare of a car headlight. She could not move, could say nothing, only gaze into his dark eyes, her breath a tight ball in her chest. From fear? Excitement? She knew not. Then he was closing the door and he was gone, and for some reason her heart gave a hard thump of disappointment.

Ellen called the following afternoon and begged Beth to come quickly up to the tarn.

'What d'you think? Pegleg has found a mate.'

'Oh, but that's wonderful.'

'There's just one problem.'

'What's that?'

'I'm not sure she cares for his bachelor pad. Bit small.'

At the tarn they watched as Pegleg demonstrated the precarious art of landing and take-off on this small sheet of water high in the cup of the mountains. He struggled, as ever, against the windstream, judging the right moment when he must put the brakes on.

'He's got his under-carriage down,' Ellen yelled. 'Good lad.'

Wings flapping madly, he missed the tarn entirely and came to a flurried halt in the reeds. His new wife appeared supremely unimpressed. She certainly declined to imitate Pegleg's clumsy efforts. Waiting patiently until he had concluded his demonstrations, she enticed him to swim with her. Preening themselves and each other, they seemed thoroughly content with their lot.

'Where do you think he found her?'

'Who knows? He's been off searching almost every day for weeks.'

'I'm glad. She's a beauty, and he won't be alone any more.'

It was comforting, sitting here with Ellen, the summer sun soothing her, making her feel lazy and languid as she watched the swans, entranced by this developing romance.

But at the back of Beth's mind was an image of the previous evening, seeing herself captured in candlelight, as Andrew must have seen her. His need for her had been plainly written in the burning gaze of his eyes, moving hungrily over her body. Never, in all the time she had known him, had she seen him look so desolate.

Yet what had surprised her most, was her own reaction to him. The urge to gather him in her arms had been overwhelming. And it had taken her hours to settle to sleep after he had gone, her body fidgeting and churning with some unexpressed ache. And for once, she hadn't dreamt of Pietro.

'Do you reckon she'll stay?' Ellen was saying, and Beth jerked her mind back to the present.

'Of course she'll stay.'

'She's playing hard to get. See how she swims away from him. Taunting him. No better than she should be.'

And Beth's giggles faded away somewhat, as the candlelit image again rose in her head. 'She likes him really, you can tell.' As she liked Andrew.

'But would you stay here if you were her? As well as being too small for a couple, it's an empty spot. Winter lasts for eight months of every year, and the wind can cut you to pieces. And it's gey lonely. No other swans or water birds of any kind for company. Bit bleak, wouldn't you say?' Then Ellen half glanced at her. 'How's your own love nest?' and Beth managed a smile.

'About the same, I'd say. Andrew is good to me. And we get on OK.'

Ellen grinned. 'Married life suiting you then?' and Beth flushed, turning her face away from Ellen's curious gaze.

'Yes,' she admitted. 'I'm sure we'll be fine.'

'You don't sound sure.'

'I am. It's just – well – it takes time, I suppose. There are one or two things we need to – well – sort out – you might say.'

'Then grasp the nettle,' Ellen said, her attention once again fixed upon the swans. 'As our new bride is doing here.'

The young female was making a valiant attempt at a take-off. She was plainly anxious about the sweep of fell which rose steeply all around, and the lack of space she had to play with on the water itself. She was beating her wings with a kind of frantic resolution, sending the water swirling. Even so she too ended up in the rushes, nose down in the sphagnum moss.

'Oh, dear. Not going well, is it?'

After several more abortive attempts she finally managed to get airborne, and for several moments circled the sky above the small tarn, beating her wings dramatically in the thermals. And then Pegleg made a supreme effort and was up there with her at the first attempt.

'They'll go now,' Ellen said, rather quietly. 'Find a more salubrious lake, with good company and better landing facilities.'

'Oh, no.'

'Life changes and you have to change with it, or you're done for.'

'But I shall miss him.' Beth watched as the pair circled once more, then flew away together, no more than specks in the distance.

'This isn't the place for them. They can start afresh, somewhere else. With married quarters.' She laughed. 'Quite right too.'

But Beth was sad. 'Bye, Pegleg,' she whispered.

And though she visited the tarn every day for a week, Ellen's warning appeared to be correct. Pegleg and his bride never did return to Brockbarrow tarn.

Beth, however, had no wish to leave Broomdale. For all it was quiet and lonely at times, she loved it here. And if she did not quite love her husband then at least she was determined to make a success of their marriage.

She owed it to him to at least try. If only she could work out quite how to explain about herself and Pietro. Grasp the nettle, Ellen had said. Well, there was surely no need to be shy with him, her own husband, and they'd been friends long enough before their marriage. But when should she broach the subject, and how?

First she must prepare her nest, secure some space for them to be alone and get properly acquainted. Lure him on, as Pegleg's new bride had done. Then having got the problem out of the way, they could then settle this other, more delicate matter.

She would begin with that dratted parlour. A newly married couple needed a place to be alone. And she meant to have one.

So she carefully devised her plans and when they were complete, presented them to him. 'Tam is bringing my things over from Broombank tomorrow. They can't find space for my stuff indefinitely, it wouldn't be fair. And I really would like to have my own bits and pieces about me.'

'Bits and pieces of what?' He looked surprised. 'Haven't we enough stuff here?'

'Yes, but it's not mine, is it? I'd like my own cushions, pictures, books and ornaments. Some crockery Meg gave me and, oh, various bits and bobs.' She smiled. 'I might recover those two old chairs in the parlour, then we could light a fire and be cosy together each evening as the nights draw in. Just the two of us. It could be our room. Don't you think Billy and Seth would agree this time? It would be so pleasant?' she wheedled.

How could it be anything but pleasant to have Beth all to himself? For a moment Andrew felt himself weaken, then an image of her, naked in the candlelight, came into his head and he felt again that burning frustration deep in his belly. The more they were alone together the more he craved for her, and the more her rejection of him wrankled. It was like living in a hair shirt. No, best to avoid close contact altogether. He tightened his lips and his resolve. 'I thought we'd settled the matter of that damned parlour. If you start doing things to it, there'll be all hell to pay.'

Beth drew in a deep breath. 'Well, I'm re-opening negotiations. I know it belonged to your mother, and was used only for special occasions, but things are different now, Andrew. We're married, and need time on our own. We can't sit every night with those two old men, kind as they are. The place is too small, too cramped, and it's driving me mad. We need space to get better acquainted, as they say back home in the states.' She laughed, trying to lighten the tension between them.

Andrew considered his wife, hungrily appraising the smooth round cheeks, still pink and girlish. The swell of her breasts rising and falling with little breaths of excitement beneath the simple blouse, and the curve of her hips in the tight blue jeans she often wore and longed, very urgently, to press her against himself and make love to her, right here, on the floor of this old kitchen. 'Aye,' he said softly. 'A place of our own would be nice.'

Her heart rose on a beat of hope. 'I'd make Billy understand. See his pride wasn't hurt. We can't live in the past, Andrew. We have to go forward, you and I. Change is inevitable.' Her cheeks were flushing to a bright cyclamen pink, in bewitching contrast to her beguiling, grey-blue eyes. It would have taken a stronger man than Andrew Barton to resist their appeal.

'Happen it's not such a bad idea,' he conceded. In his mind he'd already unbuttoned her blouse and his hand was closing over the soft ripeness of her breast, feeling the nipple harden beneath his fingers. He flinched, then his chest puffed out as he drew in a steadying breath. 'You do what you want with the front parlour, Beth, and I'll tell 'em that I said you could.'

She was so thrilled by this small victory that she flung herself at him, kissing him with exuberant delight. 'Oh, thank you, thank you. I shall make it *so* lovely and cosy.' And, as once before, they were both so startled by her impulsive action, embarrassment washed over them in a dampening wave. Then she scurried away, duster in hand, eager to make a start.

* * *

And so the parlour was scrubbed out and polished, the new curtains returned to the window, chair covers made, and Beth's pictures and bright scatter cushions set about. It transformed the room. If only it could have the same effect upon their increasingly stilted relationship, Beth knew she would be content.

Each evening she and Andrew would sit together, the old battery radio playing soft music, 'Bright Eyes', or 'I Will Survive', two appropriate hits that year. He would read his paper and Beth the latest novel she had borrowed from the library van which visited the dale every Tuesday. They looked like any other contented married couple, and if there was little conversation between them beyond farming matters, who could say that was so unusual after a tiring day's work?

Often he complained about poor prices at the mart, or fretted over some ewe that didn't seem quite right.

'We're living on the edge here,' he would say. 'We can't afford any disasters. I'll have to take her to the vet next week if she doesn't mend.'

'Ask him to come here.'

'And be charged double? Don't be daft.'

But she was content with her small achievement and it proved to be every bit as pleasant as she'd hoped for. She began at last to relax, deciding that she might even come to be happy here with Andrew, in this beautiful dale.

Through the small window she could watch the seasons slowly change, clouds boiling with fury or listlessly mellow, and the arrival of bramblings and siskins as the summer days grew shorter, the leaves dropped from the trees and the glory of autumn also passed and a winter coolness came upon the land. A scouring wind that Seth called lazy, because it couldn't be bothered go round you, would roar up the dale. But here, in the parlour, all was safe and secure and warm.

So too did their relationship become warmer. They exchanged snippets of news, laughed and joked together, even made tentative plans for the future. Dreams of what Andrew meant to do with Cathra Crag, once it was entirely his.

'I'll put in new equipment.'

'And electricity.'

Grinning, eyes meeting with a radiant sparkle. 'Aye, best generator money can buy. And more stock. I mean to grow t'best herd of Galloways around.'

'And a washing machine?' Giggling.

'TV and record player happen.'

'And who will pay for all of this?' she laughed.

'We'll get a loan. We're young and can work hard, build a good business here, don't you reckon?' He gazed steadily at her and just as steadily Beth gazed back. He was asking her if she meant to stay, meant to make a go of life with him.

'Yes,' she said, very quietly. 'We have all the time in the world to build a good life here.'

Then he gave her one of his smiles, less rare these days. 'Cathra Crag has been in our family for generations.' Going steadily downhill, a voice at the back of his mind reminded him. 'It'll take years to get it on its feet again.'

'But it could be done?'

'Oh, aye. It could be done.' He frowned, wishing he felt as confident as he sounded. It would take a life time of sweat and toil. And for what purpose, he thought with a sudden bleakness, if there were to be no future generations to pass it on to.

This marriage had not turned out at all as he'd imagined. He'd seen the warning signs right from the first of course, but hadn't taken them too seriously. He'd genuinely believed that in a few short months, weeks even, he'd be in her bed and they'd be man and wife in truth, content together.

Yet as the months had gone by they'd grown further apart than ever. Only now did there seem to be a chink of hope. And each night as he climbed the stairs to his bachelor bed, Andrew agonised over how he was to break this impasse. Should he burst in and take her, insisting upon his rights as a husband. No, too damned Victorian. And he was a poor man at courtship, no good at wooing a woman, whatever you liked to call it. One look from those cool grey-blue eyes and all hope and passion drained from him.

But he'd given her the parlour and Beth seemed more content than he'd ever seen her. Gave him quite languishing looks at times. He lived in hope that she would one night invite him to her bed.

And later, as she stood with her hand on the door knob he thought she meant to. She hesitated, glancing back at him from beneath her lashes. Was this it? Was this to be his lucky night. Dear God, he was ready for it.

'Andrew?'

'Aye?' He must remain calm, no rushing at the last fence. He smiled up at her. 'What is it?'

'Are you coming up soon?'

His heart began to pound against his rib cage, leaving him agonisingly short of breath. 'Do you think I should?'

'Well . . .' Again she hesitated. 'There's something we should discuss.'

He sat up straighter in his seat, keenly aware of every flicker of expression on her lovely face. 'If you've anything to say, Beth, I'm a good listener.'

'Yes. I know.'

He wondered if perhaps her shyness was getting the better of her, whether he should say that talk wasn't needed between them, and sweep her off upstairs. Unfortunately he hesitated a second too long and she had started to talk.

'It was only the one time, you understand. Not that anyone cares about such things these days, but you have the right to know.'

'Know what, Beth?' Had he missed something? What had she said?

It was quite beyond Beth to live a lie. He was her husband so he should be told. Should, in fact, have been apprised of her true state before ever she'd agreed to marry him. If she and Andrew were ever to have a future together, this matter had to be cleared up between them. She must purge herself of guilt. Then she would be free to take him to her bed.

And so she told him, quite bluntly, hardly daring to pause for breath, or to watch his reaction. When, in the silence which followed her words, she finally dared to glance at him, she knew that the tactic had been a terrible mistake.

His jaw had tightened and his face was set as if frozen. He gazed at her for so long without speaking that for a moment she almost began to doubt he'd taken it in.

'Did you hear me? You do understand what I'm saying? Andrew?' She reached out a tentative hand to touch his shoulder but he flinched and jerked it out of her reach. The gesture of revulsion hurt her deeply and she drew back as if scalded.

'Andrew?'

'Aye,' he said, his voice echoing the cold bitterness that gnawed at his guts. 'I understand perfectly. You're saying you gave yourself to Pietro Lawson. You belong to him and I've made a proper fool of myself.'

'That's not what I meant at all. I'm simply telling you it happened only the *once*.'

'And whose fault was that?' He stood up, towering over her, almost threatening in his anger. Hating himself for his intolerance yet he could do nothing to still the hot jealousy that surged through him. What a fool he'd been to imagine she could ever love him. 'Why tell me? Why would I want to know what you've done with him?'

'You are my husband. You have the *right*.'

Hadn't she the sense to guess how such news would tear him apart? No, like all women she thought only of herself. 'Shove your guilt on to me, you mean.'

He saw her stiffen, knew he was saying all the wrong things, but could do nothing to take them back.

'Why should I feel guilty? It was only the *once*, I tell you.' Beth was trembling, desperately searching for a way out of this awful mess.

'And if he hadn't been openly living with your sister, you wouldn't have refused him a second time, or a third, would you?'

She drew in a quick, startled breath. 'That's not fair.'

'Sounds pretty fair to me. Are you saying you weren't in love with him, despite all you told me to the contrary?'

She could hardly bear to meet his eyes and was forced to turn her gaze away, unable to deny the truth. And Andrew strode from the room without another word.

And as she lay alone in the big feather bed that night, Beth turned her face into the pillow and shed copious tears of quiet despair and felt more lonely than ever before.

The cosy evenings in the parlour were over. She told herself it was because Andrew was busy with the hundred and one tasks which kept him working long hours on the farm. Which was partly true. But that would not explain why he seemed to go out of his way to avoid her, rarely addressed her directly and never spoke her name. He took to calling her 'the wife' whenever he referred to her, which Beth hated.

'I'm not a possession,' she told him. 'Like the house, or the farm, or the car. I'm me. Use my name. Talk to me.'

'Not now, Beth. I'm too busy. Besides, I'm surprised you want to waste your time talking to a yokel like me, let alone marry one.'

'Oh, not that old chestnut again.' But he would walk away from her, head held high in that stubborn way he had and she could only stamp her foot in frustration and wonder how she could ever regain that warmth which had been developing between them and now seemed totally lost.

Slowly, painfully, the winter passed and Beth spent more nights alone in her lovely new parlour than she cared to count. Where Andrew spent his time she didn't know and didn't dare ask. She knew that he'd taken to often going out of an evening, along to the Broomdale Inn, no doubt, where he could hide his disappointment in a pint or two of best bitter.

Sometimes she heard him clumping up the stairs to his single room at well past midnight. An unheard of time for Andrew. Once, she almost went out to confront him, but heard him stumble on the stairs, swearing copiously. So she shrank back to her bed and maintained their silence. Yet he was still up at dawn. How he kept on working so hard, she couldn't begin to imagine.

She too was desperately tired, getting little enough sleep herself. Beth felt old suddenly, all the games and hopes of youth dead in her.

And each morning she would be acutely aware of Seth's curious glances in her direction, the unspoken questions in his watery old eyes, which she steadfastly ignored.

It was true that she could do with someone to talk to. Someone who wasn't too critical. If only Tess were here, or even Sarah. She still visited Ellen regularly, Sally Ann at Ashlea and Meg down at Broombank, but found it quite impossible to broach the subject with any of them. She maintained the myth of a happy marriage and felt more and more alone. No one suspected that anything was wrong, so why should she disillusion them?

She would be loyal to her husband, if nothing else. No one must know that they were, in fact, no more man and wife now than they'd been on that June day last summer.

* * *

Beth greeted the onset of spring with great relief and took to spending hours in the patch of overgrown garden at the back of the farmhouse, as if she could bury her unhappiness in it. Clumps of nettles, rosebay willow herb, bindweed and wild poppies choked the long grass. Perhaps if she could dig it all up and make a proper garden, grow her own vegetables and fruit and flowers this year, she would have achieved something worthwhile and Andrew would take notice.

And it would at least keep her occupied and help her to sleep at night, instead of worrying over the state of her marriage.

She might take up beekeeping. The honey would be useful and she could sell the excess perhaps, on Kendal free market, which still operated on Saturday mornings. The old folk tale said that you should tell bees everything. She would talk to the bees since no one else was interested in her, she thought, in a welter of self pity.

In this she was wrong for Seth quietly watched these frenetic activities with growing curiosity and interest. He saw how her eyes followed Andrew when he passed by and how his grandson rarely caught her lingering gaze. He watched Andrew's growing irritation and he wondered. Things weren't going right for the newly weds, that was certain.

Yet she was a bonny li'le thing. Not a beauty by any means but what he would call comely. Sometimes she tied one of them cotton triangular scarves about her hair to hold it back while she worked. Suited her, it did. And being outdoors so much had polished her skin to a summer brightness without coarsening it. Her cheeks glowed like ripe apples. How could his grandson not notice how she was blossoming? And why did he never admire her determined efforts to be a good farmer's wife?

Seth made up his mind to do his best to make up for his grandson's negligence by giving the young lass every assistance. Near twelve months she'd been with them, time they stopped thinking of her as an offcomer and gave her a bit more of a welcome.

He carefully instructed her in the feeding and care of calves, bought her a fresh clutch of hens since her own were past their best, so they could enjoy their own free range eggs again, and even taught her how to milk Flossie, their latest house cow. This last seemed to delight her more than anything and she readily took over the chore.

'We're not a dairy farm, so we don't have all the equipment,' he apologised.

'Oh, I don't mind. I really don't mind hand milking.'

She always seemed so grateful for his interest, so anxious to be up early every morning to milk Flossie, feed the calves and prepare a good breakfast for the men when they came in at nine after their own early chores. Nay, you couldn't help but admire the li'le lass. And in no time at all she'd scoured out the old dairy, and bowls of cream stood everywhere as she struggled to learn how to make butter, cream and cheese.

Even Billy began to take an interest in the new activity.

'What you up to now?' he enquired, the truculent edge of suspicion back in his voice. When Beth explained, his eyebrows shot up and he stood nonplussed for a whole half minute. Then he turned on his heel and vanished out the door.

'Oh, dear,' Beth thought. 'I've offended him, yet again.'

But moments later he was back, an old book in his hand. 'Here,' he said, thrusting it at her in an awkward sort of way. 'My Emily allus used that. Been in the family for generations. Was my mother's once upon a time. She set down all her receipts in it for pickling, jams and such like. And these are my Emily's muslins. You pour the curds and whey through like, once the milk has thickened. We could get a couple of pigs to use up the whey you have left. The curd you make into cream cheese and wrap 'em in paper. Emily used to add herbs an' all sorts. Don't keep right well but hers were allus so good we were happy to eat 'em oop right away. We enjoyed 'em.'

Beth clutched the precious book to her breast and smiled up at her father-in-law. 'Oh, thank you, Billy. I really do appreciate this. I don't suppose I'll ever be as good as Emily, but I'll certainly try.'

'Aye,' he said, looking fidgety, and shyly rubbing his palms on his trousers. 'Aye well, I can't stand aboot here all day. Theer's work to be done.'

It was yet another small victory. Beth made the cheese, suffering many failures before she got it right. She experimented with herbs and garlic, and her three menfolk tried and tested, and she waited in hope for a word of praise from her husband. But while the other two were ready enough to comment and show appreciation where it was due, even offer a word of gentle criticism and advice, Andrew ate the cheese with the same stolid seriousness he would any other dish she put before him, and said nothing.

Seth noted her disappointment, and the air of sadness that clung to her. She might be getting on much better with us two old 'uns, he told himself, having won us over with our stomachs like all women do, yet with her own husband there was still summat oop. He was never wrong about such things. He could feel it. The lass wasn't happy, not like when she'd first come, all bouncy and full of hope. Summat was wrong, and he wondered how best to deal with the matter, how much further he dare go.

23

Beth herself gave Seth the opportunity he needed.

He was sitting in the yard on his rush-seated chair, a fox head taking shape in his hands as he carved and whittled the horn with the edge of his knife. He enjoyed working out of doors in the summer sunshine, and watching her weed and tidy the little garden and tie up raspberry canes.

'Thoo's done a good job theer,' he told her, warm in his praise as he surveyed the neat garden with its rows of newly planted vegetables. 'Didn't know half what we'd got under all that jungle till you cleared it.'

'The raspberries are already starting to come. I shall make jam this autumn. You'd like that, I dare say?'

'I wouldn't say no,' the old man admitted. 'Your bread's improving, I'll give you that. Quite light it is now. And doan't give me indigestion no more.'

Beth laughed, enjoying the gentle banter with the old man. 'It'll be winter again soon and then I won't be able to work in the garden quite so much.' She came to sit beside him on a low stone wall, thinking of the long lonely evenings she'd have to face, yet again. 'I like to be busy. And I want to be able to contribute to the farm's finances and I was wondering what best to do this winter. Have you any ideas?'

He considered for a long time before answering. 'In the old days a wife would spin or knit. Sally Ann still knits umpteen stockings.'

Beth shook her head in apology. 'I've tried knitting and I'm not very good at it. And I could never manage to spin or weave.'

'What do you fancy doing, then?'

'I don't know. I've had various ideas and discounted most of them.' She hugged her knees, wondering if she dare broach the subject direct. She'd certainly welcome his advice. Once she'd tried to mention the idea to Andrew, but he'd said he'd no time to listen to her chatter.

'But we need to talk, Andrew,' she'd protested.

'I've nowt to say that you would want to hear.' And he'd walked away from her, as always.

That's how they were. Stilted little comments. Sniping words. Each day they seemed to grow further and further apart.

She blinked, pushing the memory aside. 'I remember Mom talking about how she loved the feel of sheepskin and fancied working with it one day, but had never got around to it. I feel exactly the same. I love the sheepskins too.'

'Oh, aye?' Noo what was cooming here, he thought. 'Thoo doesn't want to tek up sheep farming, does tha? Like your gran.'

Beth laughed. 'No. I admire Meg enormously but that's not for me, I'm afraid. What happens to the skins? Do we sell them all to the wool marketing board?'

'Aye. We get the best price we can for 'em, such as it is.'

'Are there no bits left over? No oddments?'

The old man shook his head, frowning. 'Not usually. The animal hes to be sheared in one piece.'

'Yes, of course.'

'Why? What are you thinking of?'

She took a deep breath. 'I thought about making moccasins, tiny slippers for babies and children. I could practise doing them by hand at the kitchen table during the winter. Then I could sell the slippers, to add a bit to the housekeeping. What do you think?' She waited, breath held tight, for his response.

He was silent for a long moment, then he put back his old head and gave a shout of laughter, showing all the gaps in his teeth. 'Nay, lass. Didn't I say you were a chip off the old block? Just like your mam and gran. Always an eye for the main chance.'

Beth laughed with him. 'I suppose I am, but what do you think? I want your honest opinion. If it's daft, say so.'

Poor little lass, he thought. As if she didn't have enough work to do. She must want to please him very badly. 'I would've thought you had enough on your plate with three chaps to luik after.'

'I don't mind hard work. Besides, it would be something of my own. I don't want to be a burden to Andrew.' She became eager, now that she'd parted with these private thoughts and dreams. 'I've saved up some money from my marketing and if it proves successful, I could buy a sewing machine later. Shall I risk it?'

'Why ask me? I reckon you should talk about it to Andrew. He's your husband, after all.'

The smile faded from her face and Seth watched it go with regret. 'He always seems too busy to talk these days.'

'Nay, he can spare thoo a minute for a bit of crack, surely?'

She shook her head.

'Well, that's a poor do. Anyroad . . .' He pondered for a long moment, then with a lift of his shoulders returned his attention to the fox head, coming to life in his hands. 'You weren't so shy and uncertain of theeself when you told us to tek our clogs off that first day.'

Beth smiled. 'I wonder how I had the nerve.'

'Nor did you wait for Billy's, nor my permission when you took it into your head to do oop t'parlour. So why wait for permission now? If Andrew hasn't time to talk, that's his loss. You get on wi' it. Make him proud of you, if that's what you're after. We've one or two poor sheepskins left over from the clipping. You can practise on them. If you get to be any good, you could buy 'em in quite cheap, I dare say.'

'Oh, yes,' she said, clapping her hands together with delight. 'Why not? I'll do it.'

She would make Andrew proud of her. She'd make him really sit up and take notice. Beth felt she must convince him that she hadn't simply married him for a job ticket, that she could pull her weight on the farm. She almost bounced back to her gardening, plans and designs already forming in her head. 'Look at these. I've found two blackcurrant and one gooseberry bush under all this tangle, would you believe?'

Seth chortled with rich laughter. 'Then don't go luiking under it unless you're ready to find summat that'd really scupper your little plan.' And he laughed all the more as she blushed a fiery red.

'Nay, lass. I didn't mean to embarrass thoo. Tis only life after all. There's naught new about what you and Andrew do. Thoo didn't invent it, tha knoaws. And a bairn is usually the result. Nature being what it is. Then you'd happen have to change your plans a bit.'

Beth remained silent and he wondered if he truly had offended her. What a shy mouse she was. 'Mind you, I dare say we could all chip in and help a bit more around the house. No need for a bairn to make all that much difference, I reckon. My mother allus worked hard.'

'Yes, I'm sure it could be managed.'

'Well, there's no problem, is there?'

'No, I suppose not.' There was something in the tone of her voice that narrowed Seth's eyes and sharpened his attention. She was concentrating hard on hoeing the vegetables, head bent and hair swinging forward.

'Here, you're not . . .'

'No, I'm not.' Fiery and furious.

It came to him then, quite out of the blue and in a rush of understanding, what the problem was.

By heck, so far as he knew, his grandson could still be occupying his own single room, and Beth the other. Him and Billy went to bed early, so how would they know? And neither of them would dream of intruding.

But surely not? They'd been married a twelve month or more. He watched the tide of colour flow up her cheekbones and then recede, leaving her death pale. Was this the root of the problem then? It was worse than he thought. Now how could he fettle that? He pondered the problem for a long moment, then approached it from the side, as was his way.

'So lang as he's a gentleman and doan't rush you, like' he said, a canny light of enquiry in his eyes.

'Oh no,' she said, the faintest hint of asperity in her tone. 'He would never do that. Rushing into anything is not in Andrew's nature.'

And the old man quietly waited, in case there was anything else she might wish to say.

But Beth could scarce bear even to consider the problem any more. Swallowing a lump of self pity that had come to her throat, she abandoned the raspberries. 'I'll make us a cuppa,' she announced, lifting her chin as she made for the kitchen.

And as she passed his chair, Seth reached out and caught hold of her hand with his gnarled old fingers. His smile softened as he looked up at her. 'You're a good lass. Any man'd be proud to have you as his wife. But some chaps need a bit of reminding joost how lucky they are, do y'see? They need a woman with a bit of go in her. One who can take the initiative like, if needs be. You understand me?' His pale eyes were piercing as they gazed steadily into hers and Beth felt suddenly very calm and still inside.

'Yes,' she said, rather quietly. 'I do. I understand perfectly.'

In return for Seth's kindness, and his advice, Beth took even more care of the old man. She took him a cup of tea to his bed every morning, which he accepted with wonder and delight. Decadent, he called it, making her laugh.

Ever since she had joined them here at Cathra Crag she had seen that he had clean clothes to wear every day and good food to eat, and had always found time in her busy schedule to talk with him and keep him company. She loved to sit and listen to him endlessly recounting the old days in the dale, a lifestyle that was swiftly vanishing.

Now she realised that his great age had also given him great perspicacity.

Why could not Andrew appreciate her in the same way? Why would he never find time for her? Perhaps she had been a disappointment to him but she refused to accept that what she had done with Pietro was entirely wicked. She was human, after all, and they had been in love. And so long as Pietro never returned to the dale, which he wasn't ever likely to do except on a fleeting visit with Sarah, Beth saw no reason why she and Andrew couldn't have a good life together. If only he would forgive her. She needed some hope for the future. Living in this vacuum was driving her to distraction.

Seth helped her to get started on the moccasins. He showed her how to draw out a pattern, the best way to cut the skins. And then she would thread her needle with the strips of fine leather and sew the pieces together with the warm wool inside, bringing up the heel and fitting in the apron front, threading the thong through and tying a neat bow.

At first her efforts were slow and clumsy, and after a while her fingers got sore. She relaxed her grip, easing her tension, which amazingly helped to increase the speed of her work. And all the while she was painfully aware of Andrew, half watching, half maintaining a show of disinterest, and never speaking beyond essential communication.

She practised by making a pair for each of them and Billy and Seth were touched and pleased with her efforts. Andrew made no comment whatsoever. He thanked her, put them in his wardrobe and never took them out again, so far as she was aware.

But the best part of making the moccasins was that it gave her time to think, and to plan. If she had disappointed Andrew by her early rebuff of him, and by this latest revelation, then it was up to her to put things right. If their marriage was to be saved, she must be the one to save it. As Seth had so cannily advised, she must be the one to take the initiative. She thought long and hard upon what he had said.

All she had to do was devise a plan and be brave enough to carry it out.

She took her opportunity one day in late September when the mist was thick as clotted cream in the dale, while all above the world sparkled, clear and bright.

Andrew had spent the day out on the fells with Billy, rounding up those tups they wished to send to the sales at Kirkby Stephen.

Seth's routine was unchanging. His walk over the fells in the morning, and the afternoon spent as usual in his woodshed, and in the evening he would be back in his seat by the fire, carving his latest crook handle. If he noticed any unusual activity upstairs during this day, he paid it no heed, and certainly made no mention of the fact.

Perhaps he wouldn't have been so surprised if he'd gone to investigate.

Beth, standing in her husband's room, gazed about her rather as a stranger might. At the narrow bed which she dutifully remade and tidied each morning, at his shaving brush, comb and other personal toiletries on the pine chest of drawers. The scent of him was strong in the small room. She opened the wardrobe door and fingered the few suits and jackets which hung within. Then she smiled, for inside she felt a wonderful warm feeling of anticipation, no more than a nervous flutter in her stomach. Yet it told her that everything could be all right between them, if she made it so.

One by one, scurrying and bustling, afraid he might suddenly come home early and catch her, she removed all Andrew's clothes and few belongings from his room and took them to her own. She made space in the wall cupboard for his clothes, removed her own bits and bobs from the chest of drawers and laid out his brushes and combs just as he liked them.

When everything was to her satisfaction, Beth resolutely stripped the single bed and bore the sheets and blankets away to be washed, remaking her own double bedstead with fresh linen.

Lastly, she picked honeysuckle and honesty from the back garden and set a vase of them on her dressing table. Surveying her work she found the nervousness had swelled to a breathless ache. But this was the only way she could think of. If this didn't work . . .

For a brief moment she closed her eyes, clenching her hands together in silent prayer. It would be all right. It *must* be.

The day dragged endlessly, as no other had ever done. Andrew and his father came in at their usual time for supper. The meal was eaten and cleared away and afterwards Beth sat and sewed on her moccasins while Andrew read the paper.

At nine Seth and Billy retired, as usual, and the two of them sat on, in silent disharmony. No words were exchanged between them, a sad and accustomed state of affairs.

Except that on this night when the clock struck nine thirty Beth was in such a dither of emotion, her hand was trembling too much to sew any longer. Abandoning her efforts, she set aside her work.

'I think I'll go on up.'

'Right,' he said, without glancing at her.

'What about you?'

'I'm reading the paper.'

'Good night then.'

'Good night.'

And she quietly left the room. Upstairs she flew about in a frenzy of activity, pulling off her clothes, searching out her prettiest night-gown. She'd washed herself earlier so that now she would waste no time getting into bed. She prayed he wouldn't decide to go to the pub tonight. He'd given up going quite so often as he had little money, and had to be up early in the morning. Any moment she might hear his foot upon the stair.

It took no more than moments for her to pull the pink night-gown over her head, drench herself in a quick spurt of Tweed, vigorously brush out her hair and fling herself into the big feather bed, sinking breathlessly into the soft mattress. Her heart was beating like a drum and cold terror began to creep up from her toes. What if he did not come to her? What if, when he saw that she had emptied his room, he chose instead to sleep downstairs? Dear Lord, what would she do then?

The waiting seemed interminable. Would he never be done with that dratted paper? What could be so fascinating that it kept him reading so late? In the depth of the house she heard ten o'clock strike. Was that all it was? She'd imagined it must be midnight at least.

Then at last she heard the familiar sounds, the grate being riddled, the back door opening and closing as he went off on his round.

And then the long awaited sound of his footsteps on the stair. She sank beneath the covers as she counted every one, listened as he walked along the landing, heard the sneck of the bedroom door and the aching silence which followed. Now there was only her own heartbeat, pounding in her head, blotting out all other sounds.

The snap of the sneck and her own door was being pushed open. And she hadn't even heard him come along the landing. She became aware of his presence, heard him clear his throat.

'Are you asleep?'

'No,' she said, not daring to lift her head and look at him. All she could see from this angle was his shadow flickering on the bedroom wall, cast there by the night light on her bedside table.

Another long silence which stretched out like a void between them.

'Did you do that?'

'Yes.'

'Why?'

'I thought it was time.'

He didn't ask time for what, for which she was supremely grateful. After an achingly long moment which seemed to Beth like an hour, he closed the door and the room darkened again. In spite of herself a small sob escaped her throat. Had he gone and left her? If he rejected her now, it would be over between them. She could never find the courage to go through with this again.

'Don't cry,' his voice came quietly out of the darkness, soft and persuasive. And Beth's heart seemed to melt with a longing she'd thought she would never again experience. 'Are you sure this is what you want?'

The flickering candlelight made her face glow with an ethereal beauty of which she was not aware. Andrew caught at the breath he'd been holding in his chest and quietly expelled it. Dear God, how could he go on being angry with her when he loved her so much? But he must make no mistakes. Not when he was this close.

To Beth, he was no more than an outline, his face in shadow, backlit by a trace of moonlight filtering through the curtains. 'Yes, Andrew. It is what I want. Very much, in fact.' Then she pushed back the bedclothes and waited with softly beating heart for him to come to her.

She sang as she walked over the fells to see Ellen the next afternoon. A golden light slanted through Brockbarrow Wood, illuminating leaves still clinging to the branches of rowan and ash like sparkling jewels. There was a bounce to her step which hadn't been there for some time. Today, at lunch, Andrew had seemed six inches taller and could hardly stop grinning. She'd almost laughed out loud to see Seth's quiet smile, as if he knew everything and had arranged it all single-handed. The old rogue.

Not that she didn't deny she owed him a great deal with his sly hints of advice. But in the end, having got things started, she hadn't needed to use any further initiative. Andrew had very decidedly taken control. She could never have imagined a night so fulfilling, so entirely satisfying in all her life.

If Beth had felt any moment of reluctance over her decision, it vanished the moment Andrew's lips touched hers. She'd been quite startled in fact, by the effect of that first kiss. It seemed to unleash all the damped down emotions she'd bottled up for so long.

His hard farmer's hands caressing and exciting her more than she could have believed possible.

He'd hesitated only once, at quite the wrong moment of course, just when her entire body was crying out with need for him he'd stopped, to ask again if she was sure this was what she wanted.

'Oh, yes, damn you. Get on with it,' she'd cried, surprised by her own sense of urgency. She'd clamped her hands about his neck and wrapped her legs about him, desperate to quench the yearning deep within her.

They'd come together as if they'd been meant for each other. Andrew too gentle at first, so afraid of hurting her she could feel his trembling. But his need had overcome his sensitivity and driven him into her with a passion that pleased her more than she could possibly have expected. It gave her soaring new hope for the future and she saw, at last, how lucky she was. Andrew was a good man, kind and considerate and certainly loving.

'You're quite canny really, aren't you?' he'd said as they'd lain together afterwards, both rather stunned by events.

'Are you objecting?'

A soft chuckle. 'Not in the least. I thought for a minute I was about to be evicted from my own home.' And she laughed with him, a softly loving sound, deep in her throat.

'And have you forgiven me?' They both knew that she meant more than the evacuation of his room.

'Let's say I can live with it.'

The relief she'd felt was enormous, glad that she'd made the decision, glad they could be friends again, and lovers too. Some people, even those supposedly in love, were not always so fortunate.

And this morning, he'd surprised her by waking her early and taking her again, with an increasing passion that had been a revelation. Oh, yes. Life at Cathra Crag was going to be altogether different this winter.

Now Beth walked by the tarn, sorry to see it empty but happy that Pegleg and his new mate had obviously found a happy home some place. The swan had found contentment and so had she, once she'd learned to use her own wiles. No better than she should be! And she laughed, the sound echoing through the silken mist that skimmed the water, hazing it from soft cream to dove grey.

302

Still, calm, as only a day in autumn could be, as finally her heart was.

She felt different today. Her entire outlook had changed. Optimism fizzed in her blood as she drew the tang of autumn into her lungs, savouring the taste of it on her tongue, the clean bite of cold against her cheeks. Why did she feel so different? Could one night's love-making have this effect upon her?

She came across a young couple walking hand in hand and was able to smile softly upon them without a moment's jealousy.

'Is this the way up to Dundale Knot?' the girl asked, her red hair sunrimmed against the dark of the woodland behind.

Beth directed them along the correct path and watched them walk away, the boy's arm going quickly and easily about the girl, pulling her snuggly in to his side. In return the girl slipped an arm about his waist, leaning into his shoulder and laughing up into his face. It came to her then that perhaps there might be something still missing from her relationship with Andrew, and her heart clenched with a poignant longing. But no one could have everything.

Sighing softly Beth continued to descend the steep track, slipping on the wet rough stones.

She couldn't resist making a detour close by Larkrigg, though she chose not to go up the drive. The house would be locked and she no longer had a key. The mighty boulders that littered the fell looked like miniature castles of rock, standing proud, encircled by a moat of heather. She smoothed her hands over the Gemini Stones, laying her cheek against the cold granite and again recalled the legend which had proved to be so true.

Where was Sarah? she worried. Was she married by now? Were they both well? There had been no more than a handful of postcards since that cataclysmic announcement last spring. Bright pictures showing the usual tourist spots which hastily sketched their journey through Europe. They apparently stopped wherever took their fancy, for a few weeks or months, then moved on again. Beth supposed they must find work of some sort on these occasions.

In one letter Sarah said that she was enjoying this wandering life so much, she must have been a gypsy in a previous one.

The most recent card, some months ago, had announced they're arrival in Florence, saying they were staying with Pietro's family in the pensione. Beth assumed the wedding had gone off as planned, but they made no mention of when, or if, they would visit Lakeland. An endless honeymoon apparently. Trust Sarah. Not that she particularly wanted to see her just yet. She preferred them to stay away, for the moment at least.

One day her sister would come, of course, bringing Pietro with her as her husband. Beth wondered how she would feel about seeing Sarah married to the man she had loved and wanted for herself. But then she too was married now, in truth as well as name, so what did it signify? Whatever memories still lingered inside must be resolutely ignored. Or at best disguised.

Ellen was busy with a new patient, a young peregrine falcon, eyes bright and alert, breast gleaming white in the low afternoon sun, holding remarkably still while Ellen examined it, seeming to sense she was doing her best to help.

'Mobbed out of the sky by a couple of ravens,' she explained, 'then got itself caught up in barbed wire. Lethal stuff, I hate it.' She returned her attention to the bird, spreading out each wing in turn. 'Not too much damage. A scratch or two, a few lost feathers but he could have lost a limb or worse. Have him flying free in no time. Soon as he's over the shock and got his flight feathers ready and able again.'

Beth struggled to take an interest but for once she was itching to complete her errand and rush back home. 'I've brought you some ginger snaps,' she said, handing over a tin of homemade biscuits.

'Bless you, child, how you spoil me.' Ellen grinned. 'You know all my little weaknesses.' And then her gaze sharpened. 'You're looking mighty pleased with yourself today. Feeling well, are you? You're not . . . ?'

Beth's cheeks pinked. 'No. Why does everyone jump to that conclusion whenever I'm in a good mood? But I do feel fine, thanks very much.'

Ellen curbed a smile. 'Good.'

'I can't stop long,' Beth bubbled on. 'I have to get back and start on supper.'

'You've time for a cup of tea?'

'Oh, yes, of course.'

'Not been round so much lately. Fed up with me, are you?' Ellen brewed the tea and they tested one of the biscuits each, declaring them to be a good vintage.

Beth was not insulted by Ellen's bluntness, knowing it was only her way. 'Don't be silly. I've been busy, that's all.' And told her about the moccasins.

Ellen took it all in, nodding with interest and putting in encouraging questions and comments. 'Sound's good. Life seems to agree with you at the moment.'

'Yes,' Beth said, dropping her eyelashes and shyly smiling. 'You know I always enjoy my visits, and I'll come as often as I can, but I'll be busy these next few weeks too. And Andrew says we may go away for a few days in October.' Her cheeks flushed to a deeper pink while Ellen struggled to hold back her wicked sense of humour, brown eyes wide and teasing as she innocently asked, 'Not another honeymoon?'

'Of course not. The autumn tup sales at Kirkby Stephen. Andrew goes every backend to sell his spare young rams and buy in new blood. He says I can go with him this time, for a bit of a break. Billy and Seth will look after the farm. We'll only be gone three or four days.'

The girl was as excited as a kitten, Ellen thought for a while. 'Good as a holiday, the annual tup sales,' she said, very seriously.

'It'll be grand to get away for a bit, on our own,' Beth agreed, then laughed. 'Though I expect he'll put me a very poor second to the sheep.'

'Only right and proper,' Ellen gravely agreed. 'So long as he has your permission to do so, as any good farmer's wife will tell you,' and they both burst out laughing. Then the old woman's face took on a more serious expression.

'Are you up to some less comfortable news, d'you reckon?' The brown eyes were filled with compassion and Beth's heart missed a beat. What now? She really didn't want any more bad news, not now things were improving between herself and Andrew at last.

'What is it? More trouble with vandals? Not another snake?'

'Neither. Smooth passage for me at the moment. No, I'm afraid this concerns you. And Larkrigg.'

As, deep down, Beth had feared. 'Larkrigg?' She could hear the tremor in her own voice.

'I've heard a rumour that it's been sold, buyer unknown,' Ellen quietly told her, and Beth flinched, unwilling to take it in. She'd been trying to prepare herself for this news for months. Now that it had come, she realised she wasn't prepared at all.

'Are you sure?'

''Fraid so.'

'Oh, Ellen.'

'I'm sorry, lass.'

'What am I to do?'

'There's naught you can do. What am I to do, more like? If Larkrigg has a new owner, he might not be so keen to have a daft old woman in one of his cottages.'

'Oh, I hadn't thought. How very selfish of me.'

Ellen's face softened. 'No, I can understand how you feel. You've never been selfish in your life. Wouldn't know how. But seeing the house go, is bound to hurt.'

Beth stared bleakly at her friend. 'I can't bear to think of someone else living there.'

'Then don't think about it. Let the house go. Look to the future. You've got Andrew and Cathra Crag. And the tup sales to look forward to. Go and enjoy yourself. Live a bit. You can always pretend it's a second honeymoon, can't you?'

24

And to her very great delight, Beth found it surprisingly easy to enjoy life. The weeks flew by and in no time at all she was packing a bag and they were leaving on their three day break to Kirkby Stephen, which did indeed prove to be exactly like a honeymoon. The one they should have had in the first place.

They stayed in a small, but comfortable hotel on the main street and when Andrew was busy at the sales, Beth could wander about the shops and market, or take long walks out into the countryside. The weather was not kind to them, being rather damp and squally. Typical 'Tup Sale Weather' the farmers called it. But to the new lovers, the bad weather meant they were confined even more to their room each evening, which was no hardship at all.

Andrew seemed different somehow, away from the farm and dressed in his best suit, shirt and tie. Not to mention new smart shoes instead of those dreadful clogs. His hair seemed more fair, his eyes a deeper grey and a smile never far away. He was a fine man now, broader in the chest, not so young and awkward looking as he had once been, caring and attentive, and good fun to be with. It came to Beth with a jolt that she was happy. She'd hardly worried over Larkrigg at all. And she hadn't thought of Pietro for weeks.

The only difficulty came in having to be up bright and early each morning when they'd much rather linger in bed. But the sheep had to be penned by seven, ready for judging to commence by seven-thirty, though the sales themselves did not start until two hours after that.

The small town seemed to be bursting with people the moment

they stepped outside their hotel. Farmers in strong tweed jackets, flat caps and deerstalkers, carved stick in hand, their faces inscrutable, weather beaten and lined, until they met up with an old friend when smiles would banish creases, hands would be clasped and they'd settle down for a bit of crack over a pint of beer, mug of tea, or leaning over the rail of a holding pen.

Beth was entranced by the whole business, eager to watch how things were done and be a part of Andrew's life. The air seemed filled with noise, the sing-song voices of the auctioneers, an ever-changing rota throughout the long days of selling, the deep throated complaints of rams, young and old, almost two thousand of them over the whole period, the clash of horns when they disagreed with their fellow pen-mates and the buzz of excitement and wonder as prices were reached, lost or excelled.

Andrew explained to her how he hoped for a prize for his own pair of Swaledale tups. Bashful and Dopey, he called them, though they were anything but, being fine handsome creatures whose worth would be proved once the snows had receded from the fell tops and their progeny proved.

'A good result in the show ring affects the price we'll get. And we need the money, Beth. Things are tight.'

'I know,' she agreed, and was as anxious as him as they waited for the judge's verdict. She kept her eyes fastened on their black faces with their white noses and fierce, arrogant expressions. Then a red rosette was placed on one, a blue on the other and she saw Andrew swell with pride. A good result, followed later by an excellent price at the sale. He was well pleased.

His ram lambs, sold on the Wednesday, did not do so well, prices being lower than he would have liked.

'On the whole though, a successful sale.'

'Yes,' she agreed. 'In more ways than one.' In this time together they had grown even closer.

Once, Beth had to hurry out of the way when a bunch of young rams, horns clashing, burst from behind her in an eager dash to reach the ring. Andrew pulled her out of the way just in time, safely captured in the circle of his arms.

'Don't want to lose you,' he drily remarked, his breath against her ear. 'Not when I've only just found you,' and Beth leaned against him, excited by the warmth of his body, the strength of his arms about her.

And back at the hotel that evening he proved his words, in no uncertain terms, making her gasp with new delight.

No one was anxious to leave on the last day, many farmers lingering till quite late over the last few sales. Beth and Andrew also lingered, reluctant to break the spell and return to the reality of life on the farm.

'Some won't see another living soul for weeks,' Andrew explained.

'I suppose not.'

'That's how it was with me once. Though I suppose I was lucky having Dad and Grandad, I'd much rather have a wife.' And he grinned at her, pulling her close in his arms once more, bringing a pretty flush to her cheeks.

'You'll be too tired when we get home tonight,' she chided, accurately reading the challenge in his eyes as they danced over her face in that merry way she so liked.

'We'll see.'

And he wasn't tired. Not at all.

The following year proved to be the best ever. Beth loved it here at Cathra Crag and had found a contentment with Andrew she would never have dreamed possible. If what she felt for him was not the heart-stopping passion she had experienced with Pietro, she did not in any way blame him for that. She felt older and wiser, ready to accept whatever life sent her. He was a good husband and she grew fond of him.

Nine months following the Kirkby Stephen holiday, she gave birth to a son, William, which brought Andrew much teasing from the neighbouring farmers, since he'd proved his own worth as well as his two tups.

She transformed her home, making it cosy and welcoming with no further protests from Billy, who was so delighted with his new grandson he would have given Beth anything she asked for.

Seth's fears were soothed and a generator installed. At Christmas, Andrew gave Beth a washing machine, all tied up with blue ribbon.

And later, as the family's fortunes slowly improved, they even bought a television set which Seth pretended he never watched, yet somehow knew every character in *Coronation Street*.

The old man rarely left the fireside now. His eyesight was poor and Beth insisted that Billy cut the sticks for him.

'You'd cut your own hand off one day,' she warned him.

Seth was permitted to work in the woodshed for short periods when the weather was warm, and he could go for walks, but not too far. He would often give Beth his truculent stare.

'I know when I'm licked,' he'd say. 'It's that fierce look in her eye. By heck, she's a woman and half.'

But generally he obeyed her new rules, except in one respect. Once a day, no matter what the weather, he insisted on taking his usual walk, and made it last as long as possible, going much farther than Beth liked him to. 'The fells haven't finished me yet. Nor will they.'

'You'll never change him,' Andrew warned, laughing at the tussle between his wife and grandfather. 'It's the walking that keeps him alive.'

And she would sigh and shake her head and watch anxiously as he ambled down the lane, stick in hand. Then if he wasn't back at the precise time he'd promised, she'd be putting on her coat and off searching, seeing if he'd recklessly gone too far, or climbed a stile he shouldn't and fallen over. Yet he always returned safe and well, if in his own good time, grinning from ear to ear like a naughty schoolboy.

Beth's bleakest moment came in the summer of 1982. The Falklands war had started in April but Mrs Thatcher was certain Britain would win. Pope John Paul paid a visit and the Princess of Wales gave birth to a son.

And Beth received a letter from Sarah to say that it was all over between herself and Pietro. They'd had a ferocious quarrel and gone their separate ways, which didn't trouble her in the least, she insisted, as they had never, in fact, got round to marrying at all.

The letter unsettled Beth for days. It came as a great shock to hear that the wedding had never taken place. Sarah's letters and cards had always been few and far between, saying little, and showing no inclination to come home on a visit, or to see her twin.

If I'd waited, Beth thought, would Pietro now be returning to me? And would she want him to? He'd always insisted that he loved them both.

It was too late for such troubling thoughts. She had her life here at Cathra Crag, a kind and loving husband, her precious son and, Beth suspected, a second child on the way. She was content.

And deep down was the relief of knowing that she need never see Pietro again, ever. There would be no risk of spoiling this quiet contentment, which had been so hard won.

By the end of July the Falkland's war was declared over and celebration services were held all over Britain, including the tiny fellside church of Broomdale.

'I've lived through five wars, and the invasion of Suez,' said Seth proudly. 'How about that?'

But the Falkands proved to be his last. On a day in early August, the very one on which Beth's pregnancy had been confirmed and she and Andrew hurried home with their exciting news, they found Billy waiting for them at the farmhouse door. He was all flustered and shaking, having just that minute found Seth in his chair by the fire, quite dead. The old man's hands were still resting on the last deer-headed crook handle he'd been quietly carving. He was ninety-one.

They gave him a good send-off, as Seth himself would have wished. All his family were at the funeral. His youngest sons, Billy's two brothers, who had long since left farming and taken to town life. Their children and, since Seth had been the last of four brothers and sisters, there was no shortage of nieces, nephews and cousins, together with their own prodigious brood. Beth was surprised and proud of the number who came, including many of his old friends, those who were still alive, for he had outlived most of his peers. They filled the small house to overflowing and spilled out over the farmyard and small neat lawn.

She couldn't begin to remember who they all were but was simply glad they had taken the trouble to come, for one grand old man.

'He's had a fair crack of the whip,' Billy said. 'He wouldn't want us to mourn.'

The other farmers agreed. 'We'll miss him at the farmer's meet.'

'Aye, we will that.'

'And none could make a better stick than Seth.'

'Who'll make my next? That's what I want to know.'

'A character he was.'

'They built 'em to last in that generation, eh?'

But as everyone tucked in with gusto to the ham, pork pies and apple tarts which Beth had made, she was alarmed by their appetites and laughter. It didn't seem quite respectful somehow for people to laugh at a funeral. Yet she told herself sternly that this was a celebration of a good long life, not sorrow at an old man's death. They wanted to remember him as he had once been, a vital part of this rural community in his day, but remaining busy and useful right to the end of his long life. He would be sorely missed.

'I shall always remember Seth's kindness with great affection,' Meg said, 'as one of those dear friends who saved my life during the war. If it hadn't been for him and his good wife, and Hetty and Will Davies of course, I might not have survived. I'd have starved before ever making a living from sheep. I've always been grateful for his quiet strength. Not to mention his advice.'

'He gave me lots of wise advice too,' Beth admitted, and knew she too would always remember the old man with love and pride. He'd helped her more than she could ever repay, by making her take responsibility for her own happiness. Not for the world would she care to explain the exact reason for her gratitude to Meg. 'I did my best to make his last days comfortable and content,' she finished and Meg hugged her.

'I'm sure you did. And you've done him proud today.'

Beth was glad the funeral went off without rancour or a single sour note. The next day, however, was an entirely different matter.

The first of Billy's brothers arrived before midday enquiring, without any preamble, as to the provisions in the will.

'He did make a will, I suppose?'

'Eeh, I wouldn't know.'

'Then hadn't you best find out?'

But Billy was still searching by the time the second arrived. By early afternoon the small house was crowded with members of Seth's prolific family. Nieces, nephews and cousins arrived by the score it seemed, parked their bottoms on every chair, completely commandeered Beth's kitchen and made baby Will cry with their loud voices and general turmoil.

Beth thought she might go mad with the uproar that went on

around her. As Billy continued his frantic search upstairs, several of the more impatient got going on the parlour and in no time at all had turned the house upside down. And all over their desperation to find one scrap of paper which might outline Seth's wishes for the disposal of his effects. As the fruitlessness of this search began to frustrate and irritate, voices became raised in anger, accusations made.

Only Andrew took no part. He came in for his noonday meal at the usual time, and again for his tea and in answer to Beth's long-suffering expression and half raised eyebrow, he merely shook his head and went on his way again.

It fell to Billy to confirm finally what they had all feared. Seth had left no will, no instructions of any kind as to how he wished his home, his farm or his land to be disposed of. And it didn't take a genius, Beth thought, to recognise that this meant trouble.

With difficulty and laudable tact, Andrew finally persuaded every one of his relatives to leave.

'It's too late to discuss it now. I'm tired. Dad's tired. We're all tired. I've been working all day and want my tea. My child has to be put to bed. My wife has had enough. Right?'

But it was only a reprieve. The next morning, bright and early, they were back. Every last one of them. And Beth was almost certain they had brought reinforcements. They all squeezed round the big kitchen table, elbow to elbow and fixed poor Billy with their corporate stare. Beth scurried into the back kitchen and started to brew endless pots of tea.

'Bit careless of him not to make a will.'

'He must have been ill-advised.'

'How many times did you ask him to?' Billy mourned. 'We all did.'

'You should have made him.'

'You try making Dad do aught he didn't want to.'

'I heard he had some money stashed away.'

'Not in this house.'

'Happen you've spent it.'

'Happen you'll tek that back, our Jim,' Billy said, bridling.

'Couldn't he see there'd be trouble if he didn't?'

'He never considered anything of the sort,' Andrew put in, the only calm voice in the overstuffed room. 'He was afraid of dying.

He thought if he made his will, his number would be up. That he'd die. Daft, I know, but it's how he felt and I'm sure he's not the only one with such a notion.'

A few red faces confirmed this.

'Right then,' said Cedric, the middle brother, and as a clerk in a building society considered by the rest to understand about such matters as legal documents and wills. 'There's only one answer. Everything will have to be sold.'

'*What*?' Billy sat bolt upright in his chair. 'What are you talking about? This is our home. Our livelihood.'

Beth felt herself go quite cold and one glance at her husband's frozen face offered little consolation. She sent a silent prayer that William would stay asleep in his cot upstairs. She didn't want to miss any of this.

'Not any more it's not.' This from Agnes, Cedric's wife and a woman, Beth decided, who obviously spent a good deal of time telling others what to do, when she wasn't sucking lemons. 'It *was* your home,' Agnes explained, rather sanctimoniously, hitching up her bosom as she looked down her long nose upon them all. 'It *was* your livelihood. Once. But it belonged to Dad, not you two, and now he's gone. So everything's changed, hasn't it?'

'But I'm his eldest son,' Billy protested, not able to believe his ears. 'What am I supposed to do?'

'You'll get a good slice of whatever it cuts up for,' said Cedric. 'How many acres are there?'

'Never mind how many bloody acres. It's not for sale.'

'If there's no will, the estate belongs to each and every one of us. We have a claim too. That's the law. There's no reason why you should have it all. We're his sons too, remember. And you could say that you've had the benefit of rent-free accommodation for years.'

Billy's mouth dropped right open.

'Time you retired anyroad,' Agnes said, nodding her head like one of those silly dogs found on the back seat of cars. And several voices rose in agreement.

'You'd make my family homeless?' Andrew asked, his face expressing the horror he felt, and Beth's heart went out to him. It seemed that the goodwill expressed at the old man's funeral had been buried with him. Today they only wanted to divide his spoils.

'Billy could get a bungalow in Kendal. Or a flat in one of them new sheltered schemes, couldn't you Billy?' Jim put in.

'I suppose so,' he conceded, looking uncomfortable. 'I wouldn't mind that too much.' He half glanced at his son's face, still tight with anger, and felt guilty because he'd be happy enough to retire, take up bowling and live an easier life. Only Andrew would be left with no farm, no home, nothing at all.

This consideration didn't trouble the rest of the family one little bit. 'And you,' Agnes continued, turning her attention to arranging Andrew's life next.

'Are young enough to get a job anywhere. Start summat new, or get tekken on at some other farm.'

'Which other farm? There's more work for machinery than men these days, and you know it. And such jobs as there are, pay little. I've a family to think of now. What am I supposed to live on? Fresh air?'

'I'm sure I would't know. That's for you to sort out. We've had to find us own jobs, and our sons and daughters too. Why shouldn't you? It's a tough world out there. None knows better than me the pain and suffering it can bring.' Agnes pulled a large handkerchief from her bag, smelling strongly of camphor and mentholyptus and threatening to overpower everyone within inhaling distance, and blew her nose into it with voluble mortification.

Any moment now, Andrew thought, she'd say she'd been a martyr to bad health all her life and he'd reach out and flatten her where she sat, like a great black beetle on his grandfather's chair.

'Buy a farm of your own, dear,' Cousin Alice suggested, kindly patting his hand.

'With the paltry sum I might get out of this when you've all taken your pound of flesh?'

Cedric politely cleared his throat. 'There's no reason for you to get anything,' and giving a tightly suppressed explosion of fury, Andrew flew up from his chair and started to pace back and forth on the new hearth rug.

'I don't want any of your damned money. Only a home and a living, that's all.' He hated this unsavoury disagreement about Seth's money, but his alarm for the future mounted as he saw the resolution in all their faces. Beth came to stand by his side and slid her hand in to his.

'It's all right,' she whispered, wanting him to know it would make no difference. 'We'll manage.'

'How?' he hissed back. 'Once these vultures have finished there'll be nowt but bare bones left for us to pick over.'

And she could see his point. The arguments raged back and forth throughout the morning and long into the afternoon while she cut sandwiches and brewed tea and no one paid her the slightest attention. Only Ellen's timely arrival saved her from complete collapse.

'Sit down,' Ellen instructed, sizing the situation up at a glance and at once taking charge in her bossy way. 'I'll feed the vultures for a bit. I'm good with wild animals.' And Beth sat in the back kitchen, crying her eyes out with William on her lap, listening to the tide of argument raging back and forth in the other room.

In the end the discussion came to a halt, but only because they were all exhausted. Their decision was irrefutable.

'We'll go and see our solicitor first thing in the morning,' Cedric said.

'Aye, you do that. And we'll see ours.'

And thankfully Andrew closed the door on the last protesting relative. Ellen kissed Beth, scolding her firmly to keep her feet up, brushing aside her thanks as she went off whistling into the night.

'By heck, they'd have stripped the place bare if they'd stayed another minute,' said Billy. 'Now what do we do?'

'Don't ask me.' Andrew stood in the centre of the kitchen looking as if he'd been smacked in the face by one of the big stones off Larkrigg Fell.

'I'll put the kettle on,' Beth said quietly. 'Then we can talk and start to work things out.'

But no matter how much they talked, and they did, long into the night, there seemed no solution. Seth's superstitions had left them vulnerable and unprotected. There was nothing to stop the farm being put on the market, nothing to stop them from being evicted from their own home.

The very next day their worst fears were confirmed. Their solicitor told them that if indeed old Mr Barton had not made a will, and there was certainly no record of one, then the three brothers were each entitled to a fair share of the estate.

The good news was that the nieces and nephews were entitled to nothing. But unfortunately that also included Andrew who, it seemed, had no rights either.

'But I work on the farm. It's my living.'

'You were employed by your grandfather? He paid you a wage each week. Is that correct?'

'Yes. We both of us got a wage. Dad and me did most of the work.'

'That is not at issue here,' said the solicitor, kindly but firmly. 'The point is that you took no share in the farm's profits. Neither of you.'

'No. I doubt there were many.'

'Whether there were or not, Mr Seth Barton owned and ran Cathra Crag, officially, until the day of his death?'

'Aye,' agreed Billy. 'He did the accounts, told us what he wanted doing, though we didn't allus tek any notice, we got on wi' it. Never would let go of the reins wouldn't the old fool, though he's done less himself in this last year or so.'

The solicitor sadly shook his head. 'Then I'm afraid there's no way out. The farm must be broken up and sold, and the resulting sum equally divided between the three brothers. The only way of saving the farm for yourself, Mr Barton, would be if you were prepared to buy the other two out of their share.'

'How could I do that?'

'By taking on a mortgage, if you've no ready cash available.'

Billy's face took on an expression of panic. 'Eeh, no. I'm happy enough to retire. It's my son here who it most affects.'

'Then he would have to buy all three of you out.'

'I couldn't afford to do that. The farm couldn't cover the payments,'

'Then, as I say, the end is inevitable. I extend my sympathies but this happens more often than you might think. Small farms are being sold up every week. It's the modern way, I'm afraid. Cash in hand being considered more important than land. It's very sad.'

'Yes,' said Andrew tightly. 'It is.'

Andrew gazed on his wife, her sweet homely face scrubbed as clean as a child's, snuggled beside him in the big feather bed and his heart ached. How he loved her. He'd known all along that she didn't feel the same way about him but he'd felt that he had something to offer. A home, a farm, a good way of life. Now he had nothing.

'It won't make any difference to us,' she said, reading his mind, and he heard the telling struggle to hide her fears in the quaver of her voice. 'We'll manage, same as we've always done.'

'You'll not fancy starving, I reckon.'

'Don't exaggerate, Andrew. You'll find a job somewhere. And I too can work.' Then she remembered the new life starting in her womb. 'Well, soon as the baby's born.'

'Oh, stop it.' He leapt from the bed and started to pace the small bedroom, feeling his anger rise hot and tight in his chest as he stormed back and forth, desperately seeking a solution. 'I'll not have a wife of mine with two bairns to take care of, working her guts out. What would you do? Take in washing?'

She giggled. 'I could always go begging in the streets.' But he wasn't in the mood for joking tonight.

'Don't talk so damned stupid.'

'Hush, keep your voice down. You'll wake Will.' She crept to the bottom of the bed, trying to catch his hand as he passed by on his endless pacing but he wouldn't let himself be won over, kept twitching it out of her reach, and pushing his fingers through his hair in restless agitation. Fear was hot in him. He'd lose her. Why should she sit in the gutter with him?

'Seems to me you might decide you've got yourself a pretty poor bargain and pack your bags and go,' he said, hating the bitterness in his own voice.

'Go? Go where? Why would I do that?'

'You might wish you'd married that fancy Italian instead.' It was the first time either of them had mentioned Pietro in years, and only the very extreme distress Andrew was feeling had driven him to do so now.

Beth didn't even flinch, though she was far too stunned to find a swift response.

He could feel her eyes upon him, yet nothing in her expression gave away what she was thinking. It was a pity, in a way, that she guarded her feelings so well, for it had come to her, in a rush of startling revelation, that whatever happened she would stand by him. Life away from the farm would be hard enough, life without Andrew seemed too awful to contemplate. But then he was her husband, the father of her children. She'd grown used to his little ways, his stolid patience and painful pride. And she knew how he needed her, which never failed to excite her. She got off the bed and came to him, laying her head on his shoulder.

'Andrew.' She always addressed him by his name, never darling, or love, or sweetheart. Yet there was real affection in her voice, and in the soft touch of her hand upon his cheek. 'Don't tear yourself apart in this way. Haven't we gone beyond such taunts?'

'I don't want your pity.'

'I'm not offering any. We're a unit. Where you are, I must be. That's what marriage is all about. I'm your wife, and proud to be so.' Well meaning words, yet to Andrew they were not enough. The image of Pietro was between them, as always, like a sore rubbing against the bud of their happiness. Even Beth, sensing their inadequacy, stumbled on, making matters worse. 'We have to take with a smile, whatever life throws at us, don't we?'

'And you got me, the booby prize.'

She kissed his chin, rough against her mouth as he hadn't yet shaved. 'You're getting touchy again. I need you, Andrew.'

'Do you?' He stared fiercely down at her and she laughed.

'Of course I do. I can't have your baby on my own, now can I?'

'Happen that's all you want me for, babies. All you ever wanted.'

Desperate not to rise to this latest cruel barb, Beth rubbed her cheek against his, breathing in the familiar scent of him. 'Happen I enjoy the getting of them,' and was pleased to feel him relax against her, hear his soft chuckle.

After a moment he summoned up the courage to ask, 'So you'll stop on with me then?'

'I reckon I might,' she agreed, and he knew she was teasing him now, gently mocking his Cumbrian twang. But he could hear something more in her voice, a note which caused the blood to pound deep in his belly. He wanted her, needed her so much it hurt. Sometimes he woke in the night in a cold sweat, terrified she might have packed her bags and left him. He pulled her roughly to him, desperately trying to curb the ache in his groin as he cupped the hardening mound of her stomach with one gentle hand. 'You might change your mind and leave me one day.'

'I won't.'

'Are you sure?'

'Absolutely certain.'

And as he kissed her, then carried her back to bed with a trembling urgency to make love to her until she cried out in ecstasy, in that moment of supreme fulfillment, Beth believed every word of her promise, with all her heart.

25

In no time at all a notice had appeared in the local paper, announcing the coming sale of all stock and farming equipment at Cathra Crag, to be followed in due course, date to be announced, by the auction of the farm itself.

'Oh dear,' Billy said. 'How will we face it?' And Beth waited for Andrew to reply and take charge, as he usually did.

But he remained silent, seated in Seth's old rush chair by the fire, his hands hanging loose between his knees. He was the picture of a man in complete dejection, mourning for a way of life, not simply the loss of his job. She gently brushed back a lock of his hair with the tips of her fingers. What should she do? She had a sudden urge to turn to Sarah for comfort. But even a twin could let you down. Pietro then. No, she mustn't even think of him.

Billy put his head in his hands and groaned.

Well, if no one else was going to take charge, there was only one solution. In the end you could only rely on yourself.

'We'll face this together,' Beth said, lifting her chin and feeling a rush of adrenalin flow into her veins, knowing this was no time for weakness or indecision. 'I'll make a start on the house. You'd best begin by clearing out all those barns and sheds.'

Two pairs of eyes swivelled to hers.

'Aye,' Billy said, voice doleful. 'I suppose you're right but it won't be easy. There's stuff in there that's not seen the light of day for generations. Anyroad, clearing out barns isn't going to solve anything.'

'It's a start,' Beth said brightly. 'We'll take it one day at a time, right?'

When Billy had gone she turned to her husband. 'You can start by looking through the situations vacant, and I'll go and talk to gran. She might know of a cottage we could rent.'

It was a surprise to them all, no less Beth herself, the strength she developed and pumped into them all during the following weeks.

Was this the same girl who had been left devastated at the altar, who dithered and succumbed to her sister's every whim? Was this the girl who was so concerned with offending said sister, that she was grateful for any crumb of attention Pietro could spare, even though she had stolen him from her?

Now she seemed to be the sort of woman who started a business without her husband's permission, who lured a man to her bed by devious means and now, it seemed, she could rise to a crisis without a moment's hesitation. She smiled, and baby Will grinned back at her, showing his front teeth.

'Perhaps I'm growing up, at last,' she said, 'or growing immune to disasters.' And lifting her child into her arms, nibbled his ear, making him scream with delight.

She found them a cottage to rent on Quarry Row, arranged for an estate agent to take Billy around a selection of flats and refused, point blank, to allow either Billy or Andrew to be depressed.

'We must look on this as a new challenge. This isn't the first home I've lost,' she reminded them, defiantly bright. 'So I'm an expert on the subject. I know how to cope.'

'Getting to be a bad habit, eh?'

Beth grinned. 'Apparently so. Perhaps I'm the jinx here. Oh lord, that can't be true, can it?' Her grey-blue eyes opened wide with such horror that for the first time in days, Andrew actually laughed.

'Don't start getting superstitious on me.'

Beth giggled. 'Or neurotic? I'll go back to my kitchen and shut up. Only, can you please take care of William for a few hours?'

Andrew grimaced. 'I've a lot to do. A tractor to strip down and grease. I can't have a bairn toddling round.'

Beth sighed, straining against her patience and the tiredness of early pregnancy. 'If we are to have any refreshments at all for this sale, I'd best get cracking this very afternoon. I need help, Andrew, and there's no one else, is there?'

'Don't make a fuss,' he said, a sourness creeping into his tone. 'It's not a party.'

'Billy would want it all to be done properly, in the time-honoured way. He won't want his friends and neighbours to think we're mean hearted. Now, Will?'

'I could take him for an hour mebbe.'

'That's not very much. Hardly enough time to roll out the pastry.'

'Put him down for a sleep then.'

'He's had two already while I finished emptying the loft and took the rubbish down to the tip. He's bright as a button. Look at him.'

William was sitting on the lawn watching a ladybird climb a stalk of grass. At fourteen months he was a sturdy little boy, already walking and taking an interest in everything about him, particularly anything at ground level. He held up a clover and showed it to Beth in delight.

'Very pretty, darling. No, not in your mouth. Please, Andrew? I've only two days left to get everything ready. And I can't ask Meg to have him every time I'm stuck. He practically thinks he lives there already, he's been so often recently. And she's at the auction mart today.'

'Two hours, maximum,' he grumbled, shuffling his feet and trying not to look guilty. He knew he'd piled a lot of work on Beth's shoulders these last few weeks, but then he'd spent most of it searching for work, hadn't he? Two many hours spent in the phone box, and visiting every farm he could think of who might be in need of a man, but the story was always the same. A bit of part-time milking here, the odd day with sheep there, but no full time work to be had for love nor money, and Andrew was not in the mood for compromise.

'Two hours will have to do then.' Beth sighed, her smile now very slightly forced. She knew it wasn't that he didn't love his son, quite the opposite. But his patience had worn thin. 'You'll find something soon,' she consoled him, as she had a dozen or more times. 'Or you could always take a couple of those part-time jobs. Temporarily.'

He glowered at her, his face pinched and pale. 'I hope I won't have to sink to such a level. I'm a skilled farmer, not a two-bit labourer.'

'I know, but it's a job. Money in the hand. And we have to eat and pay rent and . . .'

'Do you think I don't know that?' and he stormed off, quite forgetting that he'd promised to take William. Their contentment, it seemed, was rapidly on the decline.

The day of the sale dawned bright and clear, a bonny day that would have warmed Seth's old heart. The cars, pick-ups and vans started to arrive early, parking with difficulty on a damp field that would be churned to mud by nightfall.

All the family came of course, anxious not to miss a thing, followed by friends and neighbours ready to pay their respects to an old friend and view the end of several generations in farming, as well as keep an eye open for a bargain among the accumulated clutter. A clutch of second home owners arrived in their Rovers and BMWs, looking for bygones to adorn their rural retreats. The tourist and curious onlooker who would buy nothing, and the usual band of dealers seeking something cheap they could sell on at twice the price.

Billy was installed in a chair close by the auctioneer, to keep an eye on things and regale close friends with any homespun tales of the items as they came up.

Beth, assisted by Meg and Ellen, was inside setting out plates of pasties, scones, cakes and biscuits on trestle tables loaned by the auctioneer. Sally Ann had borrowed a tea urn from the church hall and they all set to, to dispense several dozen mugs of tea during the course of the day, and sufficient sustenance for everyone, as and when they required it.

Andrew stood at the back of the crowd which gathered in front of the auctioneer, hands thrust deep in his pockets, shoulders hunched, acutely aware of the waves of sympathy and curiosity among those present and hating them for it.

Tom Briskett had offered him two days work with his sheep up on the high fells. He supposed he'd have to take it. There'd been nothing else. His own prize beef cattle had already gone to market and sold. On that day Andrew had thought his heart would break. The sheep would be next. And when everything had gone would it be then that Beth would finally leave him?

'Now what do we have here?' The auctioneer worked his way through a miscellany of items from cocoa tins of nuts and bolts, bent hay rakes, fencing posts, bits of wood which might come in useful, parts of long lost engines and forgotten tools, and reeking bottles of sheep salve that hadn't been used since before the war. 'The first one that is,' he quipped, putting it in a box with cattle wormer and other half empty drenches and doses.

Gradually, lot by lot, everything went under the hammer. If no one bid for it, the rejected item was added to the next and the next, and so it would go on until everything was cleared and the farm and fields stood empty.

Andrew watched bleakly as Seth's precious tools were sold one by one, Billy's voice often piping up to explain their purpose to the young, check-shirted farmers who gathered about with interest.

Should he have risked taking on a mortgage, for Beth's sake? But there was little point in mourning over that now, Andrew thought. How could he ever have made the payments?

A buyer had been found for the house before auction, offering a fair price but it meant the end of its farming days. The new people, high-flyers from Birmingham were seeking a quiet bolt-hole in the country, far away from the cut and thrust of their business lives. Well, he thought grimly, they'd find quietness here all right.

Children ran about squealing, plump wives picking through linen and pots and pans, enjoying the day out. Even from this distance he could see his mother's best blue and white china glinting in the sun. It brought a sour taste to his mouth. He supposed he should be thankful that the family had allowed them first pick of a few essential bits and pieces without, as Cedric had pointed out, charging them for it. Andrew had carried them round to the rented cottage last night and his heart had clenched at the smallness of it. He'd go mad in there, he was certain of it. And Beth deserved better. Why couldn't he be man enough to provide it?

The crowd followed the auctioneer up and down the lines of equipment, set out in rows along the length of the big field. Old ploughs and seed-drills, sheets of corrugated iron, spades of every shape and size, hoes, rakes, a scythe sharpened away to a blade so fine it might snap in two and would probably end its day stuck to someone's fireplace wall.

'What on earth is that, Andrew lad?' A cheerful voice at his elbow.

He answered without thinking, his heart plummetting. 'An iron clog – patten, Seth called it, that he buckled over his boot when he was using a spade for heavy digging. Said he'd worn it since he were a lad at the turn of the century.'

'By heck, it must be that old at least. I haven't seen one of them in years. I'll bid for it.'

Andrew managed a bitter smile as the much loved patten went for a few pence to his farmer friend, together with a pair of hedging mitts. It seemed in a way to symbolise an age of slower pace, an age of stability and innocence. One which had changed only with the passing seasons and not at the dictate of politics, banks or selfish greed. His world was disappearing, piece by piece before his eyes and he could do nothing to stop it.

He was ashamed to find a shimmer of tears in his eyes as he watched the tractor go, though he was glad to see it bought by an old friend from a neighbouring farm. That tractor had been his personal responsibility, and he couldn't have nursed or cared for it better had it been able to live and breathe.

Needing escape from his emotions, he turned on his heel and strode from the field, going in search of Beth and a restorative mug of tea.

He caught sight of her through the open door of the kitchen, looking harrassed and ruffled, pressing a hand to the small of her back. He should take better care of her. She was carrying his bairn after all.

Then he saw her half turn and her pale face light up. His heart missed a beat and he wished he could see who it was who stood just behind his kitchen door and brought such a radiant smile to his wife's face. Then the person stepped forward, a young woman. Tessa? And the two of them were hugging and laughing and jumping about like excited young schoolgirls.

He was so relieved that it wasn't Pietro, Andrew sounded almost jovial as he called out her name, and didn't even flicker an eyelid when he saw she had Jonty with her.

They'd recently moved back to the dale, it seemed, after living with Tessa's mother these last years while Jonty had treatment and physiotherapy. Now he looked bright and healthy for all he was confined to a wheelchair. And his arms and shoulders were even more powerful than before, as he spent so much time working-out each day, he told them, to keep strong and supple.

The two men eyed each other with suspicion and restrained courtesy.

'We've bought one of those new bungalows at the end of Quarry Row, would you believe? It'll be perfect for Jonty.'

'Thanks to her mum,' Jonty put in, without a trace of bitterness.

Beth was delighted. Even Andrew expressed his pleasure, glad that Beth would have a friend nearby, at least. And Beth herself, who had been secretly dreading the move but had been too afraid of revealing her true feelings to Andrew, couldn't believe her luck. Having Tessa close by would make it all bearable.

'This means our two boys can be friends too. Oh, that's brilliant. How is little James?'

Tessa gave a wry smile. 'Not so little any more. They aren't babies long enough. He runs rings round the pair of us, I can tell you. When do you move in?'

'Soon,' Beth told her. Then a farmer's wife asked for two teas, scones and jam, and there was no more time for gossip.

'We'll have lots of time to talk later,' Tessa promised. 'I've so much to tell you.'

The small living room seemed to be stacked high with boxes, and tiredness finally overwhelmed her as Beth was faced with unpacking and tidying yet another new home.

William was fractious, constantly wailing and perversely wanting to crawl everywhere he shouldn't. He opened tins and boxes, tipping the contents out with cries of glee all over the floor, putting things in his mouth which Beth had to keep taking from him, to prevent him from hurting himself. And she was so weary. Every ounce of energy seemed to have drained from her body.

Billy had moved into a smart new flat in Kendal and the house which had served as farm and family home for two hundred years was theirs no longer. The last stick of furniture had been cleared from Cathra Crag, the rooms swept and mopped out, everything gone except for the big kitchen table which had been sold with the house.

Much of the land had been sold off to neighbouring farmers, save for an acre or two around the house, together with a goodly number of the heaf-going sheep which belonged to it.

And Andrew and Beth had finally moved into Number Two, Quarry Row with the last pots and pans and armfuls of bedlinen.

Try as she might, Beth found it hard not to let her mind wander back to those early days in Lakeland when she had been so young and filled with dreams. She had thought Larkrigg Hall was the answer to everything, and yet it had brought them nothing but unhappiness and disaster. She had hoped to live there, with Pietro, for the rest of her life, but it was not to be. He'd chosen her sister instead, as all men did, and she had lost them both.

And in the end Sarah had tired of him, as expected. Only it had taken too long and was much too late for it to make any difference to Beth's life. Sarah was still in Italy, still enjoying a carefree youth. And Beth was here in this rented cottage, feeling old and worn out, with nothing to call her own, and a husband who was unemployed and she wasn't even sure she loved.

Guiltily she pushed these betraying thoughts aside and opened the first box, rubbing the small of her back with a tired gesture. Why hadn't she labelled them? Where on earth had she put the kettle?

'No, William. Let mummy open the boxes. You play with your bricks.' A wail of protest. 'All right then, you can sit in the box, let me take out the flour and jams first.'

'Tractor,' he yelled, and she had to laugh as he climbed in among the kitchen groceries and started to drive the cardboard box with many vrum vrum noises.

If this tiny living room couldn't match the elegance of the drawing room at Larkrigg, at least there could be happiness in this house. If she didn't quite love Andrew as she should, then she would keep that to herself. She could try to be a good wife to him, a good mother to her children, and not allow any regrets to mar their marriage.

And if a secret part of her still held a nostalgic yearning for a certain artist's smooth-skinned beauty, and if she sometimes wondered how or where he was today, or what he was doing, she must never, ever, reveal that fact to a living soul. Certainly not to Andrew who was suffering enough at present. Struggling to shake these disturbing thoughts away, Beth set about filling every jug with flowers to bring some brightness into the cottage and cheer her.

'There, isn't that pretty?'

William was too busy tipping soap flakes all over the floor to be interested in flowers.

'Hello. Anyone home?'

'Ellen.' Beth took one look at her friend and promptly burst into tears.

'Nay, I may not be beautiful but I don't usually get such a reaction.' Shocked and distressed, Ellen wasted no time in putting Beth straight to bed with a large mug of hot tea laced with sugar and stern instructions not to move a muscle.

Then she went through the little house as she said herself later, like a hot knife through butter. Every floor swept and scrubbed, every shelf polished, every cupboard and drawer lined with fresh paper, every item orderly and shipshape.

'Amazing how I still remember what my mother taught me,' she said, laughing as she pulled on her coat. 'There's a stew in the oven. Now I have to go and feed my zoo. I'll call tomorrow to help you finish off.'

'Oh thanks, Ellen. I'm very grateful.'

When Andrew came in he never even noticed the flowers, or the fact that the house was all unpacked and tidy. He ate the stew which Ellen had prepared, bubbling with renewed energy, talking all the time.

'I'm going to see a chap over Sedbergh way tomorrow. I've heard on the grape-vine that he's looking for a man.'

'Sedbergh? But that's miles away.'

'It's work, Beth. And its a big farm.'

'I know. I'm sorry. It would be wonderful if you could find a really good job.'

'I will, trust me.'

'Oh, I do.'

He left at dawn, buoyed up with new hope and later that morning Tessa called and they sat sipping coffee and giggling like schoolgirls over silly jokes and memories of old times.

'Do you remember that goat?'

'Oh yes, milk squirting everywhere except in the bucket.'

'And Jonty chasing it half across the fell.' And they were off again, hooting with laughter.

'We won't wake William, will we?' she asked, wiping the tears from

329

her eyes and nodding in the direction of the toddler's snuffling snores. Beth chuckled.

'It'd take dynamite.'

'And soon you'll have another.'

'Yes.'

'Are you pleased?'

'Actually yes, I am. Two years between them seems about right.' Her face momentarily clouded. 'But life's a bit tough for us right now. Andrew is finding it hard to settle without the farm, and getting a good job isn't proving easy.'

'Will you find one? After the baby's born, I mean.'

Beth sipped at her tea and considered. 'I've never had any urge to be a powerful businesswoman. Look where it got Sarah. Having said that, we could do with a bit more money.'

'Let me show you what I've been up to since I last saw you.'

Tessa brought out a portfolio filled with paintings. They were mainly of birds, owls were her favourite subject, followed by peregrines and other birds of prey in full flight, or swooping upon a vole or mouse. Bold colours, strong lines, beautiful pictures. 'Jonty helps me by preparing the canvases and framing the finished pictures. He's very good at it. Do you like them?'

'I think they're wonderful. How clever you are.'

'I've sold quite a few, as a matter of fact, and hope to sell more. It's proving quite a good living for me.'

'So you made it after all. Oh, Tessa, I'm so pleased for you. You deserve some good fortune.' Beth hugged her friend and her thoughts flew to her own abandoned scheme, a bundle of half-finished moccasins stowed away in a box somewhere.

'I've made contact with several galleries who display them for me,' Tessa was saying. 'I'd love my own though. Or a studio at least. That's the only problem with the bungalow. Great for Jonty's wheelchair, but small.'

'Well, I think these are wonderful.'

Tessa sat back on the sofa and curled her feet under her. 'So, what about you? What've you been up to? Besides producing babies.'

'And looking after a farm and three men, and moving house.'

'OK, point made.'

'As a matter of fact . . .'

330

'What?' Tessa laughed. 'Oh, come on. Don't turn shy on me, not after all these years.'

So Beth brought out the tiny moccasins she'd been working on. 'These are only for practice, to see if they're any good.'

'But they're lovely. So cute. There must be a market for them.'

'I'd have to make loads, to make it worthwhile.'

'Then why don't you?'

'I did think about it. But then with the baby, and the problems at Cathra Crag . . . Now, like you, I've no space.'

'And yet, also like me, you're desperate for the extra cash.'

Beth gave a wry smile. 'Thank you Sarah.'

The two girls stared at each other and the idea was born in both their heads in the same instant.

'Broombank Mill.'

'We'd have to ask Meg.'

'Do you think she'd object?'

Beth grinned. 'No, I don't.'

A surge of hope lifted her spirits and by the time Tess left, they'd already mapped out the first steps they must take to get the project rolling. But first she had to hope and pray that Andrew would get this job.

When he returned that evening and wearily told her that the job had already gone, Beth could scarcely hide her disappointment. The spoon she had been using to serve out the casserole she'd made, slipped from her fingers and fell to the floor with a clatter.

'Oh, Andrew. How will we manage?'

'We'll manage because we have to manage,' he said, a sharp bitterness in his voice. 'I'll go and get the dole, or unemployment benefit, or whatever it's called. Like everyone else.'

'Can't you take one or two of those part-time jobs,' she tried again, her voice tentative and coaxing.

'Sacrifice my skills and my pride you mean?'

'We can't afford pride.'

'I can't afford to keep a family on part-time pay, particularly when I have to spend half the wage on petrol travelling to wherever it is, for no more than a few hours' milking. It's not economic, Beth.' Spoken with such bitterness his hurt was almost tangible.

She felt desperation claw at her throat. 'Oh, if only we hadn't lost Larkrigg Hall, everything would be perfect then, wouldn't it?'

She saw at once her mistake as his face closed with that familiar tightness. Then he reached for the jacket he'd only just taken off with jerky, angry movements. 'I wouldn't know, would I? It wasn't my inheritance, so it's nowt to do with me.'

'I didn't mean . . .'

There was cold fury in his eyes now. 'Aye, you did. You blame me for all of this mess.'

'That's not true.'

'You can't help comparing your life now with what you once had. You've never stopped mooning for the loss of that house. Even Cathra Crag wasn't really good enough for you, was it?' His voice was rising as he made no attempt to stem his anger.

It came almost as a relief to Andrew to let it out, since it had simmered all afternoon during the long wet drive and the humiliation of standing, cap in hand, begging for work and being turned away. He should have rung up first, of course, to save himself the expense and bother. Only he'd thought he was first to hear of it, and had a better chance face to face, man to man. How wrong can you be?

'No clogs in your kitchen, eh? Not for you my mother's mangle. You must have electricity. New curtains and rugs. Vaccuum cleaners and washing machines. Everything old must be thrown out and replaced with new or your own stuff from your precious Larkrigg.'

'That's not true. Besides, I only wanted to make it cosy for us.'

'All you wanted was to spend, spend, spend. Make us bankrupt, same as you did with Broombank Mill.'

She could have protested that the bankruptcy was down to Sarah, not her, but she knew that he understood all of that. He was only blaming her for everthing because he felt a failure over not getting the job.

But her silence only fuelled his guilt to greater anger. 'And I was only second best. You made that clear enough, didn't you, right from the start?'

She flinched as if he had struck her. 'Don't, Andrew. Please, don't say such a thing.'

'Why not? It's true.'

'I refuse to quarrel with you. I won't excuse myself for negligence over Broombank, though it was hardly my fault alone. As for Cathra Crag. I loved that farm, and Seth and Billy. You know I only wanted to make a comfortable home for us all.' Tears stood proud in her eyes but not for the world would she let them fall. She must make allowances. Andrew had lost everything. He was only being cruel because he was hurting.

He walked to the door and flung it open. 'It's easy for you to talk now. But you made *me* feel uncomfortable. Look how long you made me wait to make our marriage a proper one. Not until you'd decided you wanted a bairn, no doubt.'

'Oh, Andrew.' All other words choked in her throat.

'And if Cathra Crag wasn't good enough, God knows how long you'll put up with this hell-hole. Fancied yourself as a lady-of-the-manor-type up there, didn't you? Since when it's been all downhill. You should have waited for your beautiful Italian, instead of settling for a peasant. Now you're a peasant too.'

The slam of the door echoed in her heart long after he had gone.

26

'It was the most appalling row.' Beth sat in her living room with her head in her hands, Tessa seated quietly by her side while on the rug, baby William played happily with his bricks, piling them up so he could knock them down again. 'He just stormed off and I haven't seen him since.'

'When was that?'

'Yesterday.'

A long thoughtful silence while Tessa considered this unwelcome news. 'Andrew is a proud man. Always was. He'll come back as soon as he's sorted himself out.' Then more briskly, 'As for you, you have this new baby to think of. Worrying is not allowed. Getting upset will do you no good at all. And when Andrew does return, don't comment on his absence or you'll start a new row. Jonty has had some dreadful times these last few years, some really dangerous mood swings, but he's calm now and has reached a sort of contentment. And he adores James. They are great pals.'

Beth managed a smile. 'I can see he loves you. He rarely takes his eyes off you.'

'And Andrew loves you.'

'Yes.' She met Tessa's compassionate gaze. 'Sometimes I wonder how on earth I would manage without it.'

Andrew came home later that afternoon. She didn't ask where he had been. He looked grubby and rumpled, as if he'd slept rough somewhere. Probably in a barn at Cathra Crag, if she was any judge.

The next weeks proved every bit as difficult as she had dreaded. He

335

searched for work and came up with nothing. He helped Meg and Tam out when they were hard pressed, did what part-time work he could find, but none brought in much money and he absolutely refused to take any for helping out at Broombank.

'I'll not take charity.'

And no matter how much Meg insisted it wasn't charity if he was working, Andrew simply said that they were family now and you didn't make money out of family, not in his book.

Beth sailed through her pregnancy, as usual, spending hours each week chatting over her plans with Tessa. These afternoons were a happy relief in a way, since Andrew showed no interest in their project. She found his reaction disappointing.

It hurt her badly to see her husband diminished by his lack of success. He seemed to shrink in upon himself with each passing week and it worried her greatly. She felt that all she could do was to keep him well fed and try to raise his spirits. Neither of which was easy with the small income they had coming in.

One evening she placed a steaming plate of roast pork and vegetables in front of him, sat William in his high chair and settled to eat her own meal while helping the toddler negotiate his spoon from dish to mouth without losing too much food on the way. She glanced at Andrew as he made no move to start eating.

'What's wrong?'

'How come we can afford meat?'

'I bought it cheap,' she lied, fingers crossed beneath the table.

'I thought the butcher's van had stopped calling?'

'Why should it? Eat up, love, before it goes cold.' Meg had given her the pork that afternoon, when she and Tessa had called to run through some details. Not that Andrew must know that. 'Tessa called today,' she said brightly, changing the subject.

'Seems she's never away.'

'She likes to show me her wonderful paintings.'

He picked up his fork and toyed with the meat, tender and succulent in a rich gravy.

Stubborn fool, Beth thought. The smell of it must be making his mouth water.

'She sells them, you know, and is quite sure I could sell my baby moccasins.' Beth laughed. 'We talked about it all afternoon. Meg is all for it. Says we can use the old woollen mill as workshops. Tessa will take one, me another, and we can let units to other craftspeople. Tam is looking into the question of planning permission for us.' She chattered on about advertising and finding customers while hunger finally won and Andrew stolidly ate his dinner, as was his wont. When he had finished, he got up and began to pace about as if he hadn't the patience to sit with her. Beth stopped talking, mid-sentence.

'What do you think then?'

'About what?'

'About this idea.'

He went to stand and glare into the empty fire grate, hands in pockets, shoulders hunched. 'Why ask me? You seem to have it all settled.'

She stifled a sigh of irritation. He wasn't himself at the moment, and she really must make allowances. 'Is it a good idea?'

'Suit yourself what you do. It's your life. Only don't forget that bairn you carry.'

'As if I would. I could ask Sam to come back, then I'd only be part-time.'

He turned to her, his face calm. 'You don't need to work at all, if you don't want to. I've found a job,' he said, quite out of the blue.

She was so thrilled and relieved her whole body jerked. 'Really? Where? What is it? Why didn't you tell me the minute you walked in?'

'You were too wrapped up in yourself, as usual.' The way he avoided her eyes told Beth that he knew this attack to be unfair so she swallowed the words that sprang to her own defence. 'It's in the stores at Bramley Engineering.'

She set down her knife and fork and stared at him, appalled. 'Bramley Engineering?'

'That's right. I hand out tools and nails and rivets and stuff when they need 'em.'

'Not on a farm then?'

'No,' he said, irritation creeping back into his voice. 'Not on a farm. I've told you, there's no decent farm work to be had. We can't live on a bit of part-time milking here and there. I won't struggle. I have my pride.' He glanced at her face, gone pale with distress, and guilt washed through him like a great hot tide. Look what he'd brought her to. Right down in the gutter with him, begging scraps of pork off

337

Broombank to put on his table. He wasn't stupid, he knew he didn't bring in enough for such treats.

'I ate Meg's bloody roast pork but we'll have no more of it. Not now I'm a working man again. I'll buy me own in future, thanks very much. Go on, don't sit there with your mouth drooping, eat up, you need your strength too, for the new baby.'

But her own appetite had quite gone. 'A factory,' she said, and his voice rose in temper now.

'Aye, a factory. What of it? We need the money.'

'But . . .'

'Don't start, Beth. Don't start.' And pulling on his coat and cap he strode to the door.

'Where are you going?'

'Down to the Broomdale Inn. A bloke can go out for a pint, I suppose, to celebrate finding a job?' And he went, closing the door quietly behind him, a consideration which did nothing to ease her disquiet.

On the first day of February, 1983, Beth gave birth to a daughter, Emily, named after Andrew's mother. For the first time in weeks she felt as if they were a family again. She saw the pride and joy in Andrew's eyes as he bent over the baby and when he leaned over the bed to kiss her she put her arms about his neck and held him close for a moment.

'We're lucky, aren't we?'

'In some things,' he said, and deep inside she felt a tremor, almost like fear. It seemed so difficult to reach him these days, but she had no wish to start an argument, not now when her breasts were swollen with milk and her heart with love for her new child.

Billy came to coo and admire, delighted with his new granddaughter. 'You'll fetch her to see me when you start your visits again, won't you, lass? Weather permitting, of course. We don't want the bairn to catch cold.'

'Of course I will.' Beth visited Billy every week in his new flat, where he seemed to be most content. He was always interested to hear about her life, and her new project at Broombank.

Andrew still hadn't warmed to the idea. Whenever she talked about her plans he would get up and walk away, go off down the pub to spend money they couldn't afford, or for long walks over the fells. She was almost certain that on these occasions he spent the time checking over the sheep which had once been his and now belonged to others. He couldn't come to terms with his changed circumstances and she didn't seem to be making a good job of helping him.

'You two all right then?' Billy asked now, as if reading her mind. 'Andrew settled to his new job?'

'He's coping,' Beth said, dropping a kiss on to the baby's downy head, so that he couldn't read the doubt in her eyes. But Billy was no fool.

'Not farming though, is it?'

'No. It's not farming.'

She was up and about in no time, anxious to begin living her life, for all she felt dead on her feet half the time. Emily proved to be a fractious baby, her demanding cries waking Beth at all hours, and for a time she and Andrew did seem to grow closer as he showed great concern for her health.

'Catch up on your rest in the afternoons,' he'd tell her, as he watched the dark rings of tiredness form beneath each eye.

'How can I, with young Will haring about the place?'

And so Andrew decided action was called for and one afternoon Ellen's cheerful face appeared around the door, grinning widely. 'Hello. How's the wee bairn?'

'Oh, Ellen. How lovely to see you.'

'Andrew says you need help. Tell me what needs doing and I'll do it.'

'You really didn't have to give up your afternoon for me.'

'Glad to,' she said, jiggling the rim of the cot.

'Andrew is a fusspot.'

'I won't hear any objections,' he said, following Ellen into the room.

Beth smiled up at him, feeling a surge of contentment overwhelm her. She could hear the tiny snuffling noises coming from the cot, which meant Emily was sleeping peacefully for once. Hanging on to Ellen's hand was William, singing a nursery rhyme she'd been teaching him. Oh, but she was a lucky woman. She really had no right to complain. A good husband, children, and caring friends.

'I could look after this monster for a bit,' Ellen said, swooping up the squealing toddler and bearing him off downstairs.

Before Andrew left her to go back to work, he kissed the tip of Beth's nose, as he had once loved to do. For a second they looked deeply into each other's eyes and something inside of Beth stirred. She'd missed him. She'd missed those moments of intimacy they'd once enjoyed. He hadn't come near her for months, partly because of the pregnancy but also because of the atmosphere which had grown between them, like a canker.

'I'll be well soon,' she said. Perhaps he'd be more cheerful now Emily was born, and they had regular money coming in.

'Good,' he said softly, and they shared a tremulous smile. Sighing with pleasure, Beth glanced longingly at the bed, her mind more on sleep than love making at the moment. 'I think I could do with a bit of a lie down,' she admitted.

'That's why I brought Ellen.' And he tucked her in bed as if she were a child herself, kissing her brow and smoothing the sheet beneath her chin.

Everything would be all right after all, she could feel it.

Downstairs, Ellen took Andrew to one aside. 'Can I have a word. I didn't want Beth to hear, and start worrying.'

'Why, what is it?'

'I've been given notice to quit.'

'What? Tell me about it. What happened?'

Ellen glowered. 'We'll all be on the streets before long. You remember that Larkrigg Hall was sold some time back, and been occupied by tenants in recent years. String of no-goods who never did a hand's turn about the place.' Her voice rose with indignation.

'I did hear,' Andrew agreed.

'Apparently, when the latest tenant went at the last quarter day, no other was allowed in. Word is that the owner is to take up residence himself. I'd be more than curious to meet him, only he's given me notice an' all. I'm to be out by the end of the month. Rotten so-and-so.' She sniffed her disdain but behind the bluff and bluster, Andrew could detect a degree of concern. Ellen had lived in Rowan cottage for as long as he could remember.

'Oh, Ellen, I am sorry.'

'Aye,' she said. 'So am I.'

'Perhaps another of the cottages here on Quarry Row will come vacant.'

'Fat chance. And where would I put my zoo? No, there's no help for it,' Ellen said, determinedly brisk. 'I've to pack me bags, take up my birds and beasts, and go and be a gypsy for all he cares.' And she laughed, loud and hard, as if it were the funniest thing.

'What's the joke,' came Beth's voice from the door. 'I heard voices raised. Is there a problem? What are you talking about?'

Andrew swooped her around and shooed her back upstairs. 'I told you to rest, madam. We were only saying how we mean to tie you to the bed if you don't do as you're told,' and tucked her, very firmly, back between the sheets. 'Rest. For two whole hours. That is an order. Ellen is here to take care of everything.'

Beth's last waking thought was that at least he did still love her, a fact which warmed her right to the heart, and made her feel deliciously secure.

By the time she was able to come up for air from the tyranny of night-time feeds and take an interest in such things, she found Tessa already installed in Broombank Mill, having partitioned off a small area by a window where she could set up an easel and paint to her heart's content. Jonty went with her on some days to work on the frames.

'He's thinking of taking it up full time. Doing it for other people, I mean. He could advertise in the the local paper for customers. If it proves successful, he might want to rent space for a workshop too. It would be good for him to have a project of his own.'

'Absolutely. Why not? And Meg has found a young potter. So with the rent I get, I can buy whatever I need and make a start.'

But Andrew wouldn't hear of her starting work until the baby was at least six months old, and she had to admit he was right. Beth loved these early days of babyhood, but that didn't stop her from making plans whenever she could find a spare minute. She would watch with joy as her baby suckled at her breast, while her mind busily worked out how she could fix up a cot for her at the workshop, perhaps a playpen later. There was no reason at all why Emily couldn't come to work with her every day, and William too, though she might get him into a play school for a part of each day. She held Emily's hand as she suckled, dreamily studying each tiny pearl-like nail. How tiny it was. How precious.

'I've had a brilliant idea,' she told Andrew that evening, the moment he walked in the door. 'We could make sheepskin mittens as well as the moccasins. Which would make us even more money. What d'you think?'

'I see that's all you think of these days. Money.'

'Oh, Andrew, that's not true.' But it was. The workshop project had come to obsess her night and day as the way out of their mess. 'We don't want to stay here for ever, do we? I want to help, that's all. And I don't have a farm or animals to care for now.'

'You don't have to remind me.'

And she bit her lip, hating herself for the tactless remark.

But he wasn't interested in her dreams, only in what was for his tea. 'I'm tired, Beth. It's been a long day. Can we talk about this some other time.'

He went and washed at the kitchen sink as he always did, and she scurried to move pots and pans out of his way, hearing him curse as he tripped over the nappy bucket, sending water spilling everywhere. The noise woke Emily, who at once started to tune up, and something inside of Beth snapped.

'For God's sake, why can't you use the bathroom upstairs? No bigger than a matchbox it might be, but at least you'd be out of my way.'

He paused, water dripping from the tight line of his jaw as he held the towel frozen in his hands. 'The kitchen sink has always been good enough for me in the past. Does my working class background bother you?'

'Don't be silly.' Tears of tired frustration stung her eyes, feeling a burst of resentment for the awful kitchen as she mopped up the soapy water. And for the nappies she had to wash every day and find some way of drying, since she couldn't afford to buy disposables as everyone else did these days. She pushed back her hair with a damp, weary hand. 'It's just with two children, and all the accompanying paraphernalia, we always seem to be under each other's feet.'

The moment she saw his face she wished she could take the words back.

The meal was eaten in stony silence and later, her heart clenched as she watched him stand at the cottage window, knowing that he itched to be out on those fells helping with the lambing. He could see the sheep that had once been his, hear their low bleating, and the high pitched voices of their lambs and hated not being out there amongst them. They were not his responsibility now. Not his problem. He was no longer their shepherd.

Instead he was a storeman, cooped up all day in a factory and though she was glad of the work and the money he brought home, Beth feared for the way it was tearing him apart.

She went to stand beside him and slipped her hand in his. 'I'm sorry for my outburst just now. It's been one of those days.' And he must have been pleased by the intimacy, because he didn't move away.

'I was wondering if an early night might do me good,' she said, casting him a sideways glance. 'How about you?' A long pause, during which she found herself growing tense with anticipation. If he said no, and went off to the pub tonight as usual, she'd feel utterly rejected and unwanted. The need for him to make love to her had grown surprisingly in her during these last weeks, and still he hadn't touched her.

The hand holding hers suddenly clenched very hard, and she laughed out loud.

They made love that night as if they were new lovers again, each greedy for the other. Everything was going to be all right, she told herself on a tide of exhultation. Andrew would get used to his new job soon, they had their lovely children and they did get on well, they really did. Everything would be fine. All she needed was to get out of the house for a bit each day. She decided to go and see Sam first thing in the morning.

Sam declared he'd be delighted to come back and work for her.

'There's a snag though. I can't pay you until I start making some money.'

His face clouded. 'Now that is a snag. I have to eat and I can't work for you and still claim dole. I tell you what, I could advise you, quietly like, till you get going.'

'Oh, that would be wonderful.'

Sam looked pleased to be asked. 'Buy a cutting machine, you'll need one of those to cut out the shapes for the different sized moccasins. Then talk to those ladies who used to knit for the mill. There were plenty of hand knitters worked from home, till Miss Sarah laid 'em off. I reckon they'd be glad to make moccasins instead.'

'I hadn't considered that possibility. Do you think they would?'

'You can only ask.'

'Yes, I suppose so.' She was doubtful, nervous of asking, since they'd been so let down last time.

'Have you thought of getting the knitting going?' Sam said, watching her face. 'It'd be grand to see the old place working again, as it once was.'

'I'd rather not. It all seemed to go rather sour. And it would need capital, which I don't have. I've divided the building into small craft workshops and let them off. I shall take one for my moccasins. But I can't do it all myself, not with my family to care for. I shall need help. Perhaps asking the women would be a good idea.'

He nodded, his face serious. 'Some of 'em will have got other work, 'tis true. But those who haven't, might be glad of the chance to earn a bit of money. Good outwork is hard to find.'

'You're right. As you say, I can only ask.'

He looked pleased. 'Grand. And when you've got going, give me a shout. I'll tek the risk and come and work for t'same money as I'm getting now, on t'dole. You can start on the pay rises as soon as the money starts rolling in.'

Beth laughed. 'Ever the optimist.'

'Oh, aye. I've every faith in you, lass.'

And as Beth walked home through Brockbarrow Wood, trundling the pushchair up the stony path, turning right to Quarry Row before she reached the silvery waters of the tarn, she glanced back up the fell towards Larkrigg Hall, shading her eyes against the sun. She could see chunks of dark rocks jagged against a rose tinted sky.

A great deal had happened since the day of their arrival, let alone the day Sarah and Pietro had walked out, leaving her facing bankruptcy. There'd been many ups and downs since then, not least in her own marriage, but at last she felt things were going right. Baby William was a son to be proud of, bright as a button. Even Emily wasn't crying quite so much.

'Come on, princess, let's go home for a nice cup of tea. Then early to bed for you two, and perhaps for Daddy and me as well.'

A weak shaft of early summer sun glinted in the stag's one remaining eye as the heavy door swung open and the young couple walked into the hall.

'Poor chap, you'd have thought someone could have mended him by now. Bring the cases in later, I want to explore right the way through first. Coming?' The woman skipped up the stairs with conscious elegance, hoping he watched and admired. But he ignored her, concentrating on bringing the suitcases from the car and carrying them upstairs to the master bedroom. He began to unpack and unfold every garment. Seconds later she was back at the door, half teasing, half anxious as she watched him.

'Why are you doing that now? Do stop, there's plenty of time. Come and see, the house is as beautiful as ever and the garden is a blaze of colour, and weeds of course.' Sarah laughed, feeling the usual wash of uncertainty flood her as he did not even glance in her direction, mingled with a spurt of impatience. 'Why have we come if you aren't even interested in the place?'

'I am interested,' he said, lifting a suit and hanging it in the great mahogany wardrobe.

As he reached for the next one, she went to him and slid her arms about his shoulders, reaching up to stroke his face, wanting him more in that moment than she had ever done. 'Let's make love. Now. On the bed, this very minute as we used to.' There was excitement in her voice but he only walked away from her to continue with the unpacking, not troubling to reply.

Annoyance, kindled by fear brought a flush to her lovely face. 'I won't let you down, Pietro. I've promised to ask her. I'll do anything to please you. Haven't I told you so a thousand times?'

He looked at her then. A cool, dispassionate gaze across the wide expanse of bed where once she had instructed him in ways to please her. He had learned a good deal more since then, about Sarah, and about himself. 'I look forward to you putting those promises into effect.'

A small, tight silence, then Sarah giggled, desperate to relax the tension between them. 'Won't Beth be surprised when she learns we are back, and that we're the ones who bought Larkrigg.'

'*I* bought Larkrigg.'

She sobered instantly. 'O–of course. But it's the same thing really, isn't it?' A delightful pout and a bewitching smile from violet eyes which would have entranced any other man. Pietro folded a cashmere sweater.

'No,' he said. 'It is not the same thing.' He turned away from her, intent on his unpacking and for one reckless moment fear turned to rage in her breast, then seeped away, leaving her empty and shaking with insecurity, as it always did.

'Pietro? Darling?' She crept to his side, tentatively touched his arm. 'You do still love me, don't you? Still want me? It will be all right now, won't it?'

He hung his Italian silk ties on the rack, smoothing them down one by one. 'That is up to you, wouldn't you say?'

'And Beth.'

'No, it is you who must make it come right.'

'I understand, and I'm sure she'll agree. I told you, she always does everything I ask. Simply everything.' Sarah gave a bright laugh, that sounded hollow even to her own ears. 'And then we'll be OK, won't we? As we used to be. As you promised?' She came to him again and slid her arms about his shoulders, pulling him to her, lifting her lips to be kissed as she pressed her body against his. 'Show me how you love me, Pietro. I need you to show me.'

His mouth, inches from her own finally smiled, as if her words had pleased him, and the tip of his tongue slowly licked his lips. 'It is for you to show me.'

'I will. I do love you. And I want you. Now.'

'Do you beg me?'

'I do. Oh, I do.' Her eyes were glazed, eyelids drooping, all concern for her stylish suit and elegant coiffure quite forgotten in her hunger and need for him. 'I'll prove it.' She frantically stripped off all the expensive garments and tossed them like rags on to the dusty carpet. Then she knelt before him and put her hands together in supplication. 'Ask of me anything. Anything at all. You know that I will do it. I need you, Pietro. I love you. I'm so desperately sorry that I left you that time. It was only because I was mad with jealousy.'

'Jealousy is petty.'

'Yes, Pietro.'

'Many women would be glad to have me as their lover.'

'I agree, and I swear that no matter what you do, I will never complain again. All I ask is for you to let me be a good wife to you. For always. Please, I beg of you, say that you love me a little.'

'You are not crying. Where are your tears? How can I be sure you are sincere, if you do not cry?'

The sulkiness was back in his voice and her body began to tremble and shake, not simply from the cold in the long neglected room but from the terrible yawning desperation that he might turn and walk away from her, as he did once before. Only for good this time. She'd almost lost him once, she mustn't risk it again.

'Forgive me, I'm excited,' she explained. 'Coming back to our old home, looking forward to seeing Beth again. And about us, so soon to be settled, at last.' She laughed up at him and spread wide her arms, arching her back so that her breasts jiggled delightfully in all their splendour, moving apart her knees in open invitation. 'No one can make you as happy as I can. Admit it. If I spend my entire life on the mission of your happiness, I ask for no more. I will be content.'

This pleased him. He was the teacher now and had taught her well. Reaching down, he flicked at one nipple with a fingernail and smiled as it sprang to attention at his touch.

His one hope had been to cause as much disruption to this family as they had done to his. He'd been willing to try anything to that end.

His first idea had been to court and win either one of the twins to agree to marriage and then let them down at the last minute. Sarah had seemed the free spirit so he'd gone for Beth, but for all she'd been besotted by him, she had baulked at rushing into marriage, because of her past disappointment. Unfortunate.

Then Sarah, rampant for a man, had taken him to her bed and he'd been quite surprised by the pleasure of the experience. She wasn't a soft sort of mistress who required much in the way of soft talk and pampering. Quite the opposite in fact. She was inventive and demanding, with few scruples to trouble their relationship. And they'd enjoyed a good time together while the money lasted.

He'd eloped with her on impulse, not quite knowing whether he would ever marry her, but certainly intending to bring her nothing but unhappiness. Thus he had succeeded in hurting Beth and Meg O'Cleary, and Sarah too in one simple act. He could still recall the pleasure he'd felt on that day.

But it hadn't lasted. He wanted more. He might manage to inherit Broombank through her, thus damaging the whole damned family, as his grandfather and later his own mother had been hurt by them. He was not averse to any form of disruption to their well ordered, self-satisfied lives.

The months with Sarah had, however, proved surprisingly enjoyable, at least in the beginning. But still she had irritatingly refused to consider marriage and he'd been forced to let the matter drop and bide his time. Then to his fury, she had turned all moral on him, and left. And all because through sheer boredom, he had taken another lover, several in fact. But whose fault was that? How could one woman hope to keep a virile Italian satisfied?

She'd screamed at him and had hysterics, taken a lover herself, but in the end crawled back, begging him to forgive her, promising she would never fail him again.

But his weakness for indiscretions had entirely changed the nature of their relationship. It was really most amusing. Now, at last, she was willing to do anything to please him. And he could enjoy watching her suffer each and every day. Had indeed brought her home for that very purpose, and so that her family could appreciate at last the extent of his power. It gave him a kick just to think of it.

With a sigh of delight Sarah saw the excitement kindle in his eyes. He wanted her. At least she still had that hold over him.

She took his hand and smoothed it over her bare flesh, over each ripe breast, the flatness of her stomach and on down to her soft moistness. Then the compulsion which had been responsible for holding them together against all the odds over the years, took hold and drove them to a coupling, swift and vigorous, right there on the floor, the roughness of the carpet scratching her naked flesh. It was quickly over and she went into the small bathroom to shower while Pietro strolled downstairs.

'*Ciao*,' he said to the empty rooms, smiling at a memory. 'Now it is time for the *bellavendetta* to make real progress.'

27

Meg was washing down the dairy when the two figures appeared at the door. For a moment she thought she was hallucinating, then she dropped the hose pipe and ran to them, so that water went everywhere and she was soaked to the skin in seconds. She was forced to dash back to the tap to turn it off, before laughingly flying to embrace Sarah. 'How wonderful. Why didn't you tell us you were coming?'

'I wanted it to be a surprise.'

'It's certainly that. I thought you were still in Italy. Oh, I'm so glad to see you.' Meg's eyes slid past her and fixed upon Pietro, her lips stiffening as she registered again the familiar chill in his blue eyes. 'Good morning, Pietro.'

'Mrs O'Cleary.'

'Meg, please. Let's not stand on ceremony. Come inside. Have some tea. Where are you staying?' And unable to resist her curiosity, 'Are you two married or not? We've never quite been able to work it out. Do tell me everything, we're all dying to hear your news.'

Sarah brushed aside the questions with easy laughter. 'Oh, there's too much to tell all at once. First, I want to know if you've forgiven me for deserting you all. And if Beth has forgiven me. I've missed her so much, you wouldn't believe.'

And Meg smiled, pleased by Sarah's obvious eagerness to meet with her twin again, and by her evident contrition. There had been days, particularly at the time of her defection when bankruptcy had threatened, that she had struggled to feel any sort of love or forgiveness for this wayward granddaughter. Now, seeing her return to the family fold as it were, she felt a surge of maternal feeling. The girl had been young and headstrong, madly in love with this beautiful young man, living only for today as so many young people did. How could she hold all that against her?

'Beth didn't go under, if that's what you mean.'

'I know, she wrote and told me.'

'I'd say she came out of it all the stronger. As for forgiveness, you must ask her for yourself.'

'Good,' Sarah said, hardly taking in what Meg was saying. 'Where is she?'

But Meg was anxious to put Beth's case, and blithely continued with her tale as she brewed a pot of strong tea, not glancing in Pietro's direction. 'She suffered, of course, don't think for a minute she didn't. And it broke her heart to part with the house, but it was the only way to save herself from disaster, save us all from the most terrible trouble. The possibility of Broombank being made bankrupt was quite intolerable.'

'Don't make me feel more guilty than I do already.'

'But she survived. And is now doing rather well, as a matter of fact. Started working at the mill again.'

'I thought the mill was closed. That she was married to Andrew and had a child?'

'Beth operates it as individual workshops for local craftsmen and women. It's working rather well. She's got four set up already, and hopes to do a couple more eventually.' She could see Sarah fidgeting, glancing out the window, and laughed. 'She's not there now. She's at home and yes, you're quite right, she does have a child. Two as a matter of fact.'

'Two?' Sarah's violet eyes took on a clouded look, rather like a summer storm over Larkrigg.

'A tiny new baby girl, named Emily, has joined us. Absolutely delightful,' Meg said with evident pride in her voice. 'Go and see her. She won't be able to believe her eyes when she sees you.'

'I shall go this minute.' Half turning to Pietro. 'Coming?'

His eyes still on Meg, he shook his head. 'You go. I'll drink my tea and talk to Mrs O'Cleary. Fill her in on all the news.'

* * *

It was one of those mornings at Quarry Row when being a young mother of two babies seemed to be the least enchanting job in the world. William was grizzling with a cold and Emily had just regurgitated her entire breakfast all down the front of Beth's dressing gown. No doubt, Beth realised, because she'd stuffed too much down her in the first place, but it was worrying all the same.

A fitful fire struggled in the grate around two or three pieces of coal. She still had to wash and dress herself, and the children too for that matter, fetch in some logs so Will could get warm, tidy breakfast away, and face the usual mound of washing. And she could hear the first taps of rain on the window which meant she couldn't put anything outside to dry. Drat.

An hour later she had the fire blazing to a furnace, causing steam to rise from the loaded clothes horse of dripping bibs and nappies. William was still grizzling, clinging to the belt of her dressing gown as she moved about the small living room, picking up toys, rubbing a duster half heartedly about. She felt absolutely exhausted yet really should go and dress, then she'd make herself a lovely cup of coffee by way of reward for getting the washing done so early.

When she heard the light tap at her door she assumed it to be Tessa on her way to the mill and didn't look up. 'Coffee?' she asked, picking William up and smoothing his hot head with one hand while jiggling the baby buggy in an attempt to soothe the crying baby with the other. 'I was just about to make one.'

'My God. Do you live here?'

Time seemed to stretch out endlessly as Beth turned disbelieving eyes upon her sister. Sarah stood framed in the doorway of the tiny cottage, and she seemed to Beth in that moment like a vision from another planet. Wild ebony hair tamed to a fetching shaggy bob and a tan to dream of, she was elegantly attired in a snappy little suit in lemon yellow with the sexiest short skirt Beth had ever seen. William's dumper truck nestled against endless legs clad in what must be the finest of silk stockings.

Beth carefully set her son in the corner of the old sofa and tucked a rug about him before she found the strength to cross the room to Sarah. Hands instinctively tightening the belt of her dressing gown, she placed a kiss on each cheek then stood before her, heart pumping.

'Why didn't you tell us you were coming?' Was all she could think of to say.

Sarah's eyes scanned the crowded, over-heated room and laughed. 'Would it have made a difference?' Emily chose this moment to increase the volume and Sarah's eyes fastened upon the buggy. Then she was swooping past Beth and gathering the baby in to her arms.

'Oh, what a darling. How can you let her cry? She must be hungry.'

Beth watched, half amused now, but surreptitiously pushing back her untidy hair, not knowing whether to hate herself, or Sarah, for choosing this morning to do her chores before getting dressed. What a slut she must look. 'She's just sicked it up as a matter of fact. I should take care with that suit.'

Sarah didn't look in the least bothered. Nestling the tiny baby close against her cheek she turned pitying eyes upon her sister. 'I'll hold her while you get dressed, if you like. Poor lamb.' And she settled herself down on the sofa, amongst the crumpled piles of ironing and baby powder, captivating William with one of her most bewitching smiles. 'Then yes, please, coffee sounds wonderful.'

Upstairs in her room, Beth stared at her own tired face in the dressing table mirror. Too many sleepless nights with little Miss Emily. She touched imagined lines of fatigue, fingered her drooping breasts, still oozing milk. Trust Sarah to return looking like something out of a glossy fashion magazine and find me looking like the before picture.

Sighing, she rummaged through her drawer for a make-up bag, started to apply mascara then angrily tossed it back and slammed the drawer shut. She didn't wear make-up, not during the day when she was with the children. She was an ordinary mother, housewife, whatever, and proud of it. She might just put on a gingham dress and apron.

In the event she chose a favourite cotton skirt and long baggy sweater, brushed her hair till it shone and fastened it back, defiantly, with her old slide.

'I've got her off to sleep,' Sarah whispered proudly as Beth handed her a mug of coffee.

And so she had. Emily's small face, usually puckered with fury was for once smooth and angelic, for which blessed relief Beth felt a wave of resentment. 'You don't have to whisper,' she said. 'She'll sleep through anything now. William too was asleep, his head resting on his aunt's lap. 'I'll take Will upstairs.'

'Oh no, I really don't mind.'

'He has a cold. He'll pass it on to you. And he needs to keep warm.'

'It's like the Sahara in here.'

Ignoring this mild criticism, Beth swooped up her son and carried him off to his bed. Then she wheeled the baby buggy outside into a fitful sunshine, followed by the clothes horse since the rain had thankfully stopped and closing the door, turned at last to face her sister.

'Why have you come?'

Sarah laughed. 'Heavens, what a welcome. What happened to – how are you? Pleased to see you again sister dear.'

'I'm sorry. I haven't quite got over the shock of seeing you here.'

'What about you?' Sarah glanced about the room, struggling to keep the sound of incredulity out of her voice. 'Are you content with all of this?'

Beth considered for a moment. 'Yes,' she said, with determined resolution. 'I am. It's a quiet life, and if not entirely perfect in that we always seem to be hard up and Andrew can't find permanent work in farming at the moment, it's a reasonably happy one. I'm lucky.'

'Isn't it a bit – well – cramped? How do you manage in that awful kitchen?' Sarah had clearly spent the time Beth was upstairs exploring the tiny cottage. It wouldn't have taken long.

'It's a bit of a tight fit with two children but we get by. Where are you staying?'

'What about the mill?' Sarah said brightly, not answering the question. 'Meg says you've turned it into workshops.'

'Yes.' And so Beth talked about the workshops she had let out and tried to shake off this feeling of unreality that Sarah was here, back on Larkrigg Fell and sitting on her own rumpled sofa.

'And you also have a moccasin industry? You must be making a packet.'

Beth gave a wry smile. Some things didn't change.

'Same old Sarah. Always thinking about money. No, I'm not making a packet, as you call it. It is a very new, very small cottage industry, and I do have expenses. Nor have I any wish to. I'm seeking only to make a decent living, and if I can help others to do the same, so much the better.'

'Same old Beth.' An astringent quality in the voice which she refused to rise to.

'I mean to take things slowly. No risks, no disasters.'

'Not like last time you mean,' and their eyes met over the coffee mugs.

'If you like to put it that way, yes.' And as the two sisters studied each other, a smile began, growing slowly into a forgiving smile. 'We survived,' Beth said. 'But I can't say I enjoyed the experience. It was hell for a time. Even poor old Ellen was bitten by a snake so I had her patients to tend to as well as my own troubles. But she survived and so did I, though it took time. Yes, I dare say I must have forgiven you, in the end.'

'You'd forgive anything. Even of me.'

'Perhaps I had my reasons.' A small silence and then Beth continued, 'So, tell me all your news. Where have you been? What have you been up to all these years?'

'You first.'

Beth settled back in her chair, glad suddenly that she had Sarah to chat to again. She hadn't realised how much she had missed her. She chattered on, not noticing her twin's silence, telling how they came to lose Cathra Crag, of Seth and Billy, and all the happy parts of her marriage. And talking with pride about her children.

'Then there's Tessa and her paintings, and Jonty and his picture-framing business. He copes brilliantly, working hard to build a new life for himself, and they're happy. It's so good to see them together.'

A brittle little laugh. 'You sound almost jealous. I thought it was me who had a pash for Jonty Reynolds.'

'Don't be silly.' Beth tried to cover her blunder by joining in the laughter. It always made her wistful to see Tessa and Jonty together. Not because she had any feelings for him herself, but because Jonty and Tessa had attained a depth of happiness which she didn't seem able to reach. She and Andrew were content, they got along fine most of the time, but there was still something missing in their relationship. There remained a constraint between them, fuelled by the memory that she'd agreed to marry him only because she couldn't have Pietro. 'Few people find such perfect happiness,' she admitted. 'You only have to watch them together to understand what I mean. But that's enough about me. It's your turn now. What has brought you back to Lakeland?'

'Can't I simply want to visit my favourite sister?'

'Of course.' Beth's gaze was probing, taking note of the sharpness in the tone, the flawless beauty perhaps a touch drawn, the figure more gaunt. Was something wrong? 'You've told me nothing. Where you've been. What you've done. What happened to you after you left Pietro?'

'Oh that.' Sarah shrugged. 'We got back together in the end.'

Beth felt a shiver of ice run down her spine. 'You mean he's still with you. Here?'

'Naturally. Didn't I say?'

'No, you didn't.' Beth was struggling to cope with this new information, trying to decipher how she felt about it. 'So you married him after all?'

'No, we're not married.'

'Not . . . ?' She wasn't sure whether to be pleased or distressed by this news. 'But if you got back together . . .'

'Oh, Beth.' Sarah leant forward in her seat, hands clasped together as if in supplication. 'At first I didn't want to marry. Wasn't interested in commitment of any kind, as you know.'

'But you changed your mind?'

'We'd had a disagreement over – well, never mind about what now. And I walked out on him. We were apart for months and you wouldn't believe how I missed him.' The violet eyes grew misty. 'I changed during that time, Beth. I came to see that the only way I could be happy was to be with Pietro. Really with him, for always. I was ready to make that commitment, d'you see?'

Compassion pushed aside the last remnants of jealousy. 'Yes, love, I do see. We all change and grow up in time. Even you.' A small silence while she waited for Sarah to continue. When no more came, Beth casually started to fold baby clothes and lay them in the basket ready for ironing. 'So have you come home to do the deed then?'

'Not exactly. Possibly. Probably. Oh, I don't know. We haven't quite worked it out yet.'

Beth raised a quizzical eyebrow but said nothing.

Sarah avoided her probing gaze and went briskly to the window, staring out at white clouds sailing majestically by, at the sleeping baby and the washing fluttering in the breeze. 'If I had a problem. I mean, a really serious problem, you'd help me, wouldn't you?'

'What sort of problem?'

'Whatever. Anything.' An edge of hysteria came into her voice and Beth hastened to calm her.

'If I could help, I would, naturally. You're my sister.'

Sarah swung round, her face alight again, like the laughing young girl she had once been. 'You always did do everything I asked.'

'Yes,' said Beth, more thoughtfully, smoothing a matinee jacket into the basket. 'I did, didn't I?'

Sarah swooped across the room and hugged her, kissing Beth on the cheek. 'We're growing terribly dreary. Wake those gorgeous children of yours. I want to visit with my niece and nephew. We'll save all talk of problems for another day. I've only just arrived home, for goodness' sake. And I may not even have to trouble you with it, in the end. We'll see. OK?'

'Whatever you say, Sarah. Whatever you say.'

Sarah came every day after that. She helped with the children while Beth worked on her mitten patterns, and even made her peace with Sam.

Andrew's attitude to his sister-in-law was polite but cool. He watched the two sisters together with interest, but said very little. He could find no quarrel with Sarah's behaviour, yet he was uneasy. She seemed oddly secretive, though it wasn't his place to pry if Beth was content.

The worst of it was that she had brought Pietro Lawson with her. And Andrew meant to keep that young man very firmly in view.

Mostly, Sarah kept the children occupied while Beth got her moccasin project under way. She played with William, took Emily for long walks and behaved in every way as a besotted and devoted aunt. Even more astonishingly, the two sisters never disagreed, and not a single word of complaint crossed Sarah's lips. It was really quite amazing, Beth thought, how she had matured.

She talked little about the past and would say only that she was staying close by. And Beth didn't ask. She was too concerned with putting off the moment of meeting Pietro again, which she managed to do for several days. But it couldn't be put off for ever. In the end it had to be faced.

Meeting him was the hardest thing she had ever done. It came about quite naturally and accidentally, which was a relief in a way, since it was difficult to imagine finding the courage to stage a meeting.

She was walking down to the mill one bright sunny morning, Sarah having taken the children off to Windermere for the day to give them a steamer ride, and with the promise of a big ice cream at the end of it. Beth had been reluctant to let Emily go at first.

'She's too young. She'll cry all the time and ruin your day.'

'Nonsense. She's a sweetie.'

'And you've had her every day for near a week. I'm beginning to miss my own daughter.' Said in a joking manner, but with an element of truth in it. Beth hated to be apart from Emily, for all she was a difficult child.

But Sarah had protested that she could manage very well, and was Beth turning into an overprotective mum?

So she had set aside her misgivings. Baby bottles and nappies had been packed, a picnic prepared and copious instructions issued. Then she had stood and seen them off with smiles and waves, while one half of her mind wondered where Pietro was and why he wasn't going with Sarah on this trip.

Now he was suddenly here, before her, like a genie leaping from her mind.

'You startled me,' she said, trying to smile. She'd forgotten quite how beautiful he really was. Even her dreams had lied. It made her tremble just to be near him, and not for the world could she meet his eyes.

He was smiling, patting a rock by which he was standing. '*Ciao*, little one. I take the walk, as you do. It is a beautiful day, yes? Come, sit with me. I have waited long for this meeting. I wish for to say something of great importance to you.'

'I–I'm not sure that would be a good idea. And I really don't have time.' She glanced at her watch and realised in the rush, she'd forgotten to put it on. She was forgetting a lot of things these days. 'I'm sorry. I have to get to the mill and work.'

But he was taking her arm, pulling her down beside him and she felt too weak to protest. Then even more outrageously he cupped her chin in his hands and dropped a kiss on the tip of her nose, exactly where Andrew usually kissed her. She very nearly protested but that would have been childish.

'Sweet Beth, how I have missed you.'

'Not enough to return for me.' She could have bitten the words off her tongue.

'You think that I forgot you? This is what I must say to you. I never forgot. Never. Every minute I am away, I think of you. But Sarah, she need me. What could I do?' He shrugged, in that delightful Latin way of his.

Beth wanted to tell him how he had hurt her beyond endurance. He'd walked out without a single word of explanation or a simple good bye. Yet she couldn't get the words out. Pictures of Andrew kept getting in the way, confusing her. Her children's faces rose before her eyes and she kept wondering how Sarah would manage if Emily got colicky again, and why hadn't she thought to put in her gripe water. He was still talking. She'd forgotten how he always had so much to say about himself.

'You know in your heart that nothing has changed between us. Your eyes tell me this.'

'Everything has changed.'

'Why?'

She should have said because she was happily married. 'You chose Sarah.'

'Sarah chose me.'

'And you went, willingly. Now I have Andrew.' There, she had said it. 'And I'm a happily married woman.'

'Are you?'

'Yes. And you shouldn't be saying all of this. I must go.' She swung away from him but almost before she had taken one step he had caught her arm and whirled her about, making some sort of strangled cry in his throat, crying her name perhaps. Then he was crushing her in his arms and smothering her face with kisses, his mouth taking hers as it never had before. And inside, Beth felt the all too familiar and shaming sensation of burning need.

When she broke away from him her cheeks were on fire, her heart hammering in her chest. Shock, she told herself. Only shock at his outrageous behaviour. 'H–How dare you? You had no right.'

'I had the right of my love for you. Which has never died. Do not be cruel to me, Beth. I see the way you look at me. With the great longing.'

She became alarmed and backed away, trying for a laugh which came out as an odd sort of squeak. 'What nonsense you do talk. Don't play the Latin lover with me, Pietro. It won't work any more.' And now she had started talking she couldn't seem to stop. 'Andrew and I have had our ups and downs, it's true, but we are man and wife and I've never regretted marrying him for a moment. And we have two lovely children whose happiness I wouldn't risk for the world. I won't have you walk back into my life and turn it upside down in this way.' It was entirely the wrong thing to say. The delighted smile upon his handsome features told her so in an instant.

'Is that what I have done?'

She closed her eyes and drew in a slow, steadying breath. 'You know very well what I mean. Don't play the innocent, it doesn't suit you.'

'We came back for a reason. Has Sarah told you?'

'No. What reason?'

'Ask her. You love your sister. *Sì?*'

'Of course.'

'And always help her.'

'Whatever is troubling Sarah, she'll tell me in her own time. And yes, I've told her I'll always help her, if I can.'

'That is good. And me. What would you do for me, little Beth?'

There was something in his face that panicked her. 'For God's sake, Pietro, that's enough. Leave me alone.' Then she swung from him and ran away down the path, stumbling over stones and dashing angry tears from her eyes. How could he be so cruel, so uncaring of her feelings? How dare he remind her of how frighteningly easy it could be to love him?

'Beth?' Andrew stepped out of nowhere on to the path before her and she almost fell into his arms, her feet skidding on loose stones. 'What is it? Are you all right?'

She struggled desperately to gulp down her sobs and collect herself, her face feeling stiff as cardboard as she forced it into a smile. Had he seen Pietro? Worse, had he seen him kiss her? 'Of course I'm all right. Why shouldn't I be?' she snapped.

'Why were you running?'

She gave a high pitched laugh that sounded false even to her own ears. 'On my way to work, as you should be. You know how it is. I was late, and in a hurry, and hurrying downhill found myself going faster and faster till very soon I was out of control.'

Andrew stared back up the path, his eyes upon the approaching figure. 'Yes,' he said, thoughtfully. 'I can see it's very easy to let things get out of control.'

Beth's commitment to her marriage was severely tested over the following days. Every time she saw Pietro, which was more often than she would have liked, she was nervous that he might repeat that outrageous kiss. Try as she might she couldn't get it out of her mind. It reminded her of those stolen kisses out on the high fells, the feel of his arms tight about her, his fingers caressing her breast. Her thoughts got so far out of hand that she imagined he followed her, and she took to glancing back over her shoulder wherever she went, not quite sure whether she wished to find him there or not.

She remembered, too, her own shameful betrayal of Sarah. Even that didn't prevent her from starting to question herself, and her life. Was she really content? Could she truly be happy with a husband she had married without love? Each night she tossed and turned in her bed, going over and over these questions and feelings of guilt in her mind, so that her restlessness often woke Andrew, and he would be concerned.

'Are you unwell? Is it the baby?'

'No, no, I'm fine. Go back to sleep.'

She worried too about Sarah. Her sister was not at all as she should be. Always highly strung, she now seemed more edgy than ever. She'd made no further mention of the problem she'd hinted at on that first day, and Beth worried about this with increasing anxiety. Was she ill? Was that why she had come home? To deliver bad news. Oh no, please not that. Yet she could almost feel it preying on Sarah's mind.

Beth was aware too of Andrew's increasing unease. She could feel him watching her, growing suspicious. Not that she'd given him reason, but how could she say so without bringing the whole subject out into the open again, which she really couldn't bear to do.

Andrew, in his turn, waited for her to speak of it, and explain away that kiss he had so painfully witnessed. But she said nothing.

And there was no more love-making between them. From the day he had seen her out on the fell with Pietro, all relations between them had ceased. Jealousy and resentment burned in him and he knew he was becoming prickly and distant, yet could do nothing to prevent it. She'd never pretended to love him, so it was really up to her, he thought miserably, to show him how she felt now.

Beth didn't know how she felt, nor did she dare let him make love to her, in case, in her confused state, she should call out the wrong name in her moment of climax. So she made no move to rectify the situation.

Miserable as they both were, nevertheless each kept strictly to their own half of the bed. As time passed becoming more entrenched in their stubbornness, each resolving to be the one to break the stalemate.

Pietro doesn't mean a thing to me, Beth assured herself endlessly, but couldn't quite bring herself to say as much to Andrew. And in the end she had to admit, to herself at least, that Pietro's presence was disturbing her more than she cared to acknowledge.

And then Sarah casually remarked that it had been Pietro who bought Larkrigg Hall, which was where they were living now. A revelation which left her stunned and weeping with distress.

28

Ellen was sitting in the door of Rowan Cottage shelling peas into a big blue bowl when the car drew up outside her gate. She glanced up, curious to see who was visiting at this time of day and whether she should hurry to put the kettle on. Visitors were always welcome if they came ready for a chat.

When he got out of the car, unlatched her gate and walked towards her she knew, in that instant, that trouble was walking up her path. Even before he spoke, in a voice low and hard with contempt, she sensed disaster. His words, however, were entirely unexpected and stunned her into silence for a whole half minute. A state of mind from which she very rarely suffered.

'You didn't leave,' he said. 'Despite all my requests that you should do so.'

Ellen eased herself stiffly from her stool, and stood to meet him, face to face. 'Leave? Heaven help us, are you saying that you are the new owner of Larkrigg Hall? Was it you who bought the house from the bank?'

He smiled, an arctic smile which made her shiver. 'I seem to recall giving you ample notice to quit. On several occasions, if I remember correctly. Why have you not done so?'

'Because you weren't here, blast you. I don't answer to threats, particularly from absent landlords. One minute there are tenants, the next, word is the owner is coming home. Then tenants again. Never knew whether to believe it or not. So I did nothing. And why should I leave? This is my home. Where else would I go?'

'I really don't care, but go you must. I'll not have you on my land.'

'Your land is it? And who's looked after it all this time?' The shock was passing and she was angry now, feeling she had nothing more to lose by letting him see how she felt. 'You tried to get rid of me once before, years ago, when you thought I knew too much. But then I've known all along that you weren't quite what everyone took you for. I wasn't a daft young lass, in love with you, you see. Makes a big difference. Those two girls were besotted, poor lambs. And you hurt them. I could've told them many things, if I'd put my mind to it? Happen I should've done.'

His eyes were hard as sapphires. 'Yet you didn't.'

'I chose not to.'

He was thinking fast. Finding the old woman still here had been a blow. Just when everything was coming together at last, when he almost had his revenge. His final plans were in place and he would have no one spoil them.

He was successfully driving Sarah over the edge. The more he resisted, the more desperately she would do anything to win him as a husband. It was highly diverting. Beth too was as besotted as ever, though she would never agree to her sister's latest wild scheme. But it didn't matter. It mattered only that she suffered, that they both did, as he and his family had suffered in the past. And he hadn't even started on the rest of them yet. He smiled at Ellen. 'You wisely guessed that it would be a bad idea. I would not recommend you tell them anything, even now.'

'Why should I not, if I'm to lose my home anyway? Happen I don't like seeing you play one off against the other. Happen you'd be better trying to buy my silence, Mr Fancy-Pants Lawson. Exercising a bit of caution for once.'

He stepped closer. They were of a height and to his intense disappointment, Ellen showed no sign of intimidation as he glared straight into her eyes. Her mocking gaze was telling him that he'd met his match. But it troubled him only slightly. He could handle her. He could handle anyone. Given time.

'What good would you do by hurting them?' His voice was so soft she could only just make out the words, for all his closeness. After a moment or two of furious thinking, Ellen snorted, forced to agree.

'Mebbe you're right. For the moment.' She moved away, disgust curling her lips, something in her face he could only describe as triumph. 'Your friend seems to have found contentment, of a sort. Settled down nicely with our Tess, he has. Knows what side his bread is buttered. If now you've all manner of complications in your own life, you've only yourself to blame. I'll say nowt, for the sake of them lasses. But I don't see why I should disrupt meself for you. You sort yourself out, and I'll sit back and enjoy the fun.'

Dark blue eyes narrowed, his next words coming through gritted teeth. 'I have the power to silence you, believe me.'

'As you tried, and failed to do, once before.'

'I'll make sure I succeed next time. I can make your life not worth living.'

'And I yours,' Ellen told him, happily smiling. 'I'm not one to interfere, or moralise. Live and let live, that's my motto. And so long as I can stay in my little cottage, I'd have no reason to say anything, now would I? I ask only that you don't hurt anyone, ever again. Checkmate I think.'

At that moment the two girls in question were facing each other as adversaries.

'Just like old times,' Sarah said tartly. 'At each other's throats again, yet I really can't see why you are so upset.'

They stood at the head of Whinstone Force, icy waters dividing into a curtain of white lace over the dark rocks as it racketted down to the gill below. Kingcups and globe flowers starred the peat-rich soil at their feet, and a holly blue butterfly landed silently on a forget-me-not flower. Beth glared at it, unseeing. 'I'm upset because you and Pietro high-tailed it over the proverbial blue horizon and left me in a total mess. Yet all the time, he was rich enough to put everything right.'

'Hardly. Besides, the money was given him by his stepfather, to make a new start with his life. Why should he give it to us?'

Beth hesitated, for there was some sense in this argument. Even so . . . She turned impatiently away from the waterfall, the sound of it seeming to drum against her heart and she sank on to a rock, uncaring that it was slick with damp moss. 'He was happy enough to spend our money and eat our food when he was living with us and everything was going fine. So why shouldn't he help bail us out when we were in trouble?' The shades were beginning to drop from her eyes, and she didn't like what she was seeing.

Later she tried to discuss the subject with Andrew, but the mere mention of Pietro's name sent him pulling on his jacket and heading out the door, as he usually did whenever an unpleasant subject was raised between them.

'Where are you going now? Not off to the pub again? I need to talk. We both do.'

'Not now, Beth.'

'Why not now? Why do you always shut yourself away when things aren't going quite as you'd like? When will you stop being such a loner?'

But he only turned chilly eyes upon her. 'Meg lost some sheep today. I'm going to see if she's found them safely.' And Beth watched him go, tongue-tied with frustration.

It was one morning in May when she woke to find herself alone, yet it was still dark and the alarm clock had not gone off.

'Andrew?'

She pulled on her dressing gown and went downstairs. He wasn't there. It didn't take more than a moment for her to realise that he must have gone over the fells again, perhaps still looking for Meg's lost sheep. Any excuse to get out amongst the animals he loved.

Sighing, she checked her babies were still sleeping then went to make herself a cup of tea. She sat shivering in the living room, wondering if she should light a fire or go back to bed. Then Emily woke, demanding to be fed and she sat and watched the dawn break, a pink light change to pearl grey and then blue, and still there was no sign of him.

She felt utterly exhausted. Worrying over Sarah's problem, whatever it was. Worrying over Pietro, and the state of her marriage.

She glanced at the clock. At this rate he would be late for work. A small kernel of alarm started somewhere deep in her breast. Where was he? Why hadn't he told her he was going out, left a note or something? Surely he hadn't left her? Were their problems so serious?

By the time the clock struck eight, the time he should have been at Bramley Engineering, she was already dressed and tucking both children into the double baby buggy.

'We're going to see Aunty Tess, isn't that nice?' she said brightly, not wishing to frighten them with this change of routine.

She almost ran down the lane, worrying what she would do if Tessa refused to take the children. But of course she offered right away, the moment she recognised Beth's distress.

'God knows where he is but I must find him. He has to get it into his head that the sheep are not his responsibility any more. Apart from anything else, he has a job and he should be there. Now. And . . .' I have to be sure that he hasn't simply walked out on me. But she couldn't say that. Even to Tessa.

'Beth, don't worry. Andrew has been walking these fells all his life. He'll be fine. He'll be with the sheep, you know he will.'

'I'm not worried about his safety,' she said defiantly, eyes flashing. 'I'm only bothered about him losing this job.' Yet that wasn't strictly true. Fear was cold and hard inside of her, nestling against her growing anger. Tessa made no attempt to argue.

And as she climbed Dundale Knot, calling his name, she encouraged the anger to grow. It was much more comfortable than the fear. Her feet slipped on the shale and the slippy, sheep cropped turf, but she didn't slacken her pace, pushing herself harder till she had no breath left, only a pain piercing her side.

Why was he too proud and stubborn to talk out his feelings with her? Instead, he always sank into an impenetrable silence. Ever since Pietro had arrived he'd avoided her like the plague. They should learn to communicate more, as other couples did.

If he hadn't left her, had simply gone off to help Meg find her dratted sheep, he could at least have left a note. How dare he go off like this, risking his job, his *life*, over animals that were no longer his responsibility. He'd feel the edge of her tongue when she found him.

But when she did find him, lying flat on the ground, her one thought was to run to him, heart pounding. 'Andrew, what is it? Are you injured?' Oh, don't let him be dead. Please no. I didn't mean to be angry.

'Hush,' he said as she almost fell upon him. 'You might frighten her. She's stuck on that ledge.'

She stared at him, then down the side of the crag at a ewe which had got itself stranded. Tessa had been absolutely right. It was the sheep which were troubling him, and not their marriage at all. She was almost disappointed, and spoke more sharply than she intended, as a result. 'Andrew, what are you doing here? You should be at work.'

'I wish I'd brought my rope.'

'Rope? Why should you carry a rope? You're no longer a shep . . .' She stopped when she saw his face change, could have bitten her tongue off.

He indicated the terrified sheep, restlessly stamping about the narrow ledge. 'Meg's lost twenty sheep this week. I was helping her look for them when I found this one. Would you have me leave it to fling itself over the edge?'

'I wonder if you realise the risk you've taken,' Beth said, not yet ready to let her anger go, in case something worse should replace it.

Andrew's face was tight with anger as he almost spat the words at her. 'What risk?'

'Because one ewe was in trouble and needs a bit of help, you've risked losing your job.'

'And you are no doubt going to remind me that I have children to feed and a wife to keep. And I don't do it half so well as another certain person would who apparently has money to burn all of a sudden.'

Beth bit down on her lower lip, trying to remain calm. 'Why does everything have to come back to Pietro? It really isn't necessary, or fair.'

He laughed as he got to his feet, and the laugh hurt her more than his anger. 'I come up these fells every morning before I go to work, if you want to know. This morning took longer because I was helping Meg out. Have you a quarrel with that?'

Beth swallowed any further protests. She'd said enough already, probably too much. This wasn't the moment to talk about facing up to reality. 'Shall I fetch Meg or Tam? They'll have ropes.'

'No, I can move faster than you. Stay here.' He gathered up a collection of small stones and started to drop them one at a time over the edge of the precipice at either side of the ledge upon which the ewe was stranded.

'What are you doing? You'll scare it to death.'

'That's the idea. If it hears stones skittering by, down the mountainside, it'll be reminded of the long drop. See, she's backed against the rock now. You'll have to do this while I'm gone, if she starts getting restless again. We don't want her taking fright and leaping into the unknown.'

'Oh, lord. Andrew I'm not sure . . .' But he was already running down the fell, his long legs making short work of the distance. Beth lay down, as Andrew had done, then screwing up all her courage she dropped a few tiny stones at either side of the ledge. She repeated this at intervals, making sure the sheep remained where it was, shivering and clearly terrified, but pressed up tight against the rock. The responsibility seemed awesome and an eternity passed before Andrew returned, Tam with him, carrying two coils of rope and a crook.

'You can do the climbing,' Tam said. 'You're more nimble than me these days.'

One rope was tied around Andrew and he began to edge himself down over the rock-face to a good position. Beth felt herself jerk with shock.

'You're not going down there?'

Both men stared at her but said nothing, and she bit her lip, feeling foolish and desperately afraid. She closed her eyes and sent up a silent prayer. Don't let him fall, dear God. He's not in a good temper this morning, help him to take care and be patient. But she had underestimated him of course. Andrew abseiled down the mountainside as if he were walking down Kendal Highgate.

When he was dangling about eight or nine feet above the sheep he again dropped some stones at either side, to discourage it from moving.

What will I do if he falls, Beth thought, panic overwhelming her, her heart beating so loud in her ears she was sure everyone must hear it.

'Oh, do hold fast, Tam. Let me help you.'

'Don't you fret, lass. It's fine he'll be. Hasn't he done this a hundred times or more?'

'He may have, but I haven't had the pleasure of watching him do it,' she drily remarked, and clung fast to the rope along with Tam, just in case, ignoring his soft chuckles.

Using the crook like a fishing rod Andrew lowered the rope like a lasso around the ewe's head. The next minute he was on the ledge beside it, wrapping the rope around its legs, and Beth gasped out loud with fear, expecting at any moment the ewe to go mad and knock them both off the ledge, spinning them down over the crag into oblivion.

Then he was climbing back, bracing himself with the rope and was again beside her. She wanted to grab him to her, smother his face with kisses, instead she scolded him sharply.

'Did you have to go so far down? You risked your life there. And for what? A damn' sheep.'

'Aye,' he said, and his eyes upon her were still cold. 'But I had to fasten her up safe. She trusted me.'

It was Tam who eased the tense atmosphere growing between them with his soft, Irish chuckle.

'It's no more than a shepherd does every day, Beth lass. Risk his life. Out in all weathers, tending the flock, keeping them safe, and rescuing one when needs be. Now, are we ready? Heave away.'

And despite its struggles the animal was safely drawn up the side of the precipice, flustered and frightened but none the worse for its ordeal.

'You did well there, lad,' Tam said, laughing as the ewe scampered off, its dignity ruffled and no doubt its heart beating faster than it should for a while.

'Will she be all right?' Beth wanted to know, exhausted after her own efforts on the rope and at last able to show her concern for the sheep, now she knew her husband was safe.

'She'll soon settle. See, she's found her lamb already.' And they all laughed as a noisy reunion took place.

It was then that she happened to glance at Andrew's face and saw it had come alive, alight with laughter for the first time in months. Nothing could have more plainly declared his unhappiness with the state of his life than to see him transformed in this moment, over the rescue of one careless ewe. And in that moment too, it came to her as a blinding revelation that she loved this quiet man. Loved him with all her heart.

Beth was in a shiver of excitement. She had never felt like this before, waiting for her own husband to come home. It was intoxicating, as if she had drunk a whole bottle of champagne.

She made an extra effort with the meal that night. She bought some plaice from the fishmonger's van and baked an apple pie to follow. She set candles on the table, a cup of wild violets and pretty folded napkins. Then she hurried the children through their baths and off to bed early. They would have the entire evening to talk over this delicious new discovery she had made, and explore what it meant for them.

How should she tell him? How would he take it? Would he be pleased, delighted, surprised? In all their marriage she had never said the words, though she could see now that she had loved him for years. It had grown upon her quietly without her realising. He was a dear, loving man, and she adored him. It was amazing that she hadn't realised it before. No wonder their love life had always been good. And would be again.

Dazed with delight and anticipation, she bathed and perfumed and slipped into her best dress, a pretty pink silk that rippled against her legs as she walked. It reminded her that she was still young and sexy.

She would judge precisely the moment, say exactly the right words and see the light of love shine in his eyes. She felt warm and glowing all over just to imagine his pleasure. Everything was at last going right for them, her life falling into place. Andrew had a job, she had her workshops at Broombank, two beautiful babies, and they both loved each other. What more could she ask for?

Beth could hardly wait for the sound of his footsteps coming through the door. But when he did come, she saw at once that something was wrong and her heart plumetted.

'They've laid you off,' she said, taking in at a glance the expression on his face, grey with worry and bitterness.

'I've been late once too often it seems. Today, apparently, was the last straw. Told me I was unreliable. I told them they could keep their damned job.'

'Oh, Andrew.' All the strength went out of her and she had to sit down. Now they were right back where they started. 'Do you want to talk about it?'

'No.'

She slid the candles quietly back into the drawer and Andrew ate the delicious meal without comment. He didn't even notice her dress

371

or remark on how pretty she looked. Then they went to bed, each to their own side and nothing more was said. She would have to wait for another day to tell him of her discovery. This was the saddest night of her life.

Andrew had gone off early the next morning, to start all over again on his search for work. He hadn't even laid the fire for her, as he usually did. Beth had meant to spend part of the day at the mill, working on her own project, but somehow the heart had gone right out of her. Everything seemed too much effort. Nothing ever lasted. Whenever she found something or someone to love and care for, she lost it: Jeremy, Pietro, even Sarah, her own sister. It was taken from her as if by some jealous gods who couldn't bear her to be happy even for a moment. Now Andrew was slipping from her, just when she had truly found him.

The day seemed endless. As she worried over how he was faring at finding work, Emily screamed and refused to eat her dinner, William threw a tantrum and smashed his favourite truck, and Beth cut her finger on a tin of corned beef she'd opened for their lunch. Altogether a dreadful day.

When later Meg called at the cottage, Beth welcomed her with open arms.

'Am I glad to see you. I'm suffering from a surfeit of children.'

Meg grinned. 'How about a breath of fresh air then? Down the lane, or over Coppergill Pass?'

'Anything to take me away from stinky nappies and keep these little devils quiet.' They dressed the children in warm jackets against the spring breeze, tucked them into the buggy and set off along the lane, negotiated the stile with difficulty and headed uphill, over the pass.

The smooth track rose gently at an angle, with the hump of Dundale Knot glowering above. Pretty clumps of primroses pierced the warm earth, braving the risk of a late frost, and somewhere in the depth of Brockbarrow Wood, a wood pigeon cooed.

They kept to the lea of the drystone wall as they climbed, enjoying the vista of dale spread out below them. Beth could see Broombank and further down, Ashlea, where Sally Ann lived with Nick and Jan. The lush greenness of the dale, deposited by retreating glaciers, contrasted sharply with the scoured bleakness of the surrounding mountains.

'Oh, this is doing me good.'

Meg stopped, her eyes on her home. 'This is my favourite view of Broombank. I fell in love with it when I was still a girl and have enjoyed every day I've spent in it since.'

'I can see why,' Beth agreed.

'How's Andrew settling in to his new job?'

An abrupt change of subject that brought, for a moment, only the response of silence as they set off again along the path and Beth struggled to find a tactful reply. 'He'd rather be in farming, but accepts what must be.' She couldn't tell Meg that he'd just lost it because of searching for her sheep. Yet Meg's shrewd grey eyes were piercing.

'He misses the animals. That's plain to see.'

Beth nodded. 'It's hard to watch him sometimes.'

'We're very grateful for his prompt action the other morning. We'd have lost that ewe otherwise, and we're losing enough right now, one way or another.'

'Did you know he's been getting up at four every morning recently, to go out and check on them?'

Meg laughed. 'Oh, I can believe it. It's in the blood. We all curse them on freezing mornings and then wonder how we'd go on without them. Tam and I talk about it quite a lot. That incident, and others, have concentrated our minds even more lately.'

Beth cast her grandmother a sideways glance. 'Why? You've no problems, have you?'

Meg frowned. 'A few too many sheep are going missing lately. I think it must be our age. Anno domini and all of that. Perhaps we aren't up to the job any more.'

'I can't believe that.'

'We're certainly not getting any younger, much as we'd like to deny it, and it gets harder and harder to get out of bed each cold morning. Tam says, 'tis growing soft we are.' They both laughed at her fair immitation of her husband's lovely Irish accent. 'And shinning down mountainsides is less fun than it used to be, I can tell you. He's been trying to persuade me to retire for ages and I've almost decided to do it.'

Meg stopped and brought Beth round to face her. 'But I must consider Broombank.'

'Of course.' Beth jiggled the buggy gently as she waited for Meg to get whatever was troubling her off her chest, not wanting her babies to wake. After a moment Meg started walking again, but was clearly in reflective mood.

'Broombank was handed on to me by a fine old man whom I loved dearly. I scraped and worked hard to pay for it, a low price but it seemed a fortune to me, a young girl with no money but the luckpenny he gave me to go with it. I couldn't let him down you see. He always believed in me, and my own father – well, least said about Joe the better.' She smiled. 'Now I couldn't bear to lose all the work we've put into it over the years. It's a different farm to the one I took on. I'd need to know it was in safe hands before I gave it up.'

'Naturally. But you won't give up. Not yet. You're tired, that's all, after a hard winter.'

'I'm not so sure. Visiting America made me realise there are other things Tam and I can do together, other places to see. And it crossed my mind that you and Andrew might be interested.'

Beth stopped in her tracks and this time forgot all about jiggling her babies. 'What did you say?'

'Why not? Andrew is a farmer looking for a farm. We have a farm looking for a farmer. And you can continue with the mill workshops, as agreed, only it'll be handier for you if you're living on site.'

'B–but – wait a moment, I can't quite take this in. Where would you go?'

'We've decided to buy one of those new bungalows at the end of Quarry Row. We're ready for a rest, though we thought you wouldn't mind if we put in a bit of part-time labour at Broombank, without pay of course, whenever we feel up to it. Just for the love of the place.' She grinned. 'I can't let go too quickly.'

Beth's heart was beating hard against her ribcage. 'I don't understand. How could we ever afford to buy it? It's quite beyond our means. We've no money, none at all. And it would cost a fortune.'

'Did I ask for a fortune? We can talk terms.'

'But . . .'

'We're family, aren't we? Tam and I had no children of our own. But Lissa was as dear as any daughter could be. We thought of her as our own for all she was adopted, and you are hers. So why shouldn't you have it?'

For one glorious moment Beth almost accepted, on the spot. Her love of Broombank was equal to Meg's own and nothing would give her greater pleasure than to live there, with Andrew, for the rest of their days. But then she remembered. 'There's Sarah. What about my twin sister?' How could either of them have forgotten Sarah?

'Is she interested in farming?'

'No, but . . .'

'Sarah will make her own life, probably in a city, and with that young man whom I don't approve of.'

'I know you never cared for Pietro, but really he can be very sweet and kind.'

Meg was frowning, lips pursing ominously. 'We'll agree to differ on him. What I can't understand is why he had to buy Larkrigg Hall. What on earth is he going to do with it?'

'Family is important to him. Sarah says he's been given some money and wanted somewhere for them to come back to from their travels. The rest of the time he looks upon it as an investment, and will continue to let it.'

'The less we think about that young man the better, in my opinion.' Meg sounded unconvinced. 'I doubt they'll stay around here for much longer. And it'll no doubt be another year or more before Sarah calls on us again. Broombank would be of no use to her.'

'I know she's selfish and demanding, and ridiculously irresponsible at times, but she is still my sister, with equal rights and all that.'

Meg lifted her chin with characteristic defiance. 'I've made my views clear to both of you, on more than one occasion, that I do not care for Pietro Lawson.' Then she smiled, radiant and loving. 'But you've no need to worry. I'll see that Sarah is given her fair share, all in good time. Nevertheless, I believe I may be allowed to dispose of my property, together with my precious luckpenny of course, as I think fit, and on terms I think fair. Speak to Andrew. Tell him I'm not offering charity. Send him to see me and we can discuss details.'

And Beth put her arms about her grandmother and hugged her. 'Oh, Meg. I do love you.' And she danced her round in delight, making the children chortle with pleasure at the sight.

*   *   *

'No!' Andrew said.

Beth stared at him. 'Are you mad? This is a wonderful opportunity.' His face was more grimly set than she had ever seen it, lines etched deeply at each side of his mouth, drawing it ominously down, and inside she felt suddenly, desperately sick. What was happening to them? What hope was there for her marriage to survive, if he wouldn't even meet her half way.

29

'Why do you have to be such an entirely proud and stubborn man? Why, Andrew?'

'I'm surprised you need to ask. Because its nowt to do wi' me. Broombank is your grandmother's farm, not mine. I'll not accept charity.'

'Charity? I've told you, Meg isn't offering you charity. She has more sensitivity than that. She says you can come to terms and agree a fair price for stock and machinery. But yes, the house will be my inheritance. What of it? It's common sense to keep it in the family. Wouldn't you have liked your own to have done the same with Cathra Crag?'

'That was different.'

'Why was it different? Because you're a man? Because you thought Cathra Crag should come to you, and Broombank should come to me?'

He looked uncomfortable. 'Summat of the sort.'

'Oh, don't turn chauvinist on me, Andrew. We have enough problems. And what do I know about farming? I'm not Meg. You're being over-sensitive and stupid.'

'So you're back to calling me names, are you?'

Beth swallowed her anger, fighting disappointment and taking a firm grasp of his arms, gave him a little shake. 'Listen to me for a minute. Listen to me properly before sounding off in a huff. I came to live at Cathra Crag happily enough with you. Now you can come to my family home, at Broombank with me. I know you're a proud man and I love you for it but there's really no need . . .'

'You *what*?'

She gazed in dismay at the open scorn on his face, the look of scathing disbelief in his eyes. In that instant she felt cold fear clench her stomach. It was going wrong, all of it. This should have been a happy time and instead her life was falling apart. The aching void between them was growing wider, as if it could never be bridged.

'I tried to tell you before, but you came home saying you'd lost your job.' She leaned against him, loving the warm strength of his body. 'I'll admit I've never told you before, but I do love you. Oh, Andrew, it was a revelation to me when I watched you with that sheep. It came like a wonderful realisation that I've loved you all along. We didn't start off too well and I was on the rebound from Pietro and it clouded my judgement. But I do love you, I do.'

She was laughing up into his face, waiting for him to laugh with her, to take her in his arms and kiss her and say how delighted he was. Then they could go to bed and she would show him how very much she meant what she said.

To her complete horror the corner of his lip curled and his next words hit her like a rock.

'Amazing, isn't it, how everything fits so neatly into your requirements? You decide you want a bairn so you take me to your bed. Now you want Broombank, so you've decided the best way to persuade me is to tell me that you love me. How very convenient.' Then he pushed her from him and walked from the room.

They barely spoke to each other for a whole week after that. Everything had become twisted in his mind and Beth knew that nothing she could say would alter his feelings. His pride was hurt, and she was hurting too.

She cared for her children, went each day to spend a couple of hours with Sam at the mill, and spent the rest of the time sewing on her moccasins and trying not to think about the emptiness in her life.

'I'm sorry I haven't given you an answer yet,' she told Meg. 'I need to give Andrew time to think about it.'

'There's no rush.' Meg asked if it would help if she spoke to Andrew herself but when Beth declined, she readily agreed to wait, saying she'd enough to worry about right now with the sheep rustling. 'Thirty more have gone missing this week already.'

'This is getting ridiculous. And dangerous,' Andrew said, when Beth passed on the news. 'The man is out of his mind.'

'Man, what man? Are you saying that you know who it is?'

'Of course. Don't you? Think about it, Beth. We never had any trouble until Pietro and Sarah came back.'

'You're accusing my own sister of stealing Meg's sheep?'

'No, of course not.' Andrew sighed with excessive patience. 'I'm accusing Pietro Lawson of being so screwed up over losing you, that he'd go to any lengths to seek revenge.'

Beth stared at him dumbstruck. Pietro declaring he still loved her and was jealous of her husband was one thing, hating them enough to steal Meg's sheep was quite another. 'I won't believe it. I've never heard such nonsense in all my life. Pietro would never do such a thing.'

'You mean you'd rather believe him than me?'

'No, I don't mean that.' But in effect that was exactly what she did mean and they both knew it.

It was eating him up inside. She was starting on another affair with him, he could tell. Hadn't he seen them together out on the fell, the Italian kissing her right there in the open and she not protesting one little bit. Why else would she look so guilty when he'd met her on the path? Ever since that day, they'd grown further and further apart. Wouldn't let him come near her.

Andrew had always known that she didn't love him. From the first he'd accepted that he was second best. Why should he believe that her feelings had changed? Now she pretended that she'd loved him all along but had been too dazzled by Pietro's beauty and his flattering charm to realise. He didn't believe a word of it. It hurt him deeply to think so, but it seemed that his lovely Beth was every bit as greedy and selfish as her sister.

How could there be any love between them when they scarcely spoke, tip-toeing about each other like strangers, eating meals in complete silence, and sleeping like blocks of ice in the same bed.

They'd very nearly had another row at breakfast this morning when he'd told her he and Meg were planning to head up over Larkrigg to look for the lost sheep.

'Why would they be at Larkrigg? I told you. Pietro has nothing to do with all of this. Nothing at all.'

'So you say.'

'He isn't like that. He wouldn't steal. Whatever else he may be, however vain and greedy, he's not a thief'

'You know him well of course.'

'I know he is absolutely honest.'

'Yet he's kept your sister dangling for years. Why is that, d'you think? If he doesn't want to marry her, why doesn't he leave her alone? Particularly if he still fancies you. Is that the action of an honest man?'

Beth searched her mind, desperate to find the answer. But the question had puzzled her every bit as much as it did Andrew. She could think of nothing to say. 'I'll go to see him, ask him straight out about the sheep.' And Andrew laughed, his voice sounding unusually cruel and hard, as if she had again hurt him deeply by not accepting his word.

'Aye, go on, you ask him. And let me know what he says. It should be interesting.'

'Won't you believe that I no longer love him?' she burst out in a last desperate plea.

'No, Beth, I won't.'

She sank on to the sofa amid the baby clutter and put her hands to her face. 'Then there's nothing left for us, is there?'

'No, Beth. If you say not.'

He'd left her then, filled with a sudden wave of revulsion, and an overwhelming tiredness that had seeped right to the heart of him and into his bones. He'd heard her crying as he'd walked away, but if she absolutely refused to see any wrong in the man, how could he believe in her? In Andrew's opinion Pietro Lawson was deliberately trying to steal Beth from him. He'd treated Sarah appallingly, disrupted all their lives and could well be responsible for the loss of Meg's sheep. And Beth still saw him as some sort of god. Beautiful, untouchable, incorruptible.

*   *   *

Beth took her troubles to Ellen as she always did, and was surprised to find very little sympathy.

Ellen was so stunned by what Beth told her, she almost forgot the lapwing she was tending in her hand, nearly dropping the poor creature to the floor. 'You told Andrew that it was really him you had loved all along, *after* you'd asked him to accept Broombank?'

'Y-yes.'

'Dear heaven, girl, have you no sense? Can you blame him for refusing to believe you? What timing, Beth. The man has pride. No wonder he doesn't trust you. Particularly with that young fancy-pants prancing about the place, sending you wistful glances.'

'Wistful glances? I haven't seen any wistful glances.'

'Then you haven't been paying attention.' She finished fixing the splint on the bird's wing and slid it safely into a cage, then gave Beth a withering look. 'I'll put the kettle on. It's time we talked.' As they sat on the doorstep of the cottage, watching the grass grow, as Ellen described it, they did indeed talk, and it took all of Beth's strength not to run away from what Ellen was telling her.

'He's been following you everywhere, as he always used to. I've noticed. Meg certainly has. No doubt Andrew has too. However proud and stubborn he may be, he can see what's right in front of his own nose. Pietro Lawson is back to his old game.'

'Old game? What are you talking about?'

'You surely didn't imagine that you ever had a say in the course of events, do you? Young Lawson thinks only of himself. He didn't care which of you he got, because he never intended to keep either one of you.'

'I don't understand.'

'He used each of you as a pawn to make the other jealous. Playing one off against the other to make you both miserable. That was the whole object of the game, nothing to do with which of you he really loved at all.'

Beth stared at her, stunned. 'You're saying it was all *deliberate* on his part?'

'Yes, Beth. Planned most carefully to the last detail. And he didn't care how much he hurt you both in the playing of it.'

'I don't believe you.'

'It's an uncomfortable fact to take on board, I can see that. No young girl likes to think she's been used. I'm sorry to have to be the one to tell you.'

'You talk about him as if he had no heart, no feelings.'

'Mebbe he hasn't, not the same as yours anyway.'

'But he must have loved us. He was desperate to marry me.'

Ellen went to her animal feed table and picking up a knife, took out her anger in chopping cabbage leaves. She'd promised not to speak, so she wouldn't. She'd say no more than was absolutely necessary yet it hurt her to keep silent. This little lass was in danger of losing everything because of that selfish prig. She'd not stand by much longer.

'Happen he did, but though it may be hard for you to bear, lass, he could have had other motives.'

Beth sat hunched on the doorstep and said nothing, she was too busy testing herself, to see how much this new information hurt.

'It was him who smashed up my cages, and tore up my cottage. I'd guessed what he was up to and he didn't like that. He saw me as a threat and tried to frighten me off. Only I wouldn't go. He's plainly borne a grudge against your family for years, for reasons best known to himself, and he meant to inflict the greatest hurt he could. You and Sarah made perfect targets. I used to see him stalking about the woods, watching you, watching Meg down at Broombank. So I stalked him. I'm good at stalking. He was obviously planning summat in his nasty little mind. Happen he's still at it. Happen that's why he's come back.' Her quiet gaze challenged Beth who gazed back horrified.

'I won't believe it. I can't believe he was so calculating.'

'Ask Sarah. Ask her why they've come. It's for their own interests, not yours, you can be sure of it, lass. Ask her.'

'I will. I'll ask her this very minute.'

Beth went straight to Sarah. The only way to clear this up was to face her with it, head on. Her sister had never cared much for confrontations but she must face this one.

She found her chatting with Meg in the kitchen and as soon as was politic, managed to get her outside on the pretext of a walk along the lane.

Spring gentian, purple saxifrage and bright eyed stitchwort were in bloom but for once Beth paid no heed to the beauties of nature.

'What is this problem that has brought you back to Lakeland, Sarah? I'd like to know.'

A short, telling silence and then, 'OK. I'll tell you. I can't have any children. There. That's the blunt truth, plain and simple. I had an abortion when I was seventeen. Never told anyone. Mom would've gone wild. Unfortunately it wasn't of the best quality and somehow I got damaged. I'm barren. Isn't that the word?'

Beth was stunned. This was the last thing she'd expected. 'Oh, Sarah. I don't know what to say.'

'Try – I'm sorry.'

'Of course I'm sorry. I thought – I thought you were sick, or it was some sort of emotional problem that you wanted to talk over with me, something to do with Pietro. Not anything like this.' She sat on the stile and stared bleakly at her sister, her heart filled with compassion.

Sarah gave a hard, bitter laugh. 'It's both of those things in a way. Pietro badly wants a child, preferably a son, of course, but a child of either sex will do. He says it's his right.'

'His right?'

'Family is very important to him.'

'Yes, but if . . .'

'And if I can't give him one, then he sees no reason to marry me. Simple as that.' She reached up and plucking a hawthorn leaf from a branch, tore it to shreds. Beth watched her, appalled.

'But that's awful. You don't marry someone because they can or cannot give you a child. He surely can't mean it?'

'Oh, he means it all right. He's not the young boy eager for marriage any more. He's changed, or perhaps he always was this calculating, and we didn't notice. I'm not sure. Anyway, he reminds me of his riches and says he can afford to pick and choose, so why should he choose me? Unless I can give him what he wants. A family.' She turned to Beth and her face looked pinched and cold, as if it were death white beneath the tan. 'I couldn't imagine life without him, Beth. I need to marry him. Yes, me, the girl who swore never to commit herself to a man.' She gave a bitter little laugh. 'I love him, you see, and I must have him. No matter what.'

'Yes, I do see.'

She leaned on the stile and gazed out over the countryside, hearing the song of a lark getting itself into a frenzy over their nearness. 'You were quite right, there is a reason for our being here, and this is it. Pietro wants a child, and I want Pietro. And since I can't provide one, I've come to you, my own twin sister, to ask you for one. You must have the child for me.'

The silence this time was awesome, stretching into eternity. Then Beth shook her head, a tremulous smile of disbelief playing about her lips.

'You can't be serious. Is this is some kind of sick joke?'

'No joke. I was never more serious in my life. You have two children, no doubt had them as easy as sneezing and I can't even have one.' Beth watched in dismay as tears ran from the violet eyes, down over the lovely cheek bones. Sarah never cried. This must be hurting her deeply. Even so . . .

'You can't hand out children as if they were sweets. And what exactly are you asking of me? To sleep with him?'

Sarah almost choked on her laughter. 'Don't be ridiculous. He wouldn't want to do any such thing. There are ways with test tubes these days. Haven't you heard of surrogate mothers?'

Beth wondered whether the use of a test tube would make the slightest difference to Andrew's reaction, were she to have Pietro's child, and shuddered at the thought. 'I'm sorry. This has to be the most stupid idea you've ever dreamt up, Sarah. Andrew would go mad. My marriage is in trouble enough with Pietro being here, let alone this.' And getting up she started to back away, holding up her hands in defensive protest. But Sarah ran after her, jerking her to a halt with clutching fingers.

'Don't tell him. You could come away with us for a few months. Say its a vacation. You could have the baby then come home and no one would be any the wiser.' Sarah's excitement spiralled almost out of control as the idea took hold and Beth actually felt a laugh start deep in her throat. Hysteria obviously, for she'd never felt further from laughter in her life.

'Stop this, Sarah. I've heard enough.'

'I'll lose him. Do you hear me? I *must give him a child*. You *know* how I need him. Don't be selfish, Beth. You have to help me in this. You're my sister, for Christ's sake.'

'Calm down, Sarah. Things have changed.' Beth was becoming increasingly alarmed by Sarah's highly wrought state. 'There must be another way. Adoption, for instance. Please don't ask me for this, Sarah.'

'Pietro would never consider adoption. And where else can I go for help but to you, my own twin sister? You've always helped me in the past, why not now?' Beth almost expected her to stamp her foot.

Very calmy she tried to make Sarah understand. 'Because we're no longer children squabbling over a favourite toy. Or even young girls falling in love with the same man. Babies are real people and must be brought into the world with love, not as a means to win a trophy. Even if that trophy is the man you love.'

Sarah was clenching her fists into tight balls, her face screwed up with anguish, lips quivering like a child. But there was something more in that dear face. Something Beth recognised only too clearly. Fear. She couldn't help but think that if she hadn't betrayed her sister by sleeping with Pietro, he might then have married Sarah. Beth was no nearer knowing whether Ellen's wild suspicions were correct, but the whole situation seemed to be growing into a worse nightmare by the minute. And must be put right, quickly.

Putting out a hand, she gently pulled Sarah into her arms. 'I'll go and see Pietro. He can't understand the pressure he's putting you under. You take care of the children and I'll talk to him. I can do that for you, at least.'

It was risky. Striding over the fell, a fierce determination to put everything right making her cover the distance in half her usual time, yet Beth was filled with worry. If Andrew discovered that she'd visited Pietro at Larkrigg, then he might indeed walk out on her. Her marriage would be truly over. And what would she do then?

She had to take the risk. She had to know what, exactly, was going on.

Was Ellen right? When had he used her? When he'd seduced her while he was still Sarah's lover? When he'd refused to choose between them? And when he'd left with Sarah and callously abandoned her? That had been cruel and unkind. But what choice did he have? Sarah was so very highly strung and had been in need of his support.

She stopped to think about this, leaning her head against the cool surface of the Gemini Stones, letting the wind buffet her as her mind drifted back to those heady days when they'd seemed so young and powerful, imagining themselves and their love to be immortal.

Pietro had sworn that he'd loved them both equally, yet Ellen was right in that he had also hurt them both. Look at poor Sarah even now. Why was he refusing to marry her simply because she couldn't give him a child? That too was immensely cruel, yet he claimed to love her, and was only too aware how she loved and needed him.

But one other question troubled Beth. Was she herself truly over him? Was she entirely free of her own need for him?

Beth faced Pietro in the kitchen, forgetting everything she had so carefully rehearsed on the way and blurting out the first words which came to mind. 'Is it true? Did you really simply use us? Tell me what's going on here.'

He stared at her without blinking, then gave a wry smile. 'Beth, how very nice to see you. Good morning. Coffee?'

'No thanks.'

His face was as beautiful as ever, not a line to mar the olive-skinned perfection of it. The eyes were every bit as blue and clear, the line of the mouth enchanting, if more cynical than she recalled.

She watched him move about the kitchen, percolate coffee and lay a tray with neat efficiency. It might once have broken her heart to stand in this kitchen which had been her own, and know that it never would be hers again. As it would once have broken her heart to know that she couldn't have Pietro. But times had changed. She had changed. She felt nothing now, and exulted in that fact.

'Sarah came to me with some crazy story about wanting me to give you a child.' She kept her eyes on his face, watching for any flicker of guilt, completely ignoring the fragrant cup of coffee he set before her.

He shrugged. 'What is so crazy about it? You are sisters, twins in fact. We need a child. Sarah has tried but does not seem able to have one. You can have plenty. You owe her a little happiness, is that not so?' The smile challenged her, even as the brilliant blue eyes narrowed. 'I am sure she would think so, if she knew why.'

So that was the way of it. Blackmail. She sat on the hard chair and clenched her hands tightly together in her lap. It would take all of her courage to outface him and beat him at this new game. Beth thought of Andrew's love for her, and her newly found love for him, and the strength she needed came to her.

She met his gaze unperturbed, her own eyes cold. 'I seem to recall I was not alone in that sin. It was a mistake. We were young and crazy, and I'm sure in retrospect Sarah would forgive our folly.' She was sure of no such thing but had to make him believe it. 'It never happened again. We are not young and crazy any more, and no longer live a communal life.'

'All for one and one for all?' he softly reminded her. 'You think that will save you?' and he laughed.

'There are some things you can't share. Love, for one. Ellen says you never loved either of us. That you deliberately set out to hurt us, to make us jealous of each other. Is that so?'

'Ellen will say anything against me, because I have given her notice to quit. Did she tell you? I've told her to clear up her mess from my land, and go.'

Beth drew in a sharp breath. He was clever, oh yes, he was definitely clever. Who would believe an old woman with an eviction notice hanging on her? Instinctively she wanted to defend Ellen, who was perfectly capable of fighting her own battles, yet that wasn't what she was here to do. She tried a different tack. 'I owe Sarah nothing. She almost brankrupted us. Because of her selfish carelessness I was left penniless and lost Larkrigg to the bank.'

'From whom I bought it.'

'Apparently so.'

'You could have it back if you wished. Or money, if you prefer. Money is not a problem. My stepfather gives me all that I ask. That is the price of his guilt for stealing my mother.'

'Money. Can you only judge the value of something, or someone, by what you can get out of them?'

'Everyone has a price.' She was shocked to the core and answered with spirit.

'You can't buy a child, Pietro. You aren't God. And I shall no longer be the provider of whatever happens to be Sarah's latest whim.'

'You will do as she asks. Whatever I tell her to ask for, you will provide. Can you not see how ill she is? How she clings to the edge. It would take very little to send her quite demented, I think. Something perhaps, such as how her own sister betrayed her.' The cold fury in his eyes made a parody of those perfect features, made them almost frightening, and the desire to run from him was overwhelming. But Beth refused to be overwhelmed. She was thinking fast, fighting for a way out of the morass of emotion he was piling upon her.

'Ellen says you were out for some sort of twisted revenge against my family. Is that why you won't marry Sarah? How would she react, if she knew?' If Beth had expected him to be disturbed by her accusation she had misread her man. A brief look of astonishment, all too quickly masked by high pitched laughter. 'What else did she tell you?'

'Isn't it enough?'

'The old woman has too big a nose.'

'Then it's true?'

'You must decide for yourself. It is not important. I take what I want from life.'

'Then perhaps its time you stopped taking, and learned to give a little. If you want something from life you should be prepared to work for it yourself, mot demand it of others. Perhaps it's time for you both to grow up, as I have had to do.'

He moved suddenly and she flinched away, thinking he was going to reach for her, and her hand accidently caught the coffee cup, sending scalding liquid spilling all over the table, over her hand. She leapt up and he captured the hand, taking her to the sink, where he held it under the cold tap. Beth was acutely aware of his fingers wrapped around her arm, the pain of the burn nothing by comparison.

'I love my husband,' she said, needing to say it, and as she heard his soft chuckle, wishing she hadn't.

'That is good. But you love me too, I think.' One hand seemed to have crept about her waist, was pressing somewhere below her left breast, and she became intensely aware of his mouth hovering a mere breath from her own.

'Oh, my sweet Beth. Do you not realise that I have never stopped loving you? I have never forgotten your enchanting face, those wonderful moments we enjoyed together, and could again. You have only to say the word. Why do you deny it? You want it too.'

His hands moved more freely over her, touching her cheek, her lips, her hair, down over the line of her throat and breasts. 'Such a delightful and firm little body which I love to worship with my own. Did we not always make the good team, the three of us?' His lips were somewhere behind her ear now, the heat of his breath on her neck and one hand was moving over her hip, down to her buttocks, pressing her against him.

No fire seared her loins, not a flicker of desire moved within her. Nothing. Only the birth of loathing.

'Let me go, Pietro.'

Her voice was cool and flat but he paid no heed, only continued with his kneading, his hands everywhere, his breathing growing ragged as he fondled her breast, lifted her skirt.

'Pietro, please, no . . .' Any moment now he might actually kiss her, or worse.

'Please yes. That is what you really mean, little one. Yes, yes, yes.' And he laughed, nibbling at her ear, making her skin crawl. His hold on her was so fierce that for a brief instant fear flickered and panic washed through her, cold and hot by turn. What if he wouldn't release her, what if . . . Then she took hold of his hand and very firmly and dispassionately removed it from her breast as if it were a troublesome insect that had landed there by mistake. Her gaze was freezing as it met his.

'Thank you for the first aid treatment but my hand is quite recovered.' Then she walked away and at the door turned to glare back at him. 'I shall not provide Sarah with a child, only an explanation. And I hope that I can save her, from herself, and from you.'

'You will regret it.'

'Do your worst.' Then she calmly walked out of the kitchen and down the path, hoping he did not notice how her legs were shaking.

Now, she ran down the drive and was laughing as she reached the Gemini Stones, flinging her arms about one and letting the wind ripple through her hair. She was free. At last she was truly free of the hold he'd had on her. That terrible infatuation which had so sapped her strength.

Dealing with Sarah would not be easy, but must be done. Somehow her sister must be made to see how evil the man was.

Beth wondered why she hadn't seen him as he really was? How blind is love.

But even the prospect of facing Sarah's wrath didn't sober her. She was too happy, too relieved, feeling a certainty grow inside that next time she told Andrew how much she loved him, she could finally convince him that it was true. Because now, she had entirely convinced herself.

She did not notice, as she ran and skipped, and laughed, that she was watched.

Hidden in the fringes of Brockbarrow Wood, Andrew stood silently watching his wife behave like a young excited girl, and then he looked back at the house. He'd seen her go in, knew to a minute how long she'd spent there, evidently with Pietro.

What else would make her so happy? He had never made her so in his entire life, and he wished, with all his heart, that he could.

30

Andrew strode out over the fellside, intent on meeting up with the search party from Broombank, his long legs making short work of the distance. It was early, no more than six o'clock but he had no job lined up for that day so why shouldn't he spend it hunting Lawson? Nothing would give him greater pleasure.

How he'd love to catch him red-handed. What would he do with him? Beat him to a pulp. And have Beth never speak to him again? Take him to the police then. Let them deal with the idiot. Sheep rustling was a criminal offence.

He found Meg on the crag of Dundale Knot, dogs at heel.

'How could we lose nearly fifty sheep?' she said, the moment he reached her. 'The odd one perhaps, to a dog or down a crevass. But *fifty*?'

'Somebody must has taken them. It's the only answer.'

'Exactly. And in all the years I've farmed Broombank, I've never experienced this trouble before. Why should we suddenly suffer from sheep rustling? Who could be doing it?'

Now their eyes met, the still unspoken thought loud between them.

'I have my suspicions,' Andrew said, as they set off together along a sheep trod.

'Me too.'

Again a silence fell between them, broken only by the sound of their footsteps and the wind moaning over the felltops. They breasted a ridge, jumped over a patch of bog whortleberries, their boots sinking in to the damp peat and in the end it was Meg who put their thoughts into words. 'He wouldn't, would he? My own granddaughter's husband?'

'They aren't married, remember.' His voice was flat and hard.

Meg nodded, her face thoughtful. 'And he does bear us a very real grudge. Me, in particular.'

'Yes,' Andrew agreed. 'Revenge for what he feels he lost when you didn't marry his grandfather.'

Meg shook her head in despair. 'Absolutely ridiculous. What happened between Jack and me was a lifetime ago. It's dead and gone, the war saw to that.'

'But it's warped him for some reason. He thinks it's affected his entire family life. And he'll mebbe do anything he can to destroy yours by way of retaliation.' Andrew should have stopped there but head down, eyes on the pounding of his boots on sheep cropped turf the words burst from him, unbidden. 'He's even after Beth.'

'Beth?' Meg grabbed his arm and pulled him to a halt. 'What about Beth?'

And to his very great surprise he found himself confiding in this woman he'd so resented for offering him charity and pity. They stood in a cold grey dawn on Larkrigg Fell and he poured out his heart to her, telling how Beth had only married him on the rebound. How she had been besotted by Pietro and probably still was. How he'd caught them together.

'Not . . . ?'

'I saw him kiss her. Out here, on Larkrigg fell.'

Meg was thoughtful for a moment. 'And did she kiss him?'

'She wasn't doing anything to stop him.' Andrew glowered. 'More likely she found herself still yearning for him and then felt guilty. Beth would react that way. I found her running from him, obviously upset and very much on the defensive.'

'She could, of course, be entirely innocent, running away for a different reason.'

But Andrew shook his head, sunk deep in the gloom of self-pity. 'She still loves him, that's plain. I can feel the tension in her, like a wound-up spring. Then I saw her leaving Larkrigg Hall yesterday, skippy as a young lamb.' The bitterness in his voice was painful to hear.

'Have you talked to her about it?'

'No.'

'Don't you think you should?'

Andrew's frown deepened. 'I've no wish to listen to how much she still dotes on the man.'

Meg felt a surge of irritation. 'You're condemning her without a defence. She's your wife, give her that right at least. Talk to her.'

Andrew kicked at a stone, making it bounce down the mountainside for several feet before it came to rest.

'I know,' Meg sighed. 'It's none of my business. Grandmothers aren't supposed to interfere, but I love Beth, and if you love her as much as you claim then you owe her a decent hearing. Right? Isn't your marriage worth fighting for?'

Andrew lifted his eyes to Meg's and gazed at her without speaking for a long moment. Then he gave a shamefaced smile. 'You're right, Meg, thanks.'

'Good.' She clasped a hand on his shoulder. 'Have faith, lad. Have faith. Now, to business. Tam is heading over Coppergill Pass. There's a spot near there where a lorry might get. I want to check out this heaf, you head west towards the house. If I don't see you before, we'll meet in a couple of hours at the edge of the wood, by the tarn. OK? Then we can nip off home for a bite of breakfast.'

Dawn was not a time Beth would have chosen for her confrontation with Sarah, but since Sarah had decided to stay with them for a few days, she'd taken to getting up whenever little Emily cried. It had become almost a race for Beth to reach her daughter first. On this occasion Sarah was in the room like a shot, cradling the child in her arms by the time Beth climbed out of bed.

'I'll take her,' she said, and Sarah handed her over with obvious reluctance.

'I'm surprised you don't hear her the moment she cries.'

Beth carried the child downstairs and sat in her favourite spot on the sofa. Andrew had lit the fire for her, and it was warm and cosy here. She didn't bother to respond to Sarah's criticism. 'I usually make myself a cup of tea while I'm feeding, perhaps you could do it for me.'

But by the time Beth had told her sister that she had no intention of ever having a baby for her, the tea was quite forgotten and left to cool untouched in the mugs.

Sarah, as expected, was outraged. 'But I had it all planned. I've made arrangements with a clinic and everything.'

'Then you'll have to unmake them.' The sound of the baby contentedly suckling brought both girls' eyes upon her for a second and Beth's heart sank. Was this the right decision? She did care for Sarah. She really did want her to experience the joy of bearing a child, as she had.

'How can you be so selfish? How dare you refuse me? I need . . .'

'Don't tell me what you need, Sarah. I can't bear to be responsible for you any more. Listen to me for a change. I'm no longer the shy, awkward girl I once was, who always did your bidding because she was too afraid to protest. You can't make demands and expect me to provide, not now. I'm a woman, with a husband and family, and their interests must be considered as well as yours. In any case, Andrew would never agree.'

'He would if you asked him.'

'I've no intention of ever asking him.'

And to Beth's dismay her furious, haughty sister burst into tears. 'You'd deprive me of this?' she sobbed. 'You, my own twin sister?'

Beth sighed, feeling a sad exasperation at Sarah's utter selfishness. 'It's not my fault, love. And there are other solutions you could try. Have you seen a doctor? He might be able to help you. Or considered adoption? There are plenty of children in need of good parents.'

Sarah's tears dried and her face set in mutinous lines. 'Pietro would never hear of adoption.' Then, more vigorously. 'You went up to see him yesterday, didn't you? What did he say? Did you offer to run away with him?'

'Don't be ridiculous.'

'I know you still fancy him like mad.'

'I made it very clear to him that the idea was a non-starter.' Now was the moment, Beth thought. Sarah herself had given her the opener she needed. She settled Emily to the other breast and then lifted quiet eyes to meet her sister's furious gaze. 'There's something else I need to tell you. A confession, of sorts.'

'Oh?'

'About something which happened years ago, when we were still living at Larkrigg Hall. Around the time when I thought I might ultimately marry Pietro.' Beth felt her throat closing up, the words dying on her even as she struggled to find the right ones.

'Oh, that,' Sarah said, getting up and flouncing over to the little fireplace where she kicked at a piece of coal. Sparks flew up the chimney and smoke billowed out into the room. 'I've known about your little fling with Pietro for ages.'

Beth was stunned into silence for a whole half minute. 'You *knew*?'

'Of course. What of it? At least you were a woman.'

Now she went very still. 'What do you mean? At least I'm a woman.'

Sarah put back her head and let out a long and weary sigh, then thrusting her hands deep in her dressing gown pocket turned to face Beth. 'All right, you may as well know. Pietro actually prefers men, the younger and more nubile the better.'

A picture of two naked bodies caught in a pool of sunshine exploded into Beth's mind. She saw that one of them had an arm resting across the back of the other. Why hadn't that registered at the time? They'd been too busy worrying over being discovered. Dear lord, then this must mean . . . She felt herself start to shake. 'What are you suggesting? It isn't possible. We . . .'

'Oh, its perfectly possible. Pietro had a mad pash for Jonty. Didn't you guess? He was fearsomely jealous for a while when Jonty and I were, well, at each other like rabbits, as they say.' She laughed, a hollow, lonely sound.

'But I thought he was jealous of Jonty because he wanted you.'

Sarah's elegant bob shook with laughter but the tears were rolling down her lovely cheeks. 'I made the same mistake at first. And he's not averse to sleeping with me. But he grows quickly bored. Sometimes I have to almost beg . . . He prefers the cut and thrust of the chase perhaps, or simply men, to a more conventional . . .' Her sobs choked her to a stifled silence for a moment, then she struggled desperately on.

'But I still love him, Beth, and I thought if at least I could have a child, he'd marry me and I could cope. But I can see now that it was a stupid, selfish idea. I–I'm so sorry. I didn't mean to hurt you.'

'Oh, Sarah.' And Beth could only gaze in horror as her proud, strong sister sank to her knees on the hearthrug, put her face in her hands, and sobbed. 'Oh, Beth, what have I done with my life? What have I done?'

Quickly, Beth stowed the now replete baby safely into a corner of the sofa and gathered Sarah into her arms. It was some time before she became calm, Beth offering soothing words, assuring her all was not lost. 'You might yet have a baby of your own, and find happiness.'

'With Pietro?'

'That depends on you, love. And whether he's worth the agony.'

After a while Beth installed her on the sofa with baby Emily in her lap, and went to make a fresh pot of tea. And as they sipped the comforting brew they talked, quietly and calmly, sharing fears and hopes and dreams, finding them to be surprisingly similar. Both wanting a man, love, home and family, all the conventional things together with the need for personal fulfillment, though with different ways of achieving it and with varying degrees of success.

'We've both made mistakes. I had a romantic ideal of life at Larkrigg Hall and worse, I've hung on to my rose tinted image of Pietro for so long that I was in grave danger of losing the one man I really love.'

'I think I'm finally learning,' Sarah said, 'that if you treat life simply as a game you only hurt others, and really if I'm going to make anything of my life, I have to work for it myself.'

'Well that's something to be thankful for,' Beth said with a wry smile, and they were in each other's arms again, laughing and crying at the same time, and still talking, as they never had before.

Andrew had been walking for what seemed like hours, eyes scouring the distant horizon, seeking sight of a lorry, wheel tracks, or any place where fifty sheep might be gathered or hidden away. His heart raged with hatred. Why had the man come back? Why did he have to spoil everything? Perhaps their marriage hadn't turned out as perfectly as he'd hoped, but it wasn't his fault if he'd lost his job and become less of a man.

He recalled the sight of Beth as she lay in bed this very morning, her cheeks flushed from sleep, her glossy hair spread upon the pillow. He'd longed to take her in his arms and love her there and then. He wanted to believe in her love. But how could he?

He'd crept from the room without disturbing her, without saying how he had seen her leave Larkrigg the previous day, happy and laughing. How he'd almost been able to smell the man on her when she'd got home.

Sometimes he almost hated her, as if he wanted the fault to be hers. Yet he couldn't put all the blame on to her. Andrew knew that he'd suffered from the greed of others every bit as much as she had. His own family had brought him to this mess, yet somehow he couldn't prevent himself from turning his grievances upon Beth. The result, he realised, of his own inability to accept that she loved him. Yet he saw it only as pity that she felt for him, pity that he had to take crumbs from other men's tables, and from her own grandmother.

The clouds hung heavy and low, echoing his mood, and any hope of finding the sheep today was fading as rapidly as the weather. Never reliable on these fells, this one would soon turn to stinging rain.

An hour later he walked by the tarn, seeing it ruffle with a brisk breeze and shatter with the first spots of rain, as he'd predicted. He stopped to rest, leaning against a rowan, his heart sunk in gloom.

What else could he think but that his wife had become so dis-illusioned in their marriage, she'd taken to having an affair. The fact that Sarah wasn't married to that damned fancy idiot had obviously made her longing for him worse. She'd be wishing she'd waited. Andrew swallowed the pain that stuck in his throat, then punched his fist hard against the bark of the tree. Specks of blood beaded his knuckles but he didn't even flinch. He only wished it was Lawson's head.

A sound at his side brought him reeling.

'Who the hell . . . ?'

'Only me. Wet through and feeling sorry for myself.' Meg grinned at him and shook the rain from her waterproof, sending a shower of raindrops over them both. 'Hell, I'm wet.'

'Me too, now.' He laughed.

'Coffee?' She dug in her backpack and brought out a flask. It was a welcome sight. Meg poured out two cups and handed him one. 'I used to come up here all the time when I was a girl. Rarely have time these days for walking for pleasure.' She cast him a sideways glance. 'Course, if I could retire it would be a different matter. I could have a real rest then. Even doing part time would be a start. Better than worrying over lost sheep, I can tell you.'

Andrew's face remained set tight, as always when the subject was raised, refusing to be drawn. He liked and admired Meg, but an awkwardness had grown between them since she'd offered them Broombank. A fact which Meg regretted. She was fond of Andrew, stubborn as he was, and of Beth, and could only hope they sorted their differences out soon.

Neither had seen anything of note and they companionably sipped the scalding liquid in thankful silence for a few moments, letting it warm them through.

'We'll have to watch him like a hawk,' Meg said at last.

'Aye. We will.' Their eyes met through the steam of fragrant coffee. 'We need to prove what he's up to. Prove it to Beth and to Sarah too. Make them realise he's not the angel he seems.'

'That's interfering,' Meg said. 'Grandmothers aren't supposed to interfere.'

'No, but a husband can. I need your help, Meg. To save Beth from her own soft heart.'

'Aye, you're right. We'll run shifts. Keep a watch on the Hall and see what he's up to. We'll follow him everywhere he goes.'

'And catch him at it. We only have to watch and be patient.'

Meg agreed. 'No one but no one hurts my girls.'

'Let alone steal your sheep?' teased Andrew and she gave a wry grin.

'That too of course.' She gave him a measuring look. 'You've been a good help to us on the farm. We value your assistance and wish you'd let us pay you for it.'

'No. You're Beth's family. My family now.'

'And can't a family give each other things, a farm for instance?'

He remained mute and she shook her head in smiling despair. 'Still too touchy for your own good, you daft lump. Yet you see how we can be friends when we put our minds to it. We both care about the twins, and are willing to take a risk for them.'

'That's different. That's important.'

'And Broombank isn't?'

'Broombank belongs to you. It has nowt to do wi' me. I'll not accept charity.'

Meg bit back her impatience. 'But it could be very much to do with you, if you'd let it. As you've just said, we're family now.'

'A farm is different.'

Meg sighed. 'You tie me in knots. Broombank is important to me. It's been my life and I want to see it go to a caring owner. It's a good farm. Modern and sound. Plenty of acreage. A flock of near a thousand Swales and a hundred or so Herdwicks. And thirty beef cattle which I know you're interested in, and could increase.'

'Galloways?'

'Aberdeen Angus Cross.'

She could see his interest and smiled. 'Our paperwork is all in order and you'd have no trouble getting a loan for the stock and equipment. We'll even be computerised before long, so we can check feed quantities and stock breeding more carefully. We could work together, make the change-over painless.' She raised a querying eyebrow at him, wiping away the rain as it dripped from her hat and seeing he was sorely tempted. But then the obstinate line of his jaw tightened and she sighed again. 'Are you always this stubborn?'

Andrew had the grace to give a shamefaced grin. 'So I'm told.'

'Have you considered Beth in all of this? It would make her happy to live at Broombank. She loves the place.' Which, to her surprise and distress made the jaw set even tighter. She drew in a deep breath. 'All right, I'm cold and wet, and hungry for my breakfast. We'll leave it for now, till this other little matter is sorted. You take the first shift up at Larkrigg this evening, and I'll do the dawn watch tomorrow. But don't think I've given up.'

'Do you ever?'

'Not that I've noticed.' Meg's smile vanished. 'Nor will I give up fighting over the loss of fifty good ewes. In this at least, we can be partners. Right?'

'Right. Partners it is,' Andrew said, and they shook hands on the deal.

It was Ellen who proved to Beth that Pietro was the sheep rustler. She brought her from the workshop at Broombank and led her past Allenbeck, across the humped bridge and through the lower reaches of Brockbarrow Wood. Here she showed her a bridle path, little used and overgrown but wide enough for a vehicle to pass through. 'It leads right over the tops up to the Hall. And see here, tyre tracks, plain as plain.'

Even so Beth fought it. If Pietro were a thief, this would only distress Sarah all the more. 'This means nothing. Except that a vehicle has driven over this track. But we don't know what vehicle, or why?'

'I do.' Ellen fixed her with a fierce glare. 'I told you. I watch, and listen. Most folks never take the time these days. Sat all night behind this bridge, I did.'

'Oh, Ellen, you'll catch pneumonia.'

'I'll catch a thief. Saw him with my own eyes just before dawn, sitting beside the driver. A right cove he was an' all. Didn't see me a'course.' She tapped one side of her nose. 'Never let your quarry catch your scent. But I heard them laughing and saying summat about the fun they'd have again tonight.'

Beth's heart sank, unwilling still to believe the worst. However much Pietro might hate her family, however idiosyncratic his appetites, that didn't mean they could blame him for every single thing that went wrong. Besides, Sarah loved him.

Ellen was issuing instructions in her blunt, no nonsense manner. 'Get Meg, or better still Tam and Andrew, to wait here tonight and you'll have him. See if I'm not right.'

And unable to deny the truth any longer, Beth agreed.

They waited for hours. Midnight came and went and still nothing had happened. Tam, Andrew, and Beth, who had insisted on coming with them since she felt partly responsible. Sarah was taking care of her children and Meg was taking a well earned rest. She'd agreed to join them at dawn.

Beth was having difficulty staying awake and several times Andrew urged her to go home and get some sleep.

'Maybe I will. Ellen was probably wrong.'

'Ellen is never wrong. Not about things like this. If she says she saw Pietro in a lorry, then she saw him.'

'Then I shall stay here. I want to ask him why.'

Tam reached out a hand and stroked her hair. 'Go and sit beneath the bridge, darlin', out of the breeze, and try and get a bit of shut-eye. We'll wake you if the divil comes, then you can help us spit in his eye.'

And she pulled up her coat collar and tried to do just that, managing to find a patch of turf against a drystone wall that was both dry and springy. But somehow she couldn't relax. She felt as if there were two bright lights behind her eyes, making them feel all hot and red. And Pietro's face kept looming up at her out of the brightness. Somewhere in the background Sarah was crying, and all her senses were filled with a terrible feeling of doom.

Why would he steal from them? And why should he come back tonight? Questions that tormented but for which she had no answers.

She must have slept though, for she woke with a jerk, as if a hand had touched her, yet she was still alone and the wind had turned even colder. Beth shivered, one glance in the direction of the bridle path telling her that Andrew and Tam too had finally succumbed to sleep. She could see their two heads nodding, and hear Tam's soft snores.

She smiled and stretched her cramped limbs. How long had she slept? It must have been hours for she could see the glow of dawn in the sky. Beth loved the dawn, that first pinky flush of a new day. She looked up into the sky and smiled. Did a rose sky mean that it would be a beautiful day? What was the old saying? Red sky at night, shepherd's delight, red sky in the morning . . . She stopped, her sleep drugged eyes finally clarifying exactly what it was she saw. Not the pink flush of dawn at all, but the kind of ominous glow which could mean only one thing. Larkrigg Hall was on fire.

31

Flames stretched up like blood red fingers clawing at a black velvet sky, poking through the gash of burst windows and finishing in a shower of sparks that filled the air like fire crackers. Everywhere was the pungent stink of smoke, black ash choking mouths and noses, filling lungs with lethal swiftness.

'Keep back, Beth. Keep back. It's done for.' Tam and Andrew had tried beating at the roar of flames but the heat had driven them away, black-faced, coughing and exhausted. The fire engine had arrived as quickly as it could, but the distance from Kendal was great and they were too late to save the house. Larkrigg Hall was a ball of fire, a furnace of baking heat, and from it fell the burnt ashes of Beth's dreams. Yet that was the last thing on her mind now.

'Thank God I asked Sarah to stay with the children tonight. And that Meg is sleeping.'

Andrew slid his arms about his weeping wife and silently held her close.

She tried not to picture her lovely kitchen, the tiled walls cracking in the heat, the scrubbed pine table ablaze. In her mind's eye she saw the elegant little drawing room where they'd so enjoyed pasta suppers, reduced to a pile of blackened timbers. All that work, all that money spent on restoring it, for this. Andrew stroked her face and let her cry into his shoulder.

Yet inside of him burned a small fierce fire of his own.

Was she crying for the loss of Larkrigg Hall? Or was her anguish the fear that Pietro was still in there, burned to a crisp. They'd searched for him, for as long as it was safe to do so, almost sacrificing their own safety, and he'd had to drag her out screaming with distress that they couldn't just leave him to burn, for all he was a calculating thief.

Beth's sobs had calmed and she dabbed at her eyes with the palms of her hands. 'It was never a happy house. Meg was right. I shan't miss it as much as I think.' She gave a small hiccup of distress. 'But it's still terribly sad.'

'Yes,' he said, pushing back a damp curl of hair from her cheek. 'It is, terribly sad. But no one is hurt. It could have been much, much worse.'

She sighed and rested her head against his shoulder. It was a good shoulder to rely on, solid and strong. 'If Pietro isn't in the house,' she murmured, 'where is he?'

It was as if an electric current had shot through her body. Beth was out of his arms in a second, smoke sore eyes wide and frightened. She said only one word. 'Meg,' before turning and running down the fell towards Broombank as if indeed her own heels were on fire.

Pietro was sitting in the rocking chair by the wide inglenook fireplace where once the women of the house would sit and knit. Above his head ran the huge beam from where hams had once hung to catch the oak scented smoke from the fire. The embrasure now held a solid fuel range but a griddle iron still swung from a ratten crook in the corner, though no one baked oat-cakes on it these days. It being more for show in this dearly loved home, a touch of nostalgia for times long gone.

'Three hundred years Broombank has stood on this spot,' Pietro said as she walked towards him, a tautness to the smoothly tanned skin. 'A family house, *my* family, by rights.'

'Not any more,' Beth said, and quietly pulled up a stool so she could sit before him. Tam and Andrew were checking all the barns and outbuildings, to make sure no one had set a fire in any of them. She'd had to battle with Andrew to let her come in here alone to talk to Pietro, but she'd won in the end. She could only hope this decision would not put her marriage any more at risk. 'Those days are over, Pietro. Long gone. You can't resurrect the past.'

'Exactly what I decided,' he agreed, in his most reasonable tone. 'But three hundred years is a long time and if we, the Lawson family can't have it, then why should you? More to the point, why should Meg? So I have decided to destroy it.'

'I won't let you.'

He looked at her and laughed, then getting up placed the rocking chair on top of the pitched pine table. 'And how will you stop me, little one?'

'I don't know, but I will.' Beth was amazed how calm her voice sounded, when inside she trembled. She watched as he piled other items on to the table. A sewing box, two dining chairs, a foot stool and then he set about screwing up pieces of newspapers, stuffing them in all the gaps between. 'Where is Meg?' Quietly asked, her breath held like a ball of iron in her throat. The question only made him laugh all the more.

'Gone to the devil for all I care.' His eyes glittered in the light from the lamp. 'I disposed of Larkrigg Hall. Did you see it?'

'I saw it.' She drew every ounce of strength into her next question. 'Did Meg see it? Meg wasn't inside, was she?'

He didn't seem to be listening to her, yet he gazed with an aching sadness into her face. 'It is the very great pity that you would not marry me, little one. We could have had Larkrigg Hall, and Broombank too. We would have been rich, you and I, and I would have restored my family's inheritance.'

Beth was not to be diverted. 'Was Meg here, at Broombank, when you arrived?'

Then he shook his head, seeming to lose patience with her questions and almost shouted his reply. 'Meg stole Broombank from my family.'

She was on her feet in a second, facing him with equal fury. 'I won't have you say that. Meg never stole anything from anyone in her life.'

For a second she thought he might hit her as his eyes lit with shock at her spirited response. Then the upper lip curled, as she realised it so often had done in the past. And she had never noticed. 'You would be bound to take her side.'

'I take no side. I say only what is right. Meg took on Broombank fair and square. From all accounts Jack was a wastrel with no interest in the farm and entirely unfaithful and disloyal to her. He deserved to lose his inheritance.'

'You dare to attack my family?'

'I dare. I'll certainly not stand silent while you attack mine.' Grey eyes met blue in blazing defiance. They were so close she could trace every feature, every fine line of his perfect face. A face she had once loved and now loathed for the pain he had caused. Pietro was the first to break the hold, the cynical smile twisting the lips she had once kissed.

'But now, at last,' he said. 'I take the revenge. The *bellavendetta*, the quiet vendetta which bubbles and simmers for years and then boils over. *Poof!*' And he smacked his hands together, laughing. 'You miss your precious Larkrigg, I think? And Meg will miss Broombank. So I beat you both.' His delight was rather like that of a child who had given someone a special treat.

'If you wanted a fine home you should have provided it for yourself and not attempted to steal it from others, or attack them out of greed or cruel vengeance. I've seen Ellen's animals battle against man's greed and destruction of their environment. I've seen them attacked for no reason, when they were only defending their home or their loved ones. But they never gave up striving to find the haven of peace which is right for them and neither did I. I found mine, Pietro. If you did not find yours, perhaps it is because you did not deserve to.

'Larkrigg is my home no longer and I'm glad. I've no wish to return to it. I'm not a sweet, dreamy child any longer, Pietro. I'm a woman, and you might as well know . . .' She stood up and walked to the fire, holding out her hands to warm them by the blazing logs which crackled in the iron grate, while she considered her next words. She was aware that he paid her little heed, all the while continuing to add items of furniture to the growing pile, and stuffing newspaper between. It became worryingly like a bonfire ready to be lit. It made her shiver.

'Meg no longer owns Broombank.' It was a gamble, an outright lie, but a risk Beth felt she must take. He turned to glare at her and for the first time she saw a hint of confusion in those brilliant eyes.

'You *lie*.'

'No. It is to be mine. Mine and Andrew's.'

His whole body jerked and the glare from his eyes almost cut through her with their radiation of hatred. 'Yours?'

'Yes. Meg wishes to retire, so has offered it to me and I have accepted.'

There was almost admiration in his voice now. 'Damn you, Beth, why wouldn't you marry me? If I had known of this fire deep within you I'd have forced you into it.'

'No one can force me to do anything. Not ever again.'

'But I can still stir the emotions in you, *si*?' He laughed and Beth took his words as a terrible warning. Drawing a steadying breath into her sore lungs she continued, quite matter of factly. 'I'm exceedingly glad that I didn't marry you. We wouldn't have got on at all well.' She turned to him and smiled with perfect serenity. 'What a child I was. Besotted, and intrigued by you.'

Somewhere deep in the house a gust of wind rattled a window, and a door clicked shut, making her feel a breath of unease. Had he started a fire somewhere in the house? Were the bedrooms even now burning? Her nostrils were so full of smoke already, she wouldn't recognise the smell of burning until it was much too late. Where were Tam and Andrew? *And where was Meg?*

'The reason I couldn't bring myself to marry you, Pietro, was because I didn't love you. Oh, I was infatuated with you, and fascinated by your flattering, Latin charm, but it was no more than calf love. What I have with Andrew is the genuine variety. Rich and full and satisfying. I'd do anything for him, lay down my life if necessary. But you wouldn't understand selfless love, would you? You are too filled with greed and your own selfish demands.'

'It must have been exactly the same with your mother. I'm sorry if she was unhappy with your father, but she surely had a right to make decisions on her own life. I suspect it is only your assumption that she would have been happier here, probably the marriage would have collapsed anyway.'

'No, you are wrong. She dream of England all the time. She hate to be poor.'

'If that is the case then I'm sorry for her, and for you. You should marry someone because you love them, and want to be with them and make a life together, not depend upon others to provide it for you. What Meg has here, she has built herself. She owes your family nothing, nothing at all. And we won't let you take it, or destroy any of it. Ellen was right. You did use me, and Sarah, playing with one to make the other jealous. We all thought Jonty was the joker, but your games were far more evil.'

She moved towards him then, a confidence in her step which brought a new elegance to the more mature line of her slender body. 'I used to think Sarah was selfish, but she was only childishly so. You are the supreme master and have hurt her deeply. If you don't truly love her then you should let her go. No more teasing, no more using her for your own purposes. I hope she has the strength to leave you, as you deserve. But you aren't ever going to hurt us again. I won't let you.'

He snorted his derision. 'And how do you intend to stop me?'

'Enough is enough, Pietro. Even I have a limit to my patience.'

She went over to the dresser and found a pad of paper amongst the debris stuffed within its shelves. She scribbled furiously for a moment then handed it to him, holding out a pen. 'It's an IOU. You will promise to pay for Meg's fifty sheep and then you will go far away from Broomdale, and never return.'

'Or what will you do?'

'Or I will have you charged with arson, sheep rustling and anything else I can dream up in the meantime.' She smiled. 'And you know what a good imagination I have, and how desperately stubborn I can be.'

His glare should have burned her where she stood but she only continued to smile confidently, and after a moment he sulkily but obediently signed without further protest. Handing the paper back to her he walked to the door, puffing out his chest with self importance. 'I was intending to return to Italy, in any case. My point has been made, *si*? I have taken my revenge by disrupting all your lives, and I am content. I hate your damp, cold England. I shall buy a villa in Tuscany and enjoy life. This land is not for me.'

'Do that.' The paper trembled in her hand. What had she achieved? He would never return the sheep, or pay for them. But it didn't matter so long as he went out of their lives and never came back. He was right, he had succeeded in taking a warped sort of revenge. He'd broken her lovely sister, burned down Larkrigg, almost ruined her own marriage, and *what had he done with Meg*?

As he opened the door to leave, it flung wide open and in she walked, large as life. 'By heck, its cold out there, for all it's May.' Wide mouth grinning broadly on a face streaked with soot and smoke, nose glowing almost as brightly as the honey gold hair, now like a blazing oriel about her head. 'Whoever put a match to that place did us all a favour. I'm not sorry to see the end of it. Brought the family nothing but trouble and I for one, won't cry to see it go.'

A gurgle of joy bubbled up through Beth's throat. '*Meg*.' She dashed to fling her arms about her grandmother and held her tight. Andrew and Tam came in behind her, grinning from ear to ear. Beth looked from one to the other of them and became very still. 'How long have you been outside that door?'

'Long enough,' Andrew quietly told her.

'Keeping an ear on things, as you might say,' Tam agreed, fixing his piercing gaze on Pietro who backed away, startled as the family seemed to mass against him.

Beth was still hugging Meg. 'I thought . . . Oh, we thought we'd lost you.'

'Lost me? No, I'm not so easily got rid of.'

'But where were you?'

Andrew came and rested a hand upon Beth's shoulder, it felt so good she pressed her cheek instinctively against it and lifted her eyes to his, feeling a spark of recognition as their glances met. 'Meg had gone up to Larkrigg to investigate for herself,' he said, 'instead of going to bed as she promised.'

'And got herself locked into an outhouse up there,' Tam added. 'Daft eejit,' but said lovingly with his arm about his wife.

'I wasn't tired. And I wanted to help.'

Andrew gave her what could only be described as an old fashioned look. 'If the firemen hadn't found you . . .'

'Don't say it,' Beth cried. 'Don't even think it. Thank God she's safe.'

'It'd take more than a bit of a fire to harm me.' Meg held something bright and shining in her hand. 'Besides, see, I had my luckpenny with me. Never let me down yet.'

And they all burst out laughing. Then she looked across at her granddaughter, contentedly leaning against her husband, and smiled. 'Course, I'd be happy enough to hand it on, were someone willing to take Broombank and the land with it. Sarah isn't interested, I talked to her about it. She's planning on returning to America, for a rest and to reassess her life, she says.' Meg turned the coin in her fingers. 'But it needs to go to someone, as it was once handed on to me.'

Smiling, Beth gazed up at Andrew and kissed the rigid line of his jaw. 'I could only take it if it was in an equal partnership, given and accepted with love.'

And as the corner of his mouth lifted into a smile he placed a kiss on her nose, right on his favourite spot, and for a moment nothing existed but what they read in each other's eyes. Then Andrew turned his grin on Meg.

'I don't see any problem then, do you?'

And as the shining luckpenny spun through the air no one noticed a figure quietly leave the room. They were far too busy holding out their hands to catch it.